By the Shores of
Gitchee Gumee

TAMA JANOWITZ

By the Shores of
Gitchee
Gumee

Crown Publishers, Inc.
New York

"Home," by Phyllis Janowitz from *Visiting Rites*, Princeton University Press, 1982. Reprinted courtesy of the author.

Published by Crown Publishers, Inc., 201 East 50th Street, New York, New York 10022.
Member of the Crown Publishing Group
Random House, Inc. New York, Toronto, London, Sydney, Auckland
http://www.randomhouse.com/
CROWN is a trademark of Crown Publishers, Inc.

Printed in the United States of America

Design by Lenny Henderson

Library of Congress Cataloging-in-Publication is available upon request.

ISBN: 0-517-70298-3

10 9 8 7 6 5 4 3 2 1

First Edition

For David Janowitz

With much thanks, gratitude and appreciation for Betty Prashker, Amanda Urban, Paige Powell, Ruth Jhabvala, Ismail Merchant, James Ivory, Beauregard Houston-Montgomery, Julian Janowitz, R. Couri Hay, Apple Computer, Mont Blanc, Phyllis Janowitz and Tim Hunt, without whose support my work would have been more lonely, arduous and hateful than it already is.

Home

At the dinner table forks
and knives fall heavily
upon us. This is uncomfortable.

Bony fish. Chopped eggshell
soufflé. Sandy cookies.
We chew and chew. If charity

begins at home, we are on the moon,
looking through the wrong
end of a kaleidoscope,

all our crusty furniture
coming and going. The records,
stored in the basement, warped.

A waltz, moaning on the turn-table,
skewered like live meat, while
our beefy baby rocks and roars.

We hope to exchange him at Sears.
He is not what we paid for.
We think his components are rusty.

At the bureau we bequeath our several
parts. In London or Larchmont
someone who insistently awaits

our departure is dialing. Somebody
needs a stomach, an eye, a heart.
Soon someone will hear the good
news.

A man will arrive with a Kirby
to vacuum dead skin from our bed.
The world will look grisly.

No one will care.
Even at our pickled table the air
will not clear.

A stranger, reconditioned, will
chew on fingers and toes and duck
low flying silverware.

Phyllis Janowitz
Visiting Rites

By the Shores of
Gitchee
Gumee

My mother got out the box of eggs. "Oh, no!" said Leopold. He was six at the time. "Not eggs again!" He took the box from her hands and carried it into the kitchenette, where he cracked them into a bowl.

An hour later he called us all in to dinner. When we were seated he came out from the kitchenette carrying what looked like a soufflé, except since we had no soufflé dish he had made it in a glass lasagna pan. "Leopold!" my mother said. "This is amazing! How did you know what to do?"

"I watched it on TV," he said. The soufflé, or whatever it was, was a bit dry, but my mother said she would keep her eyes open at the Salvation Army Thrift Store and look for a real soufflé casserole. We were all amazed. Leopold, pleased, glanced down modestly. He had one of the largest noses I had ever seen on a child. His father had been German.

"Your father was a chef, Leopold!" my mother suddenly announced. "Did I tell you that before? Actually, I think he was a cook—from what I remember."

"Bratwurst and sauerkraut," said Marietta, twirling a strand of blond hair between her fingers. "Wiener schnitzel and kreplach."

"I thought you said Leopold's father was a cinematographer," Pierce said.

"Oh," my mother said vaguely. "Whatever." Leopold looked embarrassed. His ears were red. He did not like my mother talking about his father, which she often did, as well as the other fathers. "How I adore you," she suddenly told him.

He glanced up. "Why?" he said, almost angrily.

There was a pause. "I don't know," my mother said.

"How many calories does this have, anyway?" Marietta muttered.

"Maybe about six hundred," Leopold said, and bit his lip anxiously.

"In the whole thing?" my mother said. "Or per serving?"

"Per serving," Leopold said.

My mother and Marietta put down their forks. " *'Then they buried*

Minnehaha,' " said Marietta, gazing into space with a wild expression. " '*In the snow a grave they made her.*' "

"I could leave out the butter next time," Leopold said. "Or the cheese."

"*I* liked it, Leopold," I said.

Theodore began to sing. "When the bloom is off the rose / Then all that's left is leaves. / When the fork's held in a pose / Then it cannot hold the peas." He had a gravelly voice and sang—I thought—quite poorly. "My latest lyrics," he said. "What do you think?"

"Not bad!" said my mother. "Would one of you children fix me a gin-and-tonic?"

"Not bad?" Marietta repeated. "Mother, he's awful."

"You're right." Theodore put his head in his hands. "It is awful. I have no talent whatsoever."

Leopold, the youngest, only six, got up and gyrated his hips. "*I* liked it, Theodore!" he said, and started to sing, Elvis-fashion. "When the bloom is off the rose, there ain't no peas on the fork."

There was a knock on the door. Whenever anyone knocked on the door of our trailer, the whole place shook. Theodore often said that if we didn't get some cinder blocks to brace it, the entire trailer might go slipping down into the lake below one of these days. No one spoke for nearly half a minute. "There's somebody at the door," my mother said at last. "One of you go and answer it."

Leopold leapt up. "I was just going to make you that gin-and-tonic, Ma," he said.

Everyone else sat there. "I'm not going to get it," Marietta said. "What if it's a burglar—or a rapist?" Marietta reached into my mother's handbag and took out a compact. There was a piece of old chewing gum stuck to the lid. She powdered her tiny nose with the grimy powder puff, even though it didn't need any. Now her nostrils were tipped in white. I didn't say anything.

"Don't be ridiculous," my mother said. "Theodore, go and see who it is."

"I'm not going," Theodore said, helping himself to some more egg-and-cheese mess. "We're not expecting anyone, are we?"

"We never expect anyone!" Leopold piped from the kitchenette.

"Pierce, get the door," my mother said. She picked up a half-eaten, translucent, emerald-green sourball candy that was partly stuck to the table. Absently she put it in her coral seas.

"I'm not getting it," Pierce said. "I'm frightened."

"Aren't you children absurd." My mother scraped a burnt crust from the dish.

"How come *you* don't answer it," Pierce pointed out. He flicked his disposable cigarette lighter, then tapped the side, trying to see how much fluid was left in it.

"Maud, you go," my mother said. "It's your turn."

"Yeah, that's right," said Theodore, brushing invisible crumbs from his lapels. His pink-and-white–striped shirt was, as always, perfectly pressed. "It's your turn. You answer it."

"I'll give the orders around here," my mother said, taking Pierce's lighter out of his hand and putting it in her pocket. "Maud, would you like to answer the door?"

"Maybe he's gone by now," I said. But there was another knock. I got up.

"I'll be in the bedroom," my mother said, getting up as well.

I went to the door. It was about two feet away from the dining table, and made out of thin aluminum. "Who's there?" I said. I stared out the window. "Nobody's there." I turned away. "He must have left." I started to go back to the table to sit down again when Marietta screamed.

"He's looking in the window," she said.

I opened the door and stood on the top step. "Hello?" I said. The man stepped away from the window and stared up at me. He had very blue eyes rimmed with black; a nice, insolent coral seas; dark, curly hair; and one of our dogs, Trayf, on the end of a rope.

"This dog." He almost whimpered. "Do you know who it belongs to?"

"That's our dog," I said, stepping down and taking the rope from the man's hand. "I'm sorry. Was he bothering you?"

"I thought he was lost," the man said. "Lost and terribly ill."

"He's not terribly ill," I said. "He's a hairless dog. He's not supposed to have any fur."

"I've never seen a dog of this sort." The man looked surprised. "What kind is it?"

"It's a Xoloitzquintl," I said. "Formerly known as the Mexican hairless. The ancient Aztecs used to eat them. We found a recipe. It was for a casserole. Do you know what a casserole is?"

"Why, yes, I think so," he said. "Various sorts of stews, which you do in the oven. Why? Is that a trick question?"

"You have an accent," I remarked. "I wasn't sure you knew."

"I'm from England."

"And you have casseroles there!" I said. "In the casserole recipe we found, the dog-meat goes on the bottom, and the turkey on top. Apparently the dog-meat wasn't very tasty, so they tried to hide it underneath the turkey. My mother raises them—the dogs, that is, not turkey. I'm the one interested in poultry. Bad dog, Trayf." I started to go back into the house. The man was still looking at me with a peculiar expression.

"I live just up the road," he said. "I've rented the house up there for the winter."

"Be careful," I said, turning to open the front door. The dog squeezed in past me.

"Why?" the man said.

I looked back at him. "There are brown recluse spiders in the basement of that house."

"What are those?" he said.

"Poisonous spiders," I said, flicking my brown hair away from my eyes.

"I wasn't told about this," he said, and took a step back nervously, as if one of the spiders might be me.

"The exterminator came and fumigated—under our trailer, and in the basements of the other houses on this road. But you should still be careful." I was embarrassed at having talked so much and I went into the trailer. My mother had not yet come out from the bedroom, but the others were still sitting at the table.

"Who was it?" Marietta asked.

"It was a man," I said. "Trayf must have escaped, and was hanging around the Colemans' house. The man is renting it for the winter. He was incredibly handsome and had a very distinguished English accent."

"How old was he?"

"I'd say he was thirty-four years old," I said. "He was a manly type of guy, beautifully dressed. Clean, too."

"I like manliness in a man." Marietta smiled wistfully.

"What was he wearing?" said Pierce, who rarely said anything.

"I'm not exactly certain. It appeared luxurious, though."

Pierce raised his eyebrow. "Color?"

"Caramel," I decided. "It was a sort of pale, nubby, caramel overcoat. Possibly vicuña."

"Darn." Marietta went to the window and looked out. "I wanted to see him. He's gone, though."

"You did see him," I said. "You said he was looking in the window."

"Who can see anything out this window," Marietta said. "It's filthy." She rubbed at it with a finger. "Who wants to live in such a hellhole."

Our trailer was very tiny and dingy. "Go stay with your father," I suggested. She turned and gave me a sarcastic smirk.

"Soon all this will be behind me," she said grandly. "I shall marry the handsome Englishman and he'll take me away from all this, to his château on the Loire." She came to the table. "Is there any ice cream?"

"Why would an Englishman have a château on the Loire?" Theodore said. "He probably has a family seat in Surrey."

"Dervon," Pierce muttered.

Theodore and I looked at each other. "Where, Pierce?" said Theodore.

"Leave me alone," Pierce said, taking a pack of matches out of his pocket and opening the cover.

There was another knock on the door. "That's him!" Marietta said. She jumped up and ran to the door. The rest of us got up and crowded around behind. Even Leopold, busy tidying the kitchenette, came out wearing a floral apron, my mother's gin-and-tonic in one hand.

"Excuse me," a man said. It wasn't the same man: this one had a chunky face that could be easily sliced into luncheon meats. "I'm here today with a special offer from Minotaur Vacuum Cleaners—a free demonstration. Is the lady of the household at home?"

"I'm the lady of the household," Theodore said, pushing past Marietta.

"Ah," the man said, looking dubious. "Is your mother home?"

"Just a minute," Theodore said. He yelled over his shoulder. "Ma, there's a man here who wants to demonstrate his you-know-what."

My mother came out from her bedroom and stood behind us. She had put on a plastic Halloween mask in the shape of a bunny rabbit, and she took her drink from Leopold's hand.

"Oh," my mother said, removing the mask. "I thought you were someone we knew. Come in. What do you want to demonstrate?"

The man's expression was frightened. He was short, and, though young, had tired, houndy bags under his eyes. His suit was cheap. He was incredibly hirsute: there was even a thick pelt of hair on the back of his hands. "You're the lady of the household?" He sounded skeptical.

It was true that my mother appeared ridiculously youthful. She had huge eyes, dark and luminous, which always seemed ready to spill over with tears. They often *did* spill over; I once begged her to try and remember to collect them in a tiny vial, so that we could maybe freeze and sell the liquid for scientific research, or to a beauty-product company that didn't want to hurt animals, just make them cry.

"You must be the Minotaur Vacuum man," my mother said. "I believe I spoke to you earlier. I saw the ad in the paper for the free demonstration. Won't you come in?"

We stepped back. He carried a large suitcase, big enough to contain a cello. "Well, well, well," he said, looking around. He unlatched the case and removed a chrome machine that might have been the engine that launched a spaceship or at least a nuclear missile.

"Wow," said Pierce, going over and rubbing the sides of the machine. "Look at that."

"Thirty-five-horsepower motor," the man said, bending down beside Pierce and wiping the vacuum off with a cloth. "Enough hp to get a small car around Paris. I'm Steve Hartley, by the way."

"I've never been to Paris," my sister said. "Have you ever been to Paris, Steve?"

"You've been to Australia, though," Leopold said, giving Marietta a poke in the ribs. "I've never even been anywhere!" He turned to Steve Hartley. "They went to Australia before I was born. Tell us about your vacuum cleaner, Mr. Hartley."

Steve Hartley acted as if my mother had asked that question. He paid no attention to Leopold. "The Minotaur is able to accomplish what no other vacuum cleaner can," said Mr. Hartley. "This model is specially equipped with a glass collection chamber. Is there a mattress in the house?"

"Come this way," my mother said, leading him down the hall—what there was of it—to her bedroom. The walls were paneled in plastic that was meant to resemble wood. Her bed was covered in a lace bedspread with a pale pink lining. There was one window, with a white plastic bamboo curtain that Pierce had hung some time ago. It was a little crooked; one side no longer fully unrolled. Through the gap left on the side, the garbage cans were visible in the yard.

"I hope you don't mind if I remove some of the bedclothes," Mr. Hartley said. He pulled up the blankets and sheets and asked for the location of the electrical outlet. Leopold helped him by plugging in the machine. Mr. Hartley turned it on. It made an explosive sound and then began to chortle and yelp dementedly. "That's odd," said Mr. Hartley, yelling above the noise.

"What is?" my mother shouted.

"This is normally a very quiet machine. However, the noise is only temporary and won't affect its performance. Over time, dead cells are sloughed from your body while you sleep, drifting into the mattress. Your whole mattress is riddled with dead cells. Only the Minotaur is capable of sucking them out, without damage to the mattress."

"That's interesting," Theodore yelled.

"What is?" I said.

"Your entire past is in your mattress," he said. "If you never changed your mattress from the time you were born until you died, maybe scientists in the future could replay your existence through DNA molestation."

"What's DNA molestation?" I said.

"Where they pick on your dead cells. You know how chimps groom themselves? Similar to plucking at lice and salt deposits."

Steve Hartley ran the intake pipe over the mattress and after a few minutes turned off the machine. It shrieked and slowly the noise dwindled from an unhappy putter to an irritated cough and then stopped altogether. "It shouldn't be making that noise after it's turned off," Mr. Hartley explained, discomfited. "All it needs is a minor tune-up. Any Minotaur you purchase from us we'll be happy to tune up at any time, free of charge. It comes with a lifetime warranty. Now, I want you to take a look at this."

He was speaking to my mother, but all of us crowded around. Protruding from the back of the vacuum cleaner was a peculiar attachment: a chrome box with a glass lid. He peered in. "Let me see," said Leopold.

"One minute," said Mr. Hartley. He lifted up the lid of the box and took out a piece of cotton that had been placed in the bottom. "Look at this," he said, holding it up proudly. "It's completely gray. The Minotaur model 350 was—just in that brief period of time—able to suck out so many dead cells from the mattress that the entire cotton pad turned gray. How does that make you feel, sleeping on a mattress full of dead cells? When was the last time you even thought of cleaning the inside of your mattress?"

"That's my whole past you've got in that jar," my mother said, reaching toward him. "Give it to me."

"No, no," Mr. Hartley said nervously. "It's what they call in the industry, detritus."

2

"You know, Theodore," my mother said. "When you were talking, it reminded me of something: there's only one percent genetic difference between chimps and us. And as everyone knows, chimps are nasty, vicious, dirty animals. There are many great apes that are kind and gentle. But it's chimps who are our closest living relative."

"What about my father?" Leopold said.

"You know," said Theodore, "I bet that piece of felt was gray before you even started vacuuming."

"Of course not!" said Steve Hartley contemptuously. "You saw the white collection pad before I started, didn't you?"

"No," said Theodore, picking three or four half-eaten sourballs off my mother's bedside table where she had left them for safekeeping and putting them in the wastebasket, which was completely full. "Like I say, for all I know it could have been gray when you started."

Steve gave an angry sigh and raised his eyebrows at my mother, as if expecting assistance. "Let me demonstrate again," he said. From a compartment inside the giant-sized carrying case he removed a fluffy square of white material which he held in the air. "White," he said, putting it in the chrome box. Then he turned on the machine again.

It sounded even more furious than the first time he had switched it on, as if a hive of killer bees had suddenly been let loose in my mother's bedroom. We all crowded around the box, letting Leopold squeeze to the front, so we could watch the dead cells being sucked out of the mattress come flying into the display chamber. At first nothing happened. Then, abruptly, large chunks of cloth and foam core filled up the box. There was an upchucking noise and the engine began to groan.

"Stop!" cried my mother. "It's ripping up my mattress!"

"Quick!" said Mr. Hartley. "Turn off the machine."

It was apparent he had gotten a bit panicky, because he was the one who knew where the on/off switch was located, not us. He tried to kick the switch with his foot, but fell over the machine onto the bed.

While I was still wondering what to do, Pierce went over and unplugged the machine from the wall. Even after it was unplugged, the noise didn't stop immediately but mysteriously continued for some time.

"What have you got in there?" Theodore said. "A rodent or something?"

Leopold began to laugh uproariously. "What have you got in there?" he repeated. "A rodent or something?"

Steve Hartley quickly rose from the bed. It wasn't his fault. There was scarcely any place to maneuver in the room. Even without seven people and a huge vacuum cleaner, my mother's bedroom was the smallest area in the house, apart from the bathroom.

Our trailer wasn't exactly a Winnebago. It was never meant to go anywhere; but it wasn't cemented down, either. Our landlord, Ol' Massa Bedros Bedrosian, had told us there were once plans to build a whole trailer park. That had never happened. So there was only the one we lived in, by the shores of Gitchee Gumee.

"Sorry about that," Steve said. "Just how old was that mattress, anyway?"

"Maybe around fifteen years old," my mother said. "In any event, it wasn't new when I got it. But it was perfectly adequate. Until now."

"Oh, gosh," said Steve, "you should have told me. The Minotaur 350 is the most powerful vacuum cleaner on the market today." Averting his eyes from the mattress, he tidied the sheets and blankets back over it. "Why don't we go into the other room, and I'll show you more things the 350 is capable of?"

"I want to see the dead cells first!" said Leopold.

"Let's go out where there's more room," Steve Hartley insisted. "It's a little hot in here." He dragged the machine into the living room. Then he bent over the box and began pulling pieces of mattress out of it, which he nervously stuffed into his pocket. At last he produced a soiled felt pad. "Look!" he said, holding it up triumphantly. "See for yourselves."

We passed the square gingerly, between thumb and forefinger. "Ugh," said Marietta. Steve Hartley looked at her appreciatively. "You really are disgusting, Mother," she added. "I'm trying not to think about it." She clasped her hands to her chest and let out a piercing scream. " *'Wahonowin! Wahonowin!'* "

"Okay?" said Steve, alarmed.

" *'By the shining Big-Sea-Water / Stood the wigwam of Nokomis.'* "

"Everyone loses cells at night," Steve said, defending my mother.

"In the day, too. And, you may not know this, but the surface of your body is covered with thousands and millions of organisms."

"Do they lead rich and full lives?" said Theodore, straightening his bow tie and looking at himself in the vanity-table mirror.

"That, I wouldn't know," said Steve Hartley. "But I do know that there are special kinds of mites that live on your eyelashes. They are specifically . . . indigenous, this one type of mite that lives in between human eyelashes."

"Not me!" said Leopold.

"Everyone," said Steve.

"How could we get rid of them?" Marietta spoke seductively, in a hushed voice. "I don't care for the idea of mites in my eyelashes."

"No, no!" said Steve. He put his thumb and forefinger on his mustache, as if checking to make sure it hadn't fallen off. "They don't cause any harm—they're meant to live there."

"Did they teach you that in vacuum cleaner school?" Theodore said.

"I only do this part time," Steve said in an injured tone. "Now, if there's an outlet in here, I'd be happy to give this room a good 'cuuming."

At first it was interesting, but when he got out the various attachments and wanted to show us how the vacuum cleaner could dust venetian blinds, everyone except Mother and Leopold went into the boys' bedroom.

Theodore and Leopold slept on bunk beds, and Pierce had the single bed. There was about three feet between them. I stretched out on Theodore's bed, the bottom. "At least maybe the house will have a clean bill of health after this," Marietta said crossly, sinking down next to me. Pierce and Theodore sat opposite.

"It says it has a knife-sharpening attachment," said Theodore, looking at a brochure he had gotten from the carrying case.

"A knife-sharpening attachment!" said Pierce, taking a full ashtray from under the bed and lighting a cigarette. "That's kind of cool, huh?"

Trayf had been hiding under Pierce's bed. The dog crawled out and jumped on the bed next to the boys. "Poor old Trayf." Pierce rubbed him behind the ears, patted him on his head. He was gray, with skin that vaguely resembled that of an elephant—bumps and tiny tufts of hair sprouted here and there. He had a patch of short black hair above his eyes as well.

"Golly!" I said, suddenly remembering. "I left Lulu and the puppies in the pen in the backyard hours ago!" I leapt up, but not without knocking my head against the underside of Leopold's bunk. Marietta and Theodore snickered rudely.

In the dining room Steve Hartley was seated at the table with Leopold and my mother.

"But what would the total price be?" my mother was saying.

"I was about to get to that," Steve said. He took out a pad of yellow paper and began to write numbers in a column.

"Ma!" I said warningly. "I bet that thing's expensive." I tried to look over Steve's shoulder to see what he was writing, but he blocked the pad from my view with his elbow.

"Besides," my mother said, "none of you children ever vacuum."

"That's because the vacuum we have now doesn't even work," Leopold whined. "If we had this one, I'd use it all the time. I like seeing the dead cells on the piece of cloth in the box."

Steve chuckled. "I'm afraid the display box is just on our exhibition model only, for demonstrations. The machine you'll be receiving doesn't send the dirt anywhere but into the disposal bag."

Leopold was disappointed. "I would still use it anyway."

"How many disposal bags does the Minotaur come with?" I said.

"Ten," said Steve, crossing out some of the numbers and beginning a new column.

"If we bought it, we'd want a lot more than that—thrown in," I said. "At least a case. Free of charge."

"Free of charge?" Steve glanced over at me and his expression changed. It was an image I would never forget. He resembled a cartoon hyena clobbered over the head. His eyes turned to Xs and stars appeared to fly out of his hairy ears. It honestly made me feel kind of sick. "I'd have to get approval from my manager," he said, his voice coming out in a croak. "But I could try."

Averting my eyes, I opened the back door and stood squinting out over the lake. It was fairly ugly. There was no foliage left on the trees, except for the oaks, which always clung to their leaves even after they had turned brown and dry, like Howard Hughes refusing to allow his fingernails to be clipped. The air, the water and the land were a dreary shade of November gray. In a minute it would be too dark to see.

I could hear the puppies mewling. They were only five weeks old, and still very tender, but I couldn't bear to go back in the room with the vacuum cleaner man. I waited until the front door slammed and I could hear his car driving off before I picked them up and carried them in. Lulu followed behind, only vaguely concerned.

The others had come out of the bedroom and were sitting once again at the dining room table. "Fifteen hundred dollars!" Theodore was shouting. "What did you tell him?"

"At first I said I'd have to let him know," my mother whimpered.

"You should have told him just plain *no!*" Theodore said despairingly. "Then what happened?"

"Nothing," my mother said.

"How could you be so stupid!" Theodore said. "Tell me what happened!"

"You weren't here!" my mother said. "Quit spewing invective."

"I'm not spewing invective!" Theodore said.

"You are! You are spewing invective! *You* should have come out here, instead of hiding in the bedroom, if you were so concerned. He said I could pay in installments. He tried to get me to sign a contract right now, but I didn't do that, did I? I put it on my credit card, instead."

"You shouldn't be allowed to have a credit card!" Theodore said. "I don't know why they haven't taken it away from you! You know we can't pay off fifteen hundred dollars! I'd get on the phone right now and cancel it, only they'd probably yell at me instead of you."

"Don't cancel it, Theodore!" Leopold said. "He's going to let us have the model with the cell-collector-and-display case. No customer's ever been permitted this before. And he gave us a free present, besides!" He took a box wrapped in red paper, tied with a gold ribbon, from my mother's hand. "What is it?"

"I don't know," my mother said. "Open it."

"Why did he give you a present?" I said suspiciously. "He may want something from you, later on."

"It was a reward for allowing him to demonstrate the Minotaur," my mother said. "Even if we didn't buy it, we were entitled. Besides, if he wants something later on, one of you girls can give it to him."

Leopold eagerly unwrapped the package. "Steak knives!" he said.

"Plastic handles," Theodore pointed out.

"They were free," my mother said.

"Free!" Theodore said. "They were fifteen hundred dollars!"

"You think I'm crazy, don't you?" my mother said. "I can tell."

"He wrecked your mattress!" Theodore said. "He wrecked your mattress, we're completely broke, and you still got suckered into buying his stupid machine."

"I felt sorry for him," my mother said. Her eyes got very bright and I knew they had filled with tears, either because of her feelings for Steve Hartley, or because of Theodore's tone of voice.

"How old do you think he was?" Marietta said absently.

"Forty," I said, picking up my mother's hand, which was like a tiny claw.

"Forty!" my mother said. "Oh, no. He's twenty-eight."

"Twenty-eight!" I said. "I don't believe it. How do you know?"

"He told me," my mother said, shaking her hand free from my grasp and patting my arm affectionately. "He just does this on the weekends. He has his own computer business. He does something special with computers that nobody else knows about yet."

"Well, it must be something that nobody else wants, if he has to sell vacuum cleaners," said Theodore with a snort.

"He'll be very rich, someday," my mother said, staring pointedly at Marietta.

"He liked *me*, I believe," I said.

"We'll see about that," Marietta said, twisting her blond hair so that the bottom turned up in a flip.

"It's true he's awfully hairy," I said.

"Maybe you could shave him, Marietta," Theodore said.

"Or electrolysis," I said.

"On the back of his hands?" Theodore said, looking at the back of his hands, which were basically hair-free. "There's always body-wax."

"You girls like animals," my mother said, picking at the crusty edges that remained in the lasagna pan. "You could pretend he was a chimpanzee."

"A little chimp! A little chimpanzee!" Leopold said, jumping on and off the red-and-white–plaid couch. A cloud of dead corpuscles— or something—came out of the cushions.

"You might have gotten him to de-cell the couch," Marietta said.

"He'll be back," my mother said.

"How do you know?" I said. "I think we frightened him. Now that he's made his sale, he'll have someone else make the delivery."

"There's not going to be a delivery!" Theodore said angrily.

"He's lonely," my mother said. She got up and began to wander aimlessly around, picking up the paper cups that littered every surface, and putting them back down.

"Yeah, and he knows an easy mark when he sees one," Theodore said. "I'd cancel the order only he'll be back in a flash to re-convince you."

"Children, things are really shaping up," my mother said, blithely ignoring him. "I can see, we're in for a change in our future around here. Good things are just around the corner. Now, Leopold, where did I leave that delicious gin-and-tonic?"

3

"I wonder why Mom thinks our luck has changed?" said Theodore in the morning.

"Who knows?" I said. "She does have considerable psychic abilities." It was ten o'clock and we were waking up. My mother was still asleep in her room. She slept late. There were days when she didn't get out of bed at all. We would bring her malted milk balls, hard candy and Jordan almonds on a tray. She liked to suck the candy coating off the almonds, leaving the nuts intact, as it was lower in calories to do this than to eat the whole thing.

"Maybe it's because we got a free set of steak knives," said Leopold. "That's a good sign, isn't it?" Pierce lit a cigarette. "Those cigarettes stink, Pierce," Leopold said. "How can you smoke so early in the morning?"

"Sorry," said Pierce, but he didn't put out the cigarette. Leopold opened the door. Lulu and Trayf came in. They snuffled the floor under the table, looking for food particles to inhale. It was a warm day, for so late in the year. The ashtray was full of cigarette butts which no one had emptied.

"How late did you stay up last night, Pierce?" I said.

"I was watching a movie," Pierce said.

Marietta came into the dining room, rubbing her eyes. She apparently hadn't removed her eye makeup before going to sleep, because her eyes had two big black rings around them. Her breasts poked through her nightgown, which was pink nylon. It had been washed so many times there were sheer patches in the fabric, almost like netting.

"Good morning," I said. "Want some coffee?"

"Don't speak to me in that civil tone of voice," Marietta said.

"Sorry," I sneered.

"It was a weird movie," she said.

"Did you watch it too?" I said. She didn't answer, but I could feel her contempt at the stupidity of my question wafting across the room. The coffeepot was on the table. She got down a mug hanging in a row with others—my favorite, a white ceramic mug with an illustration of a German shepherd on one side and facts regarding the breed on the other. "Isn't there any fresh milk?" she said, picking up the can of sweetened evaporated milk with two punch holes in the lid. No one answered. I tried to waft some contempt back in her direction. She poured the evaporated milk into the mug with her coffee.

"What was the movie about, Pierce?" I said.

"It was kind of cool," Pierce said. He scratched his neck. "There was a guy that was a servant. Or something."

"And what happened?" I said.

"He lived in a big house. The family was away. There was a murder. Or at least he found a body. I don't know who did it, though. It was kind of scary."

"It was a comedy, Pierce," Marietta said. "A romantic comedy."

"Oh yeah?" said Pierce. "Cool."

"You're sweet, Pierce," I said.

"Leave me alone, Maud," Pierce said. He put out his cigarette. My mother came into the room. She was wearing a bright blue marabou robe, very fluffy feathers that were missing in only a few patches. She had a rubber pig's nose held on over her own nose with a piece of elastic and a pair of sunglasses over her eyes, upside-down.

"Very amusing," said Theodore bitterly, putting down his half-eaten bowl of cereal. "Ever try eating Rice Krispies with condensed milk? Ugh."

"It's evaporated milk," Marietta said, picking up the can and examining the label on the side.

My mother took off the sunglasses and the pig's nose. "We have to make some plans around here," she said. "I've been thinking. I have an idea."

"What?" said Marietta.

"I will reveal all in a minute," my mother said. "Somebody pour me a cup of coffee."

Leopold pulled a chair over to where the mugs were hanging. "Would you like the mug with the balloons, Mother?" he said. "Or the endangered tree frog?"

"You decide, my petulant cupcake," she said, sliding out a chair and sitting down. Trayf and Lulu came over and put their noses on her lap. "Darling Lulu," my mother said, stroking the dogs. "Where are your puppies? Soon they will be old enough to sell, and we shall be rich, rich beyond our wildest dreams."

"Is that your plan, Ma?" Theodore said. "Because I got news for you. Nobody around here is going to want to buy a hairless dog."

"How pessimistic you are," my mother said. Leopold poured the mug with the tree frog full of coffee and was about to add the sweetened evaporated milk when she shook her head. "I drink it black," she reminded him. "Unless there's a shot of something to pour in."

"There's only gin, Ma!" Theodore said. "Gin and beer! I'd get you into an alcohol rehab program, only they'd be mad at me for taking up their time, and say you had to want to do it yourself."

"Are there any muffins to have with it, then? Cakes? Sweet rolls?"

"I could bake something now," Leopold said.

"It will take too long. Look in the freezer. In the door compartment."

Leopold went into the kitchenette and came out with a plastic bag. "This?" he said, holding it up. "It's full of crumbs."

"I like crumbs," my mother said. "They are muffin crumbs, left over from a muffin. Give me the chilled crumbs. I need something to go with my coffee."

"Tell us your plan, Ma," Theodore said.

"Wait," I said. "I have to bring in the puppies. Tell us in a minute." I stood up. There was a knock on the door. A man came in. It was Edward. He reeked of booze and was wearing a beautiful pair of red-and-black cowboy boots with eagles on the side I had never seen before.

"Edward!" my mother said, getting up and going over to him. "Light of my life! Father of my youngest child! Where have you been?"

"Little Mommikins!" he nickered. "My wild filly! I missed you." He put his arms around her and they kissed, nuzzling as if they were a pair of Icelandic ponies—Edward, the shaggy stallion, entranced by our mother, who coquettishly stamped a pretty hoof, flashing her dark, equine eyes. We all watched for a full minute. Then, with a little whinny, my mother lightly reared up and pulled away.

"You stink," she said.

"Sorry," Edward said.

"Where's your motorcycle?" Theodore said.

"I totaled it," he said. "A mile or so up the road. Near the Colemans' house. Some guy I never saw before came out and helped me. I thought I must have broken something. He gave me a drink."

Now that he was detached from my mother I could see his face was pocked and reddened, probably from landing in gravel. His shoulder-length, palomino-colored hair was all matted, as if he had come down with a bad case of mane rot.

"Was he a handsome Englishman?" Marietta said. "Did he speak of me? Did I galvanize him into action?"

"He's never even met you, Marietta," I said. "It's me he desires."

"My darling!" cried my mother. "Were you hurt?"

"I don't know," Edward said, walking stiffly around the room and sitting down on the couch. The two dogs stood behind the coffee table and began barking at him. "Shut up!" Edward said. "What did I do?"

"They don't like you," Theodore said. "You should be careful. Dogs can turn feral at any minute."

"Theodore!" said my mother warningly. "Don't say that. You'll drive him away. Where else am I going to find a man, at my age, living out here in the middle of nowhere." Tears came into her eyes.

"What do you need a man for, Ma?" Theodore said.

My mother didn't answer. She sat down again at the table and began picking at the crumbs in the bag. Then she emptied the contents of the bag onto a paper plate. In between lifting the crumbs to her coral seas she sipped her black coffee. No one said anything for a minute.

"You'll be gone soon enough, Theodore," Edward said. "You don't want your mother to be all alone, do you? I'd like to marry her and be a father to my little boy. Where is he?"

Leopold got out of his chair and shuffled over to the couch. He smiled at Edward and sat down next to him. "You're not really my father, are you?" he said.

"I'm sure he is your father, Leopold," I said. "The two of you have exactly the same nose."

Leopold examined Edward's face intently. "Oh, lord," he said, and moved away from him on the couch. "You do stink."

"I'll take a shower," Edward said, but made no move to get up. "I'm not the worst of your mother's boyfriends, either."

"That may be true," I muttered. "But nobody's seen you around here in years. You can't expect to just walk back in." I was still standing by the back door, meaning to go out and bring the puppies up the stairs.

"Got any Percodan?" said Edward. "Any codeine? I'm in severe pain. I might have cracked a rib or something."

"No, we don't have any Percodan!" said Theodore. "We don't have any codeine! You're twenty-eight years old! Our mother's forty-five! You're too young to be with such an old lady!"

"Go look under my bed, Leopold," my mother said. "There may be some pills there."

"Doesn't that show that I genuinely love her?" Edward said. "Your mother is beautiful. She has a beautiful soul, that shines through. That's unusual, in a person."

"I'm touched," my mother said. "So very touched. What a lovely thing to say, Edward."

"What are you going to live on?" Theodore said.

"My disability check from Social Security," Edward said. "Things are getting worse. Maybe I'll die and your mother will continue to receive my benefits. I'll have to look into it."

"I didn't see any pills, but look what I found!" Leopold said, coming back into the room.

"My high school class ring!" said Theodore indignantly. "I've been searching for it for months!" He glared at my mother. "You stole it!"

Edward stood up threateningly. "I won't have that kind of talk while I'm around."

"Oh, shut up, Edward," my mother said.

"I'm glad your motorcycle was totaled, Edward," Leopold said. "You had no business riding a motorcycle with epilepsy. How did you ever get a license, with epilepsy?"

"I didn't check the epilepsy box, on the application," Edward said. "They probably would have figured it out eventually. I got a new license when I moved here. They haven't shown any interest in the seven years since then."

"I tell you what!" my mother said cheerfully. "Edward, you take a shower, let's everyone get dressed, and I'll drive us all to the library!"

"I'd still like to know what my ring was doing under your bed," Theodore said bitterly.

"I'll have to do some work on the car first," Pierce said, getting up. "I was going to change the transmission fluid today."

The telephone rang. "Somebody, get the phone!" my mother said.

"I'm not going to get it," Pierce said. "You get it."

"I'm not going to get it," said Marietta. "You get it." She began to declaim, over the ringing. " *'Then the angry Hiawatha / Raised his mighty bow of ash-tree.'* "

"Theodore, it's probably for you," I said. "Why don't you answer it."

"Who would call me?" Theodore said. "I hate answering the phone, anyway."

We suddenly took an interest in Leopold. He stared at the ceiling. "There's a spider web up there," he said.

"Oh, my God," said Edward. He got up stiffly and went to the phone. It was only a few feet away, on the wall by the doorway of the kitchenette. "Hang on a sec," he said. "It's for you, Evangeline."

"Who is it?" my mother said.

"I don't know," Edward said, handing her the receiver.

"Is it really you?" my mother said breathily into the phone. "How are you, my love?" She stepped into the kitchenette and pulled the flimsy door shut behind her.

"Hey, Edward, how you been?" said Pierce.

Edward walked restlessly back and forth. "Not too good," he said. "I did six months in prison on a minor marijuana charge. Really pissed me off. So, uh, your mother—has she been seeing anybody else?"

I went down the back steps. The puppies had stumbled across the yard, adventuring on their own. There was no grass in the yard, only scrubby oak trees and moss enclosed by a wire fence that was broken down in places. The lake was about forty feet away, at the bottom of a mild incline. There were some geese out today. It was Sunday. The Algonquin Military Proving Ground across the water was quiet. It took me a few minutes to find all the dogs and gather them up.

I carried them under my arms back to the bedroom I shared with Marietta. She was sitting at the vanity, stroking fresh eye makeup on top of the old effluvial deposits. "What are you doing?" I said, putting the squeaking puppies in the cardboard box.

"I'm anointing myself with unguents," Marietta said. "Mr. Hartley is on his way over now."

"How come?" I said. I peeled off my pajama pants and began to open drawers in the dresser, hoping to find something to wear.

"That was him on the phone. Mother said she couldn't afford the vacuum cleaner he showed us yesterday, and he wants to bring over a reconditioned model for sale."

"Reconditioned?" I said. "Does that mean it's used?"

"A used model, but good as new," Marietta said. "And a lot less expensive. Where are my tweezers?"

"I don't see why you're taking all this trouble. I thought you didn't care for him." I handed her a tweezers and, sitting on the edge of the bed, started to pull on a pair of purple bell-bottom pants.

"He's a man, isn't he?" Marietta said. "And Mother says he's going to be fabulously wealthy. I have no intentions of working if I can help it. To hell with the feminist movement. These are not the tweezers I want. These are the bad tweezers. Where are the good tweezers? They are mine."

"I don't know where the good tweezers are," I said. "And I don't see how you can be interested in a man who is so hairy and whose face is so meaty. Except for that minute mustache, he looks absolutely inedible. And you're so blond and ethereal. You remind me of a delicious piece of fruit, on the verge of ripeness."

"If his computer deal goes through, Steve Hartley stands to make something like thirty million dollars."

"I've always enjoyed luncheon meat," I said. "Besides, I think he's in love with me. Being loved counts for a great deal."

Marietta turned, the tweezers poised in one hand. "You think I can't woo him from you?"

"Not a chance in hell," I said dubiously. Then I thought of something else to put on. There was a wig on the floor in the corner of the wardrobe I had been saving for a special occasion. If Marietta was going to try and take Mr. Hartley from me, at least I could give her a run for her money.

I rummaged around until I found it. I put my hair into a ponytail and crammed it into the wig-cap. It was a red-haired, synthetic wig of straight, silky, shoulder-length hair.

"Bitch!" said Marietta, putting on a chintz slip-dress covered with cabbage roses, which she wore over a dull-green leotard. "With your graven beauty—and the fact that you're only nineteen years old—you can get away with anything."

I smiled smugly. Then I sat down and began to cry.

"What's wrong?" Marietta said, coming over and putting her arm around my shoulder.

"I'll never escape this hellhole!" I said. "I'll never get out of this dump, this backwater bilge."

"Yes, you will," Marietta said. "Yes, you will."

"Check under Mom's bed for your good tweezers," I suggested.

4

"You got here very quickly, Mr. Steve!" I said gaily.

"I was down the road." He looked around nervously. "I called from the gas station."

My mother was standing right behind me. "Mr. Hartley, come in!" she said. "I'd like you to meet my fiancé, Edward Schumacher. You're both exactly the same age. Maybe you could be friends."

Theodore put his hands over his ears. "God damn it, Ma, why don't you think before you speak?"

"In what way?" my mother said.

"In whatever way you are capable of thinking! Just because two people are twenty-eight years old doesn't mean they have anything in common. There are millions of people who are twenty-eight years old, and they're not friends!"

"How many people are there who are twenty-eight years old, I wonder," my mother said. She patted Leopold, who had crowded in alongside her, on the head. Now his ruffled hair stood straight up.

Steve Hartley wasn't listening. He was intently observing me. I gave him a wink. "You seem different," he noted.

"I'm wearing a wig." I smiled shyly. "And a hell of a lot of makeup."

"I don't like women wearing a lot of makeup." Steve fondled his mustache distractedly.

I stroked my mustache. It wasn't much of a mustache, really, just a few suggestive hairs above my lip. Marietta thought I should bleach them. I knew better. Probably there was a man out there searching for a woman with a dark little mustache. "Steve, I'm going to go march myself right into my bedroom and take it off," I said. "You must be a wonderful salesperson, for I've never felt such a compulsion in my life!"

Steve practically swooned. I turned and gave Marietta, who had come up behind us, a triumphant smirk. She scowled. Then she went over to Steve.

" '*I will send a Prophet to you,*' " she said, " " '*A Deliverer of the nations, / Who shall guide you and shall teach you.*' That's a gorgeous tie you're wearing, Steve. Could I examine it a little more closely?" She picked up one end of it, and, leaning forward, whispered something in his ear.

"Oh?" Steve said, eyeing me.

"What did you say?" I said. "What did you tell him?"

"Can we see the reconditioned Minotaur?" said Leopold.

Steve industriously began to unpack equipment on the floor near the door. "This reconditioned model number 275 is in no way inferior to the number 350. The model is different only in that we've moved the positioning of the on/off switch and some of the features have been streamlined. But the number 275 is absolutely every bit as good as the newer model and—I want to let you in on a secret—some of our customers feel the older model is even superior. Now, you're wondering what 'reconditioned' means. Easy: when someone exchanges their older model, every single aspect is renovated in the factory. It's absolutely brand new."

"Does the old model have the chrome display box for the dead cells?" Leopold said.

"No, I'm afraid not. What I'm going to do, if I may, if you'll show me the outlet—" Leopold plugged it in. Over the noise Steve Hartley shouted, "Listen to how quiet this machine is. See what I mean about it even being superior to the newer model? They say it's practically silent."

"How long is the cord, Steve?" I said.

"What?"

"How long is the electric cord? How far can I go with it before I run out of cord?" I caught Marietta looking at Steve meaningfully. She raised her eyebrows in my direction. She had a wistful smile on her face. She *always* had a wistful smile on her face. Even when her face was in repose, it appeared to have a wistful smile. That was her natural expression. In my opinion, this made her irresistible.

Involuntarily, Steve smiled back at her. He had no way of knowing that her smile meant nothing. He turned to me. "Six feet," he said.

"What?" I said.

"With a machine this powerful, you don't want to have a long cord getting tangled up in things," he said. "You can see the cord is heavy-duty. It's a safety feature. It would be too bulky to move around with a long cord. It could get sucked in too easily. It's one of the features we're working on."

"Oh," I said. "Can you turn it off?"

"What?" he said.

"Leopold, unplug it," I said. When it was quiet I said, "Steve, can I take it into my bedroom? I'd like to try it out alone."

"If my children would actually use this vacuum cleaner, I would seriously consider buying it," my mother said. "I didn't realize any of them were interested in vacuuming."

The machine had wheels but it was still difficult to move. "Leopold, you get behind and shove while I pull," I said. I took it down the hall to my bedroom, with Leopold pushing. Then I plugged it in. After I vacuumed for a few minutes, I shut it off. Lulu had jumped into the puppy box and was nursing the puppies. She was even grayer and flabbier than Trayf, the puppies' father. Nursing babies had done nothing for her figure. She needed a brassiere. I wondered if there were any brassieres on the market for dogs, and, if not, might this be a good invention. "Come with me, sweetheart," I said. "I have a treat for you in the kitchen."

Lulu followed me down the hall. Steve Hartley glanced up. Then he turned pale white. It made his five-o'clock shadow appear even darker. "Something terrible has happened, Steve," I said. "Perceive what your machine did to my dog."

"My God," he said. "My machine did that? My reconditioned Minotaur?"

"She had a small amount of loose fur," I said, picking her up and plastering what I hoped was a tragic expression across my face. "I thought I'd vacuum her off."

"Oh, well," he said desperately. "I'm sure it will grow back."

"See, Steve?" said Marietta, touching him on the forearm. "What did I tell you?"

"What did you tell him?" I said. "What?"

"That's a hairless dog, Steve," Marietta said. "It didn't have any fur to begin with. My sister's a pathological liar. It's sad."

"I'm not a pathological liar!" I said. "You are! Don't believe her, Steve!"

"The dog didn't have any hair to begin with?" Steve said. "It's sick?"

"Mr. Hartley," my mother said, "I can't afford seven hundred and fifty dollars for the reconditioned model. I can't afford a vacuum cleaner for three hundred and fifty dollars."

"I explained to you about our installment program?" He rummaged in his briefcase. "You'd be surprised how—"

"I'm unemployed," my mother said. "We're in debt up to our ears. I have five tiny children."

Steve got up. "I don't want to take up any more of your time," he said. "I'll get the machine."

"Let me show you where I left it, Steve," I said, putting Lulu on the floor.

"I'll show him," Marietta said. "You did all the work vacuuming the bedroom. You rest yourself."

"Marietta, I'm rested," I said, opening my eyes wide. "You look tired. You're the one who stayed up all night."

Steve turned warily to face my sister and me. "Maybe it's best if one of you brings it out here."

"I'll go," Marietta said, to my surprise. She leapt up and with a wistful smile in Steve's direction she left the room.

"We'll go too," my mother said. "Are we all ready?"

"What?" said Steve. "Where are you going?"

"We're going to the library," my mother said, clasping her hands together underneath her chin.

"Oh, Mr. Hartley!" Marietta called from the bedroom. "Could you come in here for a minute? I seem to be having difficulty."

Steve glanced down the hall. He looked worried. He looked like he was worrying about future lawsuits if he was trapped alone in the room with her.

"Slut," I muttered as Steve mustered his strength and headed toward the bedroom. "Litigious slut." He flinched, but kept walking.

The rest of us grabbed our jackets. Theodore, Leopold and I stood at the bottom of the stairs. Pierce was halfway under the 1973 GTO that was my mother's car. The metallic blue paint was chipped and rusted in spots. Edward came out behind us. He was wearing a leather motorcycle racing jacket he had left in my mother's closet ages ago. It was emblazoned in red lettering with the name FRANK WORD. "This coat smells like perfume," he said. "Who's been wearing it?"

"Gosh, Edward," I said. "Don't be so petty. How's it going, Pierce?"

"I don't know," Pierce said, his voice muffled. "There's something else wrong with it. It's going to take me a while."

"But I wanted to go to the library," I said.

My mother came out of the trailer. Her hair was standing out all over her head as if she had brushed it too hard. It might have been static electricity. She had put on a floor-length striped coat of iridescent slubbed silk. I don't know what she had on underneath. "Are we all set?" she said. "Where's Marietta?"

"She's still in the bedroom with Steve," said Theodore. He shook his head, thinking either about Marietta inside with Steve, or about the inappropriateness of my mother's coat. It was more of an evening coat than a library coat. "Pierce says the car isn't working."

"Pierce, is that true?" my mother asked. "What are we going to do? How long will it take to fix?"

"I don't know." Pierce squirmed out on his back from beneath the car. He sat up and began biting his cuticles.

"How are we going to get to the library?" my mother said. Marietta and Steve came out. Steve was carrying the vacuum cleaner in the case. There was a moment's silence while we watched them. "I'm sorry to have taken up your time," Steve muttered nervously.

"Are you going into town now, Mr. Hartley?" my mother said.

"Yes," said Steve hesitantly.

"Do you think we could get a lift from you?"

"I—it'll be kind of crowded."

"But this is your car, isn't it?" my mother said, pointing. "We can all fit." She went over and got in the passenger's side. Leopold climbed on her lap. The rest of us got in the back. It was crowded. "Leopold, jump out and tell Pierce that we'll call him later on to pick us up," my mother said. Leopold hopped out and ran over to Pierce. Steve was putting the vacuum cleaner in the trunk.

"So, what happened?" I hissed at Marietta. She smiled fiercely. "Tell me!" I said. She kept smiling and shut her eyes. Steve got into the driver's seat. I pinched Marietta, hard, on the arm.

"Get your filthy hands off me," Marietta said. Then, in a softer voice, she added, "I've asked you many times not to pinch or bite."

"I don't bite! And you were the one who taught me to pinch!"

"Are we all set back there?" Steve said, as Leopold climbed in again. "Mrs. Slivenowicz, is your seat belt fastened?"

"Can this guy drive?" muttered Theodore.

"Please, you can call me Evangeline," my mother said. "Mr. Hartley, this is so kind of you. Would you like to join us this evening for dinner?"

"I'm afraid I can't tonight," Steve said, pinning his mustache down with the forefinger of his right hand.

"What about tomorrow?" my mother said. "Both my daughters are excellent cooks."

"Hey, that's not fair!" said Leopold. "They never cook anything! I'm the one that does all the cooking!"

"Is it true, Edward, that you used to be a chef?" Theodore said.

"It is true," Edward said. He was jammed against the door next to Marietta. "I was a sous-chef at one of New York's finest restaurants. You've heard of the Old Yorktown Hofbrauhaus? But I had to stop when my epilepsy got worse."

I caught a glimpse of Leopold over my mother's shoulder. He looked pleased. "It's a very fancy restaurant, isn't it?" I said. "The Old Yorktown Hofbrauhaus. I've heard of it."

"What about this cinematographer business, Edward?" Theodore sounded accusing. "You were a cinematographer, too?"

"For a little while," Edward said. He struggled to get his arm free and wiped his forehead. "I made several documentaries in the Middle East."

"The Middle East! What was your position on the projects?" Theodore said. "Isn't that dangerous? Was this before or after you were a chef?"

"Don't talk to me for a minute," Edward said.

"Are you all right back there?" my mother said. "Edward, are you all right?"

Edward was leaning his face against the glass and didn't answer. With so many of us weighing down the car, it was very bumpy on the gravel road. After a minute or so we turned onto the paved road and the ride was smoother. I couldn't see where we were, seated in the middle between Marietta and Theodore. "Where are we?" I said. "This isn't at all familiar."

"You should get glasses, Maud," said Marietta.

"Well, this is the library," said Steve in a weak voice, as he turned to face the back. "Have a nice time!" His coral seas smiled but his eyes remained grim and desperate.

We all climbed out. "Thanks for the ride, Steve," I said.

"Thanks so very much!" my mother said.

"I just have to tell him something," Marietta said. "You go on ahead." She turned back and tapped on the window for Steve to unroll it. Then she leaned seductively over the driver's seat.

5

We went up the stairs. The library was brand new. Although Nokomis was not a big town, the library was huge. It had cost a lot of money to build. There were ramps for wheelchairs and, inside, gray wall-to-wall carpeting. There were very few actual books in the library, however. To raise funds, the librarian had held a big sale and gotten rid of most of the volumes.

Now, although there was a department to borrow CDs and video tapes, and a children's library, the main library had only four sections containing books. Reference books could not be checked out. But there were some new fiction books, some travel books, a few shelves containing biographies of movie stars and other cultural leaders, and books on gardening.

I headed for the reference section. There was a book on poultry I had only had a chance to dip into on our last expedition. The others headed off in their own directions. Theodore wanted to look up information on sackbuts, which he claimed were medieval trombones. Edward and Leopold were going to look at Bavarian cookbooks to find a recipe for spaetzle. "How exactly did you say you met my mother?" Leopold said sincerely, looking up at him as they brushed past.

It was very noisy in the library, because the town had voted to have music playing over the new stereo system, and some of the children had taken the tricycles and laser machine guns out of the children's wing and were running up and down the book section.

It was also quite crowded. It was Sunday and there was nothing to do in Nokomis. Hunting season was finished, or else hadn't begun. The nearest shopping mall was a hundred miles away. The Nokomis Shopping Mall wasn't scheduled to open for another six months, since it had taken the developers a long time to purchase the Henry Wadsworth Longfellow Preservation Land Trust from the town, which is where the money to build the library came from. The difficulty arose over a state law that prevented the developers from paying market value; they were forced to take out a low-interest government mortgage and buy the land at a price set in 1910.

The trees had already begun to come down, but no one could see how they could build a mall on the scope of what was planned and have it completed in only six months, although it was true that the new lightweight roof was designed to be rolled on quite easily. By the time the mall was built, before the lightweight roof collapsed from the heavy weight of winter's sorbet-textured snows, I hoped to be long gone to a better climate, although some very exclusive factory discount-and-remainder outlets were promised.

It took me ten minutes to locate *The Encyclopedia of Poultry*, which had been put back in the wrong place, between the library's two books on African art. There were a number of remarkable birds, with all kinds of ruffs and feathers, and others that laid blue eggs. I particularly liked the type called the Saipan Oriental Game Fowl. This was a huge chicken (the roosters matured at three and a half to four feet tall) with a very long neck, very long legs and a tiny body.

The Shamo, which was known for its cruel expression, and even crueler personality, was another interesting bird. My dream was to acquire one or two of these chickens and raise them from hatchlings, so they would bond with me. If I limited myself to one or two, I might take them with me when I left.

I was so immersed in this book that I didn't notice a man standing behind me. "I was wondering if you were going to be reading that book for much longer," he said.

"What?" I said. It was the Englishman from up the road, but he was whispering, and I wasn't certain I understood him. He was even handsomer than I remembered, with exquisite, rebellious blue eyes almost like glass marbles, and pure black hair.

"Oh," he said. "It's you. You're the girl from the trailer, aren't you?"

"Speak up!" I said. "This is the library! I can't hear you."

"I didn't mean to rush you with that book," he said.

"It's a book on chickens!" I said.

"And fowl," he said. "I'm doing some architectural renovations on the Wolverhampton estate. I wanted to see how difficult it would be for them to keep a few peafowl on the estate. I don't know if it's warm enough here."

"You should go look in the *Rare Breeds Journal*," I said. "They have plenty of ads for emus and ostrich. They would make good guards, and add drama to the estate. Now I'm interested in getting chickens, but someday, I hope to have ostrich. Or emus." He didn't respond, so I attempted to drag out the conversation. "The Wolverhampton estate!" I said. "That's what you'd call a mansion, wouldn't you? Or might it be considered an overly large monstrosity?"

"It was built in the eighteen nineties. It's been empty for twenty years. I was brought over by the new owners. It needs a lot of work."

I looked at him, speechless, trying to come up with a way to prolong things. Finally I thought of something. "You said you're from England, didn't you? How is it, these days?"

"You know, I was actually going to stop by, later on," he said. "Something did bite me, and I thought you might know if it was one of those poisonous spiders you mentioned."

"Show me the bite," I said.

"I can't, actually."

"How come?"

"It's in rather an embarrassing spot!" he said. He gave an abrupt cackle that made me involuntarily wince. Maybe that was just how they cackled where he came from.

"On your buttocks?" I said. He didn't answer. "On your manhood?"

"Buttocks," he said quickly. "Do you think I should see a doctor?"

"What does the bite look like?"

"A dot," he said. "A red dot. I can only glimpse it with a mirror. I'm a bit embarrassed to confess."

"You don't want me to examine it?"

"I haven't felt ill or anything," he said.

"You don't feel ill," I said. "That's not what happens. It's not the same as black widow spider bite. Those live around here, too."

"You're joking!"

"No," I said. "But you'd know if you were bitten by a black widow spider right away."

"What happens with those?" he said.

"Don't you read the *Reader's Digest*?"

"No," he said.

"There was an interesting article. You could look it up. The library has an extensive collection of *Reader's Digest*s. There's quite a few condensed books, too. That's how I got my education."

"It's called the reclusive spider?"

"The brown recluse spider!" I said. "There have been quite a few cases of spider bites in Nokomis. It's horrible."

"Tell me," he said.

"Okay." I closed the *Encyclopedia of Poultry* with a sigh. I could see Marietta had spotted me from across the room. I got up. "Come with me out front so I can talk without disturbing anyone. I think the librarian is glaring in our direction."

He followed me dutifully past Marietta. I gave her a smirk.

We stood outside on the front steps. The temperature had suddenly dropped and a bitter wind swept along. The Englishman smiled uncomfortably. "A bit chilly for ostrich and emus, don't you think?"

"What?" I said.

He got out a playing-card-sized silver container and started to roll tobacco from it into a cigarette. "What's your name?" I said.

"I'm terribly sorry. I'm Simon Halkett."

"I'm Maud."

"And your surname?"

"My what?"

"Your other name?"

"Maud Slivenowicz. I kept my mother's last name. Tell me, do you think God would put animals here on earth and not give them some kind of a good time? The jellyfish, the flatworm, the anemone, even the amoeba—maybe they have a lot more physical pleasure in life than we ever receive."

"I know very little about God." He sighed and lit his cigarette with a gold lighter. It took some time to do so in the wind. "The thing is," he said at last, "after I spoke to you, I remembered I had been in the basement, when a fuse blew. Later on, I felt a hard bump, which I could only see in a mirror. Perhaps it's merely a shag spot."

"Merely a what?"

"A shag spot. You know, a boil. Pimple to you."

"Perhaps." There was something so awful about the word *pimple*. It made things so much worse. If only a pimple could be called something nicer—an artichoke, for example. "It might be merely a blemish, but on the other hand it could be the bite of one of these spiders I was referring to," I said. "What happens is, one of these spiders gives you a bite. There was a plumber, he didn't even notice it. You don't, somehow. A bite, a prick, a nibble, a nip—who pays much attention? I remember once, my mother came across some kind of a scam. Anyway, she found a sort of . . . situation, in which we could all emigrate to Australia, for very little money. There were only four of us then. Well, we came back after only a short time. However, I remember we stayed in a very run-down place, which they called a hotel. And the beds had bugs! All night I was scratching, scratching. They were bedbugs! But during the daytime, I forgot all about it."

Simon inhaled strenuously. I had never seen a man roll his own cigarettes before. "But what about the plumber?" he said.

"He only came to look at the toilet," I said. "This was ages ago, before there were even supposed to be brown recluse spiders in the area. He ended up staying several years. We didn't live in a trailer then. I'm not making this up. About six months before, he had been bending over a toilet—he was *always* bending over a toilet—and he felt a sharp bite, on his forehead, which he paid no attention to. I'm afraid he had something of a drinking problem, that plumber, which is how our mother first fell into bad ways."

"So what happened?"

"At first there was a red dot. But the dot didn't go away. And gradually it became a great, big, oozing, suppurating sore." I was very pleased at having worked the word *suppurating* into a sentence. I looked at Simon to see if he noticed. He was staring at me intently, the cigarette halfway up to his coral seas. "Are you a lord?" I said.

"What?" he said.

"A lord!" I said. "A lord! By any chance, are you a lord?"

He got kind of red and abruptly began to fumble with his cigarette, trying to get it lit again in the wind. "Ah, well, I—that's beside the point, isn't it."

"Aha! So you *are* a lord."

"It doesn't mean anything," he said.

"But you are one."

"Actually, yes. But it's not really something I like to—"

"Cool," I said. "I've never met a lord before. Not a real one, anyway. Quick, crouch behind the cement wall." I gave him a shove.

"I beg your pardon? Why must I crouch?"

"I saw my sister on the top step looking for me. She's crazy. If she tries to talk to you, ignore her. It's sad, but she has a great many mental problems." He was obviously perplexed, but after Marietta had gone back in I let him stop crouching. "A real lord," I reiterated. "I thought maybe it was just something in books, you know. English books about dead personages. In fact, I've never met anyone from England before. I've met Australians, though. That's similar, isn't it? *You* know: 'Tie me kangaroo down, sport!' Right?" I gave him a wink. Simon blanched, which was rather nice, since I had never seen anyone actually blanching before, only read about it, maybe in the very same books about long-dead English people. "Of course, I was too young to remember. So. A real lord."

"Please continue about the spider bite," he said, but I had the feeling he was secretly pleased I had discovered his secret lordliness.

"Well, the plumber's suppurating sore grew worse and worse. Tell no one—but we children were, speaking frankly, rather disgusted with my mother's latest 'find'—a plumber with a suppurating, oozing sore on his forehead."

"And he drank too much," Simon said.

"There's no need to be judgmental," I said. "Anyway, to make a long story short, the sore continued to suppurate and suppurate. Finally, something had to be done. But no doctor had the slightest idea of what was wrong with the plumber. Of course, this plumber was equally well known for having no idea of what was wrong with anyone's plumbing. But that has nothing to do with this. You see, I was really too young to actually be able to remember; thus, some of this I'm forced to improvise."

"But what happened?"

"Naturally the sore had to be cleaned out, but by that time the suppuration had progressed so far that extensive plastic surgery had to be performed. The plumber used this as an excuse to get his nose fixed and paid for by his insurance, which he had always wanted, but which would normally have been considered 'cosmetic' surgery and therefore not covered under his health plan. I forget how it came about, but a young resident at the medical center had, by pure accident, collected spiders—arachnids—as a child, and instantly recognized what had transpired. The spider bite itself, you see, is innocuous enough, but the poison injected seeps through the nervous system and eats away everything in its path."

"Bloody hell," said Simon.

"And since then, the spider's whereabouts have spread. There was another woman, bitten in the leg, but thought nothing of it, and yet couldn't understand why the bite got worse instead of better. The doctor gave her antibiotic cream but it didn't go away and soon her whole leg was rotting and by the time they cleaned it out she lost half her calf. Gangrenous."

"Was this person . . . also involved with your family?"

"No. I read about it, in the *Reader's Digest*."

"Oh, God, I'd better see a doctor," Simon said.

"Even now, a lot of doctors are unaware of this insidious condition," I said. "Just make sure you keep mentioning it, and the sense of suppuration, or else they'll think it's a flea bite. Can I ask you a question?"

"Yes," said Simon.

"Who do you find more attractive—me, or my sister?"

"I was just going to say—" Simon said, a look of panic crossing his face. Before he could answer, the door of the library opened.

"Quick, crouch again!" I said.

"But why?" Simon said.

"It's my sister, Marietta! She's venal!"

However, it was only my brother Leopold. He came out with his nose bleeding all over the place. He had his hand covering it, but large splashes were still dripping over the cement steps.

"Leopold! What happened?" I pulled his hand away from his nose, which was a mistake.

"Oh dear, oh dear, oh dear," said Simon.

"Stanley Brooks punched me in the children's wing!" he said, sobbing. "The librarian told me to go and bleed outside."

"I suppose she didn't want you to bleed over the few books they
still have," I said, rummaging in my pockets. "I don't know how
many times I've told you, leave your male counterparts alone!"

"I didn't do anything!"

"Don't you have a tissue?" I asked the lord.

Simon searched frantically and handed me a handkerchief, made
of fabric. I examined the monogram. "That's unusual," I said. "A
cloth tissue. Haven't you ever heard of Kleenex? They're disposable."
I pinched Leopold's nose. "Sit down on the steps," I said. "Sit down
and lean your head back."

"Crummy bastard," Leopold said between sobs.

"Don't cry, or you'll make it keep bleeding," I said. "Where's that
knife I gave you on your birthday?"

"I didn't bring it," Leopold said. "Why would I bring a knife to
the library?"

"Next time, do so."

"How old is he?" Simon asked.

"He's six."

Simon stooped beside him. "You're a plucky little fellow, aren't
you. Would you like me to teach you some self-defense techniques?
I used to kick-box, in school."

"I don't know," Leopold said with a shrug. "Maybe."

"We'll be by tomorrow," I told Simon. "What's a good time
for you?"

"Around four?" he said hesitantly.

Leopold's nose had stopped bleeding and I hoisted him up. At that
moment the others came out of the library. "We were looking for
you," my mother said. "What's happened?"

"That asinine pinhead Stanley Brooks punched Leopold," I said.
"I'd like to go in and beat the stomach contents out of him." I smiled
sweetly at Simon. "Excuse my language. Theodore, why don't you
go in and drag him out and smash his head open?"

"Oh, God," muttered Theodore. "I couldn't do that."

"Hello," Marietta said. "You must be our new neighbor! My name's Marietta."

"Get back!" I said. "Stay away from him, Marietta! Don't hurt him!"

Simon took a step backward. Marietta came at me threateningly. "What did you tell him, bitch?" she said. " *'Down the rivers, o'er the prairies, / Came the warriors of the nations, / . . . In their hearts the feuds of ages.'* "

"You see?" I told Simon. I grew nervous that Marietta might throttle me right there.

Luckily my mother stepped in. "Girls!" she said. "Both of you are depraved. Maud, introduce me to this fellow and don't make up stories about your sister."

"You didn't stop her when *she* did," I said.

Simon gave his little cackle and introduced himself. Marietta was about to lure him into some sort of conversation when I interrupted. "Where's Edward?" I said.

"He had a seizure in the self-help section," my mother said. "He's lying down in the librarian's office. I came out to find a phone to call Pierce. The phones inside are out of order."

"Very nice to meet you," Simon said. "Hopefully, we'll meet again. But I must be going; I just want to have another quick peek at the *Encyclopedia of Poultry* before the library closes." He vanished through the door.

"He might have offered us a lift!" Marietta said with a pout.

"I don't think he understands everything that's going on," I said. "He's from another country."

"Yeah, a country that's supposed to have good manners."

"Not necessarily," said Theodore. "A lot of skinheads, Nazis and conservative Members of Parliament."

"He's not!" I blurted out. "He's a lord! That's why he talks so funny." I hadn't meant to mention this, because I could see that instantly Marietta's eyes narrowed and she bit her lower lip with a certain intensity.

"A lord!" she said. "I like lordliness in a man. *I* said he was a lord to begin with."

"See what psychic perception you children have?" my mother said. "Think how successful you could be if you put it to some use. Now we have to find a telephone so I can call Pierce and tell him to come and get us." She had a huge armload of books which she handed to me. "You linger here," she said. "I'll go and call. Who'll lend me a quarter?"

"Be careful, Ma," said Theodore, digging in his pocket.

We waited nearly a half hour on the top steps while everyone filed out. The library was soon closing. "What am I supposed to do when Stanley Brooks comes out?" Leopold said. None of us answered.

"Was he with his parents?" Marietta said, after a pause.

Leopold shrugged. "Mrs. Brooks, I think," he said. "She teaches fourth grade."

"Then we can't use physical punishment on Stanley," Marietta said. "Not if Mother gets tired of this home-schooling business and decides to send you to fourth grade someday."

"What can we do, then?" Leopold said. "How does my nose look, anyway?"

"Fine," I said.

"I want to see it," Leopold said.

"It's the same as ever!" Marietta said.

"Oh, lord," Leopold said. "Let me see it in your mirror."

"I don't know if I brought a mirror," Marietta said. "I tell you what: let's concentrate, all together, on having Stanley Brooks fall down the stairs."

"And hurt himself?" Leopold squinted, pleased.

"Could we get in trouble?" Theodore was worried.

"A big nose is nice on a man, Leopold," Marietta announced. "Women find big noses sexy."

"How do you know I'll turn out to prefer women?" Leopold asked coyly.

"Men find noses sexy too," Marietta said quickly. "Why? Do you think you'll be homosexual?"

Leopold thought for a minute. "Nah," he said. "Probably not."

"Anyway," I informed him, "you don't have a beaky nose, you have a great big blobby nose. It's very comforting. And I think it's cute." Leopold appeared slightly assuaged.

"Here's my mirror," Marietta said, rummaging in her reptile pocketbook, which was losing a few of its scales. She flipped open the compact and held it in front of Leopold's face. "See? No bigger than ever."

"You're pointing it at my coral seas," Leopold said. Marietta adjusted its position. Leopold gingerly palpated his nose with his thumb and forefinger. "There is some swelling. Should I sue?"

"If we're going to do this, we'd better hurry," Theodore said. "The library is almost closed and he'll be out any minute. Concentrate that he's going to trip on the top stair and topple down, face first. But if we're caught, I don't want to be held responsible."

All four of us closed our eyes and concentrated. "It's no good," Leopold said after a moment.

"He's right." Marietta looked around distractedly. "I'm too hungry."

"What are we going to do?" I said. "My head hurts."

"Concentrate, damn you!" Theodore said. "He'll be out any second. I don't see why I have to do this all by myself."

"Maybe if I sit down." I edged onto the freezing-cold cement wall and looked toward the door of the library. "Uh-oh, here he comes now!"

Stanley Brooks was about four feet tall and nearly four feet wide, dressed in a red sweatshirt and baggy plaid pants. His arms were too short for his body. He was followed by his mother, and Mrs. Brooks was not too different in appearance from Stanley. Stanley saw us sitting on the cement wall with the books and—waiting a moment until his mother caught up with him—gave Leopold a triumphant curl of the lip.

He was still looking at Leopold when he fell down the stairs. We had forgotten about the landing halfway down. It was still a good six-step fall, though, on sharp-edged concrete.

"Na-na!" said Leopold before I put my hand over his coral seas.

Stanley opened his coral seas but it was a moment or so before any noise came out. Then he let out a bellow that trickled downstream and fed into a bawl. "They tripped me!" he yowled between sobs. "They pushed me down the stairs, Ma!"

His mother turned and charged us in the fashion of a moose protecting her offspring. "What did you kids do?" she screamed.

"Nothing, Mrs. Barooks," Theodore said. "I mean, Mrs. Brooks."

"You bunch of druggies!" she said. "Juvenile delinquents! You shouldn't be allowed in the library; you belong in a reform school! Where's your mother? I'm going to tell her, and get the cops on you! White trash!" She turned and waddled down the steps to where Stanley was still floundering. Yanking him onto his feet, she slapped the dust off him.

"Look!" I said cheerfully. "His shoelaces are untied. If he was thinner, he could maybe see his feet." Involuntarily Mrs. Brooks glanced at Stanley's sneakers. I wasn't lying. His laces were untied. She glared up at us while we all smiled; then she grabbed Stanley by the arm and led him off to the parking lot.

"It worked!" Leopold said.

"I don't think it worked," Theodore said grimly. "It was a lucky accident. Where'd Ma go to, anyway?"

"Maybe she stopped at a bar," Marietta said.

Our mother rounded the corner. "Goodness, it's chilly!" she said.

"Yeah, well, if you didn't go out dressed in a cocktail gown, you might not be so cold." Theodore glared contemptuously.

"I had no idea you were so conventional," she said.

"I'm not conventional!" he said. "You're the one who said you were cold!"

"What happened, Ma?" Marietta said. "Did you get Pierce?"

"He's coming," she said vaguely.

"What took you so long?"

"I couldn't find a phone anywhere that worked!" she said. "They were all jammed up! Something was wrong with all of them, for a radius of at least five blocks. It took me ages to find one that wasn't out of order. Pierce has fixed the car, and he's on his way."

We waited outside in the cold for more than forty minutes while it got darker and finally the lights came on in front of the library. We were used to eating dinner at six o'clock. It was already much later. I was hungry. My mother had to go to the bathroom, but the library was closed now. The only place to go in town was in Town Hall, upstairs from the police station. I went with her to keep her company. "I don't understand what could be keeping Pierce," my mother said. "He should have been here twenty minutes ago."

"What happened to Edward?" I said.

"Golly!" my mother said, stopping in her tracks. "I forgot all about him! He never came out of the library while you were waiting?"

"No."

"And what about Mrs. Hartley, the librarian person?"

I shrugged. "I don't know," I said. "I don't think I know what she looks like."

"I think she might leave at night by her own exit," my mother said. "She locks up, and then goes out the side door to get to her car. Oh, dear."

"But where was Edward when you left him?"

"Sleeping," she said. "On the floor beside her desk in the office. You know how he goes to sleep after he has a seizure."

"How would I know?" I said. "I've scarcely even seen this fellow. He arrives late at night and leaves early in the morning. He was last around six months ago for less than twenty-four hours, and before that, six or seven years ago. The only reason we tolerate him is because you claim he's Leopold's father."

"You're saying I've been a lousy mother," my mother said.

"Don't start that," I said. "The library is closed and Edward is probably locked inside. What do you want to do?"

"I'd like to find the ladies' room," my mother said.

"Is Mrs. Hartley related to Steve Hartley, the Minotaur vacuum specialist?" I said.

"I don't know," my mother said as we approached Town Hall. "That's a thought. She might be his mother."

We walked up the stairs from the police station through a side door leading to the public toilets. There was no paper in any of the stalls. "I have some Kleenex in my handbag," my mother said.

"Hand me some," I said. "I don't see that Edward being locked in the library is any of your concern, Mother. Let him sleep it off, and they'll let him out in the morning."

"I'm not that kind of person," my mother said. "I know that's the easy route, but I've always chosen to follow the more difficult path. We'll notify the police."

"Tell me honestly." I flushed. "Is he really Leopold's father?"

"Each man has so many sperm," my mother said. "They're nothing more than minuscule tadpoles, swimming in a sticky lake. I suppose we could have genetic testing done, but who cares? It's too late."

"Was there anybody else at that time?"

"I'd have to check my diary," my mother said.

"You don't keep a diary!" I said. "You don't even know what's going on right now, let alone what the hell you were doing seven years ago."

My mother came out of the stall. "There's not even a mirror in this place," she said, turning on the tap. The water trickled out for a second and then stopped. "Do I have on enough lipstick?"

"You could use some more," I said, trying a different sink.

"Why do you mention this now?" my mother said. "I'm not sure I brought any!"

"Well, I didn't bring any," I said.

"Let's go into the police station and make inquiries," my mother said with a sigh.

A middle-aged policeman was sitting behind a desk reading a magazine, which he put away when we walked in. There was another, younger policeman in the back corner. He had red hair and a beaky nose, but was not unattractive, given my fondness for fowl.

"Hello, Evangeline," said the policeman behind the desk.

It was Harry. We called him Harry, though he preferred Mr. Nichols. I had never seen him in his uniform before. Actually, I hadn't even remembered he was a policeman.

"Oh, Harry," my mother said. "We're in a terrible situation."

He straightened in his seat. "You're not mad at me anymore?"

"Maybe a little," my mother said. "But my memories are more good than bad. Remember when we took off our clothes and smoked a joint and then put on that ridiculous record I found at the Salvation Army?" The redheaded policeman in the corner snickered. "That reminds me—did I leave the record at your place?"

"My rhumba record!" I said. "I was wondering what happened to that! That was my record! And all this time I blamed Pierce!"

"Could I have left it under the bed?" my mother said.

"Let's not go into all that now," Harry said. "I'm on duty. What seems to be the problem?"

"He was unable to consummate the relationship," my mother confided.

"Ma!" I said. "I don't want to hear about it."

"It's his prostrate trouble!" my mother said. "It's made him impotent."

"Yeah, right," Harry said contemptuously.

"How come you don't come by the house anymore, Harry?" I said.

"Because your mother's crazy!" he said. "I think she's schizo! And I'm not the only one who thinks so. None of you kids are too normal, either."

"Impotent old goat," I said, sitting down on a bench by the wall.

"Things aren't going the way I had intended," my mother said. "Harry, let's put the past behind us. You know I always found you to be a real charmer. Maybe you simply didn't find me attractive—what do I know? Though I've always believed that a real man could basically screw anything that had a place to put it."

"Evangeline, would you stop dissembling!" Harry said. "Why did you come here in the first place?" My mother stood perfectly still. I could tell she had forgotten. She began rummaging in her pocketbook.

"Look at this!" she said, taking out two candy-coated almonds, one pale pink and the other white. "I'm going to have a Jordan almond while I think." She popped it into her coral seas and began to sing. " *'Jordan River is deep and wide / Hallelujah / Milk and honey on the other side / Hallelujah.'* Would anyone else like a nut?"

"Gosh, I just thought of something terrible," I said.

"What?" said my mother.

"That Lord Simon never came out of the library either."

"Which Lord Simon?"

"You know, that English fellow bitten by a brown recluse spider who moved in up the road. He's a real lord, from Merry England."

"Bitten by a real brown recluse spider?" said Harry. "Does he know how dangerous that can be? I got some kind of literature in on the subject only yesterday. I told Fred to read it." He gestured at the roosterish character in the corner. I gave him a wink. He turned yellow.

"Hello, Fred," I said.

"What do you mean, the lord never left the library?" my mother said.

"I mean, when you were about to go and call Pierce, after Edward had his seizure, his lordship went back into the library to read the *Encyclopedia of Poultry*. I wonder if keeping poultry would help rid the area of brown recluse spiders? I think fowl eat insects."

"I don't think chickens eat bugs," said Harry.

"Chickens will eat anything," said Fred from the corner.

"Is that true?" I said. "Would a chicken, for example, eat eggs? Would it eat chicken?"

"We used to keep chickens," Fred said. "We fed them corn, but if they ever got out, you'd see they'd eat any kind of excrement they could."

It made me physically sick to hear that sort of language. "It makes me want to puke, to hear somebody talk that way."

"Me too," my mother said. "You see, Harry, you don't think I raised nice children?"

Harry shook his head in disgust. "I'm having a hard time following what's going on here," he said.

"My mother has a boyfriend—Edward!" I said. "He went into the library. He had a seizure. The library closed. He never came out. Simon, Lord Something, our neighbor from England, whose last name I can't remember, went into the library to read the *Encyclopedia of Poultry*, a reference book that cannot be checked out. He never emerged. The library's closed. There are two men trapped inside. One is epileptic. One has been bitten by a poisonous spider."

Harry stood up and smacked himself in the head with the flat of his hand. "Hell!" he said. "Who's got a key? Let me think."

"I think we have a set of keys," said Fred.

"It's not so simple," Harry said. "The library is connected to a security system. You can't open the library without setting off the alarm. Somewhere I've got a piece of paper that has the code written on it." He started opening drawers in the metal desk.

"You know what?" I said. "I'm getting a big pimple, right on my chin."

"That makes *me* want to puke," said Fred.

"Who gives a darn?" I said.

"Maud!" my mother said.

"I think it's that security company that operates down on Route 13. Fred, where's the number for Universal Security?"

"Don't you remember, Lieutenant, they were broken into last week? They were getting their phone number changed," Fred said. "The Universal manager said he was going to make sure this time it was unlisted."

"How do you know your fiancé is even still in there, Mother?" I said. "Maybe he left out the side door with Mrs. Hartley and went home with her."

"Went home with Mrs. Hartley?" my mother said. "You think, so soon after proposing to me, he would go home with a librarian?"

"Who knows?" I said. "Remember, he's not entirely right in the head."

"That's an idea," said Harry. "Why don't I call her? She's probably got the code. At least she can tell us if these men are still holed up in there." The phone rang and Harry answered. While he was chatting I went over to look at the signs on the wall. With my bad eyesight, I thought they were job advertisements. There was a picture of Edward, and information about a warrant leading to his arrest. He was accused of having robbed a number of convenience stores in the tristate region. "Hey, Ma, take a look at this," I said.

My mother got up and came over to examine the wanted posters. "Interesting," she said. "Tell no one."

Harry put down the phone. "Tell no one what?" he said.

"Do you think I should get my nose pierced?" I said.

"No, I don't think so," my mother said. "It will make a hole in it."

"That was Steve Hartley on the phone," Harry said. "His mother hasn't come home from the library. He wondered if we had heard anything about an accident. I'm going to try calling the library right this minute, and then we'll head on over. He'll meet us there."

"Um . . ." I said.

"Tell no one!" my mother said.

"Tell no one what?" Harry said.

"Tell no one anything," my mother said. "That's what I've always told her. If she doesn't open her coral seas, men may find her highly intelligent and mysterious."

Harry put his chin in his hand and tapped the side of his nose with his finger. He stared at my mother and sighed. "You can't fool me, Evangeline," he said. "You'd better tell me." My mother shook her head coyly. "Tell me!" Harry bellowed.

"You sound angry!" my mother said. "Are you thinking of arresting me?"

"I will if you're withholding evidence," said Harry.

"Very well," my mother said. "All right, here goes: I miss you. I'm sorry things didn't work out between us. I know it was my fault in many ways."

"That's all right," Harry said, softening. "I know now that I was at fault too. But I have somebody else now, Evie."

"Oh," my mother said coolly. "Who might that be?"

"I'm dating the mayor," Harry said.

"The mayor!" my mother said. "Not that . . . that . . ."

"Penny Drexel."

"But she must be seventy years old!" my mother said.

"You know, I'm sixty-three myself," Harry said. "Don't you think you're being kind of ageist? After all, she's closer in age to myself than you."

"Well." My mother walked up to Harry's desk and leaned across it. "Let me be the first to congratulate you." She took Harry by the lapels of his uniform, and pulling him gently forward, gave him a kiss on the coral seas.

"It's still in the early days," Harry muttered.

7

My brothers and sister were still waiting in front of the library. We got out of the back of the squad car as Steve Hartley pulled up. "I couldn't get an answer on the phone," he said. "My mother should have been home hours ago. Where is she? I got worried."

"How touching," I said. "Steve, I have something to tell you. Your mother's shacked up in there with two men."

Steve looked puzzled. Fred, the policeman whose last name I hadn't obtained, went over to my brothers and sister and asked them what they were doing there. They scowled furiously.

"What do you mean, what are we doing here?" Theodore said. "Do you think we're hanging around in the freezing cold for fun? It's not exactly the safest place, out here."

"They're with us," my mother explained. "My oldest son, Pierce, was supposed to pick us up. I can't understand what's happened to him. I hope he wasn't in an accident."

"I forgot Pierce was your son," Harry said. "In any event, he should leave my former step-daughter alone. She's only fourteen. Is he aware of that?"

"What's your former step-daughter named?" I said.

"Deirdre," Harry said.

"Pierce should leave *her* alone?" I said. "She should leave *Pierce* alone! You know how the phone always rings and there are girls giggling? That's Deirdre—and the others. I can assure you Pierce isn't interested in the least. They're harassing him, basically."

"What about my mother?" Steve Hartley said. He was wearing a really terrible ski jacket made out of dark maroon nylon. "Isn't anyone concerned?"

Harry, staring at my mother dreamily, came out of his trance. "Fred, you go around and check all the doors. Steve, you didn't happen to find the library keys anywhere in the house?"

"She has them on her!" Steve said, agitatedly pinching his mustache.

"I don't know what's happened to our set," Harry said. "I thought we had them at the station."

"Wouldn't the burglar alarm company have the keys?" Steve said.

"They've changed their number. We won't have the new number until Monday."

"And there wasn't any answer on the phone in my mother's office," Steve said despairingly.

I went over to where Theodore and Marietta were huddled around Leopold, trying to keep him from freezing. They wouldn't look at me. "Why don't you get into the back of the squad car where it's warmer?" I said. Apparently they were miffed, or peeved, or both. "It's not my fault!" I said. "Where's Pierce, anyway? He's the one you should be angry at."

They still didn't speak to me but turned and went down the stairs to the police car. "Did you hear anything coming from inside the library?" I said to their backs. I followed them to the car and tapped on the window. None of them acknowledged me. I got into the front seat. "You won't believe what's been happening," I said through the metal grille.

"You just left us standing there at the library!" Marietta said. She glared down like a sulky animal in a cage.

"Do you have any idea of how long you've been gone?" Theodore said. He poked at me between the bars. "We're probably all going to get sick."

"I'm hungry and my nose hurts!" Leopold said. He pushed up his nostrils so that his nose resembled a snout.

"There's no sign of the librarian, and we don't think the lord ever came out of the library either," I said. "Edward's locked inside. Nobody has the key and nobody's answering the phone in there."

"You're kidding," Theodore said, yanking Leopold's hand away from his nose.

"No, and there's more. We saw a wanted poster with Edward's picture up in the police station. He robs convenience stores."

"Geeze!" Theodore said. "And that in addition to dealing marijuana. I'm surprised he didn't rob us. I think this is the lowest Mother has sunk."

"Maybe not!" Marietta said.

"Oh, lord, a common criminal for a father," Leopold said, holding the tip of his nose down so that it touched his top lip. "One more obstacle to overcome."

"Did he have any weapons on him?" Theodore said, pushing Leopold's hands away. "Quit it. You'll make it bleed again."

"What's in there for him to rob?" Marietta said.

"What a stupid criminal," said Theodore. "There's no cash in there. Except maybe overdue library-book fines."

"Mrs. Hartley keeps some rare tomes in her office," I said. "In a glass case. Allegedly they're quite valuable."

"What sort of rare books?" Theodore said. He sat up and tried to peer at himself in the rearview mirror. Then he adjusted his bow tie. It ended up being more crooked.

"A complete set of phrenology books," I said. "Slightly bumpy due to water damage. I read about it in the paper—there was an article. Also, even more valuable, some first-edition witchcraft books from the eighteenth century, a two-volume Satanic bible and a first edition of *Gentlemen Prefer Blondes*."

"You think Edward steals books?"

"What's phrenology?" said Leopold.

"You look at somebody's head and can tell what kind of person they are by the shape. It's a practice out of style for the moment, but I have a feeling there might be a revival." I was impressed with my own knowledge, and I could tell the others were too, because they didn't speak for a minute.

"I find all this rather hard to accept," Marietta said.

"To think my sweet lord is locked up with an armed epileptic drug dealer/convenience-store robber and a librarian!" I said.

"He's not your lord," Marietta said. "You'll see." I peered through the grille at my sister. It was true, in some ways she was prettier than me. Her nose was just a tiny bit more refined, her jaw stronger, and her misty eyes a brilliant cornflower blue.

However, anyone who liked her—romantically—would not be interested in me, and, perhaps, vice versa. There was something about her that mentally was not all there. It was almost as if she were an invisible person. That is to say, after you had left you couldn't remember what she was like, and sort of had to make up what you imagined she was like, without really having anything to base it on. She was intangible. This made her appealing to some, but not usually to those who liked me.

Seeing her was not dissimilar to seeing a deer in the forest: the deer obviously made its own decisions and had its own ideas about who it wanted to see or where it wanted to go on any particular day, but it still seemed remarkable that such a mysterious animal could actually be responsible for its own thoughts.

My mother came over to the car. "You'll have to get out, kids," she said. "They're calling in the FBI or some kind of crack force. They can't get in the library and Harry's decided it's a kidnapping."

"Who kidnapped who?" said Leopold glumly.

"Edward apparently kidnapped Steve's mother Mrs. Hartley and the English peer. He may be holding them hostage."

"Why would Edward hold a librarian hostage?" I said.

"I've been wondering that," my mother said. "Do you think she's attractive? Whenever I've seen her, I always thought she looked rather dreary."

"Maybe he's making her read to him," Leopold said. "Sometimes she reads stories out loud, in the children's wing."

"*I* could have read out loud to him, if that's what he wanted," my mother said. "I had no idea. I'm not a mind reader! Do you kids want me to borrow money from Lieutenant Nichols so you can take a taxi home?"

"Hell, no," Theodore said. "This is getting interesting. But could you borrow enough money so we could get a pizza? We can still stay tuned to what's happening, at a safe distance."

"Pizza, pizza, pizza!" said Leopold.

We got out of the car. Fred and Harry were standing behind it. "You kids better go on home," Harry said, getting in.

"We want pizza!" Leopold said.

"Why don't you get yourself a pizza then, and your mom will join you in a while?"

"We don't have any money, Harry!" Leopold said.

"Here's ten dollars," Harry said. "Listen, can any of you think of why this Edward would be holding Mrs. Hartley and the English lord hostage?"

"He has fits," said Theodore. "He's epileptic. He gets violent. And he's hanging on your Most Wanted wall."

"Theodore!" my mother bawled.

"The man's a police officer, Mother," said Theodore. "If I didn't inform him, I could be in serious trouble."

"I've made my decision, in that case," Harry said. "I'm most definitely calling in the FBI. Does Edward have any weaponry that you know of?"

"He might have," Theodore said. Marietta and I looked at each other. "He turned up this morning. We hadn't seen him in at least six months."

Fred got in alongside Harry. "Shut the door, Fred," Harry said. "I have to figure this out."

My mother had run to the top of the library stairs and was banging on the main door. "Edward, what are you doing in there!" she shouted. "Come out now, do you hear me? They're bringing in the FBI. And one of those television programs, too."

"Come on, let's go get the pizza," Theodore said, taking Leopold's hand.

We walked down the dark streets. The town had once been a mill town, and there were four old warehouses or factories that were crumbling, with broken windows. Behind them was the polluted

Suggema River. There were a few very tall street lamps, but most of them no longer worked.

A man came running up behind us. Theodore let out a startled scream and clutched Leopold to him protectively. "Steve!" said Marietta.

"Steve!" I said. He was wild-eyed and out of breath.

"We're going to get a pizza, Steve," I said. "Want to join us?"

"Is something wrong?" said Theodore. "Are you in some kind of trouble?"

"I tell you what, Maud," Marietta said. "Why don't you go with Leopold and Theodore, and Steve and I will go to get a quick drink." She turned to Steve. "Maud is too young to drink legally. Shall we go and get your car?"

Steve appeared at a loss to know what to do. He stood beside us, staring blankly. "Steve looks hungry to me," I said. "I think he'd rather come with me to get pizza."

" '*Archly the maiden smiled,*' " said Marietta, " '*with eyes overrunning with laughter, / Said, in a tremulous voice, "Why don't you speak for yourself, John?"* ' "

"It's Steve," he said vaguely. "My name's Steve, not John. Normally, I don't drink."

"Were you very fond of your mother?" I said.

He snapped out of his coma. "I don't understand any of this," he said. "It all seems a dream. I didn't even check to see if her car is still in the parking lot. What the hell is she doing? Let's get a drink. I guess I could use one."

Marietta grinned at me and started to head back with Steve. "Do save me a slice!" she said.

"Slut," I said, and kept walking toward the pizza parlor with Theodore and Leopold.

I loved Minnie-Wawa's. It was the only restaurant in town, except for the Peace Pipe Diner, which was not only too far to walk to, but was quite fancy. I had only eaten there once in my life, an experience I would never forget. I had Fruit Cup to begin, followed by Crab-stuffed Flounder in Mushroom Sauce, with Old-Fashioned Boston

Cream Pie for dessert. "So what kind of pizza should we get?" I said.

"Let's get pizza with peppers, mushrooms, bacon, pineapple and anchovies," Leopold said.

"Ugh," I pointed out.

"We'll be up all night with indigestion," said Theodore.

"Very well," said Leopold with a sigh. "You guys choose. You will anyway."

We kept walking. After we got past the mills we came to a lot of old tenement houses, originally built for the mill workers. Most of these had peeling sides and boarded-up windows. One or two were occupied. The flickery glare from the television sets spilled past the porches onto the street. A car passed us from behind, gravel pellets churning in its wake. Leopold pointed toward the ground. "What's that?"

"Used condom," Theodore said. "Wash your hands when we get to the restaurant. Hey, what was Ma saying about a television crew?"

"I don't know," I said. "It's probably one of those crime programs, filming in the vicinity."

"This could be a break for me," he said. "What if, when they interview us, we start to sing one of the songs I've written?"

"They'll probably edit it out," I said cruelly.

"Yeah, but what if I write a song, spontaneously, about the murders themselves?"

"What murders?" I said. "You don't really think Edward is capable of murdering anyone, do you?"

"Oh, lord," said Leopold. "A murderer for a father."

"Don't worry," Theodore said. "That will really help you get into college. Maybe full tuition scholarship."

"Maybe Yale—or Brown," I said. "Maybe prep school—Andover, or St. Paul's."

"St. Paul's?" Theodore said. "I don't think so. The Cambridge School, more likely."

"Does the Cambridge School take boarders?" I said.

"Why would those places want someone with a murderer for a father?" Leopold said.

"Because there aren't enough Native Americans to go around!" I said. Leopold looked worried.

" 'The Ballad of Edward Schumacher,' " Theodore said in a musing tone. "I don't even know if I can go on TV! I have stage fright."

As we arrived at Minnie-Wawa's we saw the first of the state police, sirens blaring, going past us toward the library. "We'd better not stay long," Theodore said. "We'll eat quickly and head back; now that the police have arrived, we should be safe."

The fluorescent lighting inside Minnie-Wawa's gave everything a greenish hue. One of the light bars had a loose connection and was flickering erratically. Blinking lights could sometimes bring on an epileptic fit. I had to remember to tell my mother not to go out with Edward for pizza.

There were two men who worked at Minnie-Wawa's, Alexander and Dimitrios, a convicted child molester, which everyone knew about because there was a sign in the window that said so. "Oh, damn," said Theodore. "I forgot all about that. Maybe it's not such a good idea to go in."

I pushed Theo in ahead of me. "Hello, Dimitrios," I said. He was short and kindly. The other one, Alexander, was similar to a Greek god—he had only one arm.

"Hello, good eve-a-ning," said Dimitrios. "What's it gonna be tonight?" he said. He beckoned to Leopold to step forward. "I got something especial for you," he said.

"Go on," I said to Leopold, who was hanging back. I gave him a shove.

"An especial pepperoni stick," said Dimitrios, handing Leopold a slender pink sausage protruding from a doughy shell. "I make it myself, just this eve-a-ning. Still warm."

"Very good," said Leopold, taking a bite and chewing. I could see Alexander standing in the back, scooping a pie out of the oven on a long paddle. "We'd like a small pie with extra fresh garlic, peppers and pineapple," Leopold said. He gave me a worried squint. "It'll be different from the usual."

"Whatever," I said.

"To estay or to a-go?" Dimitrios said.

"To estay," I said.

"I'd be interested to come back and watch the preparing, if I may," Leopold said.

"Sure," said Dimitrios. "You come back here, I show you everything."

"Lordy, lordy," I said. "I'll be sitting right here watching you. If he does anything funny, Leopold, scream and kick him in the E Pluribus Unum."

"You mean if he tells a joke or something?" said Leopold.

"I'm no a child molester," said Dimitrios with a wounded expression. "I'm innocent. They arrest the wrong man, yours truly. What for I want to make sexy business with the children?"

"Whatever," I said.

"I like children, but I no want to molest them," he repeated.

"Fine," I said. Leopold scooted under the counter and disappeared into the kitchen.

Luckily Theodore had been swooning into space and wasn't paying any attention to the lurking dangers. Suddenly he started to speak. " 'The Ballad of Edward Schumacher,' " he intoned. " 'Once monkfish was a junk fish / And cowboys ruled the West. / A man ate steak and hotdogs / And thought he knew what was best. / Now they serve monkfish, in restaurants so fine / And a cowboy ain't a cowboy, unless he knows his wine.' "

"I don't see how this applies to Edward," I said.

"Wait," said Theodore. "I'm coming to it. 'Edward Schumacher was a robber / In the traditions of yore / He robbed Seven-Elevens, and thought he knew the score. / He impregnated women, and flopped around on the floor.' That's as far as I've gotten."

"I don't want to be mean," I said. "But it's not your finest endeavor. I don't think it will help your television debut."

"Seriously, be honest with me," Theodore said.

"Why don't you sing one of your older songs, that you've already perfected and is set to music?"

"Oh, you're right," said Theodore. He sat down at one of the tables and started to bite his fingers. "I'm no good, no good at all. I'm talentless! Whatever happened to Pierce? He could come and bring his guitar. That might help. I could just hide in the background, providing harmony."

"You don't even know if a television crew will really show up," I said. "But what the heck, give him a call. Here's a quarter."

Alexander came out to the counter, wiping his hands on a dish towel. "The telephone, she no work," he said.

"What's with this town?" I said. "I'm never going to get out of here. I'm trapped here. I'm eighteen years old and I'm in prison."

"You're nineteen," said Theodore. "I'm eighteen. I'm the one who's desperate."

"At least you have a marketable talent," I said.

"Marketable, schmarketable," Theodore said. "Every dropout in the country is writing songs and protesting the destruction of the environment. And none of them are afraid to perform!"

"But not in the style of Noël Coward," I pointed out.

He smiled at me tenderly. "That makes it even more hopeless."

Steve Hartley and Marietta staggered in the door. "Is there someplace I can hide?" Steve said, glancing around the room. "Does anybody mind if I go back in the kitchen?" He crawled under the counter and vanished through the swinging side doors. I could hear the sound of Alexander and Dimitrios arguing in Greek.

"What's going on?" I asked Marietta. She sat down at the table and got out a pack of cigarettes.

"Darned if I know," she said.

"Won't whoever Steve is hiding from notice his car is parked here?" I said.

"He parked it in the bushes out back."

"But why is he hiding?" I said.

"The entire FBI or some kind of cult has arrived at the library, and when we drove past it Steve remembered something about the Minotaur Vacuum Company that he didn't want to get into if he was questioned."

"Surely the FBI isn't going to be interested in discussing vacuum cleaners at this time?" I said. "Is his mother still being held hostage?"

"They've made telephone contact," Marietta said. "Edward wants to keep the Satanism and witchcraft books."

"Those are his only demands?" I said. "He didn't want the first edition of *Gentlemen Prefer Blondes*? *I* would have liked it."

"I don't know, Maud!" she snapped. "I wasn't there for more than a minute before Steve panicked. I'm starving. What's the name of the handsome one who lost his arm?"

"Alexander," I said.

"Alexander!" she suddenly screamed. "Where are you, you Greek brute! Get out here!" I looked at her admiringly. The romantic possibilities of Alexander hadn't even occurred to me.

Alexander came out immediately. "Here you are!" he said. "When you gonna marry me?"

"Things unfortunately have changed slightly," Marietta said. "I'm afraid I've met someone else. But you can have my sister instead!"

Now that she was handing him over, he didn't seem quite so desirable. "You meet someone else?" he said. "Who? That fellow who come and hide in the supply closet? I'll take care of him." He gave me a wink and then went back into the kitchen.

"What did you have to do that for?" I said. "Now he'll be swarming me."

"You take things too seriously," she said. "This is all a game."

"So it's not real?"

"It's a real game," she said.

"But I can't marry a one-armed Greek pizza chef. Pizza is too high in salt and fat to eat every night. That reminds me: Leopold, where's that pizza!" I shouted into the kitchen.

"What's he doing?" Marietta said.

"How should I know?" I snapped in revenge, trying to use her exact tone of voice. "He's back there getting lessons in how to cook a pizza from a child molester."

"You are just so irresponsible, Maud!" Marietta said, putting out her cigarette on the floor and going into the kitchen. After a pause I heard gales of laughter and what sounded as if it could be Steve Hartley screaming in pain.

"Greece looks like a nice country," Theodore said, getting up and going over to one of the photographic murals on the wall. It was a yellowed picture of what must have been Athens on a day that was particularly polluted, or else the picture had simply gotten dirty after years of hanging on the wall.

"Maybe we should go into the kitchen," I said. "I'm left out of everything. That's the way it's been my whole life. And not only will I never get out of here, I'll never be in the center of excitement. I'll never attend a gala benefit premiere of the New York City Ballet."

"You don't even like ballet," Theodore said.

"That's not true!" I said. "How would I know whether I like it or not when I've only seen excerpts on public television, and that on a tiny TV that doesn't get very good reception?"

"Pizza!" said Leopold, coming out of the kitchen with the pie. "Alexander wants to know if you like bowling."

"Let him ask me himself!" I said. "The nerve."

Theodore went behind the counter and took the pizza from Leopold. "Are you sure this is done?" he said. "It looks kind of raw."

"That's because Dimitrios allowed me to pile on the extra ingredients, free of charge."

"What's all this gooey stuff?"

"Peanut butter. Dimitrios said I can have all the pizza I want, any time I come here on my own, free of charge. He can't feed *everybody* for free, though."

"Not bad!" Theodore said. "And he didn't try to molest you?"

Leopold looked disgusted. "Try to have faith, Theodore," he said. "I can be a flirt, but basically I have no intention of being deflowered."

"Leopold, you don't even know what you're saying!" I said. "You don't even know what being deflowered means."

"The librarian read *Candide*, by Voltaire, during the children's hour," he said.

"Are you sure?" I said. Leopold nodded. "All right, what is being deflowered?"

Leopold hunched his shoulders embarrassedly. "Having your flower removed?" he said.

"Where's the pizza slicer?" said Theodore.

"Here." Leopold pulled up the leg of his blue jeans and took the wheel-shaped pizza cutter from where he had stuck the handle into his sneaker.

"Oh, Leopold, that is so dangerous," Theodore said. "What if you slice up the side of your leg?"

"No one is going to punch me in the nose the way Stanley Brooks did!" he said proudly. "As long as I live and breathe!"

"But you can't go around stabbing people," I said.

"No, but I can slice them," he said. "Edward told me I can't be tried as an adult."

"Whatever," I said, giving up. "Okay, let's see this personally made pizza!" I put a slice on a paper plate and took some napkins and the hot pepper shaker over to our table. "So, what did you end up putting on it?"

"Everything," Leopold said. "But I just put pineapple, anchovies and artichoke hearts on a few slices for me."

"Artichoke hearts!" I said. "I adore artichoke hearts! You could have put them on a piece for me too, you know."

"I could pick them off and give them to you," he said sadly.

"What happened to Steve?" I said. "I heard screams. What's going on?"

"Alexander beat him in an arm-wrestling match," Leopold said. "Should I go see if they want some pizza?"

"No need to bother," I said. "They'll come out if they want some. More for the rest of us!"

He got up anyway and came back in a minute, grinning to himself. "What are they doing back there, Leopold?" I said.

"I shouldn't say," he said.

"Tell me!" I said.

He shrugged. "They're having fun," he said. "Messing around. You know. You probably shouldn't go back there, though. You're too delicate."

"How true," I said. "Why didn't you say so in the first place?"

We were eating when three tall men wearing almost the exact same suits came in. They didn't look as if they came from Nokomis. They appeared to have arrived maybe from another planet, unsuccessfully disguised as human beings. "I can't believe the librarian would read *Candide* out loud during children's hour," I said to Theodore distractedly. "Hasn't that book been banned yet?"

One of the men moved away from the others. "Is there anybody who works in this place?" he said, annoyed. "What's going on around here?" He headed toward the kitchen.

8

"Do something!" hissed Theodore.

"Take their order!" I said.

"I'm too shy," said Theodore.

"Very well," I said. I jumped up from the table. "Excuse me," I said, my coral seas still full. "I was on my dinner break. Take a seat. Can I take your order?"

"Yes," said the most important of the three. "We'd like a large pie, meatballs and mushrooms, to go."

"Leopold," I said. "Go tell them in back. Something to drink?"

"A large Mountain Dew," said one.

"Diet Pepsi, no ice," said the second.

"No Diet Pepsi," I said. "Only Diet Coke, caffeine-free."

"Okay," he said. "Diet Coke."

"Caffeine-free?" I said.

"Regular Diet Coke," he said.

"There's only caffeine-free," I said. "Ice?"

"With ice."

"Sorry," I said. "There's no ice. Small, medium or large?"

I noticed he was beginning to act like someone harassed by a buzzing fly for too long. His pale eyes flitted irritably. "Medium," he said. I was about to tell him there was no medium-sized drink, only small and large, but I was rapidly losing interest.

"And for you?" I asked the third.

"Dr Pepper?"

"No Dr Pepper. Mountain Dew?" I spoke as sweetly as possible, to make sure the last fellow didn't feel left out.

"Sprite?"

"No Sprite."

"Then I'll have the Diet Coke, with ice."

"Ice?" I said. "I don't have the slightest idea of where they keep the cups."

I began to rummage around under the counter. "Theodore, why don't you get these men their drinks."

Theo ignored me and demurely stuffed his coral seas.

"You must be the FBI agents," I said. "I've always wondered what it would be like to have sex with a Federal agent."

The men glanced down modestly. There was a greasy sponge lying in a bucket near my feet and I plucked it out fastidiously and went to give their table a wipe.

"At first I thought, an FBI agent probably wouldn't be too good in bed. Not that I'd have anything to compare it with. But for example, Clint Eastwood. What would be the fun in sleeping with someone who constantly leaps out of bed to fire his pistol? And you FBI men would be frightened to be passionate, for fear it would reveal your feminine side. Of course, your leader, J. Edgar Hoover, was well known for dressing as a woman, so perhaps I'm mistaken."

The men appeared offended, but it might have been because the sponge smelled so foul. "Well, I can see I'm not getting much of a response," I said. "How about it? Are any of you single? One of you is kind of cute, with that thin, mean little mouth. Would you like to know which?"

None of them answered. "We got that over with quickly," said one to the others, ignoring me.

"Are you talking about the hostage situation at the library?" I said.

"How do you know about that already?" said one.

"What about Mrs. Hartley?"

"She's been taken to the hospital."

"Oh, lord," I said. "Was she raped?"

"What?" The three men looked at one another, perplexed.

"We can't talk to you about the case," said the second at last. "Sorry, but we're not at liberty to discuss it. What's your name, anyway?"

"Maud Slivenowicz."

"Your mother is Evangeline Slivenowicz?"

"Um," I said. "I guess so."

"We're not at liberty to discuss it," Theodore called to him.

"Smart-ass," said the man. "Anyway, I suppose you have a right to know. The gunman was your mother's fiancé, was he not?"

"The gunman?" I said. "He had a gun?"

"It was a toy," he said. "An Uzi from the children's wing. But there was no way for us to know."

"Is he dead?" I said.

"Wounded. Taken to the hospital with Mrs. Hartley."

"Gosh darn it!" I said. "I miss everything! I can't believe it. I saw him this afternoon. He didn't seem violent then. I can't believe he would rape an old librarian. It's disgusting. At least my mother may not marry the creep in such a hurry now. Tell me, what are your names?"

"Mark Fox," said the first.

"Chad Bushwick," said the second.

"Art Osterwold," said the third.

"What marvelous names!" I said, lying easily. "Have you washed your hands?" Across the room, Theodore, humiliated, buried his face in his hands. He was always easily humiliated. "So what about the English lord? What happened to him?" None of the men spoke for a minute. "Oh, no!" I said.

"No, no, don't get upset," said Mark Fox. "He's . . . fine."

"We hope he'll be all right," said Art Osterwold. "He was okay enough to tell me he's been to Buckingham Palace, you know, in the part that's not open to the public. I asked him."

"Did he ever meet Princess Diana?" said Mark.

"Just give me a hint—what happened to him?"

"I'm afraid we're not at liberty to discuss that," said Chad. "But I can tell you he's not dead. If that's any consolation!"

Before I could interrogate them further, Fred, the policeman, came in. "I've been trying to find you kids," he said. "I'm supposed to give you a lift home." He bowed slightly to the agents.

"Go home!" said Theodore. "I want to go back to the library! What about the *Crime Stoppers* television crew? They don't want to meet with me, do they?"

"The TV show already left and went over to the hospital with your mother," Fred said.

"There's nobody left at the library?" Theodore asked. "My mother—she's okay?"

"Half the library's smashed in!" Fred said with a chuckle. The agents glared at him.

"When you get back from giving them a lift," said Chad Bushwick, "we'd like you to come over to the Holiday Inn, in Hillsboro, and I can debrief you."

I went back to the kitchen. Marietta was standing in the corner, kissing Alexander. Leopold was on the floor with Dimitrios, in front of a Parcheesi set and what appeared to be a sandwich bag full of marijuana. A car honked outside. "I have to go," said Marietta, disentangling herself. "Steve is waiting." She picked up a large cardboard pizza box and slipped out the back.

Alexander stared after her longingly. Then he noticed me. His face darkened. "You like to see me do a push-up? One-armed. I do three hundred, no problem," he said. "Your sister, she has broken my heart. Maybe in a while I get used to you. When we have a date?"

"You should never settle for second best," I said nervously. "You would always be unhappy. I couldn't bear to think of you being unhappy! Come, Leopold, the cop is taking us home."

We got into the car with Fred. It was humiliating to be taken home in a police car, since everyone in town was no doubt expecting it. No one spoke. I didn't even have the strength to practice flirting with Fred. I realized I hated him, and he was loathsome, due to the fact that he was pathetic.

I was exhausted from the day's activities. Which was worse, perpetual boredom or constant excitement? In the end, both produced the same sensations of fatigue. When I thought that I was going to have to live through another sixty or so odd years consisting of alternating boredom and excitement, and then die, it all seemed not only pointless, but discouraging.

"I want to make sure you get inside okay," Fred said when we got to the trailer.

"That won't be necessary," I said.

"I'm coming in with you!" he said. He followed us in. "*Mon dieu!*" he said. "What the heck! It looks like you've been burglarized while you were out all this time."

I scrutinized the room. Nothing appeared any different than usual. I was about to say so, when Theodore pinched me on the arm. "Ow!" I said.

"Stay calm," said Fred. Trayf and Lulu came bounding out to greet us. Lulu was so excited she started circling the garbage can in the middle of the room. Since childhood, the dog had had an obsession with circling. If there was any object she could circle—a table leg, a chair, a cardboard box—she would go around and around, faster and faster, like a demented carousel animal. I wondered if Pierce had even remembered to feed them. "What in God's name happened to their fur?" Fred said. "I'm going to call headquarters, if I can use your phone. It looks like a major break-in. Somebody trashed the place—maybe searching for something in connection with the library bombing? But then, why torture these poor animals? I'm thinking, maybe Satanic ritual."

"The library bombing?" I said. This was the first I had heard anything about a bombing.

Pierce came out from the bedroom in a pink chenille bathrobe, rubbing his eyes. "Hey," he said. "What's up?"

"Pierce!" I said. "Where were you? You were supposed to pick us up hours ago."

"Gosh," said Pierce. "I must have fallen asleep."

"You were asleep while you were burglarized?" Fred said.

Pierce did a double take. "Burglarized?" he said. "What are you talking about?"

"Vandalized your home? Ransacked the trailer?"

He started to laugh. "This is how it always looks around here!" he said.

"You might have said something." Fred gave me a disgusted glare.

"Where's my mother?" All at once Leopold turned white. He looked pinched and weak. "I want my mother. I'm going to sleep." He staggered down the hall.

"You fell asleep?" Theodore snarled at Pierce. "How could you?"

"Sorry." He shrugged. "I knew there was something I was supposed to do, but I couldn't remember. I figured if it was important, somebody would remind me later. Does anybody else need a lift? I got the car working again. I don't think it's going to hold up much longer, though."

"You want me to take a look at it?" Fred said.

"Naw," said Pierce. "The transmission's about to give out completely, and I don't think it's worth it to get a whole new one put in, even if we had the money. The body's rusted to pieces."

Theodore switched on the TV and Trayf and Lulu, each of whom weighed about twenty-five pounds, got onto the couch next to him and tried to crawl on his lap. As soon as one managed to find space, the other climbed on too, knocking off the first one. Mentally, each still believed they were the same size they had been at six weeks of age. "What I might do, I might stay up all night tonight," said Theodore, bobbing as Trayf gave him an affectionate blow to the face with his front paw. "My nerves are shot. I doubt if I can sleep. What if we really are burglarized?"

"I might join you in staying up," I said. I sat down next to him and took off my wig. No wonder I had such a headache. Fred's eyes widened, shocked. "What are you looking at, rooster-face?" I said. How I hated him! I could see it was going to be Fred—or someone exactly like him—I was going to end up with, probably the only man who would want me. Someone ordinary who adored me, and didn't earn much money, and would make me over into an ordinary, average person such as himself.

"You can watch with us?" Theodore said. "Police protection might be a good idea."

Fred looked hopeful; then his face fell. "I wish," he said, staring at me. "But I have my FBI debriefing."

"Theodore, show the gentleman out," I said.

"That's all right," he said. "I can find my own way."

Around two in the morning Marietta came home, drunk out of her mind, and threw up in the bathroom for half an hour before I put her to bed. Around three my mother came home. Her eyes were very glittery and bright. She had an armful of library books which she threw on the dining room table before collapsing in the vinyl lounge chair we had found at the Salvation Army Thrift Store for twenty dollars.

"What are you still doing awake?" she said.

"We were waiting for you," I said.

"You should be asleep!" she said. "That way you can get up at the crack of dawn."

"Why?" I said. "Why would we want to get up at the crack of dawn?"

"To get something accomplished!" she said. "We have to mend our ways, right away. I told you things were going to start happening for us. We have to be prepared. We have to get up and begin cleaning the whole house from top to bottom. I see money coming our way. Behold!" She opened her pocketbook and took out what must have been ten lottery tickets.

"Where did you get those?" I said.

"Harry bought them for me."

"Did you get any milk?" I said.

"Milk," she said. "You children are marvelous. I can't tell you how proud I am of you."

"Why?" Theodore said, although he did look pleased, with his half-shut eyes.

My mother thought for a moment. "I don't know," she said. "It doesn't matter. I just am. Is there anything to eat?"

Leopold came out of the bedroom, yawning. "I had a bad dream," he said. "What's going on?"

"What is there left to eat, Leopold?" my mother said.

Leopold thought for a moment. "I could fry you some potatoes and onions, Ma," he said.

"I can do it!" my mother said, but she did not get up and Leopold went into the kitchenette. "Anybody else want any?" he called.

Lulu came padding out from my bedroom and followed Leopold into the kitchenette. "She wants a carrot, Leopold," I said. The dog was obsessed with carrots; she ate at least three or four a day, but they had to be peeled and sliced or she would snub them.

"I'll have some fried onions and potatoes," Theodore said. "That sounds good, Leopold."

"Me, too!" I said. "Leopold learned how to make pizza tonight; the child molester taught him at Minnie-Wawa's."

"That's fantastic," my mother said. I realized she was slightly drunk. "How's Edward? How's the librarian? How's my liege?"

"Edward's going to jail. The librarian is fine," she said.

"Was she violated?"

"Violate me in violet time, in the vilest way you know," Theodore sang.

"You didn't make that up," I said.

"No, no, she's fine," my mother said. "It was all a big misunderstanding. They were all badly poisoned, however. It was a case of carbon monoxide poisoning. The library was not only badly ventilated, someone had hooked up the heating system in the wrong way. Mrs. Hartley hadn't been feeling well for quite some time, but today was the first day it was cold enough to have the heat on all day. She must have locked up and gone back to her office, where she passed out with the others."

"That's not so interesting," I said. "But Edward is really going to jail?"

"He's a thief and a gonif!" she said.

"Same thing," pointed out Theodore, who had taken a course in Yiddish at the Adult Center for Learning the previous summer. "I still don't understand how you could expose your own children to such a bad element."

"Of course, you have to forgive him, to some extent, with his epilepsy," she said.

"Ma, you forgive everybody!" I said. "That's your problem, forgive and forget."

"No, that's not my problem," she said. "I forget, but I don't forgive. My problem is my low self-esteem. I hope you children don't grow up to have low self-esteem."

"We are grown up, very nearly," Theodore said.

"And do you have low self-esteem?"

"A mixture of low self-esteem and delusions of grandeur," Theodore said.

"Me, too," I said. "My self-esteem is lower than anybody's."

"Brag, brag, brag," my mother said.

"Voilà!" said Leopold, coming into the living room with a sizzling frying pan he put down on the coffee table. Lulu followed, proudly carrying a carrot slice in her coral seas. She jumped onto the couch and began crunching.

"Oh, look," my mother said as Leopold handed each of us a spoon.

"The forks are dirty," Leopold said. "Ma, tell us about your unhappy childhood while we eat."

"How delicious," my mother said, spooning some of the crispy burnt bits of fried onions and potatoes into her coral seas. "What a perfect, divine late-night supper."

"Mmmm," I said. "Leopold, it's good."

"Well," my mother said. "My childhood. Surely you're sick of hearing about it? Surely I've told you all about it before?"

"Never," Theodore said sarcastically, but he was interested.

"Tell the part about being rich!" Leopold said.

"When you're rich you have no understanding of how difficult it is to get money when you're poor," she said. "When you're poor, it's almost impossible to climb out of the well—the cesspool—of having no money and actually get hold of some. I can't tell you how much nicer it is to be rich than poor. There's no way I can even give you kids an idea of what it's like. Of course, we have each other, and that more than makes up for any money or material possessions in the world."

"Aw, don't give us that garbage," Theodore said.

My mother looked pensive. "You may have a point."

"People like rich people better than poor people," I said. "Rich people are popular. Who cares if it's for all the wrong reasons?"

"Okay, okay, so I was an idiot," my mother said. "But I would rather have the five of you than all the money in the world."

"Charming," I said bitterly.

"Are you so very unhappy? Haven't I been a good mother to you? I've tried my best."

"You're all right," said Theodore. "But money. How are we going to get it. How are we going to get out of this cesspool?"

"Tell us about the money, Mumsy," said Leopold. He was proudly watching us eat.

"Well, let's see. I grew up in a large mansion, similar to the Wolverhampton estate."

"Similar but bigger, correct?" Leopold said.

"I don't know if it was any bigger. It was in better *shape*. My grandfather had been a financier, and he brought home treasures from all over the world. He was also a hunter, in Africa. We had lions' heads, zebra-skin rugs, and on either side of the couch was an elephant tusk, carved, more than six feet in length."

"And where did you put your umbrella?" said Leopold.

"You know," my mother said.

"Say it!" Leopold said.

"In an umbrella stand made from a hippopotamus foot!" my mother said. "Nowadays, of course, it would all be very politically incorrect. The clothing I had! I wish I had been able to keep some of it to give to you girls. I had my own dressmaker, and a couple of times a year I used to go into New York City and tell her what I wanted. Then, one summer, when I was barely nineteen—"

"My age!" I said.

"—I was visiting some friends off the coast of Thailand—they had a place on Phuket, before it became really overcrowded and touristy. It was there that I met Pierce's father, Neldo. And after that my father—your grandfather—disowned me. I suppose I could have tried harder to make it up with him, but it was the sixties, and I was a free spirit. I told him he could keep his money and go to hell. And so I lived with Neldo out of wedlock for several years and my father was horrified, because that's not what people from our background did."

"And then you met Marietta's father," I said.

"That's right. Pierce had only just been born when I met Gunthar. A Danish ballet dancer. He has since returned to Denmark to head up his own company. As beautiful a man as I have ever seen, but cold as ice, although it sounds like a cliché. Anyway, one day you kids will have a lot of fun going to visit all the fathers in various countries."

"Who drove you home, anyway, Ma?" Theodore said. He was almost asleep.

"I took the car of the Englishman from up the road," she said. "He didn't feel well enough to drive. So I took him home and then walked back."

"I thought he was in the hospital," Theodore said.

"Ma!" I said, furious. "Did . . . something happen between you and that Englishman?"

"I'll tell you all about it in the morning," my mother said. "Now, let's go to sleep. We have to turn over a new leaf."

"That doesn't even make any sense," Leopold said. "If you turn over a new leaf, all you see is the other side of it."

9

"Rodgers and Hammerstein had a song about roasting lobsters," Theodore was saying to Pierce. It was about one in the afternoon.

"That's stupid," Pierce said. "What kind of stupid song would be about roasting lobsters?"

"It was a song about a clambake," Theodore said. "See, they could get away with it. If I tried it—forget it."

Pierce looked disbelieving. "A song about a clambake," he said. "I don't get it."

"Where is everybody?" I said.

"They took the dogs and went up to nurse the Englishman," Pierce said.

"Marietta too?" I said.

"Yes."

"Gosh darn it!" I said. "How come she drank so much and still got up before me?"

"Genetics," Theodore said. "The Danish blood absorbs alcohol."

"So did you ever figure out what happened at the library exactly?" I said.

"Kind of," Theodore said. "Want some coffee?"

"Yes, please," I said. "I'll get it, if you tell me what happened."

"I've heard a number of conflicting stories at this point. We'll have to wait for the paper on Friday to get the real story. But basically, what I think is, Edward was still sleeping it off after his fit. Leopold left a toy gun alongside him. The Englishman was either high on drugs, or was particularly sensitive to the carbon monoxide fumes. Anyway, he had gone into the librarian's office to find out if he could check out the *Encyclopedia of Poultry* even though it was a reference book. The librarian was already making the rounds, locking up. Then she came back to her office and passed out with the others from the fumes. Meanwhile, as you know, the phones were out of order. The FBI knew Edward was a convenience-store robber. When they didn't get any response, they drilled a hole in the wall and saw Edward lying there with the gun beside him, and what appeared to be a pipe bomb, and the librarian passed out with her skirt up around her waist, and they got an armored tank from the Algonquin Proving Ground to smash in the wall."

"An armored tank?" I said.

"Or some kind of vehicle," Theodore said. "You know, like what they used in Waco, Texas."

"And the pipe bomb?"

"Search me." He shrugged. "I don't even know if it was a real pipe bomb. There was a rash of pipe bombs across the country about a year or so ago. A few of them were real, most of them not."

"I guess it makes sense, sort of," I said. "But what happened to the Englishman?"

"They thought he was on the criminal side and beat the hell out of him. Some kind of wound to the genitals, I think," Theodore said.

"Oh, gosh, how awful," I said. "I'd better join the others and visit him. Is there something I can take as a gift?"

"What are his interests?" Pierce said.

"I know!" I said delightedly. "Pierce, let me have a joint or two."

"Aw, come on," Pierce said. "I don't have much grass left, and there hasn't been any around lately. You don't even know this guy."

"Listen, Pierce," I said. "Give me what you have left and I'll tell you what I've been thinking would be a good plan for you."

"Tell me your plan first and I'll consider it," Pierce said.

"What if you moved to Los Angeles and became a movie star?" I said.

"By myself?" Pierce said, but he suddenly looked very peculiar, as if something had dawned in the ooze of his primitive brain for the first time: A Thought. What we were witnessing might not have been dissimilar to viewing the first Neanderthal man to make fire; I was about to mention this, but I was afraid that, having distracted him in this crucial moment, he would never have another Thought again.

"I'll . . . I'll come with you for a short time, to help you get set-tled," I said. "Pierce, you really are the handsomest man, and it's been a long time since there was somebody around who could talk like Gary Cooper. There are a few other stars of that nature, but let's face it, most movie stars today are short with big noses and weak chins."

"Who's Gary Cooper?" Pierce said.

"Hey, Maud, that's not a bad idea!" Theodore said, and he actu-ally appeared impressed. "After he's a movie star he can help the rest of us, at least me with my music."

"But I have no idea what I want to do, so he can't help me with that," I said. "Except I could see myself marrying the English lord, and then people would respect me."

"I'm sure that's true," said Theodore. "Since women's status is still primarily based on whether or not they have a man and which man it is. But wouldn't you find it kind of disgusting to have people being nice to you because you're a lady?"

"Naw," I said. "What the hell do I care?"

"As long as they're nice!" Pierce said, and began to cackle dementedly. "Do you really think I'll have a shot at being a movie star?"

"If you keep your coral seas shut," I said.

"And lose the cackle," Theodore said. "Whenever you don't speak, Pierce, people are so impressed with you—even terrified. I've seen it happen. You have no idea. I wish *I* had that kind of effect on people."

"But how am I going to go on these auditions and keep my coral seas shut?" Pierce said.

"I'll come with you," I said. "I'll just explain, this is really too far beneath you and you don't want to talk. I expect you'll have to actually read the part you're trying out for, though."

"But he might not even have to do that, Maud, if you explain that he doesn't do well in a cold reading," Theodore said. "Gosh, it'll be fun to go and visit on location."

"Can I have the marijuana now, Pierce?" I said.

He went to the bedroom and came back holding a puppy and two joints. "Leetle puppy," he said, holding it up to his face. "Little stinky." He handed me the joints.

"One's wet!" I said.

"It fell in a little puppy piss," he said. He was as cheerful as I had seen him in a long time.

I put the joints down on the table and went into my bedroom, where I started taking all the clothes out of the closet. At least I would be better dressed than Marietta, even if she were the first to get to the lord. He was conservative in appearance—the times I had seen him—but as I could not hope to compete with the conservative English girls of his class he had no doubt associated with all his life, my one hope was to amuse and tantalize by eccentricity. Also, that was the only sort of clothing I had.

I found a pair of very tight aqua-blue satin pants (slightly longer than Capri length and only somewhat stained), and on top I selected a tight black angora sweater with short sleeves. Topping off the ensemble was a pink, hairy acrylic fake-fur jacket. That left only the shoes. I didn't want to wreck any of my good pairs by walking up the road in the mud. Marietta's feet were a size smaller than mine, though she had a few pairs I could uncomfortably jam my toes into. Still, did

I want to take the risk of incurring her wrath? Actually, that wasn't too terrible an idea, since when she saw me wearing her shoes and let loose with her guttural snarls it would cast her in a bad light.

But at the last minute I chickened out and put on some green Wellington boots, which would perhaps make him nostalgic for home, since he would be reminded of the Battle of Waterloo, in which for the first time all his fellow countrymen wore rubber galoshes. I scooped the joints off the table and started out the door.

"When are we going to leave, Maud?" Pierce said.

"Start packing, bro!" I said. "We'll be out of here in two weeks— or less, as soon as we scrape together the money."

I headed up the muddy road. On the way I saw my mother, Leopold and Marietta coming toward me. "Where are you going?" Marietta said.

"To see the Englishman," I said. "How's he doing?"

"You shouldn't bother him now," Marietta said crisply. "He's resting." Trayf and Lulu, who had been sniffing some trees, ran to me. Trayf jumped up, muddying my blue satin trousers. Lulu gave him a sharp blow—she sort of swung her teeth at him—on the side of his neck. He let out a yelp and looked at her with an injured expression. Lulu despised Trayf, except when she came into heat. At those times she found him not quite so unattractive. He was always baffled and amazed at her abrupt change in personality and the diminishment of her contempt for him.

My mother had gotten Lulu first, four years before, and though she acquired Trayf only a few months later, it was too late—Lulu had already decided she was a person, a person who did not like dogs. Trayf, naturally, adored her. Every morning the first thing upon rising he crept to her and tenderly administered licky kisses; every morning she snarled at him.

"How long are you going to be?" my mother said. "We thought we'd go and visit Edward in the hospital this afternoon, before they move him to jail."

"What time were you thinking of going?" I said.

"Visiting hours are four to eight," my mother said. "I thought we'd go at four. I don't like to drive when it gets dark. I can't see in the dark."

"If I'm back by then I'll come," I said. "Maybe I could be given the opportunity to practice my driving."

"You see even worse than me!" my mother said.

"Why don't you practice now, Maud, while it's still light?" Marietta said.

"I think not," I said, giving her a wink. "Don't wait for me, in any event!" She scowled. "Hung over?" I said.

"If you're wearing any of my clothes and I find out, I'm going to take yours and shred them with a manicure scissors," Marietta said.

"Marietta!" my mother said. "You shouldn't drink so much if it's going to give you such a nasty disposition the next day. You're not pregnant, are you?"

"See you later!" I said, leaving them to quarrel in the mire.

I rang the doorbell and waited for what seemed about ten minutes. Finally an upstairs window opened and the lord leaned out. "It's you," he said. "Listen, do you mind if I drop the keys down to you? I can't face going down the stairs."

"My pleasure," I said, and waited while he threw down the keys in a sock.

I had never been in the Colemans' house before, since the Colemans didn't like us and out of spite had called the police a number of times. They accused us of turning over their garbage pail, breaking down their fence, unchaining their outdoor dog and stealing their tomatoes. Only one of those things was partly true.

Whether or not the lord had rented the place furnished, or if it was the Colemans' old furniture, I didn't know, but either way I felt sorry for him. All the pieces were either very plain and simple and white, or crudely constructed objects like old pie safes and highboys with peeling buttermilk paint and punched-metal doors. Most of the junk must have been a hundred and fifty years old, and nobody had ever bothered to fix it up or get nicer things.

I wandered around for a couple of minutes looking at the kitsch before I went upstairs. Simon was lying in bed beneath a plain white comforter, with a breakfast tray-table in front of him. "You missed the others," he said nervously. "They just left."

"I know," I said. "They said you might be resting and that I would be disturbing you. But I didn't care."

"No, no, not at all," he said.

I pulled over an old ladder-back chair. "But, pray, what happened to you? No one will tell me a thing."

"One of your FBI agents took a disliking to me," he said. "Apparently he began kicking me in a rather sensitive region while I was unconscious."

"Gosh," I said. "I wonder which one?"

He looked embarrassed. "The genital area," he said.

"No," I said. "I mean, I wonder which *agent-provocateur*. There were three of them in the pizza parlor last night. If I had known, I would have poisoned the pizza."

"That's kind of you," he said. "But there were a good many more than three on the scene last night."

"Did you have a chance to get that spider bite looked at?" I said.

"I was so groggy and sick, I forgot to ask the doctor," he said. "Your mother was generous enough to take me home."

"Yes," I said glumly. "I forgot about that. She has a way of generously taking advantage of people. I hope she didn't take advantage of you?"

He coughed and flushed an unusual shade of pink, like a peeled persimmon. "I was so desperate to get out of the hospital, I simply left, on your mother's suggestion, without officially checking out. I hope I don't get into trouble for doing so. I don't know if my insurance will cover this fiasco."

"What kind of insurance will cover this fiasco?" I said.

"I have something called American United Guar," he said. "I'm not sure what it includes, however. And they didn't ask me last night who would be paying. Does that mean it was free of charge?"

"No," I said. "First of all, I'm sure this American United Guar doesn't cover anything. None of them do; having it is just a formality. Secondly, they'll hunt you down and make you pay. That's how it works here. But, you're a lord. Doesn't that mean you're rich?"

"Pfft, no," he said. "I'm the second son. It was my eldest brother who got everything."

"Because your father preferred him to you?"

"No, no," he said. "That's just how it works with us. Primo Geniture."

"Ah," I said. "So tell me, what did this elder lord do with everything?"

"Spent it, mostly," he said. "He's an earl, actually. He lives down in the Bahamas."

"That's fascinating," I said. "And what does Earl Geniture do, alone in the Bahamas?"

"Well, he plays golf," he said. "He has a restaurant. Actually he may be opening another in New York."

"A restaurant!" I said. "Just think, he has a restaurant, all alone in the Bahamas. Did you mention this to Leopold?"

"Your little brother?" Simon said. "No, why?"

"My brother is very interested in the restaurant industry," I said. "Perhaps at some point I might take him down to say hello. He's too young to go on his own to visit El Primo. I mean, your older brother."

"How is the poor little fellow?" Simon said. "He was acting rather glum, while he was visiting. I meant what I said about teaching him boxing. But I'm in no condition at the moment."

"You wouldn't believe how many people tell me that after I meet them. Say, I'm freezing! Don't you think it's freezing in here?"

"Is it?" Simon said. "I'm terribly sorry. I just didn't notice. Growing up in English boarding school, you know . . ."

"You poor thing! But, you must put all that behind you. I'm here now," I said, unzipping my pink jacket. "It looks very warm under the blankets. Could I get in there with you for a minute?"

"In the bed with me?"

"I'll take my boots off," I said, and kicked them across the floor.

"Well! Whatever you like! That would be delightful! You must do as you please! I'm terribly sorry—I might have suggested it myself, only I . . . I . . . well, I . . . I don't know what to say, really, I never dreamed—"

"Don't chastise yourself," I said, peeling back the covers and snuggling in.

"You certainly have an extensive vocabulary, for an American," he said, twitching.

"We had one of those calendars," I said, adjusting the pillows and removing a couple of magazines. He was wearing lavender and lemon-yellow striped pajamas.

"This is delightful," he said, after a pause. "I hope you don't think the less of me."

"What for?" I said. We lay in cozy silence for a minute until something bit me viciously under the covers and I let out a little shriek. "Do you have fleas?" I said.

He spoke at the exact same moment. "What sort of calendar?" he said.

"It was a word-a-day calendar," I said, reaching under the covers to scratch.

He screamed too, almost as if he were mocking me. I think he must not have heard my remark about the fleas, because he seemed to think I had cried out for a different reason. "Don't worry, you have nothing to fear from me!" he said. "I'm incapacitated."

"Whatever," I said with a sigh. "I won't be around for long, you know."

"I understand," he said. "But please stay for just a few more minutes. I'm quite enjoying this."

"No, not like that," I said. "I won't be in the *vicinity* for long."

"Why?" he said. "What are you talking about?"

"I'm going to Los Angeles with my brother Pierce. He's going to be a movie star. Want to come visit?"

"Why, yes!" Simon said. "I would like to come for a visit. I've never been to Los Angeles. I've intended to go there for quite some time."

"Great!" I said. "Oh, yeah, I almost forgot." I scrambled in my pocket. It took me quite a while to squeeze my hand into my tight pants, under the covers, while Simon giggled optimistically. "I brought you these joints. For the pain." I handed them over. "This one fell in some liquid. You might want to dry it out awhile."

"Aren't you heavenly," Simon said. "What did I do to deserve this?"

"You don't prefer my sister to me?"

"Your sister!" He laughed uproariously. "Your sister!"

"My sister is attractive, don't you think?" I felt slightly miffed at his contempt.

"I'm not laughing because your sister's not attractive," he said. "Your sister's beautiful, you're beautiful, your brothers are beautiful."

"I think my brother has a very good chance of becoming a top movie star, don't you?" I said. I glanced at Simon. He looked like an ethereal tuberculosis patient who wrote poetry on a mountaintop during the First World War. He had such a sensitive expression of suffering that something occurred to me. "You maybe prefer boys?"

"I've put all that behind me—I hope!" Simon said. "You know, in England things are different than they are here. That's considered a normal developmental stage. Now I think I'm ready to move on to the rather dreary adult segment of life. My little love, may I ask you a very special favor?"

"Yeah?" I said hopefully.

"Would you read to me from my most favorite book? It always cheers me up so immensely."

"Where is it?" I said. He reached under his pillow and passed it to me. "What part do you want me to read?" I said in a glum voice.

"Anywhere!" he said. "Oh, goody."

" '*Water, water, everywhere, / And all the boards did shrink; / Water, water, everywhere, / Nor any drop to drink.*' "

"Ooo," Simon said. "Yes! '*The very deep did rot: O Christ! / That ever this should be! / Yea, slimy things did crawl with legs / Upon the slimy sea.*' "

Something was making me vaguely queasy, but I decided not to examine my queasiness too closely. "I guess I'd better be going!" I said. "Thanks for warming me up!"

"You don't have to go just yet, do you?" he said, brushing my face with his long white fingers. His touch was so delicate it reminded me of one of those butterflies that feed on the tears of antelopes, as featured in a nature program on TV.

"I'm afraid so," I said, slapping away his hand. "We're going to visit

Edward in the hospital before he's transferred to jail."

"May I telephone you a bit later?" he said.

"Sure!" I said. "Call me tonight! By the way—I'm not sure how to put this and am somewhat embarrassed—I'm a virgin, technically speaking. If it's of any concern to you."

"It's not really a problem one way or the other," he said. "On the one hand, it might be nice if one of us had some experience. On the other, at least you won't notice any shortcomings of mine. Either way, how refreshingly American you are! How terrific that you're so open! Sweet Maud!"

I walked back to the trailer wondering why I didn't feel more joyful. Landing the lord had been a bit too simple; maybe women liked more of a challenge. But then, perhaps things that were meant to work out did so quite easily. No doubt there would be plenty of other obstacles to overcome—his mother, for example.

Everyone was sitting around eating baked apple dumplings. Leopold had found a full bushel basket we had picked a few months before and left out in the storage shed, forgotten until now. He had cored the ones that were still good, stuffed each with raisins, butter and sugar, and wrapped them individually in pastry crust made from the last of the flour.

"What's happened here?" I said, puzzled. It appeared there were now swarms of minute winged insects everywhere. "A hatching of some sort?"

"Unfortunately, when I carried the basket into the house to pick through them, I didn't realize there were millions of fruit flies inside," he said.

Since it was warmer indoors, the fruit flies must have decided it was spring, and time to breed or mutate or whatever it was fruit flies were good at. There were thousands, if not millions, of tiny frisky fruit flies, joyously fluttering this way and that. "These apple dumplings are fabulous," my mother said, waving her hand in front of her face to try and shoo them away. "But we really are going to have to do something about getting some groceries around here. Now that Pierce has the car working again, let's everyone count our change and empty our piggy banks, and we can try to get some food."

We all dispersed to see what we could come up with. I found three dollars in pennies, dimes and nickels in my jewelry box beside my bed. Marietta had four dollars and nine cents. Pierce, three-fifty. Theodore had nothing.

Then Leopold saved us by finding fifteen dollars left in the book of food stamps that he had been placed in charge of. My mother miraculously came up with a five-dollar bill she said would go for gas. "Leopold, add up all the money," my mother said. "That can count as your math class today."

Leopold was supposed to be on a home-schooling program my mother had decided would be better than going to regular school. The rest of us kids had to go to public school, but none of us wanted to go to college after the horrors of early education. Even though our rich grandfather—whom we had never actually met—had had his lawyers write to Mother years before and tell her that if she were willing to send Pierce away to boarding school he would pay for it, Pierce had refused, and my mother didn't have the heart to force him.

The evil old man hadn't repeated the offer for either of us girls, and though Theodore had once written to him asking for the money to take some classical music lessons, we never heard from him again after Theodore (who had signed an agreement to send in a report) notified him that the money had been spent on a Yiddish class at the Adult Center for Learning.

This was during a period of time when Theodore firmly believed himself to be descended on his father's side from the musical team of Rodgers and Hammerstein. ("More likely Leopold and Loeb," said Mother.) In addition to the Yiddish lessons, Theodore purchased a top-of-the-line food processor for Leopold, and welding school (at night) for Pierce, along with an electric guitar and squirrel-proof bird feeder designed to resemble a thatched cottage. (At that time Leopold was also briefly interested in bird-watching, but in any event Theodore never did mention buying the bird feeder to the old grandfather, just the other stuff.)

"Let's make a list of things we need to get, so we don't spend our time in the supermarket trying to remember," my mother said.

"Toilet paper," I said.

"Milk," said Marietta.

"Organic eggs," said Leopold.

"Bacon," said Pierce.

"Oh no, Pierce, we'll get bacon if we have enough money after we've covered the necessities," my mother said. "Bacon's not essential. It's not even good for you. If there's extra money, that can be your luxury request." She thought for a minute. "Leopold, write down *hot dogs*."

"Hot dogs aren't good for you either," I said.

"I know, but we're going to want one dinner with meat," she said. "Hot dogs and baked beans will provide the illusion of a meal."

"Oatmeal," said Theodore. "Oatmeal's good, if you get hungry late at night."

"Dog food," said my mother.

"Ketchup," said Leopold.

"Now add up approximately how much you think that's going to cost," my mother said.

"Around seventeen dollars, at that overpriced supermarket," said Leopold. "Maybe fourteen, anyplace else."

"Not bad!" my mother said. "Very good! I make it at approximately fifteen, since I think the hot dogs and dog food are on special this week. We have nine or ten more dollars to squander."

"I could cook a dear little chicken," Leopold said modestly.

"Good idea!" my mother said. "Excellent idea. Write down *one chicken, five dollars*."

"Cookies," said Pierce.

"All right," my mother said. "We can stop at the Day-Old Thrifty Outlet and see if there's any cake, cookies or stale bread that look nice. And your bacon—we can get that at the supermarket."

"I don't need two treats," Pierce said guiltily. "I should go get a job or something, to help out."

"You fixed the car yesterday!" my mother said. "If not for you, we wouldn't be going anywhere today! I should pay you for that!"

"Naw," said Pierce.

"Besides, soon you'll be rich," I said. "And that's when you can help us, if you haven't forgotten us by then. Better to get rich than to have to take a job in a gas station. Although I'm sure you'd be very successful in the gas station industry."

"If Pierce worked in a gas station, men and women alike would flock to that gas station," my mother said. "He's trustworthy, honest, reliable, and does not make others feel uncomfortable."

"Also, in all objectivity, he is the handsomest man I have ever laid eyes on, even more so than that Englishman," Marietta said. "I'm on a diet, from now on. Leopold, could you cook some vegetarian dishes besides hot dogs and chicken?"

Leopold squinted. "Can you give me some examples of vegetarian dishes?"

"Rice and beans are a vegetarian dish," Marietta said. "Together they are a wholesome, inexpensive, perfect protein."

"What a good idea, Marietta, to become a vegetarian," my mother said. "How did you ever come to think of it?"

"I've been thinking about it for a long time," Marietta said. "Steve Hartley and I were discussing it last night; we talked about tofu and lentils for what seemed like hours."

"Is Steve Hartley a vegetarian?"

"He hasn't eaten meat in five years," she said. "He even gave up fish recently, after he realized that the fish in his tropical tank recognized him. He thinks it's helped a lot in being so successful."

"Where's his success, then?" I said.

"He's very successful, Maud!" Marietta said. "You know nothing, you're so busy being snide. He not only gets a big commission selling vacuum cleaners, if this sale of his computer invention goes through, he could make thirty million dollars, and he came from a single-parent family with only the income of a librarian, you know. His father died when he was very young."

"Of what?"

"He was overanesthetized. They thought he had a heart defect and put him to sleep. He didn't even get to say good-bye, though he tried; Steve says he died without a murmur."

"Poor Steve," my mother said. "He must be desperately lonely. Marietta, I hope you don't break his heart."

"I know Marietta," I said. "She'll pursue him until she's got him hooked, and then lose interest."

"Come on, let's get going," my mother said. "We have a lot to do. Gas station, the hospital, shopping, and if there's any time we can go to the cemetery to examine the latest vandalism."

"Tell us one more thing about being rich," Marietta said.

"Poor people wear bright colors, rich people wear dull colors," my mother said, looking at each of us in turn.

"*Muted* colors!" we cried in unison, correcting her.

"But as long as we're poor, we're going to continue to wear bright colors," my mother said. "Unless maybe that's not such a good idea?"

"Bright colors!" we cried. "Fit for a peacock! Melon, emerald, chartreuse!"

"Brocade!" said Pierce.

"Brocade's not a color," Marietta snarled.

"I wish for all my children: beauty, brains, humor and height," my mother said. "How far will beauty get you?"

"From age eighteen to forty-five," we said. "Longer with plastic surgery."

While Mother looked at herself in her compact, we got up and danced an impromptu kind of dance, singing, "Aqua, turquoise, hot pink, tomato, baby blue," which Theodore had written some time before.

"Gosh," said Theodore. "That song needs some work."

"Tell us what's going to happen, Ma!" I said, when the singing and dancing had died down and we had all sunk to the floor, exhausted.

"Yes, Mother!" the others cried. "Give us your prediction!"

"I'm going to make my wishes for each of you," my mother said, squinching her eyes.

"Wait, just a minute," said Theodore. "Do you guys really think that song's any good?"

"Theodore!" we all hissed. "Shut up! We want the predictions!"

"For you, my youngest, the Magic Hand with Food. I see you in a chef's toque, coming out of the kitchen in New York's most fashionable restaurant—and you own it!"

Leopold nodded appreciatively.

"For you, Theodore, Your Name in Lights on the marquee of Broadway's longest-running musical."

"How long has it been running?" said Theodore.

"I don't know," my mother said. "Years. Centuries. And for you, Maud, I give you the Ability to Be Irresistible to Men, a talent that will not fade with time."

"Hey, I want that!" said Marietta.

"No, Marietta," said my mother. "You can also be irresistible, but you will Write Poems and Recite them on a Stage wearing a silver dress and a silk chiffon scarf around your head. Unless you'd prefer a career as a Mental Health Professional?" Marietta adamantly shook her head. "All right, then, Poet it is."

"But Mother. What if I can't come up with anything original to write?"

"The only thing stopping you from originality is a misguided belief that anyone is listening in the first place. Just take stuff out of old books and change a few words around—nobody will know the difference."

"Really?" Marietta preened, pleased as a satisfied cat, and for a second almost appeared to be washing her face with her paws.

"So what about me?" said Pierce.

"That's simple," said my mother. "You will become a Famous Movie Star."

"Cool," said Pierce. "Will it be a lot of work?"

"No. But each of you has to promise always to help the others, through thick and thin, and quit bickering."

"Aw, that's going a little too far," said Theodore, as we all rolled our eyes and headed out the door.

11

"What sort of car does the Englishman drive?" I said as we crowded into ours. I hoped his was new; our car had a funny smell, musty and metallic, although the seats had been re-covered by Theodore in tiger-striped fake fur. Fumes poured up from the underbelly, and Pierce hadn't been able to do much about it, though he often muttered things to himself about a catalytic converter.

There were spider webs covering the steering wheel and dashboard, which Pierce wanted to clear away, but we wouldn't let him, since all of us had become attached to the spider who lived there. It wasn't a brown recluse spider, but some other type, with a large yellow posterior, which it liked to swish provocatively. Spider always enjoyed going for a ride; we could tell by the way it waved its limbs at us. Sometimes one of us would bring it a wounded or spastic fly, tucking it in the web for a surprise treat.

"You're getting fat," said Marietta to Leopold, who was on her lap. "Look at this." She pinched him around the waist. "Love handles."

"I hate that expression—love handles," I said. "So, what kind of car does the Englishman drive?"

"I believe it was a rental car," said my mother, who was trying to back out of the drive. She didn't enjoy going backward, which she believed went against God's greater plan. "What was that? Did I run over someone?"

"I'm fat?" Leopold said. "Do you really think I'm fat?"

"Of course you're not fat," I said. "You're six years old."

"What do you know?" he said. "You need glasses. I'll increase my daily sit-ups."

"Obsession with physical appearance is a pathetic disease I had hoped my family was immune to," my mother said, narrowly missing a tree.

"Ma, do you want me to drive?" Pierce said.

"No thank you, Pierce," my mother said. "That won't be necessary. You may not like my driving but at least I drive slowly and have never been in an accident."

"I think I may have been a tree in my past life," I said. "I remember being sawed in half. It was unpleasant."

"Sit on Theodore's lap, Leopold," Marietta said. "You're too heavy and you're making me itchy."

"I don't want you on my lap," Theodore said. "I just ironed these pants."

"Everybody hates me," Leopold said.

"Sit on my lap," I said. "I don't hate you. I'm not like the others."

Leopold scrambled across Theodore and onto my lap, then curled up and put his sticky hands in a stranglehold around my neck. I rubbed his stomach, hard and round as half a little cantaloupe. "You're my Beloved," I said, and smirked in a superior fashion at the others.

Pierce turned around in the front seat. "Now you're getting as awful as Mom, always trying to be so sweet and lovable."

"Placating," said Marietta.

"Cloying," said Theodore. "Typical female of a certain age."

"Stupid reptilian morons," I said.

"Children!" my mother said. "I will not have it! Can't you try and get along with each other? Or I will get in an accident. You're all so spiteful."

"Get your hands off my neck," I told Leopold. "You're strangling me."

"If we get in an elevator, Mom has to smile and say hi to everybody in the elevator," Pierce said.

"If we go to the supermarket, she's trying to win over the check-out girl," Marietta said.

"She wants everybody to love her," Theodore said. "To prove she's the nicest in the land. It's tiresome."

"Like a female dog in a manger, that falls over on its back whenever another dog comes over," Marietta said.

"You're right," my mother said. "It is tiresome. Why don't I just act the way the rest of you do, vicious and evil? I hope one of these days when I'm dead you all wake up and realize how mean you were to me."

"I'm not mean to you, am I?" Leopold said.

"Maybe I'll dye my hair black and get two white streaks in the front, in the style of the Bride of Dracula," I said.

"Ordinary," Marietta said.

"Lacks originality," Theodore said.

"I think it sounds cool," said Pierce. "Or you could, like, dye it white-blond."

The Harry and Naomi Rosenthal Memorial Hospital was a small cement building overlooking Great Bear Lake and Gitchee Manito Nuclear Power Plant. Leopold had to wait in the lobby. We had forgotten that children under fourteen weren't allowed to visit. Only three of us were permitted in at a time. I went with the first group. Fred and another policeman had been stationed outside Edward's door.

"Is he dangerous?" my mother said.

"As soon as he's better we take him to jail," Fred said. "By the way, Mrs. Slivenowicz, I wonder—when you're finished with your visit, could I have a word with you in private?"

"What's that?" my mother said, going into the room. "Oh yes, certainly."

I tried to follow her in but Fred grabbed me by the arm. Theodore looked alarmed, but stepped around me and went ahead. "I'm going to ask your mother if I can take you out on a date," Fred said.

"What are you talking about!" I said. "Get your hands off me, you filthy pig." I yanked my arm away.

"Wait a minute, Maud!" he said, but I ignored him. "Don't try and shut the door, any of you!" he called.

Edward was sitting up in bed, his right arm handcuffed to the bedpost. With the other he was spooning red Jello. "Bail was set at a quarter of a million dollars," he said. "Isn't there something you can do, Evangeline?"

"Shouldn't both his arms be handcuffed?" Theodore pointed out.

"I can't raise that kind of money," my mother said. "Not even ten percent. Why was it set so high, Edward?"

"They say I did things I wouldn't want to mention," he said, and started to cry. All of a sudden I could see how he must have looked when he was a little boy, maybe not that different from Leopold. The outside of him might have been mean, but it was only in order to protect someone weak and helpless inside, like a father seahorse with a baby seahorse in its pouch.

"What do you mean, '*They say*'?" my mother said. "Did you do them or not?"

"My court-appointed lawyer told me not to discuss the case," he said, and his nose started to run as he cried. "Will you stick by me,

Mommy? What if I go to prison for years? Will you wait, Evangeline?"

"I don't think so," my mother said. She sat down on the edge of his bed. "There, there. Don't cry. Maud, find me a Kleenex." I handed her a tissue and she held it up to Edward's nose. He blew. Then she lay down alongside him in bed. "Somebody take this Jello away," she said. "Unless, does anybody want it? Is there any way we could carry it out to Leopold?"

"That's what I thought you'd say," Edward said.

"If you really must have the Jello, you keep it," my mother said.

"No," said Edward, "I knew you'd say you wouldn't stick by me."

"What can I say?" my mother said. "I don't want to lie to you, Edward. We had some nice times together though, didn't we?"

"I don't know," he said. "They weren't that good. Anyway, I was too drunk or drugged up most of the time to remember."

"Going to prison will give you a chance to get straightened out," my mother said. "You should count yourself lucky. You're not too badly hurt, and being in jail will give you time to do something like write a novel. Dostoyevsky had epilepsy. Maybe your lawyer can even get you off by blaming the epilepsy. Did you kill anybody during your robberies?"

"Don't tease me, Little Mommy," Edward said. "You don't think I'd do something like that."

"How should I know?" my mother said. "Just answer the question."

"I really can't discuss it," Edward said.

"Ma, this is pathetic," Theodore said. "Let's get out of here. Because you were so desperate to find a man, you picked a disgusting murderer with a mother fixation who held up innocent people who owned franchises at gunpoint. Can't you see how shabby it all is?"

Now my mother started to cry, lying alongside him in bed. "I know what you're saying is right," she said. "But I feel so bad! He was so handsome, and young, and I thought I could change him!"

I peered down at Edward. His nose was huge, his matted, sun-bleached hair sprouted in tufts, his forehead conformed to the Kennel Club's standard for the bull terrier. "You think he's handsome?" I said, laughing involuntarily.

"A noble profile. Like a Percheron. A Clydesdale."

"Horse?" It was true, in a vague way there was a certain decayed nobility to his head, like an old warhorse that had been sold to pull a vegetable cart. Not exactly top of the food chain, but with dignity nevertheless. "Mommikins," he said sadly.

"Handsome!" Theodore said. "Noble!" and started to laugh too. We laughed so hard, possibly out of tension, that Fred came into the room.

"What's going on in here?" he said. "You really aren't supposed to be in bed with the prisoner."

"She thinks he's handsome," I said, between gasps. Fred began laughing with us. The three of us stood there, doubled over, while my mother and Edward, his free arm around her shoulder, lay in bed together and sobbed.

Finally we quieted down a bit, although every once in a while one of us started up again. "Mrs. Slivenowicz," Fred said, and got very somber. "I get off duty at six, and I wanted your permission to take Maud out on a date."

"That's fine with me," my mother said, blowing her nose.

"A date!" I said. "I don't want to go out on a date with you."

"Fred de Gaillefontaine doesn't like being turned down for a date," Fred said.

"Freddy Gaillefontaine!" I said. "What kind of absurd name is that?"

"Generations ago my family came from Gaillefontaine," Fred said. "In France. We owned some kind of village there, with a château. But since then, we've been on the decline."

"Are you threatening me?" I said. "By saying you don't like being turned down?"

"No!" said Fred. "Threatening you! You scare the hell out of me. It took all my strength to ask you out. I'm not actually sure I even want to spend any time with you."

"She has that effect on people," my mother said. "She has the magnetism of both the North and South Poles at the same time."

I smiled absently. "Fallen French aristocracy," I said. "That is rather romantic. In what type of château do you reside in this country?"

"Split-level ranch," Fred said.

"Furnished with ancestral antiques that have been in your family for generations and which they have no idea of the true value of?"

"Forget it," Fred said miserably. "You don't want to go out with me, you don't have to go out with me. I think my mom got the furniture at Sebert's Discount."

"You have red hair," I said.

"I know," Fred said.

"That's a problem."

"Oh, go on a date with him, Maud," my mother said. "What else do you have to do?"

"I'd rather do anything than go on a date with him!" I said.

"He's cute," my mother said. "You're mean. *I'd* go. You don't have to have sex with him."

"Of course I don't have to have sex with him!" I said. "I don't even want to speak to him!"

"Just go to the movies or something," my mother said. "Do me a favor. Stay away from me for a few hours. You're driving me crazy."

"I'll take you to the movies *and* dinner," Fred said.

I was so shocked I was unable to speak for a minute. "I'm driving you crazy?" I said. It was as if my mother had thrown a bucket of water on me. "*I'm* driving you crazy? More than the others?"

"Yes, for some reason, today you're driving me more crazy than the others," she said.

"I wish I was dead," I said. "What's going to become of me? My own mother doesn't even like me. I have no money, no connections, no talents, I live in a trailer that isn't even good enough to be called a Winnebago. I'm nineteen years old and nothing thrilling is ever going to happen to me."

"Please stop," my mother said, blowing her nose once more and getting out of bed. "Because you're driving me crazy today doesn't mean I don't love you. You can do whatever you want. You're practically exploding with unfocused power. Whole planets could blow up! Marietta has it too: the sexual power of young females. Use your energy while you have it! I wish I was your age again, only with the brains, knowledge and wisdom that I have now. I wouldn't be hanging around the Harry and Naomi Rosenthal Hospital sobbing."

"What would you be doing?" I said, looking to Theodore for a tissue.

"I'd be out there having fun and adventures! I'd be on a date with Fred! With any luck, I'd be home before I knew it, only a little worse for wear."

"See?" said Fred. "It's only a date. It'll distract you from your troubles."

"Very well," I said, studying my tear-stained face in the mirror above the sink. "Where will we be at six so Fred can pick me up?"

"You'll meet in the lobby. This is only the beginning, Maud," my mother said enthusiastically. "You need no longer remain trapped by your fears and anxieties! If you survive this, you can do anything!"

"I'll need a few minutes to change out of my uniform and have a shower," Fred said. He gazed at me critically. "Did you bring along any other clothes?"

12

"Just forget the whole thing!" I said.

"You look fine as you are," Fred decided.

"He doesn't care for your outfit, Maud!" my mother said. "Go get Marietta and change clothes with her. She's wearing a nice skirt. The least you can do is not cause him any embarrassment, if that's what he wants."

"Yes, Mother," I said, subdued. "Whatever you say." I went down the hall to find Marietta. Steve Hartley was standing a few doors down.

"Steve!" I said. "How's your mother doing?"

"She might not make it," he said.

"You're kidding!" I said.

"No, I'm not kidding," he said. "By the way, I found a vacuum cleaner that may be in your mother's price range." He held up a brochure and a piece of paper with scribbled numbers.

"Gee, Steve," I said. "Your mother's in there dying and you're working out a payment schedule for a vacuum cleaner?"

"It's probably a defense mechanism," he said. "Is your sister around?"

"Hang on," I said. "I'll get her. Don't go away."

I went to the lobby. Marietta was standing talking to a doctor who was approximately six feet seven inches tall. "Steve Hartley is down the hall," I said. "He wants to see you. His mother is dying."

"I'll be there in a razor's edge," Marietta said without turning around.

I went back to the patients' rooms. "She's coming," I said. "As soon as she finishes seducing a doctor." Steve looked stricken. I felt awful for him. "Steve, what happened to your mother? Is she really dying? If the FBI raped her, can't you sue?"

"Oh no, it's not the FBI," he said. "She's been sick a long time."

"What's wrong?" I said.

"Shy-Drager syndrome," he said. "She'll probably need a counter-pressure device."

"How horrible," I said. "I didn't know. And to think men still want to attack her, in her condition. I feel so bad for her."

"Like I say, she's been sick for a long time. This may be the end for her."

"I didn't know her, but she appeared to be a lovely person," I said.

Steve nodded appreciatively. "I guess I'll get the house. You know, I grew up in it, and I've been living at home since I graduated. It's a big house, though a bit much for one person."

"What part of town is it in?" I asked.

"The Heights," he said, naming the nicest section.

"Is it a big white house, Victorian, with green trim?"

"No, it's a brick house, red, dating from about eighteen thirty."

"I know that one!" I said. "That's a really nice house. I've always loved brick houses."

"We never really had enough money to keep it up, in the past. My father died a long time ago and money was tight. But considering everything Marietta told me, you're very kind to show concern. Going through what you're going through."

"What did Marietta tell you I'm going through?" I said indignantly.

"I shouldn't have said anything," Steve muttered. "Well, I guess I'd better go back in. Will you tell Marietta to refrain from smoking when she gets here? The oxygen tents are on."

"Does Marietta smoke?" I said.

He was startled. "She said you practically forced her to start, on her knees."

"That sounds like something she would say. How unfair!"

"That's just what she said *you'd* say. Where there's smoke, there's a cigarette. And she was certainly smoking like a chimney the other night. It's awful."

I went to the lobby. Marietta was still talking to the giant doctor. "I didn't know you smoked, Marietta," I said. "And that, on top of the drug problem! I wish you'd stop trying to hustle these poor doctors for scrips."

The doctor, about to speak, opened his coral seas. No words came out, just some bad air. Without even introducing himself or making excuses, he rudely lumbered away. "Thanks a lot for ruining my chances, Maud," Marietta said.

"What chance would you have with a giant?" I said. "Even if things did work out, your boyish hips are much too narrow to birth any over-sized offspring. 'Nuff said?" Her nostrils flared and I took a step back. "Anyway, where's Leopold gone? You've lost him."

"A nutritionist has taken him to the kitchen, to show him how hospital food is prepared," she said.

"Let's hope he doesn't pick up any ideas," I said. "Did you know that Steve Hartley is here? His mother is dying and he's about to inherit that lovely house."

"You really have no feelings, do you," Marietta said coldly.

"That's two crushing criticisms I've received, from my own family, in the space of less than a few minutes. You're all determined to wreck my self-worth, aren't you. Take off your skirt."

"No!" said Marietta. There was a pause. "Where exactly is this house Steve is about to inherit?"

"Come with me into the ladies' room and change clothes with me, and I'll tell you," I said. "Mother said you have to. I've got a date with that awful Fred de Gaillefontaine, and he's offended by my appearance. I don't know why he didn't ask you out in the first place. Probably because he thinks you're out of his league. Little does he know."

"Now I'm supposed to put on these horrible orange Day-Glo plaid pants?" Marietta said, but she followed me into the toilet. "You get to wear this lovely cream wool skirt and spill spaghetti sauce on it, and I have to dress like a circus clown in a goldfish bowl. I can't understand how time after time you manage to wipe the smile off my face."

"The tights, too," I said. "Besides, it's not fair that you get to have genuine Danish blond hair and mine is brown."

"Chestnut," she said. "Silky chestnut locks. Mine is straw."

"This just can't be! Aaaugggh!" I said, catching a glimpse of myself in the mirror.

"You're obsessed with yourself. You think you're the center of the universe."

"Yeah, and you don't?"

"That's different."

We went back into the lobby. The English lord was coming through the revolving doors. "Hullo," he said weakly. "I'd kiss you both, but I'm terribly ill. Don't you girls look nice."

"She's got a hot date with that Fred D. Gaillefontaine," Marietta said. "She's been dying for him to ask her out. I had to lend her my clothes, she was so anxious to look good. Normally I'd never be wearing this monkey suit."

"It's quite cute," Simon said.

"Do you like it?" said Marietta. "I actually found it, some time ago, and gave it to her. Anyway, if you need any help, I'll be hanging around here, volunteering with the sick, while she's getting plastered."

"With Fred de Gaillefontaine?" Simon said. For some reason he sounded intrigued.

"A silly youth," I said. "Of the province. He means nothing to me. What are you doing here, anyway? What's wrong?"

"I realized, lying in bed, that I really should get that spider bite attended to, or, if what you're saying is true, my buttock is in danger."

"Do you feel poison dripping through your system?"

"Maud is certainly used to that," said Marietta.

"Yes!" Simon said. "As if a hypodermic needle has been permanently inserted there, connected to an IV containing some corrosive substance. Is there anybody around, perchance, to take a look at it?"

"There was a giant doctor here, momentarily," I said. "Unfortunately Marietta's aggressive tactics scared him off and he returned to his lair. It may be hours before he emerges. I tell you what: come with me into the toilet and I'll palpate your heinie."

"I'll come too!" Marietta said.

"Would you?" he said. "But what if somebody walks in on us? I . . . I'm rather modest, I'm afraid. It's the tradition in which I was raised."

"Weird," I said, thinking. "We'll use a private toilet in one of the patients' rooms. You two wait here for a second—I'll go and scout for a really sick person." I walked down the hall. When I turned around, I could see Marietta leaning forward, eagerly grasping the Englishman by the forearm.

Like a highly strung racehorse at the gate, my competitive nature took over. Around the corner a fat doctor was eating a Twinkie. There was still one left in the package. "Hi!" I said. "Dr. Johnson, how are you? I told you not to eat those Twinkies. You'll be so gorgeous, when you lose five pounds." I took the uneaten cake from his pudgy hand.

"I'm Dr. Kenmore," he said, gazing at his snatched Twinkie with mournful eyes. "You must be mistaken."

"I'm so sorry," I said. I popped half the cake nervously into my coral seas. "I was sure you were Dr. Johnson. How embarrassing. Do you want your Twinkie back?" Cream oozed out of the center and I licked it off. "Anyway, you'll be cute too, Dr. Kenmore, when you lose fifty pounds. Listen, could you do me a huge favor? I'm in a terrible predicament. Could you have my sister paged? Her name is Marietta Slivenowicz. If she doesn't come to Room 302 immediately, it will be too late. I'd be so grateful, Dr. Kenmore." I had forgotten how much I hated vanilla cakes such as Twinkies. I had consumed probably at least four hundred calories in something I didn't even like. Tears filled my eyes.

"Yes, yes, okay, fine," Dr. Kenmore said. "Marietta Slivenowicz.

I'll have her paged. Are you okay? Can I get you a cup of coffee? Do you want to join me in the cafeteria?"

"Thank you," I said. "Perhaps later, after, you know, it's over." I rummaged in my pockets and came up with Lord Simon's fabric handkerchief that Leopold had bled all over. The blood had long since dried. Daintily I wiped my nose and coral seas. "You understand," I said.

I waited until he picked up the phone receiver nearby on the wall. As I heard Marietta's name announced I scampered away. In the lobby Simon was now alone. "Here you are," I said. "Where did my sister go?"

"I'm not sure," Simon said. "She was paged."

"Follow me." When I glanced back I could see Simon limping behind. There was a wheelchair against the wall. "Poor baby," I said. "Why don't you get into it? It might lend credibility. And I can see you're in pain." He seemed skeptical. "Get in! Hurry!"

"Yes, Miss," he said. He sat down and I began to push him through the corridors, hoping to find an empty room.

There was a man lying in bed. His head was wrapped in bandages. "Help!" he said when he saw us in the door. "Help me!"

"Shouldn't we do something?" Simon said as I began to tow the wheelchair backward.

"There's no time for that," I said. I made a right and we turned down another corridor.

An old man was supported by a younger woman. "Where did you leave your wheelchair, Dad?" she shouted. Either she was very angry with her daddy for losing his wheelchair, or he was deaf.

"Where's my wheelchair?" he repeated. I gave the pair a scowl as we raced by, letting them know they should get out of our way.

"The terrible truth is, I've never really liked old people," I told Simon. "It sort of seems like their own fault that they got that way. I hope you don't think the less of me for confiding in you."

"Watch out!" he said as I nearly crashed his chair into a person coming the opposite way. "Maybe you should slow down."

"There's no time to be slow, my liege!" I said, speeding along.

"Time is of the essence. My mother always stressed the importance of getting things accomplished. 'Make post haste! Make post haste!' she used to tell us kids. We never knew what she was talking about."

For five minutes or so I enjoyed playing nurse, picking up the pace as I pushed him down the corridors, taking the corners as tightly as possible. There was no hospital personnel in sight, only patients staggering about, dragging their IVs behind them, clinging to the walls, looking for crumbs of food on the floor.

"I saw a ballerina in a wheelchair on TV," I said. "She could only wave her arms around. And there was another show, about handicapped people in Holland. They have a special house of prostitution, with equipment so they can be hoisted out of their wheelchairs to engage in sex."

"I think I'd like to stop now," Simon said, fumbling with the brake.

"Party pooper," I said, rapping his hand. We charged into a room with four beds.

"Get me some juice!" the first woman said.

"I don't work here," I explained.

"Please!" the woman pleaded. "Anything. Even a glass of water. It's been days."

"How many days has it been?" I said.

Before she could answer, a woman in another bed began shouting. "Ethel! Ethel! Ethel!" It was hard to figure out what was going on, above the roar of the TV. "Ethel! Ethel!"

"Water! Water! Please!" begged the other.

The curtains were pulled shut around the next bed. I hoped it was empty; I didn't think I could face another diseased person inside. I yanked apart the drapes. Some sort of peculiar activity appeared to be taking place beneath the bedcovers. I studied closely. It was my sister and Steve Hartley, making out. "Goodness!" I said. "What are you doing in bed? You're really sick! And you say *I* have no feelings. His mother is dying!"

"I'm comforting him," Marietta said, half-sitting. "He had me paged."

"Huh?" said Steve, pulling the sheets over his head.

"He needs me," Marietta said. "Get out, would you? In times of stress people do peculiar things, to mark time."

"You're having sex in front of all these people?"

"Sssssshhh," my sister said. "Keep your voice down. We're just having a little cuddle."

"Look," Steve said, tossing the covers aside. "We're both fully clothed. Nothing's going on."

"And you think these poor ladies enjoy the two of you grunting and humping over here?"

"They all have Alzheimer's, Maud," said Marietta. "They don't know what's going on."

"Please, make yourself at home while I'm out of town," said the second old lady. "But before I go, I'd appreciate some assistance."

"What do you want now?" I said, distractedly approaching her bedside. She reached out with an ancient arm, little more than a bone thinly draped with gray skin, and gave me a vicious pinch. "Ow!" I said.

"Fooled you!" she shrieked delightedly. "Fooled you!"

"Let's go away from here," I said, and wheeled out the lord.

"Aren't there any doctors or nurses in this place?" he said. "Maybe . . . ah, I don't know how to put this . . . maybe I'd be better off with a professional opinion." He tried to get up from the chair but I firmly held his shoulders.

In the next room were two men on their backs, in separate beds, their eyes closed. "We're merely using the toilet for a minute!" I said gaily. Neither responded. "Probably visitors taking a nap," I said. "We'll have to be quiet." I pushed the wheelchair up to the bathroom door. "Hop out," I said. "The wheelchair can't fit through."

Simon staggered into the toilet and I followed. "Shall I undo my trousers?" he said.

"How else am I going to see your steatopygic outcropping?" I said. "Take everything off and bend over!"

"Yes, Miss," he said. "But I'm terribly embarrassed."

"Act like a mensch!" I said.

"Act like a what?"

"A mensch!" I said. "A mensch! You know, a balbatisher type of guy." I had picked up a great deal from Theo without even knowing it.

"I don't quite follow you, I'm afraid," Simon said.

"No time for explanations now!" I said. "Strip, my darling."

He laughed nervously. "Would you mind terribly closing your eyes while I disrobe?"

I shut my eyes until he said he was ready. He stood bent over the bathtub, buttocks exposed. "If I inflict any pain, feel free to cry out," I said.

"I beg your pardon?" he said.

"I don't see anything," I said.

"Are you certain?" he said. "On the right, low down?"

"Is this a joke?" I said.

"What?" he said. "Oh, no! Certainly not! You don't see anything?"

"Wait a second," I said. "There is something."

"Yes?" he said. "What is it? Tell me!"

"A teeny tiny red dot," I said.

"Damn," he said. "I knew it. Whatever am I going to do?"

"Oops," I said. "Wait. It's only a speck of fluff. Red fluff."

He sighed and pulled up his pants. Then he turned around. We were standing so close together we were practically touching. Only the toilet was between us. Almost as if he had touched a turned-on electric cattle prod, his arms jerked forward. He clasped me to him. His coral seas shot out and pressed against mine.

I decided it would be polite if I wrapped my arms around him in return. We stood that way for maybe thirty or forty seconds, coral seas smacked together, before he suddenly let go and stepped back, practically toppling into the tub. "Well!" he said. "That was unexpected, wasn't it? But very nice, darling."

"You have quite a big stiff one," I said.

"Hahaha!" he said in a high voice. "You are so refreshingly forthright. I think that's what I adore most about you."

"Whatever," I said. "Let's get out of here. I don't think they've washed the bathtub in years." I opened the door and sat in the wheelchair. In the adjacent beds the two men lying in their prostate positions still hadn't moved. I wondered if I should put pennies on their eyes.

"Shall I push you, darling?" he said.

"What time is it, darling?" I said.

"Almost six," he said. "What are you doing this evening?"

"Are you asking me out?" I said.

"Why, yes," he said.

I was so disappointed tears of rage came into my eyes. "I can't tonight," I said.

"Oh, yes," he said. "I remember. You probably have too much integrity to break a date."

"I don't have any integrity," I said. "Ugh. But my mother does. She'd kill me if I did something so mean."

"I see," he said, puzzled.

"Do you think personality is connected to intelligence?" I said.

"What do you mean?" he said.

"Dogs have personalities, although it might not seem that way if you suddenly went into a room with a lot of dogs you didn't know. But gradually you would get to know the personality of each. The same if you went to a cocktail party."

"I'm not sure I'm following you," Simon said. "By any chance, do you play golf? I've played in weather this cold in Scotland."

"My point is," I said. "If dogs have personalities, then probably alligators do, too, only very subtle ones. And maybe birds do, too, and even ants. It's a question of spending enough time with each ant to get to know what he or she is really like: shy ant, retiring ant, aggressive ant, animated ant, personality-plus, the life of the party—you get my drift."

"What about tomorrow evening?" he said. "Not for golf—but to go out."

"That would be fine," I said. "By the way, what's your favorite rodent? Mine's guinea pig. Second place, squirrel and capybara tied."

"I . . . I'm not sure," he said.

"Think about it and tell me tomorrow," I said.

Simon left me sitting in the wheelchair in the lobby. I was depressed. I finally had an invitation from a man who was interesting and glamorous, and I wasn't allowed to accept. By tomorrow he might have forgotten all about me. Or Marietta might have gotten to him. After a while Fred arrived. It seemed to me he should be punished a bit, for torturing me in this way.

He had changed into jeans, somewhat pointy black ankle boots, a black T-shirt and a heavy wool tweed overcoat from some long-forgotten era such as the 1950s. I had to admit he was much improved, although now that I thought about it, there was something vaguely sexy about a man in a uniform even if it was a synthetic polymer. He stared at me. "What are you doing in a wheelchair?" he said apprehensively.

"Nothing," I said. "Got a problem with the handicapped?"

"If I'm going to spend an evening with you, you'd better act cheerful!" he said. "You're not doing me any favors."

"Fine," I said. "I'm cheerful."

"Where do you want to eat?" he said in a quieter tone.

"I don't care." I shrugged.

"What about Rumpernoogies?" he said.

"That sounds fine," I said. I didn't want to reveal to him that I had never eaten there; in fact, apart from Minnie-Wawa's Pizza and the Peace Pipe Diner I hadn't eaten out, except at home, since before I could remember.

I got out of the wheelchair and followed him to his car. It was a new car, white, with black interior.

"Wipe your feet before you get in," he said.

"Prissy whiskers," I said.

"Shut up!" he said. "It's a new car. I want to keep it clean, that's all."

Suddenly he leaned over and kissed me. I would have screamed and fought him off, except my head was spinning. The minute he touched me it was like being embalmed, only in the positive sense. It was everything that was supposed to happen when one was being kissed. I forgot where I was and became an invertebrate or lower life-form, with all the splendors of existence of a jellyfish or amoeba, simply floating in an infinity of primordial bath salts. Finally we stopped kissing and, giving me a wink, he leaned back in the driver's seat and started the engine.

"Don't try that again, you filthy moron," I said.

"Whatever," he said, backing out of the parking lot.

I pulled down the windshield visor to see if there was a mirror attached. Marietta had left a lipstick in the pocket of her skirt. "Who's guarding Edward?" I said, still trying to maintain an ordinary tone of voice, as if nothing had happened.

"Two other officers on duty," he said. "What's it to you?"

"Just curious," I sneered.

I ordered the daily special—prime rib—and a brandy Alexander. It came with a maraschino cherry. He didn't say anything, even though I was underage. The rib was thick, soft as cream cheese and red. It certainly tasted delicious, but I resolved to become a vegetarian as soon as I had finished eating. I wanted never again to be bought for a piece of meat. "Not bad," I said. "Thanks for the meal. So. Did I tell you I'm planning to move to Los Angeles?"

"Is that right?" he said. He kept grinning at me foolishly. His teeth were very white, like those of a young animal, possibly a wolf, wolverine, coyote or red fox.

"Yes," I said distractedly. "I'm going with my brother. Within the next few weeks."

"Los Angeles is nice," he said. "I might move out there."

"No, you won't!" I said.

"It's a big city," he said. "You can't stop me. I can be a cop anywhere."

"What made you decide to become a police officer?" I asked politely, remembering that the steak cost thirteen ninety-five.

"It's in the family," he said.

"Do you have any hobbies or special interests?" I said.

"Yeah, sure," he said. "What's it to you?"

"It's called a conversation," I said. "But don't answer, if you're not up to it."

"I tie flies," he said.

"How fascinating," I said.

"Who needs you?" he said. "Why do you think I was recalcitrant about answering in the first place? I knew whatever I said would be met with contempt."

"Touché," I said.

As soon as we got in the car we began kissing again. "Let's go all the way," I suggested.

"Hey, I'm not like that," he said.

Suddenly I realized the terrible direction I was headed. For whatever reason, Cupid had shot his arrow when the police officer kissed me. Cupid was a wicked sprite, releasing his nasty needles for fun; I could have told him this was not on the agenda. I had no intention of falling prey to some chemical-tipped dart. For whatever moral purpose, my body was desperate for Fred; but my mind had better sense and would surely lead me out of this booby trap.

"Do you know how octopuses mate?" I said. "The male octopus prepares the female by rubbing her all over with one of his arms. Both of them get so excited they turn red. When the male thinks the female is ready, he reaches into his cavity, takes out a few packets of semen and sticks these into the female. The only problem is, the place he sticks them is inside her breathing tube. So she figures he must be trying to strangle her, and tries to kill him."

"Gee, you're weird," said Fred. "What kind of thing is that to say?"

"You're right," I said. "You seem to think you're not weird; therefore I must be. Since you won't put out, take me home."

"You don't want to go to a movie?" Fred said.

"You're a little tease," I said coldly.

"I thought we were getting along okay!" he said. "I'm not ready to sleep with you, that's all. Where's the romance in that? I might be in love with you! I don't want to get my feelings hurt! I thought . . . we could spend some time together."

"Quite honestly? You don't have a hell of a lot to say."

"I know about the sex life of one-celled green algae," he said.

"Yeah?" I said suspiciously.

"The kind that swims around in pond water," he said. "Two algae of the same size come together and fuse. It's sex, but neither of them is male or female."

"Hhmm," I said. "Neither male nor female. That's reasonably interesting. Okay, you can take me home now."

"I don't understand," he said. "Couldn't we just have fun? I'd enjoy getting to know you slowly."

"Whatever," I said. "I can see you're already pushing for some kind of commitment, and it's not going to work." I felt kind of mean, being so mean. But I could see that my body was more demented than I had ever imagined, and was ready to lead me into all kinds of trouble, refusing to respond to an English lord and selecting a policeman who would never earn much money and might get shot during an armed robbery by someone related to my mother's fiancé. I had to get out of this town, and if I got attached to him I might never escape.

He had become sort of dazed, and drove me home without speaking. "I guess if you're that anxious to make love I could get a room at the Holiday Inn," he said at last.

"Why don't you think it over," I said bitterly. "I don't want you to feel pressured into anything. And if I did sleep with you I can see you'll get all clingy. You're right, it's probably not such a good idea."

"Maud," he said. "There's something I have to tell you."

"What?" I said.

"Your mother's boyfriend," he said. "Can't you please warn your mother—he's a very bad guy. If you don't mind, I'd like to call or stop by another time to make sure everything's okay."

I opened the car door. The car light revealed the puddles underfoot had turned to ice, white and crispy, and the mud had hardened like tired chocolate frosting. An owl, looking for mice, hooted in a griping tone near the lake below. The wind picked up and the oak leaves rattled. "You don't need an excuse to come over," I said. "Maybe my sister will be willing to have a romance. Or my mother." After I walked up the steps he didn't pull away but sat in the driveway, staring into space.

"Lo and behold!" my mother said when I came in the door. "Are you pregnant yet?"

"I have no intentions of getting pregnant," I said. "Not like some people."

"I might just be able to have one more baby," she said. "Though I admit, at age forty-five, it's getting a little late."

"Aw, not another one, Ma," Theodore said, adjusting his bow tie. "Did anybody see my mascara?"

"Use mine," I said.

"Mine is hypoallergenic," he said. "Besides, I don't like sharing. Your stuff is all grubby."

"I think mascara on boys is stupid," I said.

"How antiquated!" Theodore said. "How sexist! I use a tiny bit on the tips of the lashes only. Seriously—you think it makes me look like a jerk?"

"Are you going out now, Theodore?" I said.

"Maybe," he said.

"Where could you go around here? And what's all this stuff all over the place?"

"I'm getting my wardrobe organized for Los Angeles," he said.

"What are you talking about?"

"I've decided I'm coming too," he said. "Of course, I may change my mind at the last minute."

"I once made a nice baby with Edward," my mother said. "I wonder if there's any preconjugal-type prison visits allowed?"

"I don't think you should try to duplicate Leopold, Ma," Theodore said.

"No?" my mother said. "Perhaps you're right. He is one of a kind. The pickings are getting slim around here, though. There's always Harry, but I'm not sure I can overcome his impotence."

"There might be a kind of mini-pump you could use on him, Ma," I said.

"Maybe we should all go to California," my mother said. "I'm sorry I didn't have more children during my youth. I always thought I might have eight. Now I see that the most I can hope to squeeze in is six." She went to the window. "Fred's still out there. How come you're home so early? What did you do to him?"

"I didn't do anything!" I said.

"I'm going to invite him in," she said. "I think he's cute. If you have no use for him, I might."

"Forget about it, Ma. He won't put out."

"Maud!" my mother said. "I'm shocked. I had no idea you were that kind of a girl."

"I couldn't help it," I confessed. "He's incredibly sexy, if you keep your eyes closed. Honestly, I never experienced anything like it."

"Why do you keep your eyes closed?" my mother said. "He's very good-looking!"

"That's true," said Theodore. "I'm no judge but he looks like that Irish musician."

"If you'd listen to me, you'd see I know what I'm talking about," my mother said. "However. You save yourself for the English lord. I'll take Fred. It'll be nice to have a date for your wedding." She went out in the direction of the driveway.

"Gosh," I said to Theodore. "I know she's going to spoil everything. How can I have her to my wedding?"

"Don't worry," he said, and plugged in the iron. "English people already look down on Americans. They won't know she's not normal, for an American. Anyway, she has a short-term memory. She'll forget all about it when we reach California. You didn't see the spray starch anywhere, did you?"

"They have orange trees in California," I said, going to the window. "And avocado." I could see my mother and Fred in the front seat of his car. She must not have shut the car door. The interior light was on. "I hope she doesn't run down his batteries so much he can't leave," I said.

"Who cares about fruit trees?" Theodore said. "They have a demand for good sound-track composers out there, and all kinds of production facilities. It's a songwriter's Mecca—if you have the right connections, which I don't."

"We'll all be rich," I said. "Even Leopold—there's a real demand for little kids with homely faces for movies, sitcoms and commercials.

But unlike other child stars, he'll put the money away to open a restaurant."

"That's odd," said Theodore. "I had my good pair of cuff links right here, next to the ashtray, and now they're gone. How come stuff disappears around here so often?"

"It's Mother," I said.

"And what about you?" Theodore said. "Don't you want to be an actress?"

"You mean a movie star?" I said. "No, I don't think so. I have a talent for luring men that I'm beginning to see I might be good at. I want to marry someone rich, or else famous, though I'll settle for foreign aristocracy."

"Oh, come on," Theodore said. "Aren't you going to be terribly bored? That's not a career. I'm disappointed in you."

"Hey, do you want a cliché, or do you want the truth?" I said. "The truth is what you're getting. I can't be bothered to lie to you; I'm too lazy, and highly scrupulous."

"I don't see how you can go around telling people that that's your career ambition," Theodore said.

"What should I say?"

"How about nuclear physicist?"

"Nuclear physicist!" I said contemptuously. "That's dumb. How about Dominatrix?"

"You'd be lousy!" Theodore said. "You'd tie a guy up and then stand around talking about yourself."

"So?" I said, turning away from the window. "Wouldn't that be torture?" Theodore furrowed his brow contemplatively. "What's the word for today?"

"I didn't know you were still interested in my word-a-day calendar!" he said. "You said it was stupid!"

"I've changed my mind," I said. "It's come in handy."

"Merkin," Theodore said.

"What is it?"

"A wig for the pubic area," he said.

"Useful!" I said. "Very useful! Good word. A pubic wig. Not bad."

"I'm working it into a song," he said. "Maybe you can help."

"Pop: 'Will UB My Lady (in Red Merkin) 2Nite,' " I said. "Renaissance Revival: 'My Love Wears a Golden Merkin.' Country-Western: 'Last Night I Found My Baby's Merkin on the Bathroom Floor.' "

He shook his head. "I thought more along the lines of: Girls, get out your merkins, / At the party I'm serving gherkins / And I ain't letting any jerks in—"

"Forget it," I said. "Who would go to a party where the main hors d'oeuvre was gherkin pickles? And another thing—people will think you're being patronizing if you call them girls. And—"

"Oyez!" said Theodore. "Enough already. You're right, you're right, you're right. Don't rub it in."

I heard the sound of Fred driving off and my mother burst in. "I may have solved at least one of our problems," she said. "Fred has agreed to take two of the puppies, at three hundred dollars apiece."

"I don't believe it!" I said. "What did you do to him?"

"I have my methods," my mother said. "Now, if I can just sell the other three, we'll have enough to get to Los Angeles. I must say, Fred is very worried about my association with Edward. I think he's a tiny bit jealous. He was amazed when I told him Edward was Leopold's father."

"You *think* Edward is his father," Theodore said. "What else did the criminal do that we don't know about?"

"I can't even remember," my mother said. "Such trivial matters are beneath me. I think we should go to sleep now, so we can get up at the crack of dawn."

"I don't see why we would want to get up at the crack of dawn," I said. "However, I'll do it if you tell me how you ever convinced Fred to buy two hairless dogs."

"I do have to give you some credit," she said. "He was so upset he didn't know what he was doing. I explained to him that these dogs are the wave of the future and are better as defense dogs than German shepherds."

"Did you tell him this breed is known for having teeth that fall out?"

"No; but I explained that a hairless dog is perfect for someone allergic to dog hair, which Fred is. Six hundred dollars, kids! You have to hand it to your old mother. He's coming to get them tomorrow and bringing the check. Actually, it may be that he just wants to get another glimpse of you, Maud."

"Keep him away from me, that's all I can say. I'm so embarrassed and humiliated, Mother. Imagine, he didn't find me attractive enough to screw!"

"Now, now, he's probably homosexual," my mother said. "Are you ready to hear more bad news?"

"Yeah."

"Try and sound more excited about it!" my mother said.

"Yes!" we said energetically. "We're ready to hear more bad news!" Actually I wasn't certain how there could be *more* bad news when I didn't remember hearing any earlier bad news, but I didn't want to say this in case she came up with some fresh material.

"Marietta's engaged to Steve Hartley."

"What?" I said. "She can't be! She's only known him two days. His mother's not cold in her grave."

"No—she's not even dead yet!" my mother said.

"Where's Marietta now?" I said. "I'd like to congratulate her for beating me."

"She's spending the night at Steve's house and is coming over in the morning to pick up her things."

"This is just pathetic," I said. "Only twenty-one years old, and grabbing the first man who comes along."

"Not the first, exactly," my mother said.

"She hasn't even given the whole business a chance!" I said. "Auctioning herself off to the lowest bidder."

"If he ends up with thirty million, that's not too low!" Theodore said. "She'll forget about us immediately, I bet."

"How could she? I thought she would maybe come with us to Los Angeles; there are plenty of men out there. She could easily get a job as a car-wash attendant."

"He has a lovely home," my mother said.

"Or maybe she could get a job as a chambermaid," I said. "Though as far as I can tell, she's never cleaned in her life. She always forced me to do her jobs! Hopefully, given time, I can learn to forgive her. More to the point, what do we know about the husband-to-be, anyway? His background, his family, his religious beliefs and curious customs; maybe he's a serial killer, or a wife-beater with several slaves chained in the basement. Perhaps I should investigate."

"No investigating!" my mother warned.

"When's the wedding?" said Theodore. "What if we're in Los Angeles by then? I'd like to perform a specially written musical number. Maybe she won't want me to, though."

"As long as she's happy," my mother said bleakly.

"I never thought my own sister would do something so mundane. This isn't how things are supposed to turn out!"

"Maybe his mother won't die after all, and she'll put an end to it," my mother said. "Children, we must pray. Let's gather round."

"I thought you were all for Steve Hartley?" I said.

"Who knows what I'm for," she said. "It seemed a good idea at the time, but that was before I knew we were moving to Los Angeles." She picked up her bottle of gin. "Theodore, would you be an angel and find my can of V8 juice? I hid it someplace. Try under my bed."

Early the next day Marietta came back to collect her things. She was driving Steve Hartley's mother's car, a lemon Toyota. "Does Steve know you don't have your license?" I said.

"I have a learner's permit," she said disdainfully. "It's none of your business, anyway, unless you plan to throw yourself under the wheels."

"You can't drive alone with a learner's permit," I said.

"Do you mind?" she said, pushing past me and opening the closet. "Thank God I'm out of this dump, and away from your constant spying eye."

"Yeah?" I said. "I'm standing right here to make sure you don't abscond with any of my possessions."

"Who would want your filthy old carnival rags, anyway," she said.

"Boy, you've changed fast," I said.

"This family has forced me to change," she said. "In self-defense."

"Has Steve Hartley seen this side to you?" I said. "I bet not."

"He accepts me for who and what I am," she said. "Unlike you. I have a job now, too. That way I can support the two of us so Steve can concentrate full-time on selling his computer business."

"Great," I said. "The oldest cliché in the book and you're writing it. What's your job, anyway?"

"Cocktail waitress," she said. "With the possibility of serving meals if someone else leaves."

"Oh?" I said, secretly impressed, since waitressing was the job that terrorized me more than anything. "Where at?"

"I'm not saying," Marietta said.

"What are you so ashamed of?" I said.

"I'm not ashamed! I just don't want you turning up trying to make an idiot of me!"

"I get it," I said. "I bet you're working in a topless bar."

"No, I'm not," she said, flinging the rest of her clothes into the suitcase.

"Nice luggage," I said admiringly, as one of the puppies, stumbling drunkenly across the floor, urinated on a corner of the suitcase.

"It's Steve's mother's," she said grudgingly. "She won it at a librarians' convention."

"Nice twin set," I said, noting her coral cashmere sweater and cardigan.

"It's Steve's mother's," she said.

"She has nice taste, for a librarian."

"Why are you so nasty about librarians?" Marietta said. "You really have a very bad attitude. How disrespectful, to be so sneering about a woman who has finer thoughts, dignity and better sense than you'll ever have, always leaving your soiled mark on everything. After Steve sells his company, I'm thinking of going to school to become a librarian."

"Maybe you can become a topless librarian," I said.

"I can't believe I ever put up with this family for so long," she said. "Thank God I don't have to anymore."

"You used to like us," I said. "You've changed. You've deteriorated. You've become an ordinary, middle-aged housewife."

"Let's say good-bye lovingly," she said. "Since we may never meet again."

"When's the funeral?" I suddenly remembered.

"What funeral?" she said.

"Of Steve Hartley's mother," I said. "You know, the librarian? The one whose suitcase you're using? Whose twin set you're wearing? Whose car you're driving?"

"Her? She's not dead," Marietta said. "Actually, she's a lot better. She may be home in a week or two."

"Aha," I said. "We'll probably be gone by then. We're moving to Los Angeles. Best of luck to you, though; I'll definitely make sure you have our address, and you can join us there in the remote chance that when Steve's mother gets home she doesn't exactly appreciate you."

Marietta was about to say something snippy, but then she stopped. "Do leave me your forwarding address," she said. "I'm sure Mother will be pleased if we keep in touch."

"Perhaps we'll see one another before we go," I muttered, but she had already departed.

A short while later Fred came over to pick up his puppies. It was painfully tragic to part with them. He naturally selected the two I wanted to keep. "Hark, Lulu," I said, holding up the pups to their mother. "Say good-bye. You may never see your dear infants again."

She looked relieved. It had come as a shock to her, having children. She didn't like dogs, and didn't believe she was a dog. She believed she was a person who didn't like dogs. If she had been a person, she would have been more shameless than Marietta and me put together. Whenever a fresh man came over, she swooned. Any chance she got, she escaped to an abode where there was a man. Her appearance usually offended people (she was overweight, and being hairless made this all the more apparent) but, feeling sorry for her, they generally let her in.

Once inside a stranger's house, she would try to get into bed with them. Her expression would be mournful, in a nonverbal attempt to explain that her home life was unhappy. However, after getting whatever handouts and tidbits she could, she always returned to us; she had no one else to be disgruntled with.

At the sight of Fred, she fell on her back, legs spread, begging him to stroke her voluptuous belly. Involuntarily he began to rub. She gave him a prod with her paw to let him know she preferred a quicker play of hand. "Like this?" he asked her distractedly. "I wonder if you would mind coming for a little walk with me." Lulu jumped up and began to bark excitedly. "No, no, not you," he said. "Maud."

"Did you write the check yet for your darling puppies?" I said.

"I'm finished," he said, scribbling. "Now would you come out?"

"No," I said. "It's cold out."

"Go with him for a walk, Maud!" my mother said. She held up the check for six hundred dollars, waving it to let the ink dry. "The exercise will do you good."

"Let Leopold come with us, then," I said. "I need a chaperone."

"What do you need a chaperone for?" Fred said indignantly.

"Poor Leopold," I said. "A young boy needs to get out of the kitchen. He needs fresh air."

"I don't need any fresh air," Leopold said.

"You need fresh air!" I said.

"I'm not going to attack you!" Fred said.

"I know," I said. "But what if I attack you?"

"Please come for just a little walk," Fred said. "What are you so frightened of? I can defend myself if I have to."

"Don't be so certain," I said. "You had your chance, already."

"Like you say," he said, "it's cold out. You'll be too cold to attack. Didn't I give your mother a check for six hundred dollars? It's the least you can do. Unless you're frightened that this time I might respond."

"You're not going to respond!" I said. "Nothing's going to happen between us. Attacking you once was more than enough. Your chance is over. Finished. That's how life is. It's a lesson I hope you've learned. All right; let's go."

I grabbed Pierce's greasy work coat from beside the door and headed down the steps. The wind was malevolent, cutting into my legs and face. The trees slumped unhappily, hunched in the cold. A dankness pervaded the wintry air, a distant scent of slightly defrosted manure and leaf-mold. I was already anticipating getting out of this place, so muddy and gray, with its awful murmuring pines and hemlocks bearded with toilet paper and old sneakers that drunken frat boys had tossed around.

From across Gitchee Gumee came the sound of munitions exploding. I wondered why I had never gone over there in the past. Marietta and I could have had a nice time, testing out the men on the proving ground, though it was true most officers in the army were probably homosexual, or crippled from wounds. Still, there might have been one or two intact specimens around. Now it was too late, what with our imminent departure.

Fred came out behind me. He had the doorknob in his hand. "What are you doing with our doorknob," I said disdainfully. "Put it back, please."

"I didn't do anything!" he said. "It just fell off!"

"So screw it in!" I said. "Or aren't you even capable of that?"

He fumbled nervously. "I don't understand!" he said. "It came off in my hand. And all these little springs and wires have leapt out of it." I gave him a look of such contempt he appeared blighted. There was no need to tell him the doorknob frequently fell off. He shoved it back into the hole in the door and came down the stairs. "You'd better keep these," he said, handing me some screws and springs. "I'm sure they fit someplace, but I couldn't figure it out."

"Walk if we're walking," I said, heading out into the woods. We trudged along in silence. "Have we walked enough?"

"I thought we could talk," he said.

"Then talk."

"Don't you have any feelings? How come you're so mean?"

"I'm not mean," I said. I was stricken. Certainly I hadn't had any intentions of being mean. It amazed me that anybody could interpret my actions as such. "I have to move on, Fred. Don't you see? It's not you personally. But I've grown. I've changed. Can't you understand?"

"I thought something had happened between us," he said. "Something special. Not just to go and have sex."

"Oh, sex, schmex," I said. "I have aspirations, dreams, goals, wants, needs, wishes, desires."

"Sure," he said. "Me too. I'm a human being. But you're not giving anything half a chance."

"I can't afford to get trapped in this town with a police officer of formerly noble French ancestry," I said. "I don't want to ruin your reputation."

He paused, and I stopped too, next to a maple tree. It was a young, once sprightly maple tree whose bark had been gnawed at the base, no doubt by rodents. I sat down on the ground to examine the poor tree trunk. "By the way, what's your favorite rodent?" I said.

"I'm fond of the jerboa," Fred said. "If you bandage that bark, the tree might pull through." He sat down next to me.

To occupy myself I rummaged among the leaves. I turned up a shriveled spider, dead from its travails. "Did you know that when mating, since male spiders don't want the females to eat them, what they do is put a drop of semen on her web, then dip each of their palps into it?"

"Their palps?" Fred said.

"The spider has no mashie niblick, Fred!" I said. "You didn't think it did, did you?" I raised my eyes toward the heavens in dismay. "He has a palp at the end of each pair of legs. It's like a hypodermic syringe. He dips his palps into his semen, which he has deposited by rubbing his abdomen with a little web he has specially knit for the occasion. And when the female comes by, he shoots his sperm into her with the syringe and runs away as fast as he can before she embraces him. If she manages to embrace him, she eats him! See this little spider? It's been sucked bloodless."

"But is it fun, for the male?"

"Of course it's fun!" I said. "He *loves* the danger!" Fred leaned forward and, warily putting his arms around my shoulders, began to kiss me. It was awful, because I had the same queasy, dizzy sensation and forgot where I was. What if Simon, Lord of all Halkett, came along and saw this? He would get ideas. I pushed Fred away.

"How do you know so much about sex?" he said.

"I read a lot of dirty books," I said. "*The Sex Life of the Animals* is one of my favorite reads. Garden snails, for example, are hermaphrodites. Each has a mashie niblick in the head, and an Edith Sitwell located in an unmentionable place. They also come equipped with their own daggers. The daggers pop out of the head too. Before mating, they stab each other violently with the daggers. This can lead to fatalities. If they live through this, they have passionate sex—simultaneously screwing and getting screwed! I read their sex life is more passionate, more tender, more erotic than that of people! However, if you like, we can have a quick fling before I move to L.A." I brushed off my hands and decisively rose to my feet.

He followed me back to the house. "I don't want a quick fling," he said. "Why can't we have something more meaningful?"

"Take it or leave it."

Inside the trailer I handed the springs and sprockets from the doorknob to Pierce. "Fix it," I said. He had just gotten out of bed and was cooking eggs. "How can you stand to eat more eggs?"

"I like eggs," he said, hurt.

My mother, Theodore and Leopold were sitting on the couch. "Big excitement," Theodore said. "Mother's called the Nobel Prize sperm bank in California. She's too old—they won't have her—but we've decided to sign you up."

"What are you talking about?" I said. "I don't want a baby."

"Come on," my mother said. "Have the baby with the Nobel Prize winner and give it to me. You're young. A few weeks later you'll never notice the difference."

"With your looks and even a small amount of Nobel Prize brain we might have something," Theodore said.

"Yeah, but what if it comes out the other way round?" Leopold said. Mother and Theodore laughed appreciatively.

"Don't feel bad," my mother said, seeing I was crestfallen. "You have brains, they're just not very good ones. He didn't mean it in a negative way. We all want this, Maud. We were watching TV, just now, and they showed how they go around and collect sperm from all the Nobel Prize winners. We got so excited; that's how we got the idea."

"As soon as we get to California, you can do it," Theodore said. "Though I may be chickening out on the whole idea of accompanying you."

"It'll be fun to have a new brother or sister," said Leopold. "He or she can help with the cooking and cleaning."

"To make up for the loss of Marietta," my mother said.

"Gosh, you're all nuts," I said. "What kind of world is this to bring a baby into? The ozone layer is missing."

Nobody spoke after that.

"Please," Leopold finally said. "They make good sunblock now."

"Think about it," my mother said. "I can have a more traditional-style baby at the same time and raise them both together. That would bring my total up to seven."

"This is a nightmare," I said. "When are we leaving, anyway?"

We had forgotten Fred, who was standing by the front door, holding the doorknob, which had fallen off again, in his hand. "I'm thinking maybe I'll come with you," he said.

"You can't come with us," I said. "I told you."

"And I'm telling *you*, your mother's fiancé is very dangerous!" he said. "I haven't told you the half of it. You might even be glad I was with you."

"He can come with us, if he wants," my mother said. "If you don't want him, I'll take him. It might be a good idea to go in two cars, anyway."

"In fact, I may have to join you a bit later," he said. "I'll have to put in for a transfer, which might take a while. It's probably a good idea if one of us has a real job with an income."

"You're not one of us!" I said.

"Pay her no mind," my mother said. "*I* say you're one of us, and my opinion is the only one that counts."

"Oh, lord," said Leopold. "This is no way to bring up a child."

"What child?" I said.

"Me!" Leopold said. "A fact that nobody seems to remember. Children need discipline, stability and lots of material possessions."

"Having a police officer in the house should provide some stability," my mother said. "Don't you think?"

"What do I know?" Leopold said. "Don't they leave loaded weapons around?"

"No!" said Fred defensively. "I would never leave a loaded weapon around, particularly if there was a child in the house. If you like, though, we can join a gun club in California and I'll teach you to shoot."

"Cool," said Pierce, coming into the living room with a plate of scrambled eggs covered with ketchup.

"I forgot how much I hate guns," my mother said. "Will you keep them in a locked suitcase under Maud's and your bed?"

"How can I keep them in a locked suitcase?" Fred said. "If there's an intruder, if your fiancé is given early release, I can't take the time to find the key or remember the code. I need to have it handy."

Theodore had turned ashen. "In that case, I don't think it's a good idea for you and Maud to live with us."

"What is it, Theodore," my mother said. "Is it a premonition?"

"Yes," Theodore said. "It's a premonition of some kind."

"I'll find my own apartment nearby," Fred said in a barely audible voice. "You know, I haven't had all that easy a time of things. I grew up with practically no family, too."

"How awful," my mother said. "You had a dysfunctional family?"

Fred nodded. "We didn't know it, but my father had a whole other family in a nearby town. When we did find out, he told us that his other family was much *nicer* than ours."

"Oh, that's not dysfunctional," my mother said.

Fred was stymied. "It's not dysfunctional?" he said disappointedly.

"How can it be dysfunctional?" my mother said. "You had a mother, right? A father? Brothers and sisters? A roof over your head? An education? Adolescent dabbling in drugs and alcohol?"

"Yes, but—"

"That's a *functional* family," my mother said.

"Yes, but didn't you understand? He had a whole duplicate family in a nearby town we didn't know about—and they turned out to be smarter, and more attractive. He spent more money on them. They had better jeans."

"Were there murders? Incest? Suicides? Frequent beatings? Sexual abuse? Then I rest my case."

"Whatever," Fred said disappointedly, and sat down on the reclining chair, doorknob still in hand.

"Don't you think you'd better take your puppies and go?" I said. "You have to get them settled down in their new home. They're not even paper-trained, and they cry all night."

He tried to stand, but the reclining chair, which was unbalanced, fell over onto its side with Fred still in it. "It was an accident!" he said, his voice muffled.

"Nothing works in this house," said my mother with a sigh. "Maud, help him up. He's your boyfriend."

"He's not my boyfriend," I said. "I have better things in mind. I'm not like you and Marietta, settling for the first thing in hot pants that comes along."

"Oh, I think you're being unfair," my mother said. "You know the pickings are slim around here. I've done all right, considering that I've practically never seen a man in my life."

"That's 'cause you kept the lights off," Theodore mumbled.

"And my father did his best to jeopardize any relationship I might have had," she went on, ignoring Theo. "Honestly, should I become a lesbian? Do you think that would give me more of a selection?"

Pierce went over and assisted Fred from the chair. It took both Theodore and Pierce together to hoist the chair upright again. "Looks like you broke it," I told Fred.

"Pay her no attention," Theodore said. "That chair always topples over whenever a guest sits in it. You have to know how to balance."

Fred limped over to the table. "Poor Fred," my mother said. "Are you hurt?"

"Ma, would you really become a lesbian?" I said.

"I don't know," my mother said. "I might think about it. If the right person came along and popped the question. I can't really see myself alone and I guess that from now on any man who comes along is going to be interested in you or Marietta, not me."

"Oh, Ma, you're still so beautiful," I said. "What kind of sick old man would rather go out with me or Marietta than someone his own age?"

"Haven't I taught you *anything*, Maud?" she said.

"You know, I might have pulled something," Fred said, rubbing his neck. "I didn't break the chair or anything, did I?"

"It looks like you broke it," I said.

"It's been broken for months!" my mother said. "Why do you torment the poor man?"

"I might be able to fix it," Pierce said.

"Oh, you've said that for months. When are you going to get to it?"

"I've been busy with quite a few other things here!" Pierce said. "You know, I might like to have a life of my own, instead of having responsibility thrust on my shoulders before I'm ready."

"Gosh, that's the longest speech I've heard you make in ages," I said. "I didn't know you felt that way."

"What can I do?" my mother said. "Please don't make me feel guilty. We all have to pull our own weight. Just be grateful none of these fathers actually stuck around; there wasn't a single one of them that you liked. Wasn't it better that we ran our own family, even if we did have to work harder?"

Fred sat at the kitchen table, rubbing various extremities. "The chair ripped my pants," he said. "Darn, what time is it? I've got to take these dogs home and change for work. I have the four-to-midnight shift and Harry likes us to get there an hour early."

"Will you be guarding Edward?" my mother said.

"Yes," said Fred. "He's a strange guy, Mrs. Slivenowicz. Mood swings."

"But do they feel he's improving?"

"They don't know what's wrong with him," Fred said. "In my personal opinion, he's doing something to keep himself sick. Want to walk me to my car, Maud?"

"No, thank you," I said. I put the puppies in a box and kissed them good-bye, with lengthy instructions to Fred as to their diet, schedule and itinerary.

I was a bit blue after they had gone. I went into the kitchen; buttered toast often cheered me up. I turned the dial on the toaster to dark. Some idiot had stupidly put it on light. There was no point in doing that, because when it was turned to light the bread would only stay down for five seconds before springing up, imagining itself to be toasted. I shoved in a couple of extra-thick stale all-natural-grain slices and went back into the living room.

"Do you think we'll ever see him again?" I said to my mother.

"Who?"

"Fred!" I said.

"I thought you wanted to get rid of him," my mother said.

"You don't think I was mean to him, do you?" I said. "What if he's crying? Now that he's gone, I can't help but feel a teeny bit guilty."

"Well, don't," my mother said. "That's the weakness and failing of all women. You may have broken his heart, but quite frankly I've never heard of anybody actually dying from a broken heart."

"What about, say, a hundred and fifty years ago?" Theodore said. "Didn't people keel over a lot from broken hearts?"

"Maybe," my mother said. "I wouldn't know. But in recent history I haven't come across one case of anybody dying of a broken heart. If it did used to be a real cause of death, it seems to be a plague that's extinct. I haven't even heard of anybody's life being wrecked from a broken heart. Don't delude yourself."

"Is it that people have fewer feelings now than they used to?" I said. "I wonder if snails are still as passionate as they used to be? They say snails are more passionate than people."

Before she had time to answer something exploded in the kitchen and we all ran to look. My toast had shot of its own accord out of the toaster and both pieces were on fire. Flames were coming out of the machine and the two slices, like volcanic tufa, were on the far side of the sink, right near the Kmart curtains. "Fire!" yelled Leopold. "Fire!"

"Let's think carefully," my mother said. "An electrical fire in the kitchen can be dangerous. Leopold, you grab a utensil and push the flaming whole-grain toast into the sink. Theodore, you turn on the water. Maud, hand me that dish towel."

I passed a dish towel over to her and she beat the toaster with it. Finally the flames were put out. The air was thick with black smoke. "I begged that landlord of ours to put up a smoke detector," my mother said. "Now I won't feel so bad when we leave. I guess I'll go ahead and give him two weeks' notice tomorrow, though. That's good enough, don't you think? We're only here on a month-to-month basis anyway."

Leopold was staring in disbelief at the ravaged kitchen. Crumbs of burnt bread were everywhere, and the shooting flames had blackened the underside and front of the cabinets. "Why?" he said, looking at me plaintively. "Why did you do that, Maudie?"

"I didn't do it on purpose," I said. "I just put the toast in the toaster. I wasn't even in the room."

"It's her energy field," my mother said. "She's so powerful, toasters catch on fire. Doorknobs fall off. Chairs collapse, crushing their occupants. You've got to figure out how to chain that force, Maud, and put it to some purpose. That's your next job, otherwise it will either get worse, and the whole house will collapse, or else it will disappear and you won't have utilized it."

"I have other things to do at the moment."

"Such as?"

"Such as trying to get something to eat!" I said. "I'm starving! I didn't even get to go with you on your shopping expedition because you forced me to have a date with Fred and there's probably nothing I like to eat around here, because you were too busy trying to auction me off."

"Auction you off!" Theodore said with a snort. "You can't have an auction with no bidders."

"I had no idea you felt that way," my mother said. "You poor thing, you're weak from hunger."

Just then there was a sudden trembling, as if a mild earthquake was in progress. "What was that?" Theodore said.

"The trailer," Pierce said. He had gone back into the living room. There wasn't enough room for all of us in the kitchenette. "I hope it was just settling on the cinder blocks, and not about to topple off. That La-Z-Boy reclining chair falling over might have unsettled it."

"You'd better do something!" my mother said. "You'd better go out there and look!"

"Yeah, yeah," Pierce said. "Don't bug me. I'll look later." The trailer trembled again.

"I tell you what," Leopold said. "I could roast the dear little chicken. Can you wait an hour and a half, Maud, for something to eat?"

"No, I can't wait an hour and a half!" I said. "I need something to eat *now!*"

"What do you have to get so mad about?" Leopold said.

"She has a nasty disposition," my mother said.

"I'm hungry, that's why," I said. "And nobody would accompany me on my walk with Fred. Cupid shot his load, and it hit me."

"Was it a big load?" said Theodore.

"It was a mother load! I want no part of it, let me assure you."

"Why?" Theodore said.

"Subjectively, I'm attracted. Objectively, he's boring."

"At least Cupid is shooting his load into you over *somebody*. I don't have *anybody*. No girls like me," Theodore said.

"Plenty of girls like you," my mother said. "You just aren't paying any attention. You don't even see these girls when they do try to flirt with you."

"Things would change if only I ever get to be a famous lyricist and composer. But I'm sure it will never happen. Women would be all over me then, like Cole Porter, or Noël Coward, or Andrew Lloyd Webber."

"Leave out two of them, I think," I said.

"Besides, women are all over you now, only you don't see it," my mother said. "You figure if they're interested in you, there must be something wrong with them. All of you are in such a rush to get somewhere, you're missing the pleasures of the trip. It's the journey, remember, not the destination."

"Cool," said Pierce.

"Aw, don't give us that hippie/Zen stuff, Ma," said Theodore.

15

Pierce said he would walk with me up the road to my rendezvous with Simon. "Hey, you might as well come in with me, too, if he's home," I said. "I don't even know if he remembers we're having a date."

"Why don't you call him?" said Pierce.

"Oh, no," I said. "I don't like the telephone. I hate using the phone. Besides, what would I say?"

"Yeah," Pierce said. "I know what you mean."

We trudged along in silence. There was a car parked off the road, under some trees, but nobody was in it. I figured it was probably those girls, hoping to spy on Pierce. He was oblivious, however. If there was a reason he had wanted to walk with me, he wasn't communicating. It might take him a while to come out with it, if he ever did. In the distance the munitions blew up. "Usually they don't shoot them off this late in the day," I said, looking at my watch.

"Yeah, that's right," Pierce said. "Usually they stop by now, huh?"

"They usually stop around four o'clock," I said.

"Four o'clock?" Pierce said. "I guess I never pay that much attention. It's just a noise going on in the background."

"You know, Pierce, even the female starfish loves her children," I said.

"Huh?" Pierce said.

"Actually, I don't know if she loves them—but she sits with her arms around them, the babies and fertilized eggs, too. It's the lowest form of life that exhibits maternal instincts. But that's all it is, an instinct. Unless, of course, it's love."

"The starfish looks after her children, huh?" Pierce said.

"Another interesting thing about a starfish is, if it wants, it gets divorced."

"From the father?"

"No," I said. "From itself. If it gets bored, or full of self-hate—then all of a sudden it might just . . . *uuuuhhhh!* rip itself into two pieces. And whichever organs are missing from the halves grow back again, so there are two complete starfish, which go their separate ways."

"That's kind of a good idea," Pierce said. He paused to light a cigarette. He had some difficulty. It was windy, and without gloves his hands must have been half frozen. They were red and chapped.

"You must start wearing gloves, Pierce," I said.

"How come?" Pierce said.

"A movie star can't have red, chapped hands."

"Oh yeah?" Pierce said. "You think so? That's kind of what I wanted to ask you about."

"What?"

"Do you really think I have a chance at being a movie star? Or are you just saying that?"

"I really think so," I said. "Haven't you seen yourself in the mirror?"

"Sure, all the time," Pierce said. "But there's plenty of guys out there who are good-looking."

"You have something more than good looks. You have animal magnetism. Look down the road." We turned to the parked car we had passed some yards back. The four girls must have ducked down as we went by. Now they were sitting up, mouths open, like peeping tomtits in a nest. Seeing we had observed them, they flung themselves back out of view again. "Who's that?" I said.

"Where?" said Pierce.

"In the car."

"In the car?" Pierce said. "That's those girls."

"Right," I said. "Who else has carloads of girls waiting in the road just hoping to get a glimpse."

"I don't know," Pierce said. "You think they came to see me?"

"Pierce," I said patiently. "Girls follow you all over this town.

There are always carloads of girls parked to look at you. Why do you think the phone rings all the time and nobody's on the other end?"

" 'Cause of me?" Pierce said. "Cool." We walked along the road for a time. I kept my eyes on the ground for arrowheads. I had read that Indians once inhabited the region. This was next to impossible to believe. Native Americans were highly intelligent. It must have been a really dumb tribe to choose an area where most of the year it was either fall, damp and gray; winter, when it was damp and cold; spring, damp and muddy; or summer, when there were mosquitoes, black flies, deerflies, horseflies, green flies, gnats and poison ivy.

"If I were a Native American, I would have selected a different vacation spot, at least," I said. "Maybe Fort Lauderdale."

"Yeah," said Pierce. "So, uh, you think you'll get one of those emus you wanted before we go to L.A.?"

"Oh, I don't know," I said. "It might be kind of hard to drive an emu cross-country."

"You think?" said Pierce. "You could get a small one though, couldn't you? Or if you want, I could make a hole in the car roof." He shrugged. "Whatever. Well, uh, I guess I'll go back now."

"You don't want to come with me and see if the lord is home and visit for just a little while?"

"To visit the lord with you?" Pierce said. "You think that would be okay?"

"Sure. It'll be good for you to hang with the lord. These English people have all kinds of connections. They're like the Mafia. Maybe he knows some producer in Hollywood who can help."

"Okay," Pierce said. "I found half a joint in my pocket. It might be kind of old, but we can smoke it. You sure it's all right for me to come with you?"

"Why not?" I said. "It's my date. He has to do what I say."

"That's kind of cool, huh?" Pierce said.

I knocked on the big front door. The Colemans had covered it with a steel grid, saying they needed extra security with us as neighbors. "Is the lord in?" I called. After a pause the gate swung open and Simon smiled weakly, revealing a coral sea of pearly teeth.

"How nice of you to stop by!" he said. "I was hoping you hadn't forgotten." I couldn't help but be charmed by his insolent expression. Wrapping himself in an oversized paisley shawl, he sprawled indolently on the couch. We stood examining him for a moment before we plunked ourselves down. "I'd kiss you hello, but I'm still a bit poorly. And I'm feeling shy in front of your handsome brother," he said, looking down at his buffed nails and then biting them.

"So, um, you're a lord, huh?" Pierce said awkwardly.

"Mmmm," Simon said.

"So what's that like?" Pierce said.

"What do you mean?"

"Well, um, do you have to do things?"

"You mean, are there lordly duties?" Simon said. He picked up a pink emory board.

"Yeah, I guess," Pierce said. "Hey, could I use that on my fingernails when you're done?"

"By the way," Simon said. "I meant to thank you for the joints yesterday. That was excellent grass. Would you mind terribly my asking whether it would be possible to obtain any more?"

Pierce stared at me. "He wants to know if you can get him some more marijuana," I said.

"I got half a joint in my pocket," Pierce said. "It might be kind of stale, though."

"Shall we smoke it now?" Simon said.

"You can keep it," Pierce said. "I got to get going."

"Must you be leaving so soon?" Simon said desperately.

"I'd like a drink," I said grimly.

"I should have offered you one!" Simon said.

"That's all right," I said.

"No, no, entirely my fault. What would you like? I haven't got a whole lot at the moment, I'm afraid. There's gin, and a bottle of champers. Would you like a glass of champagne? I've put it on ice specially."

"That sounds okay," I said. "Is it, ah . . . nice and sweet?"

"It's rather a dry champagne, I'm afraid."

"That will have to do."

"So listen, I'll see you around," Pierce said, leaving the half joint on the coffee table and moving toward the door.

"Awfully nice of you to drop by!" Simon said, getting out from under the coverlet. "Stop anytime!" He looked longingly after him. Finally he remembered me. "Yes. Goody. You're here. Come with me into the kitchen, won't you, darling, while I open the champers?"

I trailed behind. "Is it that you prefer my brother to me?" I said. "I can get him to come back, you know, and I could leave."

"Beg pardon?" Simon said. "Really? Oh, no. No. Your brother is very attractive, but you're the one I have the crush on. I think. It's just that . . . I'm very nervous around you, so I thought I might feel calmer if we weren't alone together."

"Oh yeah?" I said. "You're scared of me?"

"Petrified," he said, opening the champagne with a pop. He handed me a glass. "Well, here's to us."

"Did you know the blood fluke lives in a state of permanent copulation, inside a chicken? That way they don't have to bother spending time looking for a mate. After the male and female fluke find each other—quite by accident, in the chicken's throat—they live happily ever after. The only one who's not happy is the chicken. Could we sit down already?"

"Yes, Miss." The bubbles burst, and Simon poured out more champagne. We went back to the living room. Simon got under his blanky. "Read to me?"

"Yeah, yeah." I picked up his little volume and opened it at random. " '*I fear thee, ancient Mariner! / I fear thy skinny hand! / And thou art long, and lank, and brown, / As is the ribbed sea-sand.*' "

"Oooh, I get all shivery just thinking about it. Darling, there's something I've been meaning to ask. I have to go back to England for a few weeks. Would you like to come with me?"

"What?" I said.

"Would you like to come with me when I go to England?" Simon said.

"I'm sorry," I said. "What did you say? I was just thinking about a hermaphrodite fish parasite. It's rather special."

"Was it a bit presumptuous of me to invite you to go on a trip? You barely know me."

"Did you just ask me to come with you to England?" I said.

"I'm sorry."

"That'd be great!" I said. "I've never been to a foreign country. Except Australia. How much would it cost? I have twenty-four dollars in a special education savings account."

"You don't have to worry about that," he said. "I'd make the arrangements."

"Great! Only, it's just that—" I hesitated. "I promised my brother I'd take him to Los Angeles."

"Damn your integrity!" he said petulantly, and then collected himself. "He's a grown fellow. He could go on his own." He slid over to me and put his arms around me. He was so handsome it nearly brought tears to my eyes, but he smelled slightly of old cheese, and I shook myself free of tender sentiment. "It would be such good fun if you would! I'd love for you to meet the parents."

"Gosh darn it!" I said.

"Surely your brother can manage perfectly well without you?"

"I don't think so," I said. "He's very sensitive. He'd never get over the disappointment; he'd never trust anyone again. I promised I'd make him a star."

"The thing is, from my point of view, this is all quite unusual," he said. "I'm experiencing feelings I simply wouldn't have believed existed in me a few days ago. Perhaps I might come with you to Los Angeles, assist you in seeing your brother properly settled in his new life, and then we could go to England together. I know my mother and you will get along famously." He chuckled to himself. "We call her the Sacred Monster, behind her back."

I took a sip of the champagne. It was a terrible disappointment, like so many other things. In my mind I thought it was going to taste like liquid gingerbread mixed with dancing fairies or demonic sprites. However, it was merely sour.

"You don't mind that it's dry, do you?" Simon said, biting his lip. "It's Cristal. I've got some caviar for us, too."

I said nothing but watched Simon with what I hoped was a grave expression. His blue eyes were fringed with thick lashes, so profuse it appeared he had painted on eyeliner beneath his lower lids. What an idiot he was. He knew nothing about me, had no clue as to what I was *really* like. Thus far he had seen only the good side of me, and he obviously could have cared less whether or not I had a brain in my head. Now he was ready to take me home to meet his parents! He had simply based his opinion of me on my physical appearance, and made up a story to go along with the illustration.

What if I had weighed four hundred pounds and been fifty years old? He wouldn't have bothered to speak to me, even if inside I was exactly the same person. Why did people assume that the inside and the outside were in any way related? With Pierce, for example—girls always imagined he was deep, and men always decided he was a hoodlum, when in fact, after years of study, I could safely say there was simply nothing going on inside at all. "You look so thoughtful," said Simon, lifting his glass.

"That's because I'm having a thought."

"What are you thinking?"

"It's a thought-in-progress," I said. "And there are two parts to it."

"What's the first part?"

"That I'm going to burp."

"Hahaha!" He giggled merrily. "But seriously. Don't be shy. Any of your thoughts would be interesting to me, no matter how trivial."

"Leave me alone!" I said. "I'm still thinking, and you're interrupting. If you make one sound, I'm going to bludgeon you."

"I beg your pardon?"

"Bludgeon you over the head and run like hell out of here!" I said. "I have no qualms about it."

"Bloody hell!" he said admiringly. "You sound exactly like the Sacred Monster, only she puts things differently, of course. Are you quite serious? Do you mean what you're saying?"

"No, not really," I said. "I never mean what I'm saying. I was thinking, and I can't think and speak at the same time, so I just opened my coral seas and words came out." He had backed off to the other side of the couch and was looking at me coyly. "Maybe I have a brain tumor," I said. "Or maybe it's just that my mother brought us up all wrong: we were never taught which cutlery to use, nor to lie and act phony. She encouraged us to say exactly what was on our minds."

"It doesn't matter, darling," Simon said desperately. "We'll get you taken care of."

"This is how I am!" I said with a glare.

"Oh, I like it, very much," Simon said. "You see, I was brought up quite the opposite. Anyway, I'm afraid I'm a bit of a masochist. Look, you've gotten me aroused, when you spoke of using a cudgel on me. It's rather painful, still."

"What about our date?" I said. "Might you be taking me to try some cuisine?"

"Oh," he said with a disappointed sigh. "You want to go somewhere. Of course. That's natural. I understand. The only problem is . . . would you mind very much, if you drove? I'm afraid with my derriere in its present condition . . ."

"My pleasure," I said.

"Good, good," Simon said. "That was my only concern. Do tell me: what is it you like to do? Where do you go for amusement?"

"There's nothing to do around here!" I said emphatically.

"Feeling a bit peckish? Shall we just have dinner?" He checked his watch. "It's actually nearer tea time than dinner, but I don't suppose there's anywhere to have tea—"

"Yeah, let's go get dinner," I said. "Unfortunately, apart from Rumpernoogies, I doubt there's a place in the province that will be up to your standards."

"Rumpernoogies it is, then! Oh, what fun."

We got into his car. "By the way, how do you start this thing?" I said.

"Hahahaha!" Simon said with a giggle. "You are amusing. I was wondering, would your brother be able to get us some other drugs? That might be something to occupy us, don't you think?"

"This town has pretty much dried up, for drugs," I said. It was obvious he wasn't going to offer me any assistance. I slammed on the gas and turned the key in the ignition. The engine started with a peculiar whine. Then I put it in reverse and began backing up. Unfortunately a tree came out of nowhere and hit the back of the car. "Darn it," I said. "I hate it when they do that."

"The thing is," said Simon. "I could use some drugs for more than recreational purposes. I could use a painkiller."

"Are you in pain?" I said. I was properly aimed now, and headed down what vaguely looked like the road.

"Maybe you should get a little further toward the middle of the lane," Simon said nervously. "And put on the headlights."

"Whatever," I said.

"I still am in a bit of pain, you see," Simon said. "Actually it's my buttock. I know you said you didn't see anything, but it's rather uncomfortable."

"I have a solution," I said.

"What's that?"

"Why don't you buy one of my mother's puppies? The ancient Aztecs used to keep these dogs to draw out poison from the body when they were sick."

"What would I have to do?" said Simon.

"Sit on it."

"A puppy. Of course, I can't take it with me when we go to England. Quarantine, you know." He let out a shrill scream.

"Golly!" I said. "Don't screech like that! We can board the dog for you."

"The mailbox!" he said. "The mailbox!"

"Do you have a letter to mail?"

"You almost hit it!"

"Oh, don't worry," I said. "There are plenty more. They're all over the place, in *this* country."

"I think perhaps I'll drive. If I could borrow your sweater or something to put under my right side."

"The dogs are only three hundred dollars each," I said. "You should get two, that way they can be company. There's still one—or two, we're not certain—males left. In the event that you return to England to live, you can breed them and make a fortune. The market's probably saturated around here." I glanced over at him. He was attempting to impersonate a sweaty, yellow sponge. What had happened to that insouciant, devil-may-care grin? Maybe he actually was sick. He clutched his knees, assuming crash position. "Are you okay?"

"If you could pull over . . ." he said.

"So you'll take the pups, then."

"I'm really more of a Labrador retriever–type personality. I hope this won't offend you, but you don't know how to drive, do you?"

"I can drive!" I said. "It's just that I can't see."

"Perhaps that spot just ahead would be a good place for you to pull over."

"Are you going to get the puppies?" I said.

He screamed again. "Pull over!"

"Brute," I said. "There's no need to address me like one of the servants." The car came to rest at a telephone pole. Though the pole had struck the car quite forcefully, luckily it had dented the hood only slightly, from what I could see. For several minutes we didn't speak. In the growing gloom the wind whined, out of tune, through the winter wheat—whatever winter wheat was, I had never been entirely certain. The landscape was gray, and the hills covered with mud and cow manure.

The metallic odor of skunk, probably a roadkill, wafted through the crack at my window-top. Several cows stood uneasily in the gloom on top of a crest. They were black and white, unless they were Port-O-San toilets that had been left there by workmen constructing a housing development. I decided against asking Simon, although I was mildly curious. "Labrador retrievers are boring," I said at last.

"Look at that waitress!" he said. "She looks like a guard at the state penitentiary."

"That's Ellen," I said as she came toward our table. "She used to be a guard."

"Are you serious?" he said.

"She was an ex-wife of Harry, one of my mother's boyfriends," I said.

"Hi, Maud!" Ellen said. She put the menus in front of us. "Who's the catch-of-the-day?"

"He's a lord from Halkett, England."

"Is that right?" Ellen said. "I have quite a few lords on my family tree. I've been working on it for twelve years. You wouldn't believe some of the people I'm related to. Did you ever hear of Lord Lucan? He's a distant cousin. He's living over in Oswego."

Simon laughed shrilly. "Very amusing," he said. "Finally, an American with a sense of humor."

Ellen looked at him suspiciously. "What's so funny?" she asked.

"Ellen, would you bring me a whiskey sour with two cherries?" I said.

"Maud, I can't bring you anything to drink. I know you're underage. So don't even ask. What'll his highness have?"

"I wouldn't mind a perfect martini," he said.

"He'll have a whiskey sour, Ellen," I said. "In a Coca-Cola glass. And a martini chaser on the side."

"Fine," she said. "Peruse the menus and maybe I'll be back."

"She's nice, don't you think?" I said.

"She's unusual," Simon admitted. "My God, will you look at this menu? How extraordinary!"

"I think I'll have Rumpernoogies' Chicken-fried Steak Special," I said. "With the choice of two vegetables."

"Where do you see vegetables?" said Simon.

"In the box in the right corner." I read the selections out loud. "Vegetable Sides: Home-style Mashed Potatoes, Idaho Baked Potato, Extra-thick French-fried Potatoes, Our Own German Potato Salad, Deep-fried Golden Onion Rings, Sweet Corn Niblets."

"Please don't take this the wrong way, but I would feel better if you didn't introduce me as a lord," Simon said.

"Oh, lord," I said. "Were you lying, about being a lord?"

"No, no," he said. "But it's embarrassing for me."

"You shouldn't be embarrassed!" I said. "You know, my family used to be very rich. On my mother's side. My grandfather. But he disowned us. If he dies, though, there's a chance we might inherit everything."

"And how does it happen that your grandfather is so wealthy?"

"He stole a Vaseline-type patent. It was shortly before World War Two. During the war his product was in demand for lubricating guns. Then it became a beauty-product ingredient. But he had a falling-out with my mother. I've never met him."

Ellen came back to the table with Simon's whiskey sour and martini. There were several mushrooms in the martini. "I don't know if that's perfect," she said. "But it's as good as I can do it. Have you decided?"

"I'm having Rumpernoogies' Chicken-fried Steak Special," I said. "My vegetable choices are the mashed potatoes and French fries."

"*Two* kinds of potato, Maud?" said Ellen.

"Oh, very well," I said. "I'll have the mashed potatoes and the corn."

"By any chance, are there any green vegetables available?" Simon said.

"Green vegetables?" said Ellen. "As in, the color green?"

"Yes."

"Such as?"

"Anything, really. Courgettes? Mange-touts?"

Ellen squinted. "I'm not following you."

"Um," Simon said nervously. "It needn't be green; just a different sort of vegetable. Aubergine? Lady fingers? Flageolets?"

Ellen looked at me. "You know what he's talking about?"

"I think he's into some kind of S and M."

"I don't like that type of language," said Ellen.

"What I mean is, do you think the chef could prepare a marrow? Or a swede? Even some spring greens—"

"I never heard of those things. Did you see we have deep-fried onion rings?" she said.

"I suppose what I'm hoping for has green leaves, stems, florets,

twigs or seeds; but I'll settle for whatever you've got other than potatoes, corn or the ubiquitous *fried*."

"Let me check," she told Simon with the smile reserved for the
mentally stupid.

"So," I said. I leaned across the table and took the whiskey sour. I
tried to think of something to say. "Here we are. And you certainly
are handsome." It didn't come out quite as Marietta would have put
it. I tried again. "You *certainly* are handsome."

"Thank you. You, too. Beautiful, I mean."

"But, for a man, you may very well be more handsome than I am
as a woman."

"Do you think?" Simon said. "Oh, no. I remember the first time
I saw you."

"Yes, I remember the first time I saw you. I don't have much of a
memory, but after all, it wasn't that long ago."

"No, it wasn't, was it."

"And to think, you came all the way from England to fix up the
Wolverhampton mansion and ended living just up the road! It's sort
of unbelievable, don't you think?"

"I suppose it is, actually. You know, there's something you may be
able to help me with."

"What's that?" I said breathily.

"I've had the devil of a time getting these contractors over to re-
build the estate. I agree to their prices, pay a deposit, get them to
commit to a completion schedule, and I never see them again. What
am I doing wrong?"

"That's just how things work around here," I said with a slight tone
of disappointment, since I had thought he was about to propose.

"I can't believe that! Is there some American system for getting
things done that I simply don't understand?"

"Maybe you hurt their feelings," I said.

"Do you think? But what could I be saying? Is it that I sound patronizing? *You* said I was addressing you like one of the servants. This
fellow—I've already paid him a fortune to redo the roof. He's never
turned up. Now I can't even get him on the telephone!"

"What's his name?"

"Bedros Bedrosian," Simon said. "I suspect he's Armenian. He supplied excellent references, though."

"Yes," I said. "He's our landlord. Old Bedros Bedrosian. You never can get him on the phone except during his office hours."

"His office hours?" Simon said eagerly. "When are they?"

"Every other Thursday, from six until seven in the morning."

"That's it? Those are his office hours? I didn't even know roofers had office hours. But what can I do to get him to start the job?"

"I suppose there's a chance he's Leopold's father," I said thoughtfully. "In which case he would owe child support. You might threaten him with that."

Ellen came back to the table. "We only have what's listed on the menu," she said. "You could have a salad, though."

"Brilliant!" said Simon with relief. "What salads do you have?"

"What kind of salad?" said Ellen. She sighed wearily. "Didn't you read the menu?"

"I didn't see any salads listed."

She stared at him in complete disbelief. "You didn't see the salads listed?"

"No," said Simon. "It was awfully silly of me not to notice, wasn't it."

She shook her head. "There's the Oriental Stir-fried Steak Salad. That's stir-fried steak on a bed of California iceberg lettuce garnished with radish slices and crispy Chinese noodles. There's a Taco Salad with iceberg lettuce and over a quarter pound of hamburger meat, on a bed of fried taco chips. There's Rumpernoogies' Own German Potato Salad, and there's the house salad."

"House salad! What's in that?" Simon said desperately.

"It's just a salad," said Ellen. "You know—lettuce."

"With what sort of lettuce?"

"I believe it's iceberg," she said. "I don't think we have any other kind."

"That'll be fine," Simon said. "And then I think I'd like the Rumpernoogies' Famous Fried English Fish and Chips. What type of fish is it?"

"It's frozen."

"Yes," said Simon. "But of what type?"

"It's fried English fish, I guess. You want me to go check?"

"That won't be necessary!" he said. "I'll take it, whatever it is."

"You should have just said so in the first place," Ellen said irritatedly. "You want the house salad and the Fried English Fish and
Chips. What kind of dressing you want on the salad?"

"What kind do you have?"

"We have Spicy Mexicali, Oil and Vinegar, Ranch, Blue Cheese,
Italian, Creamy Italian, Lo-Cal Italian, Thousand Island, French,
Russian, Roquefort and Honey-Mustard-Yogurt dressing."

"The Spicy Mexicali dressing, on the side, please."

"You want the salad to start? How about you, Maud? You want
something to start?"

"I think I'll have some French fries to start, Ellen."

She came back a minute later with a plate of limp, white fries and
a bowl containing almost white iceberg lettuce, two slices of cucum-
ber and a pale pink tomato wedge, all covered in thick, lumpy glue.
"Mr. Oo, the owner, just arrived and wants to come over to say
hello."

"Who?"

"Mr. Oo," said Ellen. "It's a Chinese name. Spelled W-U, pronounced ooo."

"Do send him over," Simon said. He took a bite of his salad. After
Ellen had gone he said in a timid voice, "I distinctly asked for Spicy
Mexicali dressing on the side. This is Blue Cheese dressing."

"Don't you like blue cheese?" I said.

"I don't like the lumps of cheese," he said.

"I like the lumps!" I said. "Why don't you pick out the lumps and
wrap them up in your napkin, and I can have them later."

Mr. Wu came over. He was a Chinese man of immense age, and
average height. "I know your mother," he said.

"Who doesn't?" I said.

"So," he said. "How do you like my restaurant?"

"Such a blessing!" I said.

"In what way?" said Mr. Wu.

"Just that there's a civilized place to dine in the vicinity," I said, smiling in what I hoped was a sophisticated, woman-of-the-world-type fashion.

Mr. Wu looked pleased. *"Gehakteh leber iz besser vi gehakteh tsores."*

"Meaning?"

"Chopped liver is better than miserable troubles."

"Old Chinese proverb?"

"It's Yiddish! I thought you knew. Hey, your sister is working out real good."

"What?" I said.

"You didn't know that either? She just started waitressing at my other franchise operation."

"You're kidding!" I said. "I don't believe it. *'I know a maiden fair to see. / Take care! / She can both false and friendly be / Beware! Beware!'* "

" *'From the water-fall he named her, / Minnehaha, Laughing Water,'* " said Mr. Wu. "You also recite that stuff?"

I shook my head. "I was just testing you," I said.

"Maybe you'd like to waitress for me, too," he said.

"No thanks," I said. "I'm not going to be around this dump for much longer."

"And you're the English lord!" Mr. Wu said. "Very nice to meet you. *Gelebt vi a har un geshtorben vi a nar.*"

"Meaning?"

"Lived like a lord and died like a fool. Mind if I join you? Let me buy you both a drink." Mr. Wu slid over next to me on the banquette and affectionately nuzzled my ear. *"Nit utlecher vos zitst oiben-on iz a pan.* Or: Not all who sit at the head table are aristocrats." He grinned at Simon. "Don't take me seriously, sonny. It's in my nature to find your weak spot and needle it." He picked up my hand. Then he gestured across the room to Ellen and pointed at the drinks on our table. "Bring them another round of whatever they're having, Ellen," he said. He kissed the back of my hand. "Okay by you?"

"Yes, thank you," I said.

"I think I might switch to beer at this stage," said Simon. "What type of beer do you have?"

Ellen rolled her eyes, which shone like mercury from an old-fashioned broken thermometer. "In bottles or cans we have Miller,

Michelob, Budweiser, Bud Light, Coors, Coors Light, Amstel, New Amsterdam." She stared distractedly around the room; other tables were filling up. It appeared Ellen was the only waitress in the place. "Rheingold,* Beck's, Samuel Adams, Heineken and Genesee Cream Ale. Draft beer we have Michelob, Amstel Light, Carlsberg, Bass and Anchor Steam."

"I'll try the Rheingold, please."

"Listen, honey," said Mr. Wu, "I shouldn't say this, but I can't help myself. Leave the *goyisheh kopf* and go out with me. I've seen you and your family around town for a long time. Your sister is a real *shaineh maidele* and her quoting poetry has been a big help at the restaurant. I'm thinking of getting the staff to dress up like regional Natives, though I'm not sure if I can get away with it in today's cultural climate. Now, as for your mother—" He wetly kissed the fingertips of his other hand. "A marvelous woman. Next, we come to you. Are you prepared to hear out my opinion?"

Ellen put down the new round of drinks and left. Simon's drink was in a frosted beer mug. He took a gulp and put it back on the table so clumsily it toppled over and three-quarters of the contents spilled before he was able to right it. "Faugh!" he said. Trembling like an aspen leaf, he frantically guzzled what was left of my original whiskey sour. "That was no beer!" he said, sort of chortling. "What was it?"

Ellen came back to the table carrying a bowl of salad and another martini. "Here I am again!" she said cheerfully. "I'm sorry! I brought you somebody else's salad a while ago. This one's yours. I put the Spicy Mexicali dressing in a mug." She picked up the beer mug to show him. "Hey, where did it go?" She glared suspiciously into it.

"The crazy guy drank it!" said Mr. Wu. "What are you doing with a schlemiel like this?"

"I didn't know it was salad dressing!" Simon gasped. He made a face. "How vile!"

---

*A Note to the Reader: My beer is Rheingold, the dry beer. Think of Rheingold whenever you buy beer. It's refreshing, not sweet. It's the extra-dry treat. Won't you try extra-dry Rheingold beer?—Author.

"Oh, stop *krefkeying*," said Mr. Wu, annoyed. Simon made a terrible face again.

"Heimlich maneuver?" I suggested, preparing myself. He shook his head violently.

"I'll get him some more," said Ellen. "Here's his martini. Oh, nuts. He wanted a beer, didn't he? What kind did he say he wanted?" Simon didn't answer. "You want me to tell you again what kind we have?"

"Please, could I have a glass of water?" he managed to blurt. His eyes were an even more intense blue now that the white part had turned watery and red.

"Doesn't he sound like Oliver Twist in the musical?" said Ellen proudly. "How I loved that show! I even went to New York City to see it." Looking panicky, Simon reached across the table and swigged my fresh whiskey sour.

Simon took Mr. Wu's drink and gulped that down as well. "My *sake*!" he said indignantly, as Simon fumbled witlessly around the table. When at last his fingers blindly found his martini, he snatched it up and drank it in one inhalation. "Another round, Ellen," said Mr. Wu with a disgusted expression.

"What were you drinking?" said Ellen.

"I was drinking *sake* on ice," said Mr. Wu. "But I think I'd like a Bailey's Irish Cream on the rocks."

"Please," said Simon in the voice of a bullfrog half-flattened by a car while trying to cross the road to deposit his milt on top of a string of fresh spawn. "If I could just have a glass of water."

"I always thought *sake* was a Japanese drink," I mused.

"I don't know what's gotten into me," said Mr. Wu. "Arrested adolescence or something. Since I worked so hard all my life I never got a chance to have any fun. I came to this country thirty years ago—I was just a kid, really—and went straight to work at Bernstein's Delicatessen. On Delancey Street. You know it?"

He lifted my hand to his cheek, rubbing it across his skin. "*A maidel iz vi samet—aderabeh, gib a glet.*" Then he glared at Simon. "You know what that means? A maiden is like velvet—come on, fondle her!"

"Ooh," said Simon, clutching his head. His coral seas hung partly open, perhaps with incredulity that men found me so desirable, or perhaps from consuming a coral sea of salad dressing by accident.

Ellen brought over two drinks and put them down in front of me and Mr. Wu. "Darn it!" she said. "I keep forgetting young Oliver's water." Simon peered into the various glasses—most of which were empty, since he had drunk them—and at last made a sorrowful whimper.

"I think, Mr. Wu, he wants to be alone," I said.

"So tell him to go!" Mr. Wu said. "Honey, I've been waiting outside your school for you. I was hoping you'd be at the St. Vitus' Dance."

"I graduated two years ago."

"That explains why I never see you."

"This is wild. And to think this is happening despite the fact that I don't have very large breasts and grew up in a trailer."

"Gold glitters even in the mud. You know, when I came to this country I was younger than you. I worked twenty hours a day, seven days a week, and sent money back to my family in China. I never kept anything for myself. My kids are grown now, my wife died two years ago. Now it's time for me! *Besser a misesseh lateh aider a shaineh loch.* You know that expression?" I shook my head. "No? I'll tell you: Better to have an ugly patch than a beautiful hole."

Simon drank Mr. Wu's Bailey's Irish Cream. "Is she coming back with my water? She really is a sadist." He spoke in a new, high-pitched tone I had never heard him use before. "I think we've had just about enough of this. Haven't we, Maud?"

I shrugged. "We're not really making a very good showing tonight, are we," I said severely.

"No, Miss," Simon croaked. Mr. Wu, looking impatient, hummed to himself under his breath.

"A word: I don't know how things work in *your* country, but over here acting like a performing baboon and drinking salad dressing isn't exactly the best way to get girls. Oh, what am I saying? Over here you can do *anything* and you'll get girls."

"No, no. You're right," said Simon, chastised. "My fault entirely. I'll be fine just as soon as I can get a drop of water."

"Just relax, would you?" I said. "So which place do you own where my sister's working, Mr. Wu?"

"The Pau-Puk-Keewis Cocktail Lounge. It's on the highway, just near the entrance of the Sacred Lodge Casino and Resort-Hotel. You know, they serve no alcohol on the reservation, so the tourists stop at my place to get loaded before heading into the old Ponemah burial grounds to gamble, buy tobacco and birdwatch. Give a pig a chair and he'll want to get on the table."

"Maud, I really think we should go."

"The first time you said that it was smart, the second time it was cute, the third time you get a sock in the teeth," said Mr. Wu.

"I've had quite enough of this!" said Simon.

"Yeah, yeah," I said. "In a minute. This is getting kind of interesting."

"Will you excuse me?" Simon got up and staggered off. I examined the empty glasses. He had apparently drunk two (or three, I wasn't counting) martinis, three whiskey sours (mine), Mr. Wu's sake, a large glass of Bailey's Irish Cream and a salad dressing chaser. This was truly not fair, since I had been anticipating having at least *one* drink on what I figured would be my first real, glamorous date.

"So what do you say? Your friend is gone. A dog without teeth is just not a dog. Come out with me."

Suddenly something occurred to me. "Were you telling the truth when you said you waited outside my high school? Has this infatuation been going on a long time, or is it something that came over you quite recently?"

"When there is wind outside, the garbage flies high."

"Another Yiddish saying?"

"Yiddish, Chinese, who remembers? Truth is found only with God, and with me only a little. No, this infatuation actually just hit me recently. It struck me like I don't know what."

"Ooo," I muttered. "I bet it was my mother's wish, the one making me irresistible to men. The wish got granted."

"What?"

"Nothing. Listen, Mr. Wu, you're too old for me. Simon's right. It's not that you're not attractive to the type of girl who likes elderly father-figures, or to decrepit women who are actually your own age. Let's try to understand: you labored as a waiter in a sweatshop, under terrible conditions, when you first came to this country. Now you're ready to party, having finally figured out what it means to be an American. Well, you're not making up for lost time with me, amigo. I have other plans."

"You're saying you don't want to go out with me?"

"Yes!" I said. "You're ancient!"

"She who has the ax gives the whacks!" he said, sliding out of the banquette just as Simon returned, wiping his coral seas. "No wonder your sister is more popular than you. I won't forget what you did. I could have helped you." He gave me an icy glare and stomped toward the cash register.

"Hey!" I called after him. "What's the matter with you?" I felt stricken, the same sensation I had when once I picked up a limp butterfly and all its powder came off on my hand and I realized it would never fly again.

"What happened?" Simon said as Mr. Wu walked away. "What an odd bloke!"

"I just said he was old," I said. "He's antique! He must be in his fifties. His forties, anyway."

Simon grimaced, as if he had caught me secretly torturing a cat with an umbrella and was sorry and alarmed to learn that I wasn't a good Girl Scout. "Oh dear. He's a bit of a rum cove, but that probably wasn't a very kind thing to say."

Ellen came to the table with Simon's platter of English fish and my chicken-fried steak, two glasses of water and a beer for Simon. "Here you go," she said. "Sorry about that."

Simon drank both glasses of water in succession. "That's better," he said. "I could still taste the salad dressing, even though I finally went to the men's room and drank from the spigot."

"Oh, you didn't!" said Ellen.

"I did, indeed," Simon said.

"Around here, we don't drink from the tap," Ellen said. "The Gitchee Manito Nuclear Power Plant waste feeds into the reservoir system."

"How can they allow that to happen?" said Simon, spluttering.

"In return we're going to get five manatees when the temperature in the water reaches eighty-four degrees. Don't worry! I'm sure you'll be okay."

"We'll be able to tell later, when the lights are off," I said. "So what the hell's wrong with Wu?"

"What's wrong with Wu? What's wrong with *you*? He's pretty mad, Maud," she said. "What did you say to him? You'd better look out. He's in quite a snit."

"I just said the truth!"

"Marietta certainly gets along with people better than you do. She always knows just the right thing to say. I'm kind of surprised that there are two sisters in the same family with such different social skills."

"He's old! I can't help that! What's the big deal?"

"He's extremely sensitive, Maud!" said Ellen, looking wistfully in Mr. Wu's direction. "Now I'm worried."

"Maybe you should go and apologize?" Simon said.

"Why?" I said defensively. "Why should I go and apologize? For speaking the truth? Aren't you jealous, Simon?"

"No, no," he said, lifting up a fish-fork of fish with the wrong hand. "I'm really not the jealous type. He is a peculiar man, but I would hate to think you hurt his feelings." He looked at the fish skeptically, then chewed and swallowed. "Scrummy nosh!" he said with surprise.

"I'm not even hungry anymore," I said, pushing my chicken-fried steak away to one side.

"Please, Maud, won't you apologize?" said Ellen. "What if he takes it out on your sister? What if he takes it out on your family? What if he comes over in the middle of the night while they're asleep and burns down your trailer? Or pushes it into Lake Gitchee Gumee?"

"Exactly," said Simon, nodding in agreement as he ate.

"Food okay?" asked Ellen.

"Spiffing," Simon said. "I'd be curious to sample your chicken-fried steak, if you're really not having any." Ellen quickly slid my plate toward him. "Tell me, why would anyone fry a steak as if it were a chicken?"

"I never thought of it that way before," Ellen said admiringly. Involuntarily she sat opposite Simon and stared at him with a moony expression. She didn't even notice water from her pitcher was spilling out onto the floor.

"It sounds a bit dodgy, doesn't it?"

"Oh, I could listen to you talking for hours," Ellen said with a sigh. "Whatever it is that you're saying."

17

"We can hang out at my house," I said when we were in the car. "We can watch TV and talk to my mother."

"What fun," said Simon dryly.

"What does that mean?" I said. "Are you, like, saying you do stuff differently in England? That you'd, like, be playing snooker or organizing a child-hunt or something better?"

"No, not at all!" Simon said. "I just hoped . . . how embarrassing . . . that you might like to come back to my place for a little cuddle."

We turned out of the parking lot and headed down the road on the left side. A car came toward us, honking, and it was only then Simon realized what he was doing and swerved to the other side. "Oh, bugger!" he said. "I forgot where I was." He took a deep breath. "You distract me so much I don't know what I'm doing."

"And you had the nerve to criticize *my* driving."

"Curious," he said as we continued. "The car seems to want to pull to the left of its own accord. It's more than that I simply forgot. Something internal must have been damaged when you hit that telephone pole."

"*I* didn't hit the telephone pole. It came out of nowhere and struck the car. No one could have foreseen it."

"There's a rest area ahead," Simon said. "I'm going to pull over, if you don't mind."

"Don't even think about trying to make out!" I warned. "These rest areas are laden with psychopathic killers, just waiting for the unsuspecting."

"I thought I'd get out and see if I could repair the damage to the bonnet." The rest area was a quarter mile or so down a little exit road. The headlights illuminated three huge garbage cans, overflowing. Loose garbage was piled around the bottom and sides of the cans as well—paper bags from fast-food restaurants; an oversized Crisco container; empty soda and beer bottles; opened cans of pineapple rings; globes of crumpled aluminum foil; a huge, partially shattered pumpkin; a stack of what might have been tattered porn magazines featuring appendages, or gardening magazines depicting fruits and vegetables.

A big raccoon, snout covered in tomato sauce, peered belligerently up at the car. Beside the trash heap a metal sign on a post stated DUMPING OF HOUSEHOLD REFUSE PUNISHABLE BY LAW.

" '*There always is a fire now,*' " said Simon, " '*and where the ashes have grown cold / Lover Boy and I walk quietly / around the beer cans tires and broken clocks . . .*' "

"Rabies is on the rise," I said.

"How dreadful," Simon said. "And all this garbage!"

"It's because the town charges the residents two dollars per bag they collect these days. If the police don't catch you, you can leave garbage here for free. You have to make sure there's no identifying information inside the bags, though, or they let it ripen and return it to you."

Simon went around to the front of the car and opened the hood. Something caught my eye among the filth and I got out. A huge chicken coop, made of chicken wire and wood, about six feet long and in incredibly good condition, was lying on its side.

"Simon, guess what?" I said. "This would be perfect if I ever get a chicken. I want it." I started to drag it away from the rest of the garbage, but it was almost too heavy for me to move. I pulled it a few inches through a pile of entrails and orange peels before I gave up. "I need some help!" I said. "My arms are too weak."

Simon slammed the car's front lid. "I don't know what to do," he said. "I suppose I'll have to take the car to a garage. Oh, no! Watch out behind you! The animal!"

"What animal?"

"The sort of badgerish thing," he said. "The one you said was rabid. I think it's leering at you. I don't think it likes you touching its garbage. Come to the car, my darling."

"Not until you help me move this chicken coop into the trunk," I said. "It's probably too big to fit, unless we drive with the trunk open."

"It's awfully dirty," Simon said, apprehensively approaching the coop. "Mightn't it be harboring some disease?"

"Maybe," I said. "Maybe it's infested with spiders. Or that thing you can get from birds—micturition or something."

The rabid raccoon, eyes glittering demonically, stood on his back legs, knocking over a bag of garbage, which split open. Then he shuffled off to a cardboard box and began flinging desiccated buffalo wings in our direction.

"What's all this?" I said, as books cascaded out from the ripped bag. There was a nearly complete set of Time-Life Cooking Encyclopedias shimmering in the early evening moonlight, everything from *Classic Candy* to *Pork*. "Why would somebody junk these perfectly useful books?" I said, opening to a page that listed seven recipes for Divinity.

"What have you found?" said Simon.

"Hey, there's a lot more books, too." I pushed the cookbooks to one side. "A whole slew of books on Satanism! I wonder if this was the stuff stolen from the library?"

"Let's have a look." Simon tried to take them from my hands, but I denied him his *droit du seigneur*.

"This one looks pretty rare—photographs from *Rory's Midget Circus of 1934*. How cute! Here's a picture of a trained kitty-cat act. Midgets are dressed as lion tamers! A midget in a clown costume is being shot from a cannon. A Saint Bernard dog is pulling two twin girl midgets in a little sleigh!"

"Let me see!" Simon pleaded.

I clutched the midgets to my bosom and picked up another volume. "Here's a real old book on witchcraft, complete with pentagram flow charts and more than eleven-hundred-and-one easy spells you can do at home!"

"Could I have a peep, when you're finished?"

"We've got to take this stuff home with us, even though it appears to be stolen."

"Shouldn't we call the police?"

"No!" I said. "Finders keepers. It's in the garbage. In this country, that means nobody wants it. Oh, there's loads of interesting things—" I tipped out the contents of another box. In it was a purple Fender Stratocaster guitar, with the name Jimi Hendrix scratched, apparently by hand, into the front; a biggish-sized oil painting of a clock and a pizza hung over a washing line in the middle of a weird desert; a small red leather box containing a whole lot of jewelry, mostly enamel-and-gold cuff links and a few rings with diamonds, emeralds, rubies and sapphires; also a square, heavy metal box. "Lots of really pretty cuff links in this box," I said.

"May I see?" said Simon, a bit meekly.

I handed him the metal box instead. "Here," I said. "You look in this one. I haven't even opened it yet. The box is nice—is it brass? Or bronze?"

"It's quite heavy," said Simon, impressed. "It's a very nicely done object. Whatever could it contain?" Opening the lid he let out a yell.

"What's in it?" I said.

"Ashes," he said. "Ashes, and what appears to be a number of teeth. Five bicuspids, to be exact."

"Oh, I doubt that."

"Look for yourself! It's full of ashes—I'm not lying."

"I believe you when you say it's full of ashes, but I don't see how someone like you could possibly know your bicuspids from your tushes."

We started loading the trunk. It took quite a few trips. "Maud!" Simon shouted.

"What?" I said, dropping an armful of books, which landed on his shoe.

"Bloody hell!" he said with a sharp intake. "That's the old gouty foot!"

"Sorry," I said. "Is that why you were shouting?"

"No," he gasped, hunched over. "The raccoon! It's coming toward us."

"Wow," I said. The raccoon, even outside the immediate glare of the headlights, had incredibly uncharitable eyes. "I don't think he likes us. He looks wasted."

Simon hoisted the chicken coop into the trunk. "Let's get out of here," he said. "This is frightening me. And I seem to have pricked my finger with a rusty spindle of some sort." We paused, gazing into each other's eyes.

I got into the passenger seat. "Get in!" I said. "Quick! The spavined creature is directly behind you." Simon flung himself into the car. "I've never seen a raccoon behave so aggressively," I said. "You know, I just remembered, if a rabid animal drools, and you touch the saliva, you can get rabies."

"Just from touching saliva?"

"That's right," I assured him. "A child died that way in Kwasind. One day, hiking cheerfully through the woods, her hand, complete with small, open wound, brushed against a saliva-covered leaf which a squirrel had lubricated. The circumstances were unusual, but not impossible. For you see, when you have rabies, you drool uncontrollably. Therefore, everything we've just touched may be covered with rabid sputum."

"Bloody hell!" said Simon.

"One other thing: when did you last have a tetanus shot?"

"A tetanus shot?" said Simon. "Why, I can't even remember."

"You'd better get one, then," I said. "And fast. Lockjaw is an incredibly painful death, even for an English person with an upper-class accent."

Everyone was at the trailer except Marietta, finishing up what looked to have been a delicious *boeuf bourguignon*, aka Irish meat stew. There were chunks of potatoes, some mushrooms and a colossal heap of bright green spinach on Pierce's plate.

"Leopold, look what I found for you!" I said. "There's something out there for everyone! But you guys are going to have to carry the chicken coop in—it's too heavy."

Theodore and Pierce got up. Simon came in the door, arms piled high. "Mrs. Slivenowicz, I hope this isn't a terrible nuisance."

"Are you moving in?" she said.

"I beg your pardon?" Simon said. "Oh, no. We found a load of discarded items at the rest area that your daughter, Maud, thought might be entertaining."

"Have you eaten yet?" my mother said. "Would you like some of this delicious *boeuf bourguignon* my son made?"

"Actually, I did eat, but I'd love a taste, if there's any extra," Simon said. He glanced at Pierce's plate. "Particularly if there's any more spinach."

"No more spinach!" said Leopold. "But there's this." He handed him a jar that had been on the table for several years. "Nobody's been able to get it open. Maybe *you* can. It's called Gentleman's Relish."

Simon scratched his nose, examining the ancient jar someone had once found in a bin of sale items. Leopold leapt up and returned a moment later with a full paper plate of stew, which he placed in front of Simon. Then he sat opposite, anxiously watching his expression.

"Oh, this is delicious," Simon said. "This is simply wonderful. Perhaps—do you think I might have a bit of bread? Would that be inconvenient?"

"No, it's not inconvenient," my mother said. She turned to Leopold. "Get him some bread, Sonny. Let him eat while the boys carry in the rest of the stolen items."*

---

*The mother here is reflecting on the life and adventures of Ma Barker, who had trained her sons to be criminals. Was Ma Barker really to blame? This seems unfair. Far more likely, Ma and her gang were deprived of nutrition and decent employment opportunities; Ma was left with no alternatives for supporting her family other than to abet these cruel, unthinking louts—"boys" to her, but to the rest of the world, brutish, typical men.

"Ma, we don't know if it's stolen!" I said. "It's garbage."

"That's right, Maud," my mother said. "You done good."*

Leopold handed Simon a beautiful white roll** and both he and my mother went back to watching Simon eat. He dipped the bread in the gravy. "Tell me, Leopold—these beautiful white rolls—surely you don't make them yourself?"

"We buy day- or week-old bread at the Thrifty Outlet and I scrape the mold off it," Leopold said. Simon put down the white roll. "The *boeuf* in the *bourguignon* was half-price because it was the last day it could be sold. But I don't see what difference it makes, anyway. It's all old to begin with. They had a program on about meat, and even if it has a big pus-filled abscess they just chop out the abscess and sell the limb to the supermarket. Potatoes—I like potato skins, but because they ship potatoes in unrefrigerated trucks, potatoes, more than any other item, are saturated in pesticides. The mushrooms— they were given to Mother by a Korean friend of hers. He grows them. We hope."

"He grows them?" said Simon, putting down his fork.

"We hope he *grows* them and doesn't *pluck* them!" I explained. "You see, when he first moved to this country from Korea, he went out in the woods one day with his wife, and his wife's friend, and his mother-in-law. Lo and behold, in the woods they found some mushrooms that looked just like those they used to eat in Korea! So they picked the 'shrooms, went home and cooked them. He had to take a phone call, and by the time he hung up, his wife, his wife's friend and his mother-in-law were on the floor in convulsions. You see, even though the mushrooms looked the same as the kind they used to pick and eat in Korea, they were not the same. Two died. One needed a liver transplant."

"Do tell us a little something about your background, Simon,"

Ibid.

***"Near Heidi's plate lay a beautiful white roll." (*Heidi: Her Years of Wandering and Learning*, by Johanna Spyri, translated by Louise Brooks.) Leopold loved the story of Heidi, and made a practice, whenever he could, of serving beautiful white rolls.

my mother said. "Are you a good lord, or a bad one?"*

"Not a frightfully good one, I'm afraid," said Simon, picking at a bit of spinach from Pierce's plate.

"Oh, dear," my mother said. "I could wash that off for you. It fell on the floor, earlier. When Pierce picked it up, he put it back on his plate. The dogs don't like spinach, or they would have eaten it. Watch out for hairs."

"The mushrooms our Korean friend grows aren't the same kind at all," Leopold said helpfully. "Finally, the wine I use is Manischewitz."

"Very tasty," said Simon, staring into space.

"Isn't he handsome?" my mother said. "And I love his accent."

"Ma!" I said. "Can't you see you're embarrassing him? Leave him alone and look at what else I've dragged in."

Theodore and Pierce lugged the chicken coop between them, and dropped it on the floor. A cloud of grayish-white dust rose from the interior and blew out and over the room. "Cool," said Pierce.

"How filthy," my mother said. "That's dried chicken droppings. You can get a disease from bird droppings. What did I always tell you kids about dried chicken droppings?"

"You can get a terrible disease!" we all cried.

"What was the disease you said I could get?" asked Simon in alarm. My mother was about to answer when the entire trailer began to tremble. The floor tilted in two directions—downhill and uphill.

"Quick!" Theodore said. "Everyone run to the opposite side of the room!"

We all looked at him. "You run, Theodore," I said.

"To balance it!" Theodore said. "To balance it, you idiot."

Something odd was happening not just with the floor, but with the ceiling as well, which seemed to be going in the opposite direction,

---

*The scholarly reader might be advised to consult *The Wonderful Wizard of Oz*, by L. Frank Baum, for the source of this literary allusion. For a similar example, see page 152, when Simon pricks his finger on a rusty spindle. He and Maud instantly recollect the tale of Sleeping Beauty, but neither dares mention anything to the other.

like a cardboard box folding up. Leopold let out a thin, high-pitched wail. "Ow!" I said, putting my hands over my ears.

"My chocolate soufflé!" Leopold said. "It was my first attempt."

"Is it going to fall?" my mother said.

"Yes!" Leopold said.

Simon began to scramble to the far side of the room, but he didn't appear to be making much progress. "Get to the far side!" he said.

"That's what I just said!" Theodore shouted. "Get on the other side of the room!"

"My beloved dogs!" my mother said.

"Where are they?" I said.

"In the bedroom," my mother said. "Go get them, quick!"

"Quickly, my lord!" I said, pointing at Simon.

"Maud, go with him," my mother snarled. "He can't manage two grown dogs and the puppies by himself."

"Why do I have to go?" I said. "I'm frightened."

"What about Trayf, and Lulu, and the puppies?" Pierce said.

"They're in the bedroom!" I said.

"You're kidding!" said Pierce. "I'll go get them."

"Quick!" Theodore said. "This place is slipping. This is no joke. One of us should call for help."

There was a pause. "Why don't *you* call, Theodore?" my mother suggested.

"*You're* the mother," Theodore said. "I tell you what: I'll dial." He picked up the receiver. "It's not working!" he said, jabbing the buttons. "Our wires must have been pulled out. All of you, we better get out of here!"

"My Cuisinart," Leopold said.

"Forget the Cuisinart," my mother said. "Simon's right. Party's over! I want you out of the house, now!"

"Simon!" Theodore said. "*I* was the one who said it. I never get any credit."

My mother tried to pick up Leopold but he really was too big. She half-dragged him uphill, toward the door, and frantically yanked. "It's jammed!" she said. The TV toppled off the stand and the couch, in slow motion, began to slide across the floor. "We're trapped!" my mother said. "I don't blame you, Maud."

"Why would you blame me?" I said.

"For bringing all that junk in!" my mother said.

"Oh, G. Dash D., I wish I were dead," I said. "I'm blamed for everything! Nobody likes me. Everybody likes Marietta better than me; and she gets to be prettier, too!"

Dishes and pans crashed in the kitchen as the cabinets apparently flew open. We almost always used paper plates, since china or plastic had to be washed twice—once before use, to get off the old food, and then again when it was time for the next meal. At least now that would never even be a consideration. "I don't think Marietta's prettier than you, Maud," Theodore said, trying to hold onto the television.

"Really?" I said.

"You're more unusual looking. Marietta's beautiful, but in a more usual way. You're beautiful in an unusual way. The two of you would appeal to different types. Especially once you don't have pimples."

"I only have one pimple!" I said. "I *knew* everyone noticed."

"That's because you talk about it, and you keep touching your face and drawing attention to it!" my mother said. "Come on; quit brooding about your looks and help me get the front door open, or none of this will make any difference."

"Just who was my father, anyway?" I said.

"There's no time to go into that now!" my mother said.

"I smell something funny," Pierce said, coming back into the room with Trayf squirming under one arm and a duffel bag in the other. "I've got the puppies in the bag. They were scared witless."

"You smell something?" my mother said.

Leopold took a deep sniff. "It's the gas!" he said.

"Oh my God, you're right," my mother said. "It's the propane. The line is leaking. We've got to get out of here or it's going to explode."

"You guys have a good sense of smell," I said, crawling on the floor, which by now had become nearly vertical. It was fortunate that quite a few things were built in, such as the table; I grabbed it by the base. "I don't smell anything. I'm surprised, Pierce, that you can smell anything, smoking cigarettes all the time."

"Pierce, you smoke cigarettes all the time?" my mother said, grabbing Leopold's arm as he began to slip out of her grasp. Pierce looked at me with narrowed eyes.

"Ooo," I said. "I'm frightened. Don't hurt me, Pierce. You're going to be a good movie star."

Pierce looked sheepish. "Yeah?" he said. "You think so? I got to try and remember what I did just then."

"He's not going to be a movie star if we don't get out of here!" my mother said. "The door is stuck. Simon, you take the dogs. Pierce, break down the door."

Simon took the duffel bag and Trayf's collar. "Is this all of them?" he said.

"Lulu!" I said with a wail. "You forgot Lulu!"

"She was under the bed," Pierce said. "I couldn't get her out. You know what she does."

"So you just don't bother to mention it!" I said.

Simon handed me the duffel bag and gave Trayf a shove in my direction. "I'll rescue Lulu, my beloved," he said, exiting down the hall. We all looked at one another but none of us spoke. There was a pause, and then the terrible sound of Lulu snarling. This was followed by a shriek and stream of expressions.

Pierce tried to pull open the door. It didn't budge. "It won't open," Pierce said.

"It's stuck," I said.

"You think it's stuck or something?" Pierce said. He gave it a kick but nothing moved.

Simon stumbled into the room with Lulu in his arms. He held her awkwardly. "I'm afraid she bit me."

"Lulu would *never* bite," my mother said.

"You won't report her, will you Simon?" I said. "They put dogs to sleep after three attacks. If you report her, she doesn't have a chance. It's death row."

"Ma, what do you want me to do?" Pierce said.

"The window!" my mother said. Pierce went to the window, but it too was stuck. "Break it!" she said.

"You want me to break the window?" Pierce said.

"Break it!" my mother commanded again.

"You're not going to be mad, are you?"

"No!" my mother snarled.

Leopold was crying. "I'm scared."

"Don't try breaking it with your fist, Pierce!" my mother said. "Use an object!"

"All right, all right," Pierce said. "You don't have to get so mad." Pierce looked around the room but none of us could see anything that might be useful in breaking a window. "The guitar!" my mother said. "Take that purple guitar and smash the pane with it."

"Not the Fender Stratocaster!" said Pierce. "Here, I'll smash it with this suitcase." He started to take the duffel bag from me.

"Not the duffel bag the puppies are in!" my mother said. "Oh, God, you don't have a brain in your head."

"So what do you want me to use?" said Pierce, glaring.

"Maybe there's something in your pocketbook, Ma," I said. "Where's your purse?"

"I don't know!" my mother said.

"You're holding it, Ma!" said Theodore.

"Oh," said my mother. "Let me look. I don't know what I'd have in my pocketbook that could be used to smash a window, though." She unzipped the side compartment. "Here's a hammer," she said, taking it out and handing it to Pierce. "I wondered why my bag was so heavy, all this time."

"Is that my hammer?" said Pierce. "Where was it?" He smashed the pane a couple of times. "It's made out of plastic, not glass," he said. "I can't break the damn thing." But after a few more blows the entire window, frame and all, gave way and fell out. "I don't know," he said, peering through. "We're pretty high off the ground now, on this side."

"Jump!" my mother said. "Jump! You'll have to catch the rest of us when we follow."

Pierce slung one leg over the empty frame. "It's going to be a tight squeeze," he said. "I'm going to have to scrunch down. I'm thinking, can I get both legs out of here at the same time, is the problem."

"You can do it," my mother said as the trailer gave way a little more.

He tried to get the other leg up through the window frame. "Hey, where's my cigarettes?" he said. "Did I leave my Marlboros on the table?"

"I see them," Theodore said. "They rolled into the corner. Want me to get them? I don't know if I can reach! This is awful! Help! Help! Nobody's taking any of this seriously except me!"

"I have tobacco," said Simon. "Would you like a roll-up?"

Pierce patted his pocket. "That's okay," he said. "Luckily I got an extra pack." He took out a cigarette and a lighter. "Here goes nothing," he said, putting the cigarette in his coral seas and squeezing his left leg up to his chest.

"Pierce!" my mother said. "Don't light that cigarette!"

"Aw, Ma," Pierce said. "Leave me alone, would ya? I don't smoke that much."

"You'll blow us up! The gas!" my mother said.

Pierce slid the lighter back into his pocket. "Oh yeah," he said. "That's a point. Well, here goes nothing." He jumped, unlit cigarette still dangling.

"Push Trayf over to me," my mother said. Then she pulled herself along the floor, still dragging Trayf by the collar. With great difficulty she got Trayf's front paws up to the sill. "Jump, Trayf, jump!" she said.

Trayf looked at my mother with a hurt expression and slumped into a ball. "He thinks you want him to commit suicide," I said.

"Oh, you dumb dog," my mother said. She yanked him up by his head, and pushing with all her strength, got his front end out the window. "Pierce, you'll have to catch him!" she said. "The dog is coming through! Did you hear me?"

There was no answer. My mother peered out over the dog's backside. "Pierce, where are you?" she said.

I staggered to the window and looked out alongside my mother. Pierce was nowhere in sight. The drop was at least ten feet to the ground.

"Pierce!" I screamed. "Hurry up!"

"Where did he go?" my mother said.

"I see him," I said. "He's coming back."

"Pierce!" my mother said. "What is wrong with you? Catch the dog and don't move one step!"

"Did you still need me?" Pierce said. He walked toward us.

"You're an idiot!" I said.

"If you talk to me like that, I'm leaving."

"There's no time for squabbles now," my mother said. "Pierce, I'm going to drop Trayf down to you, and I want you to catch him."

"You're going to throw the dog out the window?"

"He's probably stoned," I said.

"Pierce, listen carefully," my mother said. "After you catch the dog, I want you to put him on the ground and stand there while the rest of us jump."

"Okay," Pierce said.

"Get back inside, Maud," my mother said. "You're not helping."

"Not if you don't want me to." I backed off. My mother slung the dog out the window. Pierce put him on the ground and Trayf began to bark excitedly. He was looking for Lulu. My mother grabbed her and put her out next. Trayf gave her a good sniffing, to check that she was okay. She sneered disdainfully and shuffled away.

"Now, Leopold," my mother said. I yanked Leopold out from under the table. It was hard to pry his hands loose from the table leg. He was crying. My mother lowered him out the window. "You go next, Maud," she said.

"Hey," Theodore said. "My librettos! I can't leave those! I don't have any copies." He staggered down the hall. It looked like it should have been fun, but probably wasn't, to walk down the hall on what had once been the wall. There was another *thwump!* as the trailer dropped down the hill a bit farther.

"Theodore!" my mother wailed. "What are you doing? Are you all right? Maud, get out of here now!"

I went to the window and looked out. The ground seemed very far away. I got my legs up and grabbed the edge of the sill. My feet were still miles off the ground.

18

"She's had the wind knocked out of her," my mother was saying. "Or maybe it was the gas? Get up, my darling. We have to get away from here in case the whole thing erupts."

Someone was kneeling over me. "Are you all right, beloved?"

"Get away from me," I said. "I'm going to puke. You make me feel suffocated."

"Oh, thank God," my mother said. "She's fine." I opened my eyes. I could see the English lord, skulking in the gloom, as if he were wearing a cape and I had hurt his feelings.

It occurred to me I shouldn't let him get away. What if I were in love with him, but simply hadn't realized it yet? "Wait!" I called after him. "Come back! I didn't know it was you. I'm chilled. Lie down on top of me before I go into shock. I need treatment."

My mother hammered on the side of the trailer. "Theodore, where are you? Hurry! I'm begging you!" The trailer slipped a few more feet farther away. "What am I going to do? I can't even get back in. Do you think he's passed out, too, from the fumes?"

The flimsy construction toppled off the cinder blocks. "Mrs. Slivenowicz!" Simon shouted. "Get back! Get away! It's on the rampage!"

"My son!" my mother shouted. "What about my son?"

Our residence began to slide down the hill on its side, headed for the shores of Gitchee Gumee. It shook like a cardboard shoe box as it rattled over rocks and stumps, crushing the dainty wire fence at the back of the yard. "Theodore!" my mother yelled. "Oh, Theodore!"

Pierce began to run down the hill after the trailer, followed by Simon. "It's heading for the Big-Sea-Shining!" I said, starting to run.

Suddenly there was a splash. "It's gone in the lake!" my mother said. "He'll drown."

We got to the bottom of the hill. The trailer had come to a halt, half in the water. "Lucky it stopped," I said. "The water gets real deep, about five more feet out."

"Is it going to blow?" Pierce said, approaching cautiously.

"I don't know," my mother said. "Can it explode while it's in the water? Theodore would know. Oh, Theodore, where are you? Are you alive?" She kicked off her bunny slippers and, hoisting her bathrobe, stepped into the lake.

"What if he hit his head and is lying unconscious on the floor?" I said. "He'll drown in his own vomit."

"Pierce, do something," my mother said.

Pierce scrambled into the water and climbed up the side of the trailer. The window was now on the roof. He turned, waved and slung himself in. I gave the side of the trailer a little shove to see how firmly it had come to a stop. It hadn't come to a stop at all firmly. It started to float out into the lake.

"What did you do?" my mother said. "What did you do?"

"I just gave it a little tap!" I said. "I hardly touched it!"

The trailer looked like a peculiar houseboat. "Do something!" my mother said. "Stop it!"

Simon walked into the water and out to the trailer. The water came up to his hips. "It's freezing," he said. "We have to act fast." He grabbed a corner, but now that it was in deeper water he couldn't get a grip, and the trailer kept floating farther out. "I'll try and join them inside," he said. I watched as he tried to climb up the side. He couldn't; the water was too deep.

My mother plunged in after him. "My son!" she said.

"Mrs. Slivenowicz!" Simon said. "The water is freezing cold. You'd better get back on shore! You'll develop hypothermia!" The trailer floated farther out on the lake. It was too dark to see much. I stood some distance behind my mother. She had still not come back out of the water. Her legs would probably have to be amputated. Simon stood on shore, shivering. After a minute a dim figure emerged from the window.

"Is that you, Theodore?" my mother said. The figure dragged himself along the top of the trailer. Then another figure came out. "Pierce!" my mother said. "Are you all right?"

"It's going down!" Pierce said. "The water's coming up inside fast!" He stood, but Theodore lay in a heap.

"What's wrong with Theodore?" my mother said. "Is he hurt?"

"He's acting kind of strange," Pierce said. "I think he's taking a nap."

"Put him over the side and I'll swim out," Simon said.

Pierce looked over the side. "Geeze, we floated a long way out," he said.

Simon ran back into the water and started swimming to the trailer. Pierce appeared to kick Theodore, although it was difficult to tell exactly. Theodore's limp body rolled into the water. "Oh, gosh, is he all right?" I said. "What will I do without him? Or if he's permanently brain-damaged? What if he's scarred, timid and fearful for life? What will I do? He's the only one I have to talk to."

Simon pulled Theodore to shore. We ran to them. "My arm," said Theodore. "My arm—and my head. The TV set fell on my head. Then it hit my arm. My arm is broken. I'll never play the keyboard again."

The trailer made a glugging sound. We turned around to look. Pierce was still perched on one descending edge. "Jump, Pierce," my mother said. "It's sinking! Swim to shore!" Pierce appeared paralyzed or frozen.

"I'll get him," I said. "He has these little moments."

"The water is freezing cold, Maud," Simon said. "I'm not sure I'm strong enough to go back in. Are you a strong swimmer?" His face was blue.

"Not very," I said.

"I'll go," my mother said.

"You can't go!" I said. "You're tiny. Pierce is huge. You're going to swim out and lug him to shore in your bathrobe?"

I walked into the water. It was so cold it was almost inhuman, but the murderous edge was missing—no doubt the runoff from the Gitchee Manito Nuclear Power Plant had raised the temperature to a degree. Still, we were not ready to receive our manatees just yet.

I walked out five or ten feet and then the ground dropped and I had to swim. By the time I got out to the trailer, maybe seventy-five feet away, I knew I wasn't going to be able to get back to shore. I hoisted myself up next to Pierce with the last of my strength. The trailer was only a foot or so above the water's surface. "You're all wet," Pierce said suddenly. "What's happening?"

"Not much," I said.

"You got wet, though, somehow," Pierce said. "You better take off your clothes, or Mom will kill you. I'll give you mine." He put his motorcycle jacket around me.

"Thanks, Pierce," I said. There was a pause. "How are we going to get back?" I said.

"I don't know," he said. "I don't think I can swim."

"You can't swim?" I said. "It's true, I've never seen you in the water. How come?"

"I just never learned," he said. "You really think I've got a shot at being a movie star?"

"If we make it out of here," I said. "How long do you think this thing is going to stay afloat?"

"If we don't move around too much, another five minutes."

"We're going to die, aren't we," I said. "It's going to sink and we'll freeze and drown."

"You think there's, like, anything after death?" he said.

"I hope so," I said. "But I don't know."

"You don't know, huh?" he said. He took out a cigarette and fumbled with the lighter. It took him a few tries to get a flame.

All of a sudden there was a *whoosh!* and a booming sound. An invisible force catapulted me off the side of the trailer and into the water. The whole thing had exploded. "Pierce!" I said, gurgling. "Where are you?" I started swimming for shore, flaming debris all around, still looking for my brother.

Finally I made it to land, in a curious state somewhere between birth and death. "Where's Pierce?" my mother said.

"He's out there," I said, draining and replacing my shoes. "Were you aware he can't swim?"

"He's drowned!" my mother said, sobbing.

"No, no!" Simon said. "Look!" What was left of the trailer was in flames. My heart sank. But then, in the smoky light, I could make out our front door, which was floating like a raft, with a large bulk on top. "It's Pierce!"

"Paddle for shore!" my mother said. "Paddle!" He seemed to be staring at the sky.

"He's out of it again," I said. "Maybe *he* has epilepsy."

"No," my mother said. "He just has a lot of thoughts, my poor baby. They distract him. This way, Pierce! Paddle this way! We're over here!" He suddenly came to, and began dreamily paddling in our direction. "I told you kids not to smoke," my mother said.

"All my compositions!" Theodore said. "My best work. It can never be duplicated. It was the best I could do, and it probably wasn't even any good."

"You'll remember them," my mother said. "You'll write more. Where's Leopold? He's probably lost in the woods. Or kidnapped. Who knows."

"No, I'm not," Leopold said. "I'm right here. Look! It's going down for the last time." We turned away from him and watched the trailer on the water. The flames shot up in one last feeble attempt to draw attention to themselves; then the whole thing sank, claimed at last by the bottomless Gitchee Gumee. The water burbled. No one said a thing. Finally Leopold spoke. "Well," he said. "That's that."

There was a shriek at the top of the hill. Marietta came running, golden hair flying in the gloom like a shimmering kangaroo rat trying to escape a great horned owl.

"If you've come to visit, you're too late," I said.

Pierce got his raft to shore and joined us. "Oh, my darling big brother, you're soaked," Marietta said. "I guess you lost your clothes in the wreck of the *Hesperus*. Too bad you don't like wearing dresses. I'd let you borrow my things."

"Are you making that offer to everyone, or just Pierce?" said Simon.

"Where *are* your things, Marietta?" my mother said.

"They're in my car," she said. "I was about to move back home, only now I see I don't have a home. '*Lo! how all things fade and perish!*' "

"At least Maud and I can get something dry to wear," my mother said.

"You're going to take all my nice things!" Marietta said. "You're going to ruin them, no doubt. What the hell did I come for? And I suppose you all talked about me while I was gone?"

"Oh, we spoke of little else," I assured her bitterly.

"Who?" said my mother.

"I don't even know why I came back!" Marietta said.

"Why did you?" I said.

"We can get warmed up at my place, and change into Marietta's clothes," Simon said. "Although it's freezing cold. Maybe I can make a fire."

Marietta sidled over to him. "That would be divine," she said.

"Where's Steve Hartley?" I said. "Oh, Marietta, this time you'll surely go to jail. You were lucky the other times that the poor fellows partially recovered." I looked at Simon to see if he appreciated this, but he was busy returning Marietta's generic smile. Struggling to make her eyes appear heavy-lidded and sloe, she was too distracted to hear me.

"I don't want to talk about it," she said.

I couldn't believe the hideous way they were mooning and gibbering at each other. "I'm going to be sick!" I yelled. Petulantly I stamped my foot, which until then had been lying quietly, damp and unhappy, in its wet shoe.

That snapped him out of it. "Oh, beloved, how are the innards?" he said.

I felt soothed immediately. He had such a way with words. Each sentence came out perfectly roasted in English accent, topped with a bit of imperialism. "Thank you so for asking, my darling!" I said with a sigh.

Theodore lay on the ground, groaning weakly. "Get up!" my mother said. "Don't just lie there, you slut. You'll freeze to death." She grabbed him by the arm and hoisted him to his feet.

"Ow!" he said. "My arm!"

"The one I'm grabbing?" she said.

"No, the other one."

We trudged up the road in the dark. I carried the bag of puppies. Trayf ran ahead. Lulu followed behind grumpily. She didn't like going for walks, particularly in the dark. This expedition was proof positive at last that we were all crazy. But at least her puppies weren't harassing her. "We should have just driven," Marietta said, walking beside me. "Did you see my little Mustang?"

"How did you get a Mustang?" I said.

"I leased it," she said.

"They'd never let you lease a car!" I said. "You don't even have an income."

"The car dealer, Tiny Sunday, felt I was responsible," she said.

"I don't believe you," I said. "What did you do to show him you were responsible?"

"One brief moofty-poofty," she said. "It hardly took a second."

"Ah," I said. "So what are you doing back here, anyway, with your suitcase? Had a fight with Steve?"

"He's immature," she said. "A grown man, living with his mother. Besides, he was boring. And he wasn't very good in bed."

"Girls, if I've told you once, I've told you a thousand times," said my mother, catching up with us, "all good men are bad in bed and boring. What are the ancillary correlations?"

"All interesting men get boring soon; all bad men are not much good in bed, either," we chanted.

"Exactly," said my mother. "You mustn't judge men by the same standards as women. They don't have any standards. Men—let me be fair, *most* men—are immature because most men are optimists."

"And being an optimist is a sign of immaturity?"

"Of course. Think about it."

"Ma, not to change the subject," I said. "But it's a shame all the stolen goods sank in the trailer."

"I know," she said. "Maybe the *Encyclopedia of Satanic Rituals* brought us bad cess? Normally I wouldn't approve of our accepting stolen merchandise."

"Why?" I said.

"Because we'd be caught."

19

At Simon's, Leopold made hot chocolate. "You should keep cocoa in the freezer, not the cupboard," he said. "There are a lot of dead bugs in the box."

"The people who lived here before left it," Simon said, sneezing and coughing at the same time. "Oh, dear. I do hope my catarrh isn't returning. Tell me, is the cocoa safe? What sort of bugs are in it?"

"Let us pray they weren't larvae," I said. "Larvae can hatch in humans. Did you know that the blood fluke *Bilharzia* lives in pairs, inside your intestines and bladder? The male is shaped like a sausage-casing, and the female lives inside him."

"I was thinking of joining that," my mother said.

"What?"

"The Daughters of Bilharzia."

"Is that like the D.A.R.?"

"Similar."

"Ma!" said Theo furiously. "*Bilharzia* is a disease, like schistoso-miasis. You're thinking of the Daughters of Bilitis. That's an orientation. Like Friends of Sappho."

"Disease, orientation, what's the difference? Who cares, as long as you're having fun."

Theodore clucked and leapt up in disgust. I was still chilled to the bone. Trayf, shivering, came over and jumped on my lap, trying to get warm. He had quite a few pimples on his back, something the breed was known for. "Are the puppies dead in the duffel bag?" I said. "Someone should check."

"I'll make us a fire," Simon said, jumping up.

"I was counting on getting our security deposit back," my mother said. "I hope the landlord doesn't expect us to pay for the damages."

"Damages!" I said. "Damages! The trailer's not damaged. All he has to do is dry it out."

"I think it's time for us to move on," my mother said. "I could have stayed here quite happily for some time longer. I always thought there was a reason for us to be here. Something we were supposed to learn, perhaps. But now I think, the hell with it."

"I've learned a lesson," I said. "After that near-death experience, plus losing everything I own, I see how precious life is, and how little material possessions mean." I smiled sweetly at Simon.

"Oh, Maud, I can't tell you how happy it makes me to hear that!" my mother said. "Life is so precious, it's true. If I've said it once, I've said it a million times."

" *'From the sky the sun benignant / Looked upon them through the branches, / Saying to them, . . ."Rule by love, O Hiawatha!"* ' " said Marietta.

"Also true, Marietta," my mother said. "Oh, children! You don't know, when you have a baby, that twenty years later you're still going to be dealing on a daily basis with a whining, screaming, spoiled brat. When I hear you say that life is precious, or quote such poetry, after all these years in which you girls have done nothing but express rage, bitterness, ingratitude and a seeming dislike for the whole experience, I must say I'm shocked." She came over and hugged me. My mother had rarely been physically affectionate before. She was freezing cold. "Would you make me a cocktail, my darling," she said.

"A cocktail for a corpse," I said. "Leopold, the gin is in the kitchen."

"I'm not the slave!" he said.

"Oh, Leopold, of course you're not the slave," I said. "You're the sweet, good and kindly one." He looked gratified. Handing me a mug of chocolate, he went back into the kitchen.

"This is all a bit much for me," Simon said, wheezing and muttering to himself as he bent over the fireplace and lit a bit of newspaper stuck under a log. "Oh, blimey, there's something alive in here. I hope it's not a mouse."

"We have to make some plans at once," my mother said.

"Leopold, this hot chocolate is delicious!" I called.

Simon began to pull the flaming papers out from under the wood. "Thanks," Leopold said, coming out from the kitchen with the bottle of gin. "I added a square of real Mexican chocolate to each mug. I used the cocoa, and made it with sugar and milk. There's no sense in even bothering with that prepackaged hot chocolate stuff."

Wisps of smoke floated into the room. Simon stood up, rubbing his hands together. "Whatever was in the fireplace, it scuttled away," he said. "I'll just put everything back in and relight it, I guess. I don't really know how to make a fire. I can't even move my fingers."

"Didn't you have fireplaces in your castle where you grew up?" I said.

"I'm afraid my chilblains are troubling me, after that dip. I've never been much use with this sort of thing, anyway. You know, I was at boarding school a good deal of the time."

"He means that they had servants who made the fires," my mother said. "I've read about it, in literature."

"Something's on fire!" Theodore said vaguely. "Help!"

"No, no, not really," Simon said. He sat down on the couch.

"He must be the same size as you, Marietta," I said. "Your skirt and cardigan fit him perfectly." I moved over and snuggled up beside him. Marietta came and sat down on the other side.

" '*Still he did not leave his laughing, / Only turned the log a little, / Only made the fire burn brighter, / Made the sparks fly up the smoke-flue,*' " Marietta said, glancing darkly up at Simon from beneath her unnaturally dark lashes.

"Oh, what are you banging on about?" I said. "You're getting worse than ever. Ma, did you know she got Tiny Sunday to lease her a car by giving him a moofty-poofty?"

"Whatever," my mother said.

Simon looked at Marietta thoughtfully. "I was just going to put on some trousers," Simon said. "I do have my own clothes, upstairs. This wool skirt is a little itchy."

"I'd love to come up and see your wardrobe," said Marietta.

"Isn't anyone going to take me to the hospital?" Theodore suddenly blurted. "You live in a dream world, Ma! Our home is destroyed, we have no money, no insurance; one daughter can't even make up her own poetry, but recites 'Hiawatha' while giving blow-jobs; your other daughter has no morality, no compassion and terrible fashion-sense; you have a twenty-two-year-old unemployed son completely lacking fortitude; another who, at the age of six, is put to work like a scullery maid without a scullery; my arm is broken and I probably have a concussion!"

"I must say, I'd be quite interested in hearing a bit of 'Hiawatha,' " said Simon.

"I think that's unfair, about the fashion-sense," I said.

"Don't blame me," my mother said. "If a tree falls in the forest and hits you over the head, you don't hate the tree!"

"You don't hate the tree?" Pierce said.

"Aw, this is pathetic!" Theodore said. "*You're* pathetic."

"Please do not speak to me in that tone of voice," my mother said. "I'm sure you're right. But you'll find you get more accomplished if you read the Dale Carnegie book—*How To Win Friends and Influence People*—that I gave you years ago."

"That book must be fifty years old!" Theodore said. "Half the pages were missing! It was completely out of date! It has nothing to do with anything!"

"You'll find certain things don't change," my mother said. "All right, if we all put our minds together, we might be able to think."

"Doubtful," said Theodore.

"What are we supposed to think about?" I said.

"What we should do!" my mother said.

"We should get in the car and head for California!" Leopold said. "Doesn't Pierce have to get there to be a movie star?"

My mother smiled at Leopold, impressed. "Good idea," she said. "We'll stop on the way and have Theodore's arm reattached. Now, who's coming?"

"I don't know if I can go to California," said Theodore. "In all honesty, I'm kind of scared."

"Ah," said my mother. "I see. So you lash out at me out of your own fear. Would you rather stay here?"

"On my own? Without any place to live? What would I do? How would I survive? No, I'll come along—reluctantly."

"I don't know," Pierce said. "It's a long trip, huh? And you'd want me to do a lot of driving, huh? I'm kind of used to it here." We ignored him.

"Let's see," my mother said. "If you're coming, Simon, that makes three cars."

"My car is a rental car," Simon said. "If you don't mind, it might be better for me to return it. That way I can drive out with you and fly back."

Suddenly Marietta took charge. "Some of us will go in my car, and you can return your car, Simon, and we'll pick you up there. Then we can take Theodore to the hospital. We'll drive like blazes from pillar to post, and be in California in no time flat."

"*I* can pick Simon up at the car rental agency," I said.

"Just meet us at the hospital," Marietta snarled. "Mother, Theodore and I will go in my cute, new car, stopping en route to collect Simon. You, Pierce and Leopold will go in the old Hupmobile."

"Why do I have to go in the old Hupmobile?" said Leopold. "What's a Hupmobile, anyway?"

"It's a picaresque name for our old wreck. You throw up in cars," Marietta said. "If you're going to do it again, it might as well be in a place that already stinks. Now, you guys go straight to the hospital. That way Pierce can use the extra few minutes for any necessary tune-ups. Then you can take Simon—if he still wants to travel with you."

Leopold, Pierce and I walked down the road to where our trailer used to be. Trayf came with us. As we got into our car, Simon drove by. "I'll see you at the hospital, beloved!" he called from the window.

Thirty seconds later my mother leaned out the passenger window of Marietta's Mustang. "Meet you at the hospital, kids!" she said. "Let's rendezvous in the emergency ward! Pierce—"

"Yeah?" Pierce said.

"Tell me, where are you going to meet us?"

"At the hospital?" he said.

"Which hospital, Pierce?" she said.

"I don't know," he said. "I don't remember the name of it. The sicko-hospital."

"The Harry and Naomi Rosenthal Memorial Hospital, Pierce!" my mother said.

"Yeah, yeah, yeah," Pierce said. "I know. I'm going to have to do some things to the car, before we get going. Most of my equipment went down with the trailer. I don't even know if I can fix it with the tools I've got in the trunk."

"We'll worry about that when we get there," my mother said. "The main thing is, not to worry, but to try and enjoy life."

"Huh?" Pierce said, as Marietta revved the engine and sped off.

"I'm freezing," I said.

Pierce turned on the radio. "I kept meaning to put a better radio in the car. I knew there was something I forgot, on my mind." We drove for a while in silence.

"Are you okay back there, Leopold?" I said. "You're awfully quiet."

"I don't feel good," he said. "I'm carsick. I'm scared."

"You're not scared," I told him. "You're excited. You're too young to tell the difference between fear and fun. They're practically the same thing. That's why you're having trouble."

"Turn here, Pierce," Leopold said. "Make a right, to get to the hospital."

"I should never have agreed to let Marietta collect the lord from the rental agency," I said. "If she says something bad to Simon about me, or tries to take him away from me, I'm going to kill her."

"You don't even like that lord," Leopold said.

"Oh, Leopold," I said. "In the old days, marriages were arranged. Since there doesn't seem to be anybody doing the arranging for me, I have to arrange it myself. The lord is handsome, with huge, lustrous eyes, shiny hair, a beautiful complexion and strong hindquarters. Though he probably has a fair amount of insanity on both sides of his family, a girl of my background can't afford to be all that choosy. By the way, just what is my background? Did Mother ever mention to either of you just who she thought my father was?"

"I think he was some kind of gypsy," Pierce said.

"Oh, no," I said. "Not a gypsy. Maybe your father was a gypsy."

"No," said Pierce. "I think she said you had the gypsy blood."

"I'm not going to argue with you," I said. "But you're wrong."

"Anything would be better than the father I got," said Leopold. "I suppose we should say good-bye to him, at the hospital."

"That's right!" I said. "I forgot, your poor dad is in the hospital, malingering. You and I can dash in while Pierce is fixing the car."

"I'm hungry," Pierce said.

"My *boeuf bourguignon* didn't fill you up?" Leopold said.

"He's probably smoked a joint since then, Leopold, and has the munchies!" I said. "A gypsy. Where would she find a gypsy? I don't see any gypsies around."

"I think it was a Rumanian gypsy," Pierce said.

"Oh, God," I said. "What that means is, in reality he was probably a violinist in a restaurant, claiming to be a Rumanian gypsy. You guys were never in Rumania, were you?"

"I heard she took everybody to a Rumanian restaurant, once!" said Leopold.

"We went to Poughkeepsie when I was three or four," Pierce said. "That would have been around the right time. It was just after Phuket. We must have eaten in a Rumanian restaurant, in Poughkeepsie. Was there belly dancing? That's probably where it happened."

"Oh, lord," I said. "What were you doing in Poughkeepsie?"

"I don't remember," said Pierce. "I think we were lost."

"What an extremely glamorous and romantic occurrence," I mumbled as we pulled into the Harry and Naomi Rosenthal Memorial Hospital Parking Lot. "Just like a fairy tale. Of course, it's hard for me to believe you had any existence at all, before I was born."

"I don't feel so good," Leopold said.

"What's wrong?" I said. "Are you going to throw up?"

"I'm worried about Theodore," Leopold said. "His arm hurts. And his head is broken."

"I hope they don't have to amputate it," I said.

"What does that mean?"

"Remove it," I said. Leopold started to cry. "Just kidding," I said. "Come on, we'll go find him."

The others hadn't yet arrived at the emergency ward, which didn't really surprise me since they had to meet Simon first at the car rental. Knowing Marietta, she would do anything to prolong her time with Simon and prevent him, agonizingly, from rejoining me. "We'll visit your daddy," I said.

"Children under fourteen aren't allowed," Leopold reminded me.

"That doesn't matter," I said. "Visiting hours are over."

We had to go back out and around the corner to get to the main entrance. There was a security guard seated behind a desk. "Visiting hours are over," he said.

Abruptly I let out a hideous groan and fell to the floor, flailing. The guard ran out from behind the desk. He knelt down next to me. "Are you all right?" he said. "What's wrong? Did you fall?"

"Please," I moaned. "Get help. Find a doctor." I waited until he had run through the lobby before I got up and dusted myself off. "Hurry up," I told Leopold. "We don't have all day, you know."

"But Maud," he said, looking pinched. "What happened? Are you all right?"

"It's okay, sweetie," I said. "I was just testing that man for preparedness."

Fred de Gaillefontaine was sitting on a chair outside Edward's room. He stood when he saw us. "Oh, no," he said. "It's you."

Before I had any idea of what was going on, my body had flung itself into his arms, and our coral seas were kissing passionately. "Ugh," said Leopold.

"Go in and visit your father," I said, disentangling myself. "You have lipstick all over your face, Fred. It doesn't go with the uniform. At least not that shade. Maybe more of a pink?"

"Whatever," he said, and began kissing me again.

"This is awful," I said, simultaneously attempting to push him away while taking a step closer. "What if my fiancé sees us?"

"Oh," said Fred. "Are you engaged?"

"No, but I plan to be," I said.

"Who's the lucky fellow?" said Fred.

"A hypochondriac English lord, with homosexual proclivities and a background of drug addiction," I said. "I love him dearly; he's extremely refined, with an acutely effete sensibility, not like you in the slightest."

"I hope you'll be very happy," Fred said, nuzzling. "I heard the other day he had leprosy."

"Interesting," I said. "How did you come by that?"

"He was here earlier, and I heard two of the doctors discussing it.

They don't know what's wrong with him. If it's what they think it is, at any moment rotting appendages and flesh will start to drop."

"Aw, I don't want to hear," I said. "He's got a suppurating, oozing sore on his buttock, and that's enough for me." Fred backed off. "I didn't sleep with him or anything," I said. "Not that it makes any difference—he just showed me his spider bite."

"That's not what the doctors say," Fred said. "*They* think it might be leprosy. He worked with the poor in India."

"I don't believe it!" I said. "My fiancé would never work with the poor. But if the urge ever strikes him now, he's got me."

"Mmm," said Fred, leaning forward to graze along the northwest territories of my ear.

"I must be going," I said. "I've got to grab my little brother before his father gives him more recipes."

I left Fred in the hall and went into the room. Leopold was in bed with Edward. Edward's arm was around Leopold's neck. "Sweet," I said. "I'm glad you two are getting along so well."

"Don't move, or I'll choke him," Edward said.

"What a mean daddy," I said.

"I'm serious," Edward said. "Tell the cop to come into the room." Leopold gagged, I suppose to show his father's sincerity.

"Oh, very well," I said. "Fred!" I called. "You'd better come in here." Fred popped brightly into the room.

"I've got the kid," Edward said. "I'm going to strangle him until he's practically unconscious. Take your gun out slowly and put it on the floor. Now give me the key to the handcuffs."

"What the hell's all this stuff on the dashboard?"

"That's our spider and his splendid web, Edward," I said. "Please don't choke Leopold so tightly around the neck. Do you have any other children?"

"Get rid of the spider. I hate lousy spiders."

"Not our beloved spider!"

Leopold gagged. "Hey, man," said Pierce. "That spider isn't hurting anybody. It's part of the family. Anyway, what if there's roadblocks and things? You should get in the trunk, Ed."

"Oh, what good thinking," I said.

"Yeah?" Pierce said, pleased. "You think? And, uh, you should take Leopold with you in the trunk. That way if the police stop us, you can use him as a hostage."

"That part was kind of stupid, Pierce," I said.

"I'm going to get in the trunk," said Edward. "And I'm going to take Leopold with me. If there is a roadblock, and the police stop us, and you say anything, the kid dies. Or, if you decide to drive straight to a police station, or any other smart ideas."

Edward and Leopold got into the trunk. "Please don't shut me in here! I'm scared," bleated Leopold before Edward put his hand over his coral seas.

"No, no, Leopold," I said, trying to comfort him. "Remember what I was telling you before, about fear and fun being the same thing? You're still having fun, sweetie." Pierce, looking bleak, closed the lid.

"You didn't have to suggest he take Leopold hostage," I told Pierce.

"You probably have a point," said Pierce. "But at least give me some credit for saving the spider."

"I didn't even think you liked that spider."

"Oh," said Pierce. "Oh, yeah. What are we going to do?"

"Just drive!" Edward's tinny voice came through the back seat. I could hear what sounded like Leopold, sobbing.

"So, like, where are we going?"

"To Los Angeles, Pierce," I said. "Remember? The others will know to meet up with us there." We drove for a while in silence, except for Leopold's muffled weeping.

"You really think I have a chance of being a movie star when we get to L.A.?" said Pierce. "It seems like kind of a far way to go."

"I've told you before, I do," I said. "I just have a good feeling about it. Oh, dear, that poor Officer Freddy de Gaillefontaine. How embarrassing for him when a nurse finds him like that, handcuffed to the bed. What if she takes advantage of him? He hates that. What did you make him take off his clothes for, Edward?" There was no response.

"What's your good feeling about me based on?" said Pierce.

"Just that I don't think they'll have seen anything like you in L.A. *I've* never seen anything like you. See, it's more than your looks or personality. You have an aura."

"An aura, huh?" he said. "But that's not a problem, is it."

"Do you mind if I get in the back and sleep?" I said.

"That's cool," he said.

I climbed over the seat and lay down with Trayf in my arms. Leopold had stopped crying. I could hear his and Edward's voices, a low murmur oozing from the vinyl. "Boy, I didn't think Mother's boyfriend would turn out to be so evil," I said. "This one really takes the cake."

"Hey!" said Edward, a bit more loudly, from the trunk. "I can hear you up there! What did you just say?"

"I said you make really good cake! Didn't you once do a lemon-poppyseed thing?"

"Yeah? Well, don't try anything funny."

"But Edward, he's your own son!"

"You know how much semen I produce on an average day? Enough sperm to populate the entire planet. You don't really expect me to care about each one of them on an individual basis, do you?"

"Watch your language," I said.

I must have dozed off. A few hours passed; when I woke I was nauseous and hungry. For a moment I forgot where we were or what we were doing. Outside the window it was dark. "What time is it?"

"I don't know," Pierce said. "I don't wear a watch."

"Do we need gas?"

"Oh, no!" said Pierce.

"What?"

"We need gas! The tank says empty. Damn. What are we going to do?"

"Um," I said. "Do you see a gas station?"

"Yeah," said Pierce. "There's a gas station, up ahead."

"Is it open?"

"It says open twenty-four hours."

"That doesn't mean anything. Does it look open?"

"Yeah. But I don't want Edward to get weirded-out or something."

"Edward?" I called. "Are you two—and enough sperm to populate the entire planet—okay back there? We want to stop for gas, so don't get nervous."

"What time is it?" said Edward.

"We're not certain. But it's still dark out, so that usually means it's nighttime."

"Okay," said Edward. "You can stop. But only as long as it takes to get gas. Keep driving. When it gets light, I want you to pull over and open the trunk."

While Pierce filled the tank, I took the dog and wandered to the toilets. "You know, I don't feel so good," I told Trayf, who wagged his tail sleepily and lifted his leg on a dumpster as if it were all a dream. "I must have gotten sick from swallowing the waters of Gitchee Gumee by accident."

The women's toilet was locked. I went into the other one. It was loathsome beyond belief. Even Trayf looked offended. "Tell me, Trayf—what sort of people be these, to befoul a room so clearly marked with their own name?" Trayf didn't respond, just wrinkled his brow and looked worried. I turned on the water in the sink and hoisted him up so he could drink straight from the tap. This was a skill he had learned from Lulu.

Then I washed my face. How quickly I had aged. The first bloom of youth was gone, plucked, crushed and dried for potpourri. Suddenly, an idea struck me over the head. I gingerly removed the lid of the toilet tank. This was a spot where guns were often kept. If I could find one, I could open the trunk and shoot Edward in the genitals, rescuing my brother and preventing any more of Edward's sperm escaping to populate the planet. But there was nothing in there, neither a gun, nor a stack of bills, nor an Ever-Bleu Tidy-Boy Bowl Cleanser disk lasting up to three months. So I went back to the sink and scrubbed my hands and face again, trying to force the bloom of youth back into it. A bulb in winter could be tricked into flowering by storing it in the refrigerator. I kept the water turned to cold.

For a second I thought Pierce had driven off without me, but then I spotted the car over by the air pump. He winced when Trayf and I reached his side. "Heh-heh," he said. "For a minute I almost forgot you were here."

"I bet you would have just driven off without me!"

He grinned nervously. "Naw," he said. "Heh-heh."

"Yeah," I said. "Hey, are you sure we're headed the right way? Don't you want to ask directions?"

"I did! When I paid for the gas. I don't have much money left, by the way."

"What directions did you ask for?"

"I asked where Los Angeles was," Pierce said. "The guy didn't really know. I'm sure we're okay, though. There's only one way out of Nokomis."

We returned to the car. "Do you think Leopold's all right back there?"

Pierce rapped on the trunk. "You guys okay in there?" he shouted. The gas station attendant stared sharply through the bullet-proof glass of his protective booth.

From the trunk came Leopold's dampered voice. "I want to get out!"

"Soon it will be dawn, and you can emerge!" I said. We got into the car. "Poor little Leopold. What a brute of a father. He's forced us to set off for California prematurely. We're down to our last few dollars, no clean clothes, no credit cards, no decent music—this is crummy."

"We're in deep trouble, huh?" said Pierce as we got back onto the highway.

"I hate that expression," I said. "If you're going to be a movie star, you should do it with dignity. You should be larger than life, not less—a sleek panther, stalking through the jungle like a tiger. That's what being a movie star's all about, you know." Pierce looked baffled, which was as close to a thoughtful expression as he was capable of. "You have some hairs in your nose that you should do something about, too," I added.

"Oh yeah?" he said. "Like what?"

"I don't know! Tweeze them! Clip them! Train them into a to-piary poodle!"

"We'll have to buy a scissors," he said. "Huh? You think we'll see somewhere that sells scissors?"

"Pierce," I said. "I'm having a nervous breakdown. I'm unable to deal with this just now."

"You brought it up!" he said. After that we didn't speak.

Around dawn I thought we passed a sign. "What did that say?"

"B-Plus Truck Stop in a mile."

"Edward!" I shouted. "It's almost dawn! Can we stop in a mile?"

"Cool," said Pierce. "We can get breakfast."

"We're not stopping to get breakfast," I said. "We're stopping to let them out of the trunk. If we get something to eat, we really won't have any money left."

"You want me to drive with dignity?" he said. "I gotta eat!"

"All right, all right," I said. "I don't even know if they're alive back there. Pull over."

We pulled into the lot. "I sure hope I left my extra jacket in the trunk," he said.

"Why?" I said. "Are you chilled? You're not getting sick, are you?"

"No, but I've got to keep up my image. I usually keep my best black motorcycle jacket in Mom's trunk. You said I should look like a tiger. I need the right accessories for that. Man, I lost a lot of good stuff in the trailer when it went down. You think I'm ever going to get it back? Like, are there salvage operations for that kind of thing?"

"Oh, for heaven's sake," I said. "Your image. Give it a rest. What about Leopold? And his murderous, spermatozoid father? Let them out, for crying out loud."

Pierce took out a comb and flipped down the mirror on the wind-shield visor. "God damn it," he said. "I wish I had taken a shower. My hair's all slimy. It's that friggin' Gitchee Gumee water."

"No, it's not," I said. "It's that outdated grease you put on your hair. You should drain your head on paper towels. Quit being so self-absorbed."

"Yeah, like you're not." He went around to the back of the car. I followed. "Oh, no."

"What?" I said.

"I don't have the key to the trunk."

"What are you talking about? You have the car key."

"Yeah, but I don't have the key to the trunk!"

A faint voice wafted toward us eerily, like a talking sardine left on a shelf of emergency survival supplies. "Let me out!" The voice bore only a distant resemblance to a younger, once-confident Edward.

"How could you have lost the trunk key, you dumb idiot!"

Pierce's lip curled. "Apologize!" he said.

"I'm sorry," I said. "You're not an idiot."

"That's better."

"It's just that I'm worried about Leopold. Maybe Edward's done something. Maybe he's suffocated him. Or given him the wrong ideas about sex, so that later in life he'll frequent prostitutes and be unable to see women as real people and not objects."

"Leopold, are you still alive in there!" Pierce said. "Answer me!"

"I want to get out of here!" Leopold said.

"Can you remove the back seat?" I said.

"Oh, yeah," said Pierce. "That's an idea. I could see if I could re-move the back seat. Part of one is removable. I had to take the bolts out, a while back. I don't know about the rest. But at least they could get air."

We opened the doors and Pierce removed one of the seat cush-ions; then he unscrewed the metal plate on the lower left. Trayf tried to assist, barking and digging with glee and his front claws. Pierce peered down to look through the crack. "How you guys doing in there?"

I heard a squeal coming from Leopold. "Quit kicking me, Dad!" he said.

The bottoms of his little shoes came into view. "Look, Pierce!" I said. "Grab his feet! Pull him out! Breech delivery!"

Leopold just managed to squeeze through. "Oh, my darling petal!" I said, grabbing him and kissing him. "My tender pet! My parasite! Are you all right?"

"Quit it," Leopold said weakly, shrugging me off. "I'm hungry. I'm thirsty. He made me pee out a rusty hole."

"Come on," I said. "I'll take you in and get something to eat. Poor tadpole."

"Screw you."

"Hey!" Edward yelled. I looked through the narrow hole into the trunk. I could see an eye. "What about me? Let me out."

"Can't you get through?"

"No! Take out the other seats!"

"Someone might see you."

"I don't care! I'm claustrophobic!"

"You should have thought of that before! Now it's too late. The other seat-backs are bolted in. And we've lost the trunk key."

"What am I going to do?"

"I tell you what: we'll go in and have a nice leisurely breakfast, and try and figure something out. Maybe there's a guy in the restaurant with a crowbar."

"Please, will you bring me back a Coke? And a candy bar?"

"You want Coke? Or Diet Coke? Or, what about Nature's Majesty?"

"I don't know! I don't know!" Edward said. "Did you have to go through a lot of roadblocks? Have there been police looking for me? I'm in heavy difficulty, huh?"

"Nobody's looking for you. Don't worry. You can stay in there forever."

"I don't want to stay in here."

"I don't believe I've ever eaten at a genuine truck stop before," said Leopold, when we were seated at the counter. "I'm quite interested in seeing the menu."

"Get whatever you want, little buddy," said Pierce. "I've got fifteen bucks left."

"You two guys are so good-natured," I said. "You, Leopold, locked in a trunk all that time by a psychopathic father and not uttering one complaint, and you, Pierce, never thinking twice about it."

"I am kind of good-natured, huh?" said Pierce.

"You should both order whatever you want. Just make sure it's the cheapest thing on the menu."

"Why do I have to get whatever's cheapest?" said Pierce. "Why don't you get it? I did all the driving."

"I know," I said. "But Pierce, we don't have much money! The point is, to make it last."

Pierce and Leopold selected the Breakfast Special for $1.99: Two Farm-fresh Eggs, Country Ham Slice (though they could have elected Two Crispy Strips Bacon or One Sausage Patty or Two Links instead), coffee, orange juice, toast, grits and gravy. "Grits and gravy. Now that is something I've never tried before," said Leopold with satisfaction. "I thought it was more of a kind of Southern thing. Yet I've always wanted to try it. What is it, anyway?"

"It's, you know, something gritty," I said. "They usually give it to chickens. Italians eat it, and ostrich and emus *must* have their grits; you see, they none of them have teeth. So they need the grit in their stomach to do the work. Oh! I guess my dreams of getting a chicken or an ostrich or an emu or a rhea—which is the same thing in South America—won't be realized for a long time, now. My future has moved so far away. I don't even know now what it was about chickens I found so appealing. The small, alien eyes, and the beak. A certain coldness of character which is so refreshing, in a world of too much false emotion. You know, maybe I'll get the fried chicken basket for breakfast."

Pierce let out a snort of disbelief. "See?" he said. "I told you. The fried chicken basket is six-ninety-nine and you make us get the cheapest item."

"Maud," said Leopold in a worried tone. "Do you know how fattening fried chicken is?"

"You know what? You're right. You're right and I was wrong. I'll have the pancake breakfast."

Pierce took out his cigarettes. There was only one left in the pack. "Would you repeat that?" he said.

"I'll have the pancake breakfast, twenty-two-seventy-nine. Oh, I see what you're getting at. No, it's only two-seventy-nine. That's okay, isn't it?"

"Not that part—the first thing you said."

"I said, you were right and I was wrong."

"I can't believe it!" he said. "You're the first person who ever said that to me! You don't know what it's like, all the time from when they put me into the slow class in fifth grade and treated me like a criminal."

"That's lousy!" said Leopold, slurping his chocolate shake through a straw. "How come they put you in the slow class, Pierce? They shouldn't have put you in the slow class. That's lousy."

"It was lousy," Pierce said. "They make you memorize poems by Byron over and over and over. Because they think you'll feel better about yourself if you know something intellectual. *'Mouth which marks the envious scorner, / With a scorpion in each corner, / Turning its quick tail to sting you / In the place that most may wring you—'* "

"You're talking about the poetry of Lord Byron?" I said. "Handsome Lord Byron, author of darkly romantic poems, with his profuse black hair and handsomely sculpted head?"

"He was a comedy writer who had something wrong with his foot, and a gland problem that made him fat. That's what they taught us in Special Ed. The teacher said if there was one person who should make us feel better about ourselves, it was old George Byron."

"Are you positive about this? He wrote comedy?"

"Yeah, mostly. *'Eyes of leadlike hue, and gummy; / Carcass picked out from some mummy—'* " Pierce started to pick his nose. "They made me memorize the whole friggin' thing. That's how come I figure now I'm going to have trouble memorizing my lines in those acting jobs. My head's already filled up. Hey, my nose hairs—are they really visible?"

"Quit it!" I said. "Or I'll scream and scream and won't know why or when to stop."

"You think we should maybe get Trayf a Breakfast Special to go?" Leopold said.

"All right; but will he eat ham?" I said. "I know he hates bacon and sausage. He'll probably hate ham. He might not even eat the eggs, if they've been near it."

"We could tell them to leave out the pork," Leopold said. "He won't know that it's still not kosher."

"Okay," I said. "Good thinking."

Pierce yawned. "I'm about to crash out," he said.

"Have a cup of coffee," I suggested. "So, Leopold, what did you and your father talk about? What's he really like?"

"He told me that homosexuals should have died out by now, because they can't multiply."

I thought for a moment. "Maybe they can't multiply," I said. "But they can be fruitful."

21

"You don't think *I* have homosexual tendencies, do you?" said Pierce at the cash register, while he paid our bill and bought cigarettes.

"A dog doesn't care if he's screwing a *leg*," I said. I slipped a Kit Kat bar, a packet of Milk Duds and a box of Jujubes into my pocket for Edward.

"Oh yeah," said Pierce after a pause, sounding puzzled yet pleased. "That's right." He picked up an item from a display on the counter while we were waiting for change and Trayf's meal. "Hey, look at this! *Our Own Version of Crystal Methamphetamine.* Cool! Over-the-counter speed. It's really expensive, though."

"Pierce!" I said warningly. "Remember our limited cash flow. I tell you what: I'll say mean things to you every couple of minutes. That should make you irritated, which will keep you awake."

In the car I put the Styrofoam tray on the back seat and watched Trayf delicately wolf the eggs on buttered toast. Leopold and Pierce stood behind the car, arguing about how they were going to get the trunk open. An awful eye abruptly appeared in the hole. "Hey!" Edward said. "What smells so good? Did you bring me breakfast?"

"Oh," I said. "I nearly forgot. Hang on." I took the candy out of my pocket and showed it to the eye. The eye vanished and a hand appeared. "Save some chocolate for the rest of us!" I said, sitting on the seat. "So tell me, Edward, what did you really do?"

"I didn't do anything," Edward said. "It was somebody else. They're just trying to frame me."

"Let's speak about you in the third person," I said. "Maybe that will help. I know a lot of serial killers prefer to speak of themselves in the third person. What did he do?"

"He twiddled the librarian," Edward muttered. "While she was unconscious."

"But Edward, why did he do that?"

"He hates people!" Edward said. "He hates people and wants to have power over them!"

"That makes sense," I said. "I know what *I* would do, if those were my feelings. But why do you think he does it?"

"Because people think they're better than he is. The only person he never hated his whole life was your mother, and even she started to get on his nerves."

"My mother was much older than he."

"I told my little mommikins, 'You may be old, but rest assured as long as I'm on this planet you'll never go in a nursing home. You'll live with me.' My only stipulation was, she would have to stay in her room, until I tell her she can come out."

"Maybe everybody acted like they thought they were better than him because they *were* better?"

"No! Even the lowliest welfare recipient takes one look at him and two minutes later she's giving him one of those patronizing, condescending, superior smiles. But it was her children, really, who wrecked everything. If he could have been with your mother without those rotten, unpleasant, sulky, spoiled, worthless children around, things might have gone a lot better in his life. But probably it wouldn't have worked out, anyway. Nothing ever has."

I let him rattle on while I went around to the back. Pierce was screwing the trunk lock with a Bic pen stripped to its shaft. "Damn," he said. "This isn't doing a damn thing." He tried to pull out the pen, but it was jammed tight.

A man wearing a baseball cap came toward us across the lot. "That guy is fat," said Pierce, kicking the car.

"Sssshh," I said. "It could happen to anyone. You never know if you might wake up one morning and find yourself in that condition."

"No sugar!" said Pierce.

"Oy," said Leopold. Trayf began barking furiously, lunging at the rear window. The man came closer.

"He shouldn't wear blue horizontal stripes, nor a too-tight T-shirt, if he wants a slimming effect," I said as he got nearly on top of us. "Oh! Yes, I see your point. It's not his shirt; he really is fat!"

"Hi there!" the man said.

"It's terrible," I said, by way of explanation. "I'm not able to see without glasses, which I don't have. On the other hand, it makes the world a nicer place, to a certain extent."

"Are you kids having trouble?" the man said. "I was watching you, from inside the diner. What happened, lock your keys in the trunk?"

"No," I said.

"I've got a crowbar in my car," he said. "You want to borrow it? You can break the lock."

"We're fine," I said.

"Help! Let me out!" said a stifled voice. "I'm trapped in here!"

"What's that?" the man said.

"Nothing."

"What are you doing?" the man said. "Who's in there?"

"The father of my little Brer Rabbit here," I said, pointing at Leopold. "His father *asked* to ride in there. He told us, 'Whatever I say or do, no matter how I plead or beg, please, Brer Rabbit, don't let me out of the trunk.' "

"At this point I'm not even certain he's my father," Leopold said. "Honestly, I don't feel any connection. Wouldn't you think I would feel something, if I was originally one of his sperms?"

"I don't believe you," the man said sternly. "I'm going to go get the crowbar." He set off at a slow, gelatinous jog across the lot. The air was fresh, so early in the morning, as if it couldn't remember what a disaster the globe had become. In the scruffy fringe of trees surrounding the bald asphalt, larks and nightingales happily chirped, gearing up for the day's heaping teaspoon of stale crumbs.

"Quick!" I said. "Let's get out of here!"

"Huh?" said Pierce. "What's the matter with you? That guy only said he wanted to help."

"We don't want any help. If he lets Edward out of the trunk, what are we going to do? Fred was right. Edward's dangerous: he has an inferiority complex. Only in his case, it's no complex. It's simple. And people who are inferior enjoy smashing up the lives of their betters, in the hope of bringing them down to their level. He has no qualms. He's qualmless! He'll probably accuse us of kidnapping him. Then we'll have to accuse him of certain things. The police will want to get involved. It might lead to incarceration for some of us, and a foster home for the remainder. This could cause a delay."

"So what do you want to do?"

"I know," said Leopold. "Tell the man to open the trunk, and when Edward gets out, we drive off."

"Good idea. What about though, if he shows up in around ten or twenty years, a broken wreck of a man, and accuses you of abandoning him?"

Leopold thought for a moment. "I'm not sure."

"In that case, we have no choice. We'll go through with your plan. Pierce, you get in the back and go to sleep. Leopold, do you know the story by Hands Christian Andersen, where the statue in the town square had its eyes—originally made of jewels—plucked out, and could no longer see?"

" ' "O, I shall be your eyes for you!" cried the little sparrow,' " said Leopold.

"That's right, Leopold: the little sparrow helped the poor, blind statue when he could no longer see. Then winter came and the bird froze to death."

"Why?"

"Because the bird was so loyal he wouldn't fly south for the winter, remember? Well, you must be my loyal sparrow. Get in the passenger seat and direct me. We'll need help in being prevented from being hit by other objects along the highway."

"What about you? What will you be doing?"

"I'll be driving! But first, I'm going to take care of the situation." Grabbing the keys from Pierce, I started the car, trying to cause it as little pain as I could. Somewhat daringly, I left it in neutral and dashed across the lot to the fat guy. He was trudging along with his proud red-tipped crowbar—at least, I hoped that was what it was. "Kind sir, this is so kind of you," I purred. "I think if you just gave the lock a good prod with your instrument, it would fly open."

As he followed me, he smiled affectionately, probably pleased at being able to help out, and that I had succumbed to his wishes and was no longer fighting him off as I had done at first. Then he raised his crowbar above the helpless trunk, as man had done since time immemorial. "Oh, gosh!" I said. "I forgot something in the car. I'll just run and grab it—don't wait for me to begin your wanton act of destruction."

I got in the car. Pierce was already snoring in back. "Okay, Leopold," I said. The car rocked as the man hit the trunk with the crowbar. "You look out the side window and tell me the moment Edward gets out." There was another wallop to the back.

At that moment the trunk flew open, obscuring my view in the rearview mirror. "Hatch open," Leopold reported. "Father stepping out."

"Is he fully out? He didn't leave a leg behind?"

"Fully emerged," said Leopold. "He's talking to the fat man, now. You'd better step on it, Maud!"

I put my foot to the gas and we whizzed out of the parking lot with the trunk still open. "I can't see, Leopold!" I screamed. "You'd better help me get onto the highway!"

Pierce sat up in back. "What the hell's going on?" he shouted.

Leopold was leaning out the side, looking back at them. "They're trying to run after us!" he said.

"I doubt they'll catch us on foot," I said as we pulled onto the interstate highway. "But, just to be sure, I'm going to go faster than the speed limit by two miles, as we merge into the left lane. Might I be hitting anyone?"

"Maud, speed up when you merge!" Pierce shrieked. "You're cutting someone off!"

"I don't like going fast," I said. "It seems unnatural, and hard on the automobile." Horns began to honk on both sides; either they were trying to tell us our trunk was open, or they didn't like my driving.

"All right, listen to me: as soon as you see a sign for a rest stop or a gas station, you're going to pull over so we can close the trunk," Pierce snarled. "Then I'll drive."

We drove in silence for a few miles, the air punctured by nothing except Leopold and Pierce's agonized groans and yelps. "What the hell's wrong with you guys?" I said. "Was it the breakfast specials you ate?"

"Are you blind?" Pierce said. "I told you to pull over when we passed a gas station. Didn't you see the sign?"

"I saw a sign, all right," I said. "But it didn't mean a thing. The letters were all blurry. How can they do that to people and expect it to be helpful?"

They insisted there was a rest area coming up ahead. "Was that really so terrible?" I said, when they had guided me into an empty parking space.

"You scraped off a lot of paint on the car to your right," said Leopold.

"The driver had no business parking his car so close to mine," I said.

"I'm pissing my pants," said Pierce. "I don't even see a toilet. Some lousy rest area. I'm going in the bushes. Come on, Trayf." He dashed off, followed by the dog.

"I guess I better go too, while I have the chance. I'm surprised Pierce had to go so badly. You don't have to go, do you, Leopold?"

"I'm staying here," Leopold said.

"Okay, I'll leave the keys. Men and boys usually never have to make *le pee-pee*. I've often wondered, what kind of a G. Dash D. would make it so much easier for men to urinate than women and then also deem it almost unnecessary for them to ever have to go?"

"God never gives us men more than we can handle," Leopold pointed out.

When I came out of the bushes the fat man had parked his red Bronco alongside our car, and was standing on the dead grass talking to Leopold. "Why did you lock your father in the trunk?" he was saying to Leopold in an angry voice.

I ran across the dead grass. I grabbed Leopold and pulled him protectively away from the man. "We're not even sure that man is his father!" I said. "It could have been any one of a half dozen people. We don't know. And it wasn't Leopold's idea to lock his acquaintance in the trunk!" Then I saw that Edward was in the man's Bronco, slumped over in the front seat. "What's happening?" I said. "Is he having a fit? Or did you shoot a round hole neatly in his head, in a place we can't see?"

"What?" the man said. "What are you talking about? He's just upset. You kids were merciless with him. He was crying."

Suddenly Edward sat upright. He opened the door of the Bronco and, leaping out, looked blindly around, uncertain as to where he was. Then he ran to our car, jumped in, started the engine and backed out of the parking space. He spun the car around, burning rubber, and took off out of the rest area and sped down the highway.

Leopold and I looked at each other. Leopold shrugged. The man seemed to be waiting for us to say something. We stood in silence. Pierce came out of the bushes. "I took Trayf for a little walk," he said. "I think he's thirsty." He walked over to what had been our parking space. Then he squinted. "Where's the car?" he said.

"Um," I said. "Edward took it."

"Who?"

"Edward?" I said.

"Oh," said Pierce. "Where did he go?"

"Search me."

"You can hardly blame him," the man said. "After what you kids did to him? And it *was* his car."

"It wasn't his car!" I said. "It was my mother's car. My mother claimed to be his fiancée. He was a criminal, and not even a very good one. That explained why, whenever he showed up, he always had nice cowboy boots, a new motorcycle, an eelskin wallet, Louis Vuitton luggage, you name it. Eelskin! Even kangaroo, in my estimation, would have been preferable, though still a little flashy. He kidnapped what might have been his own son, in order to escape from the hospital."

"What hospital?" the man said suspiciously. "He said you kids would make up stories."

I started to sob. "My life is just a hellish misery!" I said. "I didn't think things could get any worse than living in a filthy, dirty trailer, with a bunch of misfits that I was actually supposed to be related to. But now I see I had no idea of the depths in store. I want my mother."

"I had no idea of the depths in store, either," Leopold said. "And for me this is just the beginning. You're old, already. You don't have that much left to go through." He started to cry. "I want my mother."

"Copycat!" I said, bawling.

"Hey, hey!" the man said. I could see that tears had come into his eyes as well. "Don't cry. Maybe there's something I could do to help."

"Oh, shut up!" I said. I turned to Pierce. "What are we going to do now?"

"About what?"

"Pierce," I said. "Think: we have no money. Our car has just been stolen. We're stranded in a rest area on our way to California."

"This isn't on the way to California," the man said. "Where were you coming from?"

"Upstate New York," I said.

"This has nothing to do with any route to California."

"So where is it a route to?"

"Key West," said the man. "Miami. Orlando. Florida."

"Liar! Liar! Pants on fire! Nobody even asked you."

The man leaned back against his Bronco and looked at me professorially. "I welcomed Christ into my life a long time ago," he said, in a confidential tone.

"Who needs to hear from you?" I said. *"Gonza k'nocker."*

"Hey, hey!" the man said. "I don't need to hear that."

I ignored him and addressed Pierce and Leopold. "Let's get to the point. What do we have to sell to get some cash?"

"Trayf?" Pierce said. "I don't want to sell the dog." Leopold began to cry more loudly, wiping his nose on his sleeve.

"No, not the dog!" I said. "I don't even think anybody would want him. What else?"

"The car?"

"Edward stole the car, Pierce! Remember?"

"I don't know then," Pierce said.

"Our bodies!" I said.

"Oh, yeah?" Pierce said. "We're going to be hustlers?"

"I don't want to be a hustler!" Leopold said.

"No, you're not going to be a hustler," I said. "You're too innocent and virginal."

"I'm not virginal," Leopold said. "It's too late. I've heard it all. My dysfunctional family sold me down the river long ago, by not acting normal."

"You'll tell me about it later. We're not selling your body, anyway. That's where I draw the line. We'll sell my body, we'll sell Pierce's body, but not children or dogs."

"Because nobody would want my body?" Leopold said, starting to sob again. "Nobody would want it, because I'm too fat!"

"Maybe I could help," the man said. "Are you kids Christian?"

"Filthy pig," I said. "Leave my little brother alone."

"That's not what I meant," the man said, cringing.

"You might find some guys that want to have sex with you for money," Pierce said, looking around. "But I don't see any girls here that want to."

"You're missing my point!" I said. "I doubt you're going to find any women."

"You said I was like a movie star!" Pierce said.

"You are," I said. "But there aren't a hell of a lot of women on the North American highway system looking for movie-star-like men to purchase sexual favors from."

"So what, then?" Pierce said.

"Men!" I explained. "Men pay other men, to give them moofty-pooftys. Like this guy." I gestured to our new friend. "You want to?"

"You can't be serious!" the man said.

"Okay," I said. "You want to pay him to give *you* a moofty-poofty?"

"Where were you brought up?" the man said, vaguely, as if he did not know what else to say. "You're not Jewish, are you? Oh, let me help you find the Lord."

"He's in the other car, with our mother," I said.

"You should go back to your mother!" the man said. "Where is she? I'd like to report her; they should take you kids away from her."

"And you call yourself a Christian!" I said.

The man shut his eyes. "I think you're under a lot of stress," he said. "I tell you what: you think you would feel calmer if I bought you a meal?"

"Didn't we just have breakfast?" I said.

"Hey, I could eat," Pierce said.

"Breakfast was ages ago, Maud," Leopold said.

"It's lunchtime now," the man said. "You can keep me company while I eat."

"Couldn't you just buy us lunch and sit at a separate table?" I said.

"If I'm going to buy you lunch, it's because I'm trying to help you get straightened out."

"Oh, very well."

We got into the Bronco. It was new, and had a lovely artificial odor of newness. The newness sent Trayf into a frenzy. He liked his cars to be aged. I was sitting in the back and couldn't control him. He insisted on licking the entire back of the man's seat. I had never seen him do this before. Luckily the man put on a tape of white people singing gospel music, so the sound of Trayf's slurping was drowned.

It was quite a while before we found a place to eat. The diner had real home-style cooking. "I'd like to try the meat loaf, with a side order of mashed potatoes and stewed okra," Leopold said decisively, closing the menu.

"That sounds good," said Pierce, shutting his menu.

"Pierce!" I warned. "You know, most major motion picture stars of today are vegetarians."

"Is he a movie star?" the fat man said. He really hadn't said a word in a long time. He just seemed too pleased that we were accompanying him to be able to speak.

"He's going to be," I said.

"Where are you kids from?" he said with a shiny smile.

"Objection! I said we'd eat with you, I didn't say we'd talk to you," I told him. "Especially not with that moronic line of questioning."

There was a silence.

I poured a lot of ketchup on my meat loaf. It was very good, heavily spiced and peppery. Pierce looked longingly across his grilled cheese and tomato sandwich at my plate. Leopold tasted his thoughtfully, trying to determine the ingredients. "I wonder how my family is doing?" he said.

"Me, too," I said. "There are so many questions left unanswered. Is Fred still handcuffed to the bed after all this time; did he get in a lot of trouble; does he still think of me with the same intensity that came so close to ruining his life earlier? Mother: what sort of difficulties has she gotten everyone into now? Marietta: is she molesting my lord, taking advantage of his weakness? Theodore: is he suffering? And so forth." The man was jiggling in his seat opposite. "Sir, are you touching your private parts?"

"Is this really how young women of today talk?" he said.

"Yes!" I said. "Where have you been?"

"Pocahontas County, West Virginia," he said. "My wife died six months ago. I've been driving around visiting relatives. Half the time I don't even know what I'm doing. I never thought I would outlive my wife. It's strange, my meeting you this way. I can't believe we're sitting like this, having lunch. Edward told me so much about you. I don't know if I should be saying this. At breakfast, when I first saw you through the window of the diner, something strange happened to me."

"What happened to you, Monsieur?" Leopold said.

"What exactly did you have for breakfast?" I said.

"I haven't even introduced myself!" the man said. "I just realized, I know so much about you—you don't even know my name!"

"That's okay," I said.

"My name's Bob," the man said. "Bob Hittite."

"Aren't you going to eat your lasagna, Bob?" said Leopold. "You haven't even touched it. The menu said it was homemade."

"Funny," Bob said. "I've done nothing but eat, since my wife died. When I turned to the Lord, I turned to food. Now, all of a sudden, I'm not even hungry. I could stand to lose some weight, I guess."

"We'll wrap it up for later," I said. "Let's get to the point: you're a Christian."

"I want to tell you what that's meant to me!"

"Does it mean you want to give us some money?"

"No, no—" Bob said.

"Yeah, I get it," I said. "You'll give me the money after I put out. Let's get it over with."

"Oh, hey, hey!" said Bob. "With all that's been happening, I gather you're not yourself. You've gone a little loony; like me, after my wife died. Now, meeting you, I wonder what I could have been thinking of. Did you know, we were married for nearly forty years? And I don't even know what I saw in her to begin with?"

"Children?" I said. He shook his head. "So, there's no one to make any claims on your estate. Perhaps after I take you out in the parking lot, you'd like to think about rewriting your will."

"Oh, you poor crazy one! I turned my spiritual possessions over to the Lord. Financially, I'm in very good shape; I invested heavily, year after year, in UPS from the moment it was an employee option. And I worked for UPS for forty-two years."

"You worked for the United Parcel Service for forty-two years, and you're calling *me* crazy?"

"I don't follow you."

"Bob," I explained. "Don't you see, you've just spent your whole life making boxes go in circles? We've got to be going." I got to my feet. "Come on, guys. We'll bring Bob's lasagna to Trayf. Thanks for the eats, Bob!"

"Wait!" cried Bob. "What are you kids going to do?"

"We're going to stand in the parking lot until one or the other of us finds somebody who wants to pay for sex. If nothing happens in a few hours, we'll be reduced to selling Leopold. You wouldn't want to baby-sit him until then, would you?"

"I don't need a baby-sitter," said Leopold.

Bob leapt up. "You really are serious! Don't even think about it! We're going to go now. I'm going to take you to a motel."

"Gosh!" I said. "I don't even know how much to charge for overnight! I'm sure the whole business side of things will get easier in time."

"Your first job, Maud," Leopold said proudly.

"I just remembered," I said. "Did you know there was a type of squid, and at a certain time of year—mating season—all the mashie niblicks of the squids fall off and swim *by themselves* through the ocean until they find the female squids? On moonlit nights, the Polynesians go out and row through a sea of squids' self-propelled mashie niblicks. Isn't that beautiful, Bob?"

"What's a mashie niblick?" said Bob. "Some kind of golf club?"

"It's a man's private Wurlitzer!" I explained loudly.

He ignored this. "Do you know how to pray?" he said.

"Of course!" I said. "Basically, whenever you want something, you whine and nag to an invisible presence, who some folks say is imaginary."

Bob's coral seas had parted, apparently so horrified the upper lip no longer wanted to touch its lifelong companion, the moist, prissy lower. His tender face, pale, poreless-skinned, resembled a pufferfish, taut and swollen with air. "Please don't talk like that," he said.

"Why?" I said. "Is there something you're not telling me? Like, maybe you're God, and I've hurt your feelings?"

"Stop," said Bob. "Oh, please, honey; you don't mean it."

"Do you want to pray now, Bob? Go right ahead. Don't let me stop you. I have my own thoughts. What I'm wondering is, do the Polynesians net the squids' mashie niblicks and eat them? Because, if so, that seems weird. On the other hand, the squid is considered edible by many; and one never hears of it being necessary to remove the mashie niblick first."

"You can cook squid in ink," Leopold said. "I think. And I never read in a cookbook, *remove the squids' mashie niblicks first.* Not like *peel and devein the shrimp.* But I have a lot to learn, about cooking."

"No, no!" said Bob. "Listen to me: I'm going to get you kids one room in a motel, and I'll stay in another. It's later than you think. Tonight, I want you all to join me in prayer. Tomorrow, I'll drive you to my home. It's in the town of Minnehaha Springs, in the Allegheny Mountains. I see I've been sent to you for a purpose. I'm going to help. The little one, that Edward calls Leopold and you call Brer Rabbit, can go to school; your older brother can find work in a gas station—or something—and I'll help him to find a place of his own. You can keep house for me, Maud; but don't worry—it won't be much work, I can see you haven't been brought up that way. I've already got a cleaning woman, comes in every two weeks, and if you like, I can get her to visit more often."

"Hmmm," I said thoughtfully. "Oh, Bob. You're too kind. You know, I really should confess: I was incredibly terrified when I propositioned you. I had hoped my first time would be different."

"I don't need you to lie to me, Maud," said Bob. "I'm going to save you. I can see you need it."

22

I woke Pierce, Leopold and Trayf before dawn. "Get up!" I said. "We've got to get going." The room smelled of mildew and disinfectant which at some stage in their history had mutated and conjoined, forming a rapidly growing disinfectant-scented mildew. I went to the window and pulled back the greasy polyester curtain. It was still dark out, the nearly empty parking lot badly illuminated by one or two floodlights.

"We don't have a car, Maud," Leopold said. "Remember?"

"Yeah," said Pierce, snickering sleepily, his eyes half shut as he fumbled for his cigarettes. "We don't even have a car."

"I know that, you dumbo!" I snarled. "You're going to have to hot-wire Bob Hittite's Bronco!"

"Oh," said Pierce, sitting up. "Are you serious?"

"Yes, I'm serious!" I said. "Get moving!"

"So what if this guy, like, calls the cops or something?" Pierce said.

"He's not going to call the police," I said.

"How do you know?"

"He's a Christian," I said. "Besides, I'm going to write him a very special little note, explaining everything."

"That's cool," Pierce said, pulling on his jeans over his boxer shorts and lighting up. He sat on the edge of the bed for a moment, smoking meditatively. "Whose car are we hot-wiring?"

"Bob Hittite's Bronco!"

"That guy from last night? The one that made us pray? Hey, what'd you pray for? I forgot to ask you. I prayed for a really big film role with a salary of ten million dollars."

"That's right, Pierce," I said. "Bob Hittite is the retired United Parcel Service employee who wants to make me live in a little house in Minnehaha Springs with an apron, while you work in a gas station and live in an apartment above a grocery store and Leopold goes rabbit hunting or something."

"Oh yeah?" Pierce said. "That doesn't sound so bad. I didn't know Leopold liked rabbit hunting."

"I wouldn't go rabbit hunting," called Leopold from the bathroom. "The rest sounds fun, though. It sounds like the way real people get to live."

"Really?" I said. Suddenly, briefly, I could see myself living in a little house with Bob, even though he was so much older. It was an alternate reality, similar to being carried off by alien life-forms to a darling log cabin dating back to 1874. This new life would provide me with stability. I would have some babies, with great big fat jolly cheeks; and chickens who loved me and clucked eagerly at my arrival; possibly emus or ostrich, which I would occasionally allow into the house; I might learn to ride a tiny, very pretty gray Arabian filly I had raised from a colt.

It was as if a doorway along a corridor full of doors, all previously shut, had swung open, revealing a glimpse of only one of many parallel universes. But having peered in, I now wanted to keep going down the corridor, hoping to look inside other doorways.

Wasn't it more interesting to simply look than to have to live out the entire existence waiting on the other side of the door? Of course, there might come a time when I had walked down the corridor and, looking into the rooms and finding none to my liking, would find I had exhausted all the possibilities and the remaining doors were now closed.

However, since that wasn't going to happen, I decided not to accept Bob's tempting offer. "Poor Bob!" I said when we were back on the road. "I hope he doesn't try to come after us."

"We took his car," Leopold pointed out.

"Oh yeah," I said. "You're right. Well, he could rent one or something. I got him to give me some money last night, but it sure won't last us very long. I should have taken his credit cards, but that could get us in trouble."

"Can we get some coffee or something?" Pierce said wanly. The sun was beginning to come up. The light was in that transitional stage, between night and day, like two different bottles of food coloring fighting it out in a saucer alongside an Easter egg. The eight-lane highway was empty. Pierce pushed in the cigarette lighter in the dashboard. "Gee, I don't know what's wrong with me this morning. I guess maybe I'm not used to being away from the family, huh?"

"Me, too," said Leopold.

"Me, too!" I said. "I can understand that Leopold and I are homesick, but at your age, Pierce, you shouldn't even be living at home. You should be off stealing cars professionally. You're very good at it, by the way. I wonder if Mother picked a criminal for your father, too?"

"I thought he was Italian," Pierce muttered.

"You're sweet, Pierce," I said.

"Shut up! Shut up!" said Pierce.

"Do you know who's the strangest member of our family?" I said.

"Me?" said Leopold.

"Me?" said Pierce.

"No," I said. I looked out the window. I could tell we were on the road, and the pinkish-purple hue of six-thirty A.M. predominated, but beyond that I couldn't see much else. I supposed I really should consider getting glasses, or perhaps contact lenses in a shade of pink or blue.

"Theodore?" said Leopold. "He's not strange, just talented, and completely lacking in confidence. That makes it hard to tell the difference. Mother's not strange, she just doesn't have a brain in her head. Actually, that's normal. Are you talking about the fathers? But we've never even met most of them, or at least, nobody can remember. You're not referring to yourself, are you?" There was a pause and Pierce and Leopold snorted simultaneously with derision.

"I was talking about Marietta."

"Marietta!" they said, and Leopold added, "What's so strange about her?"

"She's not like a person."

"She's like a person!" said Pierce. "Similar to, anyway."

"What I mean is, she's like a chameleon. Think about it. What's her personality?"

"I don't know," Pierce said. "What's anyone's personality?"

"Most people, they have a personality. Take you. You're quiet. What they list as The Silent Type, a House Guest type of guy. Probably very spiritually advanced, since basically you have no ambition whatsoever. You just take what comes your way. Theodore: sensitive, and cowardly. Leopold—"

"Yes?" said Leopold eagerly.

"Bubbly, warm, full of curiosity; but you secretly believe yourself to be a homeless waif, of a dysfunctional family. Wrong! Mom: like a child who never grew up, trapped in an adult's body. The child stayed the same age, maybe around ten years old, but the body kept growing older, and more things were expected of this adult, whom people didn't realize was really still a mental child. That child was able to fool people, to a degree, because over the years she's gathered experience, though not necessarily wisdom."

"That's kind of harsh, isn't it?" Leopold unrolled his window and craned out, inhaling fresh air. "Where are we, anyway?" he said. "I wish you wouldn't smoke so much, Pierce."

"Perhaps; but not all that uncommon. Only Marietta doesn't fit any description. She just changes her personality to whomever she's relating to. But it's not like she's doing that on top of her real personality. No, when she's at home with us, she's a blank slate. She projects an aura of mystery, only when you pry off the aura, you learn there's not really any mystery underneath. She completely lacks any originality whatsoever! That's why men love her. They can make up whomever they want to be with. They see in her what they want. But the truth is, all they've spent time with is a wistful smile and a blank expression."

"When are you going to let us get breakfast?" Leopold said.

By now it was probably around seven-thirty. The sun was up and the early-morning commuters and long-distance haulers were beginning to infiltrate the highway.

"We can stop!" I said. "But first, look out the back and make sure Bob Hittite didn't call the police, who are chasing us, or rent a car of his own and catch up to us."

"I don't see anything," said Leopold.

"Good," I said. "Then why don't you keep your eyes open for a place."

"What about that truck stop?"

"What's it called?"

"C-Plus Eats," Leopold said.

"Let's wait until we find a B-Plus or even A-Minus," I said.

"Maud, can I ask you something?" Leopold said.

"Sure, Leopold," I said. "You can ask me anything. I have to take over your education, at least for the time being."

"That we stole this man's vehicle, and left him all alone in a motel, when he wanted to help us and take us home with him—was that right?" Leopold said.

"Um," I said. "Not when you put it that way. Try looking at it differently. Here's this fat guy: he's bored, and probably never did have too much excitement in his life, what with being married and having a job and living in a house. Meeting us was a lot of fun for him! He was the one taking advantage of *us*."

"How?"

"People like that are like lampreys, getting their kicks by draining it from other people. Besides, if I had been just a little more desperate and beaten-down, I would have given up and gone off to marry him. I bet there are a billion women in his hometown who swoon at the sight of him, whom he completely ignores. But he saw me as an exotic import whom he would acquire as a status symbol, because I looked helpless and in trouble. He deserved what he got."

"Oh," said Leopold.

Trayf, curled up on the seat alongside me, decided to have a stretch, flexing his spine and various legs in typical yoga positions. Then he stood with his front paws on my lap and yawned in my face. A gust of morning dog-breath wafted at me, hot and zoo-like. His few remaining teeth studded his mottled gums like a hippo's molars. When he was finished yawning he closed his snout and forced it under my hand with quick upward pressure, so that I got the message he expected me to pet him, immediately.

"Maud?" said Leopold.

"What is it, my darling bunny."

"When are we going to find Mom and the others?"

"We're meeting up with them in California," I said. "Remember? In Los Angeles."

"Are there palm trees in Los Angeles?"

"That's right."

"Maybe we're there already, then," he said.

"Do you know where we're going to meet them in L.A.?" Pierce said.

"We'll find them," I said.

"Los Angeles is supposed to be a big place. Leopold, will you look in the glove compartment and see if there's something to eat?"

Leopold opened the glove compartment. "I wonder how our spider is doing," he said. "I hope my father knows not to brush him away."

"We'll just hang out, where they have the stars in the sidewalk," I said. "Sooner or later they're bound to turn up."

Leopold had begun to snuffle. "Leopold," said Pierce with a sigh. "I'm sure the spider is okay. He was a tough spider. He can handle himself."

"That's not why I'm crying," Leopold said. "I want to go home."

"You don't have a home," I reminded him.

"I want my mother and brother and sister and Lulu. I want a home."

"Hey," said Pierce. "Can't you just forget about them?"

"Oh, Pierce, what a wise thing to say," I said.

"You're saying you think I sound too harsh?" he said.

"Not at all," I said. "I think you're being too kind to the little six-year-old." Leopold sobbed even louder.

"Leave me alone," said Pierce. "You're getting him more upset!"

"It doesn't matter!" I said. "What matters is, when you say something, Pierce, it sounds true. True and fresh, as if it has never been said before. You have that quality."

"I said, leave me alone!" Pierce said. "Leave me alone, or get out and walk!"

"I wasn't making fun of you!" I said. "I meant it."

"Don't make her get out and walk, Pierce!" Leopold said with a scream.

There was a pause. "So, you think we'll find Marietta and Theodore and Mom and Lulu and the puppies where the stars are in the sidewalk," Pierce said.

"Oh, yes, and the lord, too," I said. "And possibly even Freddy. Either where the stars are in the sidewalk; or on the beach in Venice; or in Spago's, Morton's or the Ivy at lunch; or Frederick's of Hollywood; waiting for us at the bottom of Laurel Canyon, or the Colony at Malibu."

"Boy, you really sound like you've been there!" Pierce said.

"I watch the nightly news on TV," I said. "There's little else on."

"Palm tree," Leopold said in a flat tone. "Palm tree. Palm tree. Palm tree. Another palm tree."

"So how much money did you get from old Bob?" Pierce said.

"Only thirty," I said. "He only had credit cards. He said if I came home with him, he'd give me some of his stock in UPS. I don't know what I'd do with a stock! Anyway, this should get us breakfast and gas; we'll have to figure out what to do for tonight. Leopold, did you just say something about a palm tree?"

"They're everywhere!" Leopold said. "All along this part of the highway outside Fort Lauderdale."

"What are we doing in Fort Lauderdale?" I said.

"We're not in Fort Lauderdale," said Leopold. "We're outside it. Where is Fort Lauderdale, anyway?"

"Fort Lauderdale's in Florida."

"I've heard of Fort Lauderdale," Pierce said.

"Pierce," I said coldly. "Was it your intention to take us to Fort Lauderdale?"

"What do you mean?"

"What I mean is, what are we doing in Fort Lauderdale, you idiot!" I said. "Weren't you listening yesterday when that guy Bob told us we were headed to Florida? Why did you start driving south this morning? You should have started heading west, not farther south. Nobody could be that stupid! Why weren't you watching the signs?"

"You didn't tell me what signs to watch for!" Pierce said. "You don't tell me where to go, you just expect me to drive this car and not even get any breakfast and bitch about my smoking cigarettes and then say that *I'm* getting Leopold upset and call me stupid! *You're* stupid! And don't call me stupid again, unless you want to get out of the car and walk!"

"I will!" I said. "I will get out and walk! Who needs you!"

"No!" screamed Leopold. "Don't go, Maud! Don't leave me!"

"Fine!" Pierce said. "Leopold and I will be better off without you, slut-bitch! You want to get out? Get out!"

He pulled off onto the shoulder. It was a dangerous spot to pull over. The shoulder was barely half a car's width. There was a tall cement wall along the edge. I opened the car door, scraping it against the cement, and got out. Pierce leaned back and across and pulled the door shut. I could hear Leopold screaming at the top of his lungs.

The red Bronco signaled, and, moving back into the stream of traffic, drove off. I could just make out the dog's face pressed against the window, and what looked like Leopold scrambling over the seat, as if by hurling himself into the back of the Bronco he would be closer to me. Then the car disappeared into the current of traffic and vanished in the stream.

It was very hot with the cars whizzing by. I had no sunblock, and I knew it was only a matter of minutes before my skin began to fry, separating from its under-layer of flesh the way Leopold's roasted chickens crisped and sizzled in the oven. My life was a mess. My eyes filled with tears, each one a perfect pear and probably filled with peculiar life-forms if I had been able to take a look under a microscope.

I stood for a few seconds, immobile, only the huge saline gems crashing down my face. A passing car honked at me, and if it were possible for a honk to sound like a leer, this one did. Then a car slowed almost to a halt, nearly causing an accident. A man leaned over and yelled at me. "Get in! I can't stop here for long!"

I shook my head. This was no time to acquire a new boyfriend, especially one who appeared middle-aged, drove a Chevy Caprice and liked to get his dates on the highway. It wasn't even a new Caprice; it had been a Caprice for a long time.

Walking along the shoulder, as close to the concrete wall as possible, blinded by tears, I wondered how long it would be before someone got distracted and plowed into me, a direct hit. I would have to live in a wheelchair and compensate by developing strength in my upper arms. In time I might be provided with one of those trained monkeys, who were taught to make lemonade and play the organ for their handicapped or challenged owners. Just thinking about it made me cry harder. What kind of life was that for a monkey? Another car pulled over. "Need help?" a man yelled.

If I had had a weapon I might have accepted one of the next five or six offers. Probably I would have been able to put any one of my attackers in their place with what my mother called my rapier-like half-wit; but did I really want to settle in the greater Fort Lauderdale region, trapped in a wheelchair with only my monkey and a man as companions?

Pierce had left me off a half mile from an exit. That was fortunate, though I still had not come up with any specific plans for what I was going to do in the few remaining moments before the accident. I started to walk down the exit ramp. In a car it might have seemed a short distance. On foot, though I kept trudging, I didn't seem to be making any progress at all. "How much?" a boy screamed. "I'll give you a thousand dollars."

This cheered me up quite a bit. At least someone out there recognized my value, though there were probably more cosmopolitan cities and more fashionable historical periods in which to begin a career as a courtesan; formerly, in, say, turn-of-the-century Paris, handmade lingerie might not have been all that expensive, whereas now not only would it be prohibitive, but I would hardly be willing to spend all my hard-earned cash on something that few men would even notice, no matter what price they were willing to pay for my company.

But it was nice nevertheless to be so irresistible; and that I was receiving so much attention from those who couldn't even see my face, just the back of my head and veiled limbs, indicated my magical powers of attraction were growing stronger—unless I had a hole in my pants in an unmentionable place. I gave my tush a quick pat, just to check. There was a lot of honking going on behind me. I didn't look around. It was probably another cretin yelling something lewd, or offering me assistance.

Since it was obvious I was going to have no choice but to turn to prostitution, I would just have to knuckle down and accept it; on the other hand, I saw no reason I could not ease into it more gradually rather than commence on an exit ramp.

The car slowed alongside me. I tried to think of something devastating to say to the driver, something that would humiliate him, put him in his place, make him see how badly he was behaving, and yet long for me all the more.

"Get in!" two voices yelled. One sounded like a child, high and fluty. I looked out the corner of my eye. It was Pierce and Leopold. Leopold was in the back. I got in the front passenger door. Pierce drove on. Leopold sobbed behind. I didn't speak. I looked out the window. Then I examined myself in the mirror on the windshield visor. My face was smudged and dirty. My raveled tangle of knotted hair was unraveling. These men who had been honking at me were definitely sickos. I could not believe, the way I appeared now, that anybody normal would want to sleep with me. I didn't even have any makeup to repair the ravages. I began to cry, accompanying Leopold in the back.

"I'm sorry," said Pierce at last. I didn't answer.

"What did you do that for, Pierce?" Leopold said, still bawling. "You frightened a living crap out of me."

"It's *the*, Leopold," I said.

"Huh?"

"He frightened *the* living crap out of you," I said. "Not *a*."

"It makes more sense to say *a*," said Leopold.

"I said I was sorry!" Pierce snarled.

"Give me a tissue," I said, sniffling.

Pierce rummaged with one hand by his feet and handed me a roll of toilet paper. "I took it from the motel this morning," he said proudly.

"Fine," I said, blowing my nose with a loud crow.

"So what do you want to do now?" he said.

"I don't know what Florida has in the way of industry apart from citrus," I said. "What else is Florida known for?"

"Alligators," said Leopold. "And retirement communities. Mother and I wrote for the literature a while ago."

"Pierce could be an alligator wrestler, and I could make belts and wallets," I said. "But we don't really have the necessary skills. And we'd need money to retire. We could maybe earn some money as migrant workers. I don't think I want to be a prostitute."

"How come?" said Leopold.

"All that dressing and undressing," I said. "I came to the realization, when I was dumped and abandoned by my own family along a completely strange highway, that I'm not interested."

"So," said Pierce. "We'll be migrant workers. That's cool."

"Thank goodness Mother isn't with us," I said. "I bet she would love to seduce those migrant workers. We'd have another little one on our hands in no time."

"But is it citrus season?" Pierce said.

"Believe me," I said, "our mother doesn't care what season it is when she sees a man."

We had continued down the exit ramp off the highway and were now traveling on smaller streets that in fact were almost exactly as wide as the highway, only with stoplights. "Maybe you should make a right, and we can get off some of these highways for a change," I said.

But when Pierce turned we were on another highway, almost exactly the same. "Let's find a country lane," said Leopold.

At the next light Pierce made another right; but it was no different.

"It might be one of those states that are completely paved over," I said.

"Are there states in the United States that are completely paved?" asked Leopold.

"Oh, definitely," I said. "Or, if not a hundred percent, ninety. There's Florida, most of Texas, New Jersey, California, Massachusetts and several others. In some cases, say, Massachusetts, the city of Boston takes up ninety percent, and the other ten percent is NO PARKING signs and Japanese industry. Texas: shopping malls, and a few fields for steers."

"How do you know?" said Pierce.

"We learned it in school," I said. Now the road widened again, exactly like the road we had just turned off: six lanes of cars, with what I assumed to be office buildings, drugstores, copy shops and banks on either side. Between a Pet Food Express and a Chinese restaurant was a twenty-story building with what appeared to be a fountain or a lake in front. "Leopold, what did that sign say?"

"Cross-Creek Hotel Inn," he said. "Maybe there are alligators in that fountain. Could we check it out?"

"Good idea," I said. "Pierce, stop!"

I went into the lobby. What appeared to be a young boy was standing behind the reception desk. I peered at him more closely. He wasn't so young, and was handsome in a way considered desirable by American standards: he had a weak, stupid face, blue eyes set closely together and dirty blond hair. He looked like he skateboarded, or skied, or golfed; anyway, some type of sport that required expensive equipment needing constant updating, and trips to spots that were very crowded with others practicing the same activity, requiring steep admission fees.

He was taking his time getting off the phone; it sounded like he was on a personal call. I stood in front of him tapping my fingers. There was a stack of brochures on the registration desk and I leafed through. A place called Butterfly World housed more than five hundred different kinds of butterflies and their larvae. An ad for the Weeki-Wacki Lounge and Supper Club said the lounge had been in operation since 1957. Real Polynesian performers danced nightly, and there was a photograph of a Mexican waiter holding up a suckling pig on a platter in front of a philodendron. Maybe a job in one of these places would be a better option than a career as a migrant worker?

I unbuttoned the top three buttons of my blouse and leaned forward on the counter, an old family tradition. The guy wore a nameplate that said BRIAN TRISTA, and, in smaller print, "ASSISTANT MANGER."

Brian put down the phone and looked at me. "Can I help you?" he said.

"Perhaps," I said. "Are you the assistant manger?"

"Yes," he said. "The manager."

"Do you have any rooms available for this evening?"

"Let me check," he said, and went over to the computer. I leafed through the rest of the brochures. The World's Largest Discount Shopping Mall Outlet, occupying over five hundred acres, was located nearby. With products from major department stores, at the lowest prices anywhere. On Saturdays and Sundays a special flea market was held inside the compound. I glanced over at Brian. He was still doing something on the computer.

"Sorry," he said, seeing me watching him. "We've been having a little trouble with the computer."

"But you must know if there are rooms going to be available tonight," I said. "Don't you have something in a book? Written down? On paper?"

"No," he said. "Give me a minute here." He pressed all kinds of buttons and keys. I glanced through a pamphlet about Parrot Land. Here parrots from around the world rode bicycles in an open environment, planted to resemble a jungle. Admission was twenty dollars. It was hard to figure out exactly where the place was located, and though I would have liked to take Leopold there, it was best if I didn't show him the brochure but waited until we had all gotten rich. "I don't know what to say," Brian said, scratching his eyebrows. "By any chance, would you want to come back later? I'm sure the computer will be working by then."

"First of all, even if you have a room available, what are the rates, and do you allow dogs?"

"I can't tell you the rates, because that's on the computer, and the rates fluctuate, depending on what our headquarters decides, and what rooms are available. But yes, we do allow dogs, provided you don't let them in the rooms."

I ignored this. "Brian," I said. "What if you gave me a room now, and I paid you when the computer starts working again."

"I couldn't do that," he said.

"It would be bending the rules," I said. "But you look bendable. And I'll give you the cash in the morning."

I had to insinuate he was going to have a lot of fun coming his way, and that I would make it well worth his while. Finally we struck a deal. He said that if we went away for a few hours, he would sneak me in. He could get in a lot of trouble: if, for example, a convention was booked to fill the entire hotel, and they suddenly arrived expecting their confirmed reservation; or if his boss came in from one of the other Cross-Creek Hotels and decided to make a surprise room inspection.

But if I would go out with him that night, and promise to give him the cash the next day, he would risk his career. If it was a really fun date, he might even be able to lend me some money.

"So now all we have to do is hang out for a few hours," I told Pierce and Leopold back in the car. "In the meantime, we should try and start collecting some money. Any suggestions?"

"Didn't you get a lot of cash from Bob Hittite last night?" said

Pierce. "Anyway, I'm hungry. Let's eat first and then figure it out." He began to drive down the highway. "Hey, here's a pizza parlor." He pulled into the lot next to a supermarket.

"All right, these are our priorities," I said. "We need to come up with at least twenty dollars; and we need food. Here's the plan: Leopold, you go into the supermarket and get us lots of snacks for the room and the car, so we won't get so hungry and desperate. Here's five dollars. I'll go hang out in the front of the supermarket, until I see a single man buying groceries for one. Then I tail him out and proposition him. If necessary, I'll have to return to my scheme of prostitution; but hopefully I can simply get him to give me money."

"What are groceries for one?" said Pierce.

"You know, like a Hungry-Man TV dinner, a quart of milk or a box of frozen burritos."

"Oh, God, don't talk like that," said Pierce. "You're making me even more hungry. Leopold, try to get me a frozen Hungry-Man TV dinner, will you?"

"But Pierce, how will you heat it up?"

"I don't care," Pierce said. "I kind of like how they taste, frozen. What am I supposed to be doing, while you guys do all this?"

"I tell you what: you'll go to the pizza parlor, order a slice of pizza and a Coke; and get a slice for Trayf, too. Then hang out in front until we come to get you. While you wait, you can be on the look-out for someone to proposition."

"Proposition in what way?"

"Sexually!" I said.

"I don't think I'm going to be real good at this," he said.

"Don't worry," I said. "You just sit in front and eat your pizza. And pretty soon some weird guy will come along and ask you a question about the dog. You make sure you answer him. Be nice. And then he'll want to know if you want to have sex."

"Are you sure?" Pierce said. "At a pizza parlor at a Florida strip mall at ten-thirty in the morning?"

"Of course!" I said. "Have you any idea, the undercurrent of things that are going on, all around us! This is exactly what is going on. There's a world of people acting in a manner that is publicly considered to be normal; and then there's the undercurrent, or what is known as the underbelly of America, happening simultaneously. For the time being, we're joining the underbelly."

"So when the guy wants to know about sex, what do I do?" Pierce said.

"He's going to first see if you want to go back to his place. You don't. That takes too long. He'll probably say it's only five minutes away. That means it's more like a half hour to forty-five minutes. You say you have an appointment, but indicate that alley in back. All you have to do, Pierce, is go down that alley and stand around while he gives you a moofty-poofty. Get a newspaper first, or something, if you want some distraction."

"Stand around while he gives me a moofty-poofty," Pierce repeated.

"What exactly is a moofty-poofty?" said Leopold.

"A moofty-poofty is where a man—or a woman, but more frequently a man—takes the mashie niblick of another man and, putting it in his coral seas, sucks on it," I said.

"Ugh," said Leopold. "Weird."

"But Pierce," I said. "Make sure you tell him you need fifty bucks first. Don't wait until afterward. And if Leopold and I come back, and you're not there, we'll wait for you; but remember, try not to forget about us and leave!"

"I wouldn't do that!" said Pierce indignantly.

"You want me to write it down for you?" I said.

"Okay," said Pierce with a sigh. "That might be a good idea."

"Tell me once more, what am I supposed to buy?" said Leopold.

"Little vittles. Small, healthy snacks—organic carrots and candy bars. A TV dinner for Pierce. Dog food. Five dollars won't get you very far, though; see if you can find some stale food for half price, or beg the stock clerk to put a cheaper amount on things just for you. I know you'll be very good at this. Just act like you know what you're doing; but whatever happens, *you don't know me*. You've never seen me before in your life, get it?"

"But why?"

"I don't think one can pick up men while a little kid is following one around. Promise you'll pretend you don't know me?"

"No, Maud!" said Leopold, throwing himself around my knees.

"It's just temporary," I explained, which seemed to assuage him.

Leopold and I headed for the supermarket. Pierce went toward the pizza parlor. "Hey!" Pierce called. I turned around. "Is this life?"

"It's similar to it," I said. "It's like life, but not exactly. It's more of a parallel track."

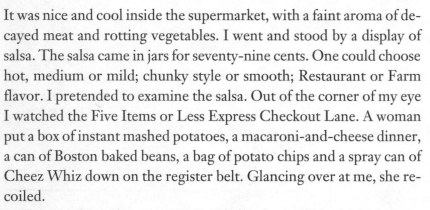

It was nice and cool inside the supermarket, with a faint aroma of decayed meat and rotting vegetables. I went and stood by a display of salsa. The salsa came in jars for seventy-nine cents. One could choose hot, medium or mild; chunky style or smooth; Restaurant or Farm flavor. I pretended to examine the salsa. Out of the corner of my eye I watched the Five Items or Less Express Checkout Lane. A woman put a box of instant mashed potatoes, a macaroni-and-cheese dinner, a can of Boston baked beans, a bag of potato chips and a spray can of Cheez Whiz down on the register belt. Glancing over at me, she recoiled.

"Is something the matter?" I said, involuntarily looking down at myself to make sure I was still wearing clothes. But I was fully dressed, though it was true I was somewhat grimy, and my harlequin trousers with the sequins were maybe a little loud. I could not help my dark gypsy blood; after all, this was probably why I craved color. I flushed with embarrassment.

It occurred to me I had no business being embarrassed. *She* should be embarrassed. *She* had somehow managed to solidify her hair into a solid mouse-colored helmet, smooth on top, with a fringe of Bozo curls at jaw level. *She* was the one wearing squarish, pale-pink plastic glasses, which gave her the appearance of an octopus pressed plaintively against an aquarium. *She* was the one wearing black rayon trousers, white mini–high heels and a blouse covered with red-and-green tulips being molested by orange-and-yellow hummingbirds.

How foul. I wondered if I should follow her out into the parking lot and knock her down and steal her groceries. Then I pictured her lying on the ground, afterward, looking at a spot of grease on her hideous blouse and crying. So: my brother Theodore was wrong—I had compassion after all! I could hardly wait to see him again, and describe the experience to him, and make him eat his words.

Still, she had no business staring at me. There had to be some suitable punishment for such behavior. I wondered if it would pay off, if I were to approach her and find out if she had ever given up a child for adoption, and then pretend I was that child and had tracked her down. If I was the wrong age, there was always Leopold or Pierce. And even if she had never given up one of us for adoption, at least she might feel sorry enough for us that she would invite us home and feed us and put us up for a few weeks.

Then I spotted a more likely prospect: a very old man by himself. He wore a red-and-blue–plaid cap, with a fuzzy fluff-ball on the top, possibly an announcement of the cessation of the male sex drive, or a warning for women to keep their distance.

I judged him to be approximately eighty years old. He took his items out of the basket: a Hebrew National salami, a can of pike fish, a container of what might have been coleslaw and a clear plastic tub of already-prepared gelatin, the type that had been kept in the deli counter for so long one knew it had developed a crust—red, studded with hard, bright-yellow fruit nuggets. Like a lioness examining an aged, crippled wildebeest on the veldt, I took a step closer.

I could already picture his car in the parking lot of my mind: something oversized and old, with low mileage, possibly an '81 Oldsmobile—Achieva? What if I were to follow him out and hop in when he opened the door, telling him that I had never done anything like this before, but that when I saw him I was possessed.

Then "Lew" would take me to his condominium on the second floor, dark and smelling of tuna fish, burnt toast and urine. The furniture, purchased by his wife when she was still alive, shipped from the Bronx to Florida, dark mahogany and dull green baize, whatever baize was. Probably his daughter, living nearby, already had the deceased's jewelry (this was a bit of a disappointment!) and came over every other afternoon to lecture her father about giving up driving, and make sure he was eating properly, adhering to the famous tuna-fish and orange-juice diet, beefed up with a dollop of sour cream and cottage cheese.

That I did not have the moral strength to pursue my imagination made me feel like a failure. I decided to press on; I made a quick reconnaissance mission up and down the aisles. There was a lone man in Frozen Food. I crept up behind.

From the back he had a bald spot and wore a dark blue suit with lumps in the shoulder pads. He was putting an assortment of frozen meat and cheese ravioli, Healthy Choice dinners and Green Giant Japanese-style vegetables into his cart. I felt like crying once again, at my plight and his. But he was a good forty years younger than the crippled wildebeest, more like a middle-aged eland or gnu, and even a lazy lioness did not choose to dine on old sinew when a juicier haunch was available.

I pursued him stealthily down Paper Products and Cleansing Supplies, past Baking Products and Coffee and Tea. He paid for his items and with a bag under each arm headed out into the parking lot in what appeared to be the direction of a black sports car.

He was gaining distance. I put on a final burst of energy and loped toward him just as he opened the trunk of his car. "Excuse me!" I said breathlessly. He turned around, raising his arms protectively. I bared my teeth in what passed as a smile for the human race, but meant something quite different for predator and prey. "I know you're going to think this is a little weird," I said. "I've never done anything like this before. I couldn't help following you out of the supermarket. I find you incredibly attractive."

"What?" he said.

So the old gnu had a hearing problem. "I said, I find you incredibly attractive!" I shouted.

He looked nervously around the lot. "I heard you. I just thought I was hearing wrong."

"Oh, I'm sure you hear that all the time," I said.

"No," he muttered.

"You think I'm weird," I said. I waited for his response, but my first blow had struck; he was too stunned to speak. "I have a crush on you!" I continued. His eyes misted with a fine film or fuzz. It was the same expression I had seen in the eyes of helpless television critters, when, singled out from the herd by the carnivorous predator, they seemed to abandon hope, give up and stand hypnotized by fear or destiny instead of continuing to attempt to flee. "I passed you in the aisle and I felt all this magnetism coming from you. I couldn't help but follow you out here. I'm sure this must happen all the time?"

"No, no!" the man said. "Not really. I really don't know what to say. Are you sure you have the right person?"

"You didn't notice something when I walked past you?" I said. "Like a sort of tidal wave or something?" If only it had been Fred I had found to accost here in the parking lot; he never would have been such a sucker for this kind of idiocy, but would have dished back to me double what I had dealt.

"I, well, actually—" The man shifted his groceries and fixed his glazed stare on my sequined trousers, which in fact were sassily tight, and shedding sequins.

"Anyway . . ." I said. "I never would have forgiven myself if I didn't say something. You probably have to get back to your wives and kids . . ." I turned and began to walk away, attempting the Marilyn Monroe tiptoe that Marietta and I had practiced for so many hours, but which only Marietta had perfected. When I did it, it was closer to the shuffle of a girl about to lose her underpants.

"Wait!" the man said. "This is very odd. I can't really believe you're serious. I don't know what to do, in this situation. I'm divorced!"

"You're kidding!" I said. "I didn't know." I tried to look moistly at him, as wetly and sensitively as a beautiful Swiss Jersey cow, breath sweet with clover; but it was hard to make such a quick transition from the mesmerizing stare of the predator to the dewy, vapid expression of the gentle cud-chewer. The man sort of recoiled and tilted his head, puzzled. "I guess I don't really have anything much to add," I said. "I'm awfully glad I did tell you that, though."

"Look," he said desperately. "I've got these frozen groceries I should put away. But, um, I could meet you later on, say, for a drink."

He peered at me. "You look about sixteen. Are you sure this isn't a trick?"

"Sixteen!" I said, rolling my eyes. "I know, I do look young for my age, but you go too far. Do you really think a sixteen-year-old would have the confidence or the skill to say these things to you?"

"Okay, okay!" he said. "I believe you. So, what about it? You want to meet tonight?"

"Oh, gosh," I said. "I'm not sure of my plans. I tell you what, though: if you like, I'll have a quick breakfast with you. Of course, you've got all these groceries to put away . . ."

"Breakfast?" the man said.

"Silly me!" I said. "It's lunchtime, huh?"

"Oh, what the heck!" the man said. "Let the stuff melt! I've got to eat, anyway. You want to grab your car and meet me?"

"Your car is a Corvette, it appears," I said. "I might prefer to go with you; you can drop me back here, afterward."

"Sure," he said.

"That is, if you don't mind waiting for one minute; I've forgotten something in the supermarket."

"Okay," he said.

I dashed across the lot and back through the automatic doors. "Leopold!" I bellowed.

"Yeah?" a voice piped and he popped out from behind the salsa display.

"Hurry up!" I said. "What's keeping you? We have to go."

"I could have gotten more, if you hadn't rushed me," Leopold said irritably. "I went to the deli counter and bought a quarter-pound of pastrami, a dill pickle, smoked salmon and sliced Italian salami."

"Are you nuts?" I said. "Those things aren't going to keep! I thought you'd buy things in cans, or bags, or jars—things that wouldn't need to be refrigerated immediately!"

"So this is the thanks I get," he said, annoyed.

"Whatever," I said. "Right now, you're accompanying me with some guy to lunch. He owns a black Corvette. When we get to the car, you get in the back—quickly, so he doesn't complain. Take the stuff out of the bag and store it under his seat, so the guy thinks we're very poor and hungry."

"We are poor and hungry!" said Leopold.

I ignored this. "He's going to give us a lift back here, to Pierce, after lunch."

"Who is this guy?"

"I don't know," I said. "It hardly matters. What's important is, he may be able to help us. We're going to need all the help we can get, within certain limits."

The man was already behind the driver's seat. He leaned over to unlock my door. Then he saw Leopold, standing behind me. He squinted, as if hallucinating. It served him right; a better-quality man would have gotten out to open my door for me, instead of just leaning over so crudely. I opened the door, and in one motion slid my seat forward and shoved Leopold into the tiny back cranny. "Hello! Who, uh, who's your little friend?"

"Cool car!" said Leopold. "New? What's this baby seat doing back here?"

"Just, uh, push it over to one side. I have my baby on the weekends. It's not really the best car, if you have kids. But I wanted to treat myself to something nice, after the divorce. It's been kind of messy."

"I hate a mess," I said, as something hit the back of my foot and I kicked it away. "What's your name, anyway?"

"My name's Bill," he said. He had half-turned in his seat; he couldn't seem to stop staring at Leopold, who in fact was behaving rather oddly, bent over and scrambling around like a lemur on the floor; then I remembered I had told him to defortify himself by taking out the food packets and hiding them; he must have shoved the packets too far under the seat, which was what hit my ankle. "Bill, ah, Brinkman."

"Oh, Bill!" I said, trying to distract him, and rubbing some dirt off my neck. "I'm Maud. Maud Slivenowicz. And this is my little brother, Leopold. I hope you don't mind; I couldn't leave him alone in the supermarket. You don't mind, do you? You have a child of your own. Look me in the eyes, Bill, and tell me you're not angry."

He had the face of something that hadn't fully hatched, or had been forced from its cocoon a bit prematurely: buggy eyes far apart and slightly protruding, tiny nose with big nostrils, slim coral seas almost as if a slit had been carved between the teeth but the addition of lips had been forgotten, or not had a chance to form. "So, uh, I guess I don't have too much time," he said. "Is there somewhere specific you and your little brother would like to go?"

"Somewhere close," I said grandly. "I'm afraid I really don't have much time, either." I pointed across the highway. "How about that spot, just there?"

"Where?"

"Just there!" I shook my head sadly, dismayed at how slow Bill was.

"Fresh Springs Medical Center?"

"Oh," I said.

"There's a couple places just beyond. Is that what you meant? The Bamboo Sliver? That's that new Chinese/Japanese cuisine; but since we're both in a rush, we could just have a drink, and your brother could have a soda or something."

"Oh, I think there's enough time to eat," chirped Leopold helpfully. "I've always wanted to try the new Chinese/Japanese cuisine."

The restaurant was empty and dark. A curious odor, raw fish and pesticide combined, waltzed up my nose. The tiny Korean hostess greeted us at the door. "What do you want?" she said.

"Table for three, please," said Leopold with the assurance of an old incarnation who had dined out for many lifetimes.

"We probably won't have time for much," Bill said. "Maybe just drinks and a snack."

"Menus, please," I said.

The menu was ten or fifteen pages long. "You know, I wish I had time to hang out with you guys, but—"

"I'd like to try the ten-course Banquet Special," Leopold said decisively, snapping shut the menu. "It sounds fascinating, don't you think? Seaweed and dried bonito flakes with miso dressing; shrimp egg roll; eel, mackerel and tuna sushi; sweet-and-sour pork; eggplant tempura; chow mein; nabe yaki udon; egg foo yung; salmon sashimi; choice of stewed litchis and pineapple tidbits or bean curd or green-tea ice cream."

I began to feel slightly nauseous. Might I be pregnant, from simply sitting on a seat that was unclean? "I doubt you'll like raw fish," I said. "It's usually an acquired taste, acquired by people who like cocaine."

"I've always wanted to try it," said Leopold wistfully.

"So just get some raw fish!" I said. "Poor old Bill Brinkman is looking kind of weird. Maybe Bill Brinkman can't afford to buy a poor little homeless boy a ten-course banquet."

"It's okay," Bill muttered.

"Aren't you a dear!" I said. "So, I think in that case I'll have the Scorpion cocktail in the skull-shaped mug that can be purchased for an additional $7.95, and following a dozen sweet-and-sour ribs, will move on to Peking Duck with extra pancakes so we can all share?"

"This is a lot of food," said Bill. "Are you guys sure you can eat all this?"

"We can always get anything left over wrapped up to go. Don't you just love those little boxes Chinese food comes in? Bill, you look tragic. I can tell you probably think I go around accosting men all the time, trying to get a free meal. Quite the opposite! Quit thinking that way! In the years to come, you'll regret that thought, for I would find it beneath me to get a free meal from a man. Without sounding arrogant, any normal man would be thrilled to buy me a meal, and would know I was doing him a favor. When we passed in the aisle, as I mentioned before, I felt a wave of something unique, and otherwise I wouldn't have troubled myself with you."

Bill looked slightly less morose. "I can't say I noticed then," Bill said. "But I noticed now. Almost an emanation, which probably doesn't happen when you're on your own, or I'm on my own, but when we come together, it's almost like a really weird force field."

Leopold, drinking from his water glass, started to choke. I gave him a little kick under the table. "Quit kicking," he said.

"It's true, Bill," I said. "What you're saying is true." I swilled my

Scorpion, trying to prevent myself from calling him a stupid idiot, at least until after the bill was paid. He was too dumb to see that *I* had my own force field, but *he* didn't have a force field. What he was noticing—finally—was *my* force field, and trying to take credit for it. I drank some more of my Scorpion. "I like your glasses," I said at last. "I can't help but find a man wearing glasses very sexy."

"I thought you didn't like glasses, Maud," Leopold said.

"I love glasses," I said.

"Then how come you won't wear any?" Leopold said. "You said you hate how people look in glasses, and that's why you didn't want any."

I tilted up my skull-shaped mug for the final sip. "I'd like another of these, if you don't mind."

Bill gestured to the waiter, pointing at my drink. "Tell me," he said. "What is it you and your, ah, brother are doing here?"

"We're on a trip," I said. "You know—traveling."

"Vacation?"

"No," I said. "Life."

"I don't follow."

"A vacation is when you take a break from regular life and do something different. This isn't a break from our life. This is what we do."

"So you just, uh, travel around?"

"Why don't you tell me what *you* do," I said. "You probably just stay in the same place, am I right? Doing . . . don't tell me: let me guess. Are you . . . an Account Executive?"

"No," said Bill.

"Senior Vice President?"

"Noo."

"Junior Vice President?" He shook his head. "Program Director? Business Manager? Director of Sales and Marketing? Financial Analyst?"

"Actually, I'm a dentist."

"Periodontal?" I said. Bill nodded. I put my hand over my coral seas.

"Hey!" said Leopold in disbelief. "What's this?" The waiter had brought over a wooden cutting board on top of which were a number of cubes and lumps of pale pink and gray flesh.

"That's your sashimi!" said Bill. "You dip it in the wasabi and some of that soy sauce."

"Oh, lord!" said Leopold, gagging. "It's not cooked."

"I told you," I said. "What did you think 'raw' meant?"

"Not *this*," said Leopold. "What a rip-off. A restaurant that doesn't even bother to cook the food. Maybe I'll try the Lake Tong Ting Triple Treat instead. Lobster, prawns and scallops in a special egg-white sauce."

Bill looked at his wristwatch. "Kids, I'd love to stay, but I have to get back to my patients."

"Let me get right to the point," I said. "Could you lend me a hundred dollars?" I leaned forward and clutched his hand. "Please don't think me a terrible person. I'm desperate. Until I saw you—and was hit by this *thing*, a passion such as I had never known—I was seriously considering prostituting myself. That was how desperate I was; I would do anything to take care of my little brother."

Bill recoiled, shocked. "You picked me up hoping to get money out of me."

"Oh, no," I said. "As you may remember, I tried to walk away. This *thing* between us was too much to handle. But you insisted on a drink."

"I didn't insist! You are some kind of little con artist."

"Now I know why your wife divorced you," I said. "Poor woman. However. Let's assume that—as you in your paranoid state of hostility toward women are insisting—I really am a con artiste. Isn't this a more interesting afternoon than just putting your groceries away?"

"No," he said sulkily. But he had a flushed look, and leaned forward to take a sip of my Scorpion.

"See?" I said. "You're already starting to exist a bit more."

"What are you talking about?"

"Before, I could have wiped you away with a blackboard eraser. You were practically invisible. But now you're beginning to take on characteristics."

"That's not true!" he said. "I always had characteristics. *You* didn't exist before."

"Wrong," I said. "*You* didn't exist before."

"You tricked me into taking you and your little alleged brother out to lunch, and possibly more, and I say *you're* the one who didn't exist."

"He has a point, Maud," said Leopold.

I glared at Leopold. "If that's how you want it, Bill," I said. "As far as I'm concerned, you're a figment of my imagination; but I'm happy to go along with Figment's own needs."

"Figment!" said Leopold, chuckling to himself. "Figgy. How are ya, Figs?"

"Do you want to tell me about periodontal surgery, Figgy?" I said. "Do you want to tell me about your unhappy marriage?"

"No," he said. "I guess I'd like a drink. I'll have a beer, I guess. I don't usually drink. I gave it up, pretty much. I used to have a little coke problem." He glanced up at me, as if trying to impress me. "So, you were making all that stuff up, about the waves between us?"

"Bill," I said sternly. "I've been almost completely honest from the moment I met you. I'm incapable of lying successfully. Ask my brother. You don't feel something between us?"

He rested his hand on mine for a moment. "How old are you, anyway?"

"Eighteen," I said. Leopold let out a chortle. I squinted at him. "How old are you, Billy?"

"Forty-three," he said. "Why? How old did you think I was?"

"Oh, gosh—not that old!" I said. "So what do you say, Bill. Could you help us out?"

"How much did you want? A hundred dollars?"

"That way my little brother and I could stay in a hotel tonight; I know life is going to look a lot better in the morning, for I've heard people speak of this, though as far as I'm concerned, life usually looks a lot worse in the morning, when you realize you have to get up and it's going to be at least twelve hours before you can respectably go back to bed again. Also, if you wouldn't mind, another forty or fifty or even a hundred on top of that, so we could get gas and have something to eat tomorrow."

"I'm just supposed to give you my money!" he said. "So what's in it for me?"

"Oh Bill, how could you?" I said. "I really thought you were above that sort of statement. I'll pay you back. I'll mail you the money. Or would you prefer some sexual transaction? Poor little Leopold. I guess he could wait outside in the hall." My eyes filled and some hot tears slid down my cheek. "Don't you see, Bill, I'm desperate. I'm only eighteen, and I've never done anything. But I don't see what choice I have, if that's how you want to be."

"No," he said irritatedly. "Here's one-fifty."

"Try to sound more cheerful!" I said. "You know, a good deed never goes unrewarded. You should feel good, doing a good deed." I blew my nose on the napkin.

"I'll come with you to your hotel," he said.

"We have to pick up my brother on the way!"

"You said *this* is your brother."

"Our other brother," I said, taking the money. "Thank you, Bill, thank you!"

Pierce was standing in front of the pizza parlor, a bit grim and definitely Heathcliffish, except I don't think Heathcliff had a pink-and-gray pimpled hairless dog at his side, although it was true I had only seen the movie starring Laurence Olivier, who never really did a thing for me, lacking the animal magnetism that Pierce constantly exuded. He managed to exude it even now. I waved at him from our Corvette. "Who's that?" Bill said.

"That's our brother," I said.

"Yeah, right," Bill said. "You really are some kind of hustler."

"He is!" said Leopold. "He is too our brother."

"We're taking him to Hollywood to be a movie star," I said. "There's only one thing he's missing that those Hollywood movie stars have got."

"What's that?"

"An agent."

"And I'm going to open my own restaurant," said Leopold. "There's only one thing those Hollywood restaurateurs have got that I haven't got."

"What's that?"

"Financial backing!"

"And me, I'm going to get to California and have adventures!" I said.

"Yeah?" said Bill. "And what are you missing?"

"Nothing!" I said. "Except . . ."

"What?"

"Well, my other brother—not the one who's here—says I don't have morals or compassion. But I don't see what good that'll do me, anyway. Having those are kind of a handicap, not an asset."

25

"Cool car," said Pierce, coming over with one hand looped around the dog's collar. Trayf wagged his tail with relief when he saw that Leopold and I were inside. For a dog, he had an extremely expressive tail: he was able to wag it warningly, threateningly, weakly, gleefully, pleadingly and so forth, depending on the situation. It made me kind of wish I had one, though then I might wind up in tricky situations where my face was looking happy but my tail was giving away my true state by hanging down feebly.

Pierce was busy caressing the roof and hood. "Can I have a ride?"

"Sure!" I said. "Bill gave us enough for two nights at the Cross-Creek Hotel Inn, all expenses paid. He'll give you a ride over and I'll drive the Bronco back. Any luck?"

"I'll tell you later," Pierce said grimly.

I hopped out and took the car keys from Pierce. I had Leopold wait in the Bronco with Trayf while I went back into the supermarket and bought dried dog food, three bottles of Nature's Majesty and many snacks. "Which way to the hotel, Leopold?" I said.

"Two blocks on the left, Maud," Leopold said. "Don't turn the wheel while you're backing up!" He screamed. I heard a scraping sound. "Stop, stop!"

"Quit shouting at me!" I said. There was a crunch.

"Um," Leopold said, quieter now.

"Oh, well," I said. "I don't think I caused any major damage. We should probably just keep going."

Pierce and Bill were standing out in front of the Cross-Creek Hotel Inn, fondling Bill's car, talking and laughing like a couple of human beings. "I was just telling your brother, why don't I put the hotel room on my credit card, and that way you can use the cash for other things," Bill said.

"Oh no," I said. "I would feel indebted to you, if you started spending money on me on your credit card. It leaves a nasty paper trail. It would be better for you to give me any extra cash, instead."

He rummaged in his pocket. "Your sister just about wiped me out," he said, giving Pierce a sympathetic, admiring glance. I wondered how Pierce managed to attract so much male admiration; really, in some ways, more than me. Those men who were not frightened or threatened by Pierce took to him instantly; if they could ignore the hoodlum aspect of him they trusted him in a way that nobody trusted me. He was a man's man, as much as a woman's man. Yet men had only to get one glimpse of me and decide I wasn't to be trusted, even if they were mesmerized. "See how nice you're acting to my brother," I pointed out. "Relaxed and comfortable; whereas, with me you acted like a piteous victim, being taken advantage of."

"You could stay at my house, and leave your brothers in the hotel," Bill said.

"Hey!" I said. "You're pressuring me; and just at a time when I'm trying to evolve, struggling up the ladder of becoming a better person. If that's what you want, of course I'll spend the night with you; but it won't be by choice."

"It was just a suggestion," Bill said, sulky. "To let you know I'm not being taken advantage of."

"You don't happen to have any grass?" said Pierce. "I could buy it off you, now that we have some cash."

"Not much," said Bill. "But I'll let you have whatever I've got. If you want to come by the office later I'll tell you what I do have: nitrous oxide. Laughing gas. You want to come over and try that? You can try and figure out why it's idling so fast, at the same time."

"Cool," said Pierce.

"See you in a while!" Leopold called gaily, following me into the hotel lobby.

Brian Trista was still on duty. "Hello," I said. "I'd like my room now, please."

He peered behind me. "Who's this?" he said.

"My brother," I said. "He'll be accompanying us later on our date." Pierce came in behind me, followed by Trayf. "My other brother, and our dog. The dog is sick. You said dogs are allowed; I'm taking him upstairs now, to nurse him."

"What's wrong with him?" said Brian.

"All his fur fell out, just like that," I said. "I hope it's not contagious, but I've heard people can get it from dogs. Pierce! Check the parking lot to see if Bill is still there. I've decided to take advantage of his credit card, after all; if he's already left, give this manger our money."

Our room was on the sixth floor. A sour, stale odor blew from the air conditioner, as if a previous guest had once abandoned a cheese sandwich there to ripen. Trayf jumped onto one of the double beds and began to lick himself with loud slurps and snuffles. He looked sulky and peevish.

Pierce was first to use the shower. Leopold lay on the bed next to Trayf. He folded his hands over his chest. I knew he was pretending to be an Egyptian sarcophagus.

I pulled back the curtains. The room looked onto a vast field of tiny houses. Each house was exactly alike, one story, square, with a lanai leading to a garage. In back of each was a screen gazebo containing a tiny swimming pool. On a patch of lawn was one palm tree, curiously shaved of all except one cluster of fronds. "I don't want to hang out here," I told Leopold's corpse. "This place is psychically debilitating. We have to get to California, before I end up married to a dentist."

Pierce came out of the bathroom, wrapped in a tiny white towel, loincloth style. "Hey, you know what that guy Bill was saying? He could probably help me get a job at the place he takes his Corvette. They do work on all kinds of sports cars—Jaguars, Ferraris, Lotus,

Lamborghini. There's a lot of rich guys down here—doctors for the old people. It might not be a bad place to hang for a few months, while we get our act together."

"Wrong answer!" I said. "And I hope you didn't use up all the towels, because I'm going to wash my hair." I flicked on the television with the remote so I wouldn't be so lonesome. One could expect little in the way of companionship from brothers, who were basically useless. Maybe I could find some kind of educational program; I raced through the channels. It was awful, not being educated. I saw now I knew nothing about fine dining, such as how to use chopsticks. I knew nothing about the history of motion pictures—let alone current and recent releases. I needed help, and maybe some of it would rub off on Pierce and Leopold. How would I be able to carry on a conversation of any merit when we reached California? They would all laugh at me when they realized I didn't know the difference between sushi and sashimi and the various directors.

"Hey!" said Pierce. "Could you slow down? I wouldn't mind watching some of that golf. What is it, the Senior Tournament of Stars?"

"What happened to you, anyway, while Leopold and I were selling ourselves to the dentist?" I said, changing the channel to a program about alien abductions. We watched for a moment, coral seas open.

"Those aliens are really sick," said Leopold, propping himself up on pillows as he got more comfortable.

"I don't want to hang out here," I said. "This place is psychically debilitating."

"Look at this!" He reached into his pocket and took out two twenties and a ten.

"Wow!" I said. "Not bad! Who gave it to you?"

"It was just like you said. I hung around and got a slice of pizza, then I brought out a slice for Trayf."

"What kind of pizza did you have?" Leopold said.

"A plain slice," Pierce said.

"That's kind of boring," Leopold said. "How was it?"

"Not too bad," he said. "I'm still hungry, though. Did you guys get any food?"

"Oh, no!" said Leopold. "I left the salami and smoked salmon and the other stuff under his seat!"

"Don't mention it," I suggested. "Anyway, I bought a few things. Taco chips, salsa, crackers, Cheez Whiz."

"Anything sweet?"

"Twinkies and Sugar Pops."

"Sugar Pops!" Pierce said. He rummaged through the grocery bags until he found the cereal box. "So this guy comes along, starts talking about the dog and gives me fifty bucks."

"What kind of guy?" I said.

"I don't know. A guy with some kind of accent, I think."

"How old was he?"

"I don't know. Middle-aged? I think he was some kind of foreigner. When I told him I was traveling with my sister and little brother, and we were broke, he gave me fifty dollars. He said he hadn't seen a dog like this since he was a child in his village."

"And he didn't want to give you a moofty-poofty?"

"He didn't seem to."

"Boy, we must be under some kind of lucky star," I said. "Maybe the others—or Theodore, anyway—are directing psychic energy at us, to force people to give us money. Are you sure he didn't maybe give you a moofty-poofty and you're just too embarrassed to tell us?"

"Huh?" Pierce said, fixated on the TV.

"Never mind," I said. "Gosh, I'm hungry. Somebody give me a Yodel. Or did I get Ring Dings? Either way." I tore open a packet and munched the artificial chocolate goo. Never had a chemical substance tasted so delicious. "Remember that divine dish you once invented, Leopold?"

"The one that wasn't supposed to have any calories?"

"No, not that one."

"The one with the eggs?"

"No."

"I thought you liked the one with the eggs."

"I did! But that's not the one I mean. I'm thinking now of the dish utilizing garlic."

"Oh, yeah!" he said happily. "That was good, wasn't it? Except, I remember, nobody would play with me at the Audubon Society day camp. I wonder if we'll ever be someplace where I can cook again."

"Poor old Leopold," said Pierce. "This is no life for a kid, huh?"

"I wonder if I can remember how to do the thing with garlic," said Leopold. "The other thing—with the strawberries and garlic—that sure wasn't a success!"

"Every experiment can't be a success," I said. "So tell us, Pierce—what really happened?"

"I told you!" Pierce said.

"Honestly, now. This guy—I bet he wanted something for giving you fifty dollars."

"No," said Pierce. "Oh, wait, there was one thing."

"What?"

"When I'm a big star, he wants to come and visit me on the set."

"Yeah?"

"I told him, that's cool," said Pierce. "He can come and visit me on the set. Maybe he was a Chinese guy."

"Surely you'd know if he was a Chinese guy?"

"I wasn't paying attention. Maybe he was a black guy. He told me where he was from. I think he said he was from Trinidad."

They stayed up all night watching TV and at three o'clock the next afternoon were still asleep. I went out with the dog three times—making a lap around the parking lot—and on my own twice: once I bought a local newspaper from a machine, and another time I crossed the highway, but finding nothing different there, I came back.

This time Brian Trista, "Assistant Manger," was on duty again at the front desk. "What happened?" he said. "I thought you were going to go out with me last night."

"Yeah? The deal was, I'd go out with you if you'd let us stay for free and I'd pay you today. Instead, I had to go and hustle and humiliate myself with a dentist to get money."

He ignored this. "So. Traveling with your boyfriend?" he said.

"My brothers," I said.

"Oh yeah?" he said. "Planning to be in the greater Fort Lauderdale region long?"

"I'm glad you think it's so terrific," I said. "But it's really none of your business."

"Wait!" he said. "I could help, if you're going to be here awhile. Maybe I could put in a word with my manager and you could get a job here."

"I don't think that's quite what I had in mind for myself," I said, and went back upstairs.

Even when I slammed the door and tried to open the window to let in some fresh air, which I couldn't, Pierce and Leopold—who were sharing one of the beds—didn't wake up. I was restless. Rummaging around, I found a Bible in a drawer, and flipped it open. I had never really spent much time with a Bible before, finding it to be very thick and too long in appearance. There I read the following: "The LORD is long suffering, and of great mercy, forgiving iniquity and transgression, and by no means clearing the guilty, visiting the iniquity of the fathers upon the children unto the third and fourth generation."

This made me extremely nervous. It wasn't bad enough that my mother had picked up a waiter in an Eastern European restaurant whose only aspiration was to torture diners by playing the violin, but according to this book, I was going to be punished for something this guy's grandfather had done. No wonder my life had been so tough.

Now that I was away from my old life, I was able to look back on it and see how truly happy I had been, even though I hadn't felt that way at the time. The nights we all sat around the table, eating tuna-fish sandwiches and getting spots on the pages of our library books, none of us speaking to anybody else, just silently turning the pages of educational material on subjects such as how to improve one's psychic ability, memoirs from the last functioning leper colony, recovering from a brain tumor and accounts of cannibalism. That had been bliss.

I took a shower and washed my underpants in shampoo, sobbing to myself as I remembered the old days and tried to adjust the taps, which one minute blasted freezing-cold and the next scalding, no matter what I did. For some reason I had an ill-conceived idea that Fred would somehow manage to track me down and rescue me from this situation, although I knew that was impossible, since he had not yet made detective grade on the police force.

Pierce and Leopold woke around four. Leopold went to the toilet. Pierce sat up, rubbing his crotch. "Where are we?" he said.

"I don't know where you are," I said. "*I'm* in Fort Lauderdale, because you were too stupid to read the road signs." I got back into bed, snuffling. As soon as Leopold came out of the bathroom, Pierce went in, slamming the door. Just then the phone rang. Nobody knew we were here, unless Fred had found us after all. I quickly picked it up.

"Hi! This is Bill Brinkman. Is this Maud?"

"Yeah," I said. "What do you want?"

"I was going to come and get you and take you out to dinner tonight, remember?"

"Either you thought you asked me but in fact you have trouble communicating with women, and never bothered to actually invite me, or you did ask me but I wasn't even listening. Which do you think it is?"

"You weren't listening? But you said okay, I thought."

"Whatever. Of course, I'll bring my brothers. I do remember you invited us to your office, to ply us with drugs."

"Well, ah, sure," Bill said. "Right. Where did you want to go. Ideas?"

"I want to go to the Weeki-Wacki Lounge," I said.

"What?"

"Don't you know it? How long have you lived here? It's a Polynesian restaurant with a nightly floor show and the flavor of the South Pacific."

"Yippee!" said Leopold, who had been listening intently while rubbing Trayf's belly.

"Oh," Bill said. "I think that might be . . . kind of a tourist place."

"It's a tourist place, Leopold," I said.

"I don't care!" Leopold said.

"He doesn't care, Bill," I said.

"Would it be genuine Polynesian food?" Leopold said.

"Would the food be genuine Polynesian food, Bill?" I said. "Leopold's interested in trying different cuisines."

"There's a kind of nice little Italian place—"

"Oh, we want something special!" I said. "What about this Medieval Feast and Nightly Tournament I saw advertised? Leopold, how would you like to try medieval food?"

"Where did you see this place?" said Bill.

"In a brochure about the Fort Lauderdale area. Who cares if it's touristy. I'm a tourist! Besides, it's set in an authentic replica of a Spanish castle. I've never been to a Spanish castle. If it's authentic, that should be like the real thing."

"I tell you what," Bill said. "Why don't you kids meet me at my office, and then we can decide. Maybe your brothers will just want to go to Bubba's Bar-B-Que and play pool, and you and me can go off on our own."

"Bill," I said softly. "There's just one thing."

"What?"

"I don't have anything to wear. Only the filthy, out-of-style, last-season's clothing I have on. I don't want to embarrass you in public. Might there be some way you could provide me with a new outfit?"

There was a pause. "I guess so," he said miserably.

"Well, sound cheerful, you old tightwad," I said, and hung up. "Is it that dentists are anal-retentive regarding money?" I asked Leopold.

"I could use a new outfit for evening wear," Leopold said.

"I didn't want to put too much pressure on him at once," I explained, feeling guilty. "He's not the most generous of souls. I suppose, extracting teeth all day, he can't bear to have anything extracted from himself. Pierce!" I shouted at the bathroom. "Hurry up in there! We have to go. We're meeting Bill Brinkman in his office. If we hurry, maybe you can seduce his hygienist into cleaning your teeth." There was no response. "Pierce!" I said. "Answer me! Did you get drugs somewhere when I wasn't looking and have now overdosed in the bathroom, blood spattered everywhere, like in the movies?"

"I'm not coming out until you apologize," he said.

"For what?" I said.

"I don't remember," he said.

"In that case, I'm sorry," I said.

He came out of the bathroom. "God damn it, you treat me like an animal," he said. "You treat me worse than I've seen you treat spiders. Why don't you go to Hollywood by yourself and see how far you get. I'll stay here and work as a mechanic."

"No, Pierce, no!" I screamed. Leopold let out a shriek, too.

"Please don't stay here in Fort Lauderdale and work as a mechanic!" Leopold sobbed. "Please, Pierce!"

"You *have* to come to Hollywood and be a movie star!" I said. "How will we get there without you? On whose back will I be able to social-climb? What excuse will I have to be there?"

"Yeah?" Pierce said disdainfully. "Then you better act a whole lot nicer to me. *I* can survive anywhere: I could be a mechanic, drug dealer, welder, play the electric guitar in a band, you name it. You can't even *see* without me."

I sighed. "Let's go," I said.

"What about Trayf?"

"We'll leave him with the little manger at the front desk."

"Yeah?" said Pierce. "You think he'll mind?"

Brian looked stricken, but he let the dog hide under the reception desk. "If my boss comes in here and sees him, I'm screwed," he said.

"He won't make a sound. I guarantee," I said. "If we leave him in the room, he'll howl. He's frightened, poor boy. He's not used to staying in hotels. Just keep him hidden. Don't let him get near any guests." While I was chatting I watched Trayf sniff, then lift his leg against the side of the check-in desk.

Luckily Brian was distracted. "What time do you think you'll be back?" he said.

"Not late," I said. "We're just going to get high, probably, and go out to dinner, then hopefully our host will drink too much and pass out early."

"I have tomorrow night off," he said. "I switched, so maybe we could go catch a movie or something."

"That would be wonderful, Brian," I said. "Watch the dog."

"I thought you wanted to leave tomorrow," said Pierce in the parking lot.

"I didn't want to cut off all his hope entirely," I said. "Besides, if for some reason we're still here tomorrow, then we already have an entertainment plan established. He can take us all to the movies. I haven't been to the movies in ages."

Pierce unlocked the passenger door and I got in. Leopold climbed on my lap. "Oh, God," Pierce said, going around to his side of the car. "Is this any way to live?"

"What do you mean, Pierce?" said Leopold.

"You know—going from one day to the next."

"Do you have any better suggestion?" I said.

"Better than what?" Pierce said.

"Better than going from one day to the next."

"I'm not following you," said Pierce.

"Never mind," I said. "Just forget the whole thing. Let's go visit the dentist."

Bill's office was located nearby, on the third floor of a bank building. "This is my receptionist, Bethany," he said. "You were just leaving, weren't you, Bethany? I'll lock up tonight."

Bethany looked as if someone had taken a round, featureless head and photographically imposed facial attributes on it. I had the peculiar sensation of seeing a cut-out face from a magazine, with round blue eyes, snub nose and long dyed hair, walking and talking, but still one-dimensional. Pretty, but there was nothing to hang on to to remember her by. She brought her own amnesia with her, like Typhoid Mary, to inflict on others. Probably she was one of those people who remembered everyone, and anyone who saw her was embarrassed, unable to figure out who she was, or that they had met her while trapped beneath her in a dentist's chair.

"I thought you said we could get our teeth cleaned, free of charge," I said.

"I did?" Bill said.

"It must be all those drinks you had yesterday at lunch."

"I didn't!" said Bill. "I have no memory of saying anything of the sort. However . . . Bethany, do you mind terribly?"

"She can clean Pierce's teeth while you take me shopping, Bill," I said. "I assume that your receptionist and hygienist are one and the same, alternating two jobs yet receiving the salary of one?"

"She's both," said Bill unhappily. "With the divorce I can't afford to hire anybody else just now."

"I trained as a hygienist," said Bethany. She was staring at Pierce. "Golly, you look familiar," she said. "Are you on TV?"

"Poor Bethany," I said. "You must be overworked. But look—" I went over to Pierce and pulled apart his coral seas. "You don't mind staying late to help him, do you?"

She looked down demurely. "No," she said.

"Good," I said. "We'll leave Leopold behind as chaperone, or beard. In fact, why don't you clean Leopold's teeth, and then Pierce's. So, Bill, let us be off."

Bill unlocked his Corvette. "Gee, Bill," I said. "What's with your car? Something stinks."

"I can't figure it out," he said. "I had the baby last weekend, but I didn't notice anything then. I'm wondering if he didn't do something and hide it."

"Do you feed your child a lot of garlic? Or fish?"

He drove me to a nearby department store called "$20 Or Less." "This is great!" I said. "I'm not lying to you when I say that previously I've only shopped at the Salvation Army Thrift Store, church bazaars and yard sales where somebody died."

In the dressing room I changed into black fishnet stockings, a red vinyl miniskirt, a striped T-shirt and a pair of black-and-white polka-dot high heels made in China from all-man-made materials. "I'd like to wear this now," I said, staggering out of the dressing room to where Bill was hiding behind a sale rack. I gave him a wink. "How do I look?"

"Um," he said, speechless with admiration.

"Billy, let me just pick out a few other teeny tiny things," I said. I put some underpants in a pile. "Look at these," I said. "Aren't they darling? It says they light up in the dark. That could be useful, if I'm in a car accident at night, or with a group of men who need to separate me from the herd."

Since he didn't seem to be able to speak, I took this as a sign he didn't object, and I grabbed a few more T-shirts, hoping some of them were small enough to fit Leopold, and an on-sale item that was maybe a grass skirt. The bill came to a hundred and twenty dollars. "Whoops!" I said, shocked by how much I had spent. "Sorry, Bill. Can you afford it? Oh, look at that pink woolly sweater with pom-poms. It's only fifteen dollars. I'll just tuck that in my pile."

He looked fairly sick but paid. I was sad to have had to rush through the whole experience. There was some jewelry on sale, too, but I didn't want to press my luck. I fingered a bracelet made of candy-colored plastic cubes and eyed Bill, but he ignored me. Perhaps someday all this would come naturally to me, and I wouldn't feel humiliated by the procedure. I gave him my bags to carry as we exited. Unfortunately the store alarm went off. "Did you drop something in one of the bags by accident?" I said.

"I don't know what this is doing in here," he said, taking out a pair of yellow stretch-satin hot pants. "Maybe fell in the bag by mistake?" He handed it to the security guard, sheepishly. Fortunately for Bill, being a middle-aged man and professional in appearance, he was not arrested, nor even hauled in for questioning, which most definitely would have happened to me.

"You have been so good to me," I said, clutching his arm. "Look, there's the Giant's Drug Store, next door. Please let me go in there and pick up a few things. It's pathetic, to have to beg you and beg you. Just think of how terrible it must make me feel. Someday I hope you'll come and visit me in my Beverly Hills mansion, sweetie. You can stay in the cabana, when my rich husband is out of town. Then you'll look back, and realize I was a desirable commodity, which I'm not all that sure you appreciate now."

I got some lipsticks—red, frosted pink, tangerine and nude; a violet mascara; pink, blue, purple and green eye shadows; a bottle of aspirin for Pierce; and tried to get some toothbrushes and toothpaste. "I can give you those for free in the office," Bill said sullenly.

In the car I put on the red lipstick. "How do I look?" I said, unrolling the window. "Let's get some fresh air in here. It smells like a fish died, and selected your car for its mausoleum. You don't think your ex-wife threw a dead fish in here to get even, do you?"

"Maybe," Bill said. "It hadn't occurred to me."

"Does she still have the keys?"

"Actually, she probably still has an extra set. She took a lot of stuff I've been trying to get back from her. We're only separated, though, not divorced yet."

"It's awfully hard for me to think about going out with a married man," I said. "Where did you say you attended dental school?"

Leopold was sitting in the reception area, leafing through a magazine. "She's cleaning his teeth and they won't let me in," he said soulfully. "I'm locked out!"

"How awful!" I said. I went and listened at the door. I could hear no whir of the toothbrush. "Are you in there?" I said.

"Not quite finished!" said Bethany after a pause. Her voice was muffled.

"I'd like to take a look when you're through!" Bill said. He turned to me. "If you stayed in town longer, I could fill his cavities. You think he'd be interested in caps?"

"Tell me, Bill, do you screw your receptionist?" I said. "I mean, hygienist?"

He didn't respond but scuttled down the hall, followed by Leopold. "Have you ever been bitten, Bill?" Leopold said, racing to keep up. "By a patient?"

"Once or twice," he said.

"And do you follow any sports?" Leopold said, tugging Bill's ugly tan jacket.

"I like basketball," he said.

"Oh, so do I!" Leopold said endearingly.

"What do you think they're doing in there?" Bill said, unlocking the door to the other torture chamber.

"It doesn't seem to me you have much in the way of values, Bill," I said.

"What do you mean?"

"I mean, no wonder your marriage didn't last! Screwing your hygienist, picking up women in the parking lot and taking them shopping for new clothes, giving nitrous oxide to little kids . . ."

He wheeled and faced me furiously. "I only slept with her once! It was a mistake, okay? And I have no intentions of giving your little brother laughing gas."

"Oh, why not?" I said. "I don't see what harm it can do. The poor little homeless child could use a good laugh, having to sit in your freezing cold waiting room and read magazines that I suspect are years out of date."

"I can't adjust the temperature," Bill said. "It's controlled for the whole building."

"You don't have to act so mad about it! I'm just trying to figure you out, that's all. You . . . ah, you fascinate me."

"I do?" he said, calming down. "So you want to try the nitrous oxide, or what? Might as well, while we're waiting."

"Will it make me laugh?" I said. "Because I don't think I want to laugh, involuntarily. Not when nothing's funny. To me, laughing is very personal. Laughing in public, and shaking hands, seem like they should be done in private. Of course, I've never had sex, but laughing and shaking hands, are, to me, a form of public sex. Put it this way: when you shake hands, you put a sensitive part of your anatomy into a part of someone else's anatomy—and it's usually that of a complete stranger! How awful! How horrible! Might be limp—or damp—or brutal. Ugh. And laughing—wouldn't you agree that that's a state of vulnerability that's no different from, say, ejaculation?"

"Don't worry, Maud," said Leopold. "I was asking Bethany about it. She says the laughing gas only lasts for a few minutes, and it's fun. Then right after, you get a headache and feel depressed."

"How marvelous," I said. "Would it mix well with alcohol? Might you have a little champers? Preferably sweet."

"I might have a little grain alcohol," Bill said. "It came by mistake with my last shipment from the supply house. It was supposed to be ethyl."

"I guess you could give me some in one of those mouth-rinsing cups," I said. "Oh, Bill, Bill, what's going to become of me? What am I doing here, in Fort Lauderdale, with a dentist?"

Bill ignored this. "Just hold this mask over your face and breathe in," he said, rolling a large canister out of the closet. "I'll go first, to show you."

"Aren't you even remotely interested in me?" I said. "Where I came from? How I grew up? My hopes, needs, wishes, dreams, goals, desires?"

Bill turned a valve on the top of the canister and inhaled deeply. Leopold lay down in the dental chair and began to fiddle with the controls. The chair became flat and then went upright again. Bill held his breath, and finally exhaling, he gave me a fiendish grin. "I know this is going to sound weird," he said. "But I think I'm in love with you." He laughed uproariously. "God are you weird."

"You've overused that word," I said. "I don't consider that statement to be a declaration of love."

"You are pretty weird," he said. "And I wasn't planning to get involved with anyone again for a long time, except casually. But this is pretty weird. I don't feel like I have a choice. As soon as I met you, I realized I might be in trouble."

"I'm not complaining," I said. "I really am thrilled with my new clothes—but was that the finest shop in the greater Fort Lauderdale region?"

"Aren't you going to try this?" he said, tilting the mask in my direction. I put it over my snout and he turned up the valve. I was filled with an icy blue sensation. All the molecules in the room seemed to swell up, expand to a million times their former size, go white-blue and then collapse.

When I put down the mask everything was wonky. Bill looked like a hideous praying mantis, only stubbier. His eyes protruded behind his glasses, watery and glassy. "Some might think the praying mantis bears a resemblance to grasshoppers," I said. "But their large egg packets, which look like puff pastry, show they are far closer to the cockroach. Did you know they are capable of killing lizards, birds and frogs? I'm not making this up!" I grabbed Bill by the lapels. "The praying mantis eats its prey alive. Unless the front legs of the female are tied before she is introduced to the male, she'll eat him immediately. Also, she's insatiable. Even after her eggs are fertilized, she'll accept more males: first for sex, and then for lunch."

"Liar!" Bill said gleefully. In what appeared to be slow motion he wrapped his appendages around me. They no longer even looked like human arms.

"Help!" I said. "Help me, Leopold!"

"I can't get this chair to go back up," Leopold muttered, basically ignoring me.

To end up in this fashion, trapped by a half-human insect in a dentist's office! His coral seas were coming toward me. I tried to scream, but nothing came out. He attached his mouth organ to mine. I regained some measure of calm and managed to push him away. "Do you have any Listerine?" I said.

"Why?" he said alarmed. "Do I have bad breath?"

"*I* might have bad breath," I said. "Or you."

"You don't have bad breath," he said.

"So that only leaves one of us," I said. "Anyway, it's not really a very nice thing to do, is it."

"What?" he said.

"Putting two mouths together like that. One often wonders how dentists can kiss, after a day's labor. Knowing what's gone on in there. Images of plaque, tartar, gingivitis springing forth."

Bill slumped wearily on the edge of the chair. "Hey!" said Leopold. "Get off! You're crushing me!" Either Bill or Leopold had pressed the button and the chair went back into an upright position. "Let me out of here!" said Leopold, scrambling free.

"Why don't you come and sit on my lap?" Bill suggested. Apparently of its own accord, the chair went down with Bill now lying on it.

Pierce came into the office. He looked kind of smirky; he was followed by Bethany. "I'm going to come with you!" she said. "I know it's kind of dramatic, but I'm like that."

"No, you're not," I muttered.

"Hey, what's that?" Pierce said. "Oh, it's the nitrous oxide. Cool.

What do you do, just turn this little wheel?" He put the mask over his face and inhaled. "Cool stuff, man," he said between clenched teeth. He passed the mask over to me. Although I hadn't found the experience very pleasant the first time, I inhaled again. I handed the mask back to Pierce. Distracted, he put it down on the counter, not bothering to turn off the dial, so the gas continued to pour from the tank with a constant *sssssshhhhhh* sound, as if we were making too much noise and it wanted us to be quiet.

"I wouldn't normally do this," said Bethany, picking up the mask, "but I want to be in the same mental state as you guys."

"I'm going to tie that dentist to his chair," I said.

Leopold started guffawing. "That's kind of funny!" he said, taking the mask from Bethany. "Let's tie him up!"

"Good idea," said Pierce. "Let's get even for all the times a dentist has ever tortured us."

27

"You've hardly ever been to the dentist, Pierce," I said. "You're just lucky there was some kind of pesticide in the local water supply that gave us all white teeth and no cavities."

"A pesticide?" said Bill, reclining in the chair, his eyes half-closed.

Bethany took the mask from Leopold and put it over Bill's coral seas. "Do you want me to get some rope, Pierce?" Bethany said. "This is like out of the movies, isn't it, one of those Helter-Skelter things." She was doing odd things with her coral seas and jaw, clenching and unclenching her teeth. "Are we going to rob him, too, Pierce?"

"Stupid slut," I said. "Do you think he's just going to sit there while we tie him up and rob him?" But Bill had shut his eyes and lay in the chair quite passively. Either he was only partly conscious, or he was looking forward to being tied up. "Actually, now that I think about it," I said, "Mother always said that many doctors and important businessmen like to take the passive role in sex, because they've had to be such control freaks all day. She said once I would make a good dominatrix, but my brother Theodore, who's very smart, didn't feel I would be such a success."

"I'll go look for the rope, guys!" said Bethany, as if we were all on the same cheerleading team.

"Let's see how your teeth look," I said to Pierce. He opened his coral seas. "Nice and white," I said. "Almost perfect. I'm not sure you need it, but later you can think about getting them capped."

"What do you mean, capped?" Pierce said, inhaling.

"Movie stars all have capped teeth!" I said.

"Little caps on teeth?" Pierce said. "I never noticed that."

"Because the caps look just like teeth!" I said. "Do you think Bill is dead? Maybe the nitrous oxide had a bad effect on him."

"You think?" Leopold said, giggling. "It sounds like he's still breathing. Unless that's the chair." He pressed the button on the chair's arm, but instead of returning to its upright position it continued to go down, until Bill was bending backward.

"Please don't hurt me any more," Bill whispered.

"He's not dead," said Leopold. "But I think the chair is broken."

Bill tried to sit up, but, bent backward almost in two, he no longer seemed to have the strength. Finally he squirmed upright and gestured for Pierce to pass the mask. Then he lay back down. "Please make love with me, Maud," he said. "Can't you see how much I want you?"

"This guy's got a stiff mashie niblick," Pierce said.

"I didn't do anything to encourage him!" I said.

"I'm sick of my life," Bill moaned, shutting his eyes again. "I don't know how I ever got into all this garbage, sweetie—alimony payments, a private practice, a kid, a Corvette. I'll come with you guys too."

"No, you won't!" I said, stamping my foot.

Bethany returned. "This is all I could find," she said in a squeaky, happy voice, holding up a tangle of rubber hose.

"What are we tying him up for?" Pierce said. "I can't remember."

"I can't remember either," I said. "Let's get out of here. Say, Bill, could we borrow your car? For a while?"

"Cool," said Pierce. "Good idea."

"You said I could come with you!" Bethany said peevishly.

"Pierce, did you tell Bethany she could come with us?" I said.

"I don't remember." Pierce shrugged.

"Have some more nitrous oxide, Bethany," I said, clamping the mask over her perky face. Inhaling, she backed away and began to laugh.

"I know you said I could come!" she said, laughing even more. Pierce joined in.

"You two certainly seem to be having a good time," I said bitterly.

"Shoot!" Bethany said. "This is like a dream for me! A cross-country trek, Hollywood—there'll be rough times ahead as we make the climb to the top, but that will be part of the fun, won't it, Pierce? Then we can have a house in Brentwood, and probably I'll be asked to model in *Playboy*, I'll go shopping on Rodeo Drive, and attend premieres with my movie-star husband who gets ten million dollars a picture! I see him as the action-adventure type, don't you, Maud?"

"What pathetic dreams!" I said. "Dreams fit for a moron."

"Hey, Maud," said Pierce. "Are your dreams so special?"

I looked at him with contempt verging on hatred. How disloyal could anyone be! He was right, though. My dreams were also pretty pathetic. I couldn't even remember what they were. "Oh, gosh, now I'm depressed," I said. "It's just that, Bethany, I don't feel you were looking at the other half of the picture: the decline. The expensive clothes, out of date only six months later; the hideous, lavish, ostentatious, tasteless house, maintained by poverty-stricken Mexican servants who hate you; the movie-star husband's hundred-and-fifty-million-dollar-over-budget flop movie; the spoiled, stupid, nasty, unhappy children; the movie star, now forty, no longer in demand, screwing every blond bimbo he lays eyes on; you, desperate, looking for a new man in a market where men only want a twenty-year-old; and finally, California falling into the ocean."

"Let me find that grain alcohol for you," Bill said. "I never got you your drink, did I?"

He got out of the chair. The mood in the room had suddenly become bleak, though maybe it was the building's air-temperature control having a nervous breakdown. Bethany sat on the edge of the chair-ride. "So you think it's a pathetic dream," she said, putting her head in her hands. "Would you tell me, please, what a better dream might be? All I want is to have something that other people want."

"But then, you don't really want it, you just want other people to be envious and jealous of you," I said.

"Yeah?" said Bethany. "So?"

"I can't remember if I told Bethany if she could come with us or not," Pierce said.

"How will you be able to get any pleasure from something you don't really care about one way or the other?" I said. "You have to sit around, waiting to derive pleasure from other people being jealous of what you have. There can't be people sitting around feeling jealous of you every second."

"I didn't buy a Corvette to make other people jealous of me," Bill said. "I bought it because it's a beautiful piece of equipment. It's like an art object." He passed around tiny paper cups filled with clear liquid.

"Of course you did!" I said sarcastically. "Bethany, fetch me two pieces of paper and a pen." She opened a drawer and handed me a pad printed with a picture of a decayed tooth and a pen, one end of which was a toothbrush. I scribbled on the paper as I gargled. "This certainly is strong stuff," I said. "Though I suspect a certain amount of my feeling has been numbed from the nitrous oxide."

"It's two hundred proof!" said Bill. "Of course I did what?"

"What?" I said.

"You said, 'Of course you did.' " He waved his feelers.

"Oh," I said, mesmerized at his apparently permanent state of insect-hood. "You bought a Corvette to make other people jealous." Bill was a bit too fuzzy to respond. He sat down on the edge of the chair next to Bethany and I now clambered onto his lap. I nuzzled his cheek. "Of course, having that Corvette does make you extremely sexy," I said. "Here, sign these two pages—on the line I marked with X at the bottom."

"I did not buy a Corvette to make other people jealous!" Bill said in an incredibly slow voice, scribbling.

"Did too!" I said. "You can't drive more than fifty-five miles an hour, even if it does go faster."

"Okay, hypothetical situation," said Bill. "What if I bought a beautiful painting, and it cost a lot of money. Why would I do that?"

"To make other people jealous!" I said. "To announce that you have a lot of money."

"But what if I bought it because it was a beautiful work of art, and I found it very moving."

"But that's not why you'd be buying it," I said. "Because you can't sit around all day looking at a painting. The first day you owned it you might sit and look at it. But after a few days, it wouldn't have the same impact and that's when you'd have to start inviting your friends over hoping they'd admire it, so you could get secondary gratification. Then you'd begin to worry whether your investment was going up in value or declining, which would turn out to be the reason why you bought it in the first place. I'm not explaining this very well."

"I get it, I think!" said Pierce, guffawing as if I had just told a joke.

"I'm bored," said Leopold. "When are we going?" He had found a dental pick and was using it to pull up strands of the carpet.

"What if I buy a big house," Bill said. "For you and me to live in."

"You can only be in one room at a time," I said. "Anybody who buys a big house is only doing it to impress other people. If only Theodore were here! He'd be able to explain this to you!"

"But isn't it nice, if you have the money, to live in a nice place and surround yourself with nice things?" Bethany said, puzzled.

"These are external things that don't provide real inner happiness," I said. "After five minutes you see someone has a bigger house, and your nice things start looking tacky. On the other hand, you have a point."

"Then why can't I have a dream of living in Brentwood with your movie-star brother!"

"I don't want to enter into a dialogue with you," I said. "You can keep your dream; but you're not coming to California with us, and that's all there is to it."

"Pierce!" Bethany said with a whine. We both looked at my brother.

"You guys will have to work it out," he said, finishing his cup of alcohol. "I don't care one way or the other."

"See, Bethany?" I said. "This is what you're up against. He doesn't care *one way or the other*. He's completely indifferent to almost everything, except food and getting high. That's why he's going to be famous. You can never truly capture his soul."

I rose regally, followed by Bill, who staggered across the room and for some reason known only to himself, opened a pair of louvered cabinet doors and crawled in. Bethany began to cry. Looking at her sobbing over something as silly as my brother made me burst into laughter.

"Is that true, Pierce?" Bethany said. "You don't care one way or the other?" Pierce didn't respond. He poured himself another cup of grain alcohol. "You're mocking me, Maud," Bethany said, between sobs. "You think you're something special, because your heart's never been broken, but you're not. I'll show you!"

"Hey!" said Pierce, suddenly reentering our plane of existence. "I don't think that's a very nice way to talk to my sister."

"That reminds me of a song!" Leopold said suddenly. He leapt up, and began to sing in his lovely, quavery little voice. " *'My mother was a lady / Like yours, you will allow / And she may have a daughter / Who needs protection now.'* "

There was a pause. "Bravo! Bravo!" I said, applauding.

"I am nice, Pierce," Bethany said, sobbing. "It's just that your sister has made me mean. What gives her the right to think she's so much better than other people?"

"Please don't go," Bill said from his cabinet. "We can go to the Weeki-Wacki Lounge or the Medieval Torment or whatever you want."

"Oh, please say we can go to the Medieval Feast and Torment," Leopold said. "They'll serve marchpane comfits, mead, pickled meats and a lot of other things I've always wanted to try, to the music of a consort of sackbut, harp, fife and violette."

There was a silence. "What?" I said.

"Those are some medieval foods," Leopold explained. "I read it in the *History of Food* at the library. Some pages were missing, though."

"What's a sackbut?" said Pierce.

"It's a medieval trumpet, or trombone, or something!" I said. "Leopold, I'm impressed with your knowledge, but I have a feeling this place probably serves barbecued chicken and ribs. I don't think it will be quite as authentic as you think. Say, Bill, could you lend me some more money? I'll be certain to pay you back."

"My wallet's over there," Bill groaned. "I'm afraid to come out from the cabinet. Please don't say you're going away. Tell me you'll come back."

As the doors to the cabinet were similar to shutters, I felt there would be plenty of air, and I tied the knobs together using the rubber hose, leaving Bill contentedly inside. He seemed to find the darkness soothing. Bethany lay on the floor, sobbing. "Don't get up, Bethany," I said. "By the way, Bill, I'm not really eighteen."

"I knew it," Bill said. "You seem much older."

"I'm nineteen," I said. I took fifty dollars and Bill's keys from his wallet, and handed Bethany one of the pieces of paper Bill had previously signed, as we left.

"So what do you want to do now?" Pierce said.

"Bill said we could borrow his car," I said. "He wrote it down on this slip of paper. Anyway, he signed it. Get in and start driving, before he changes his mind."

"What?" Pierce said. "He's lending us his new Corvette? Cool."

We got in. The car reeked of fish and garlic. "Boy, it stinks in here," Leopold said. "I think his kid must have pooped a long time ago. Unless . . ." He ducked down and removed something from under the seat. "Phew! Should I keep it, or throw it out?"

"So what are we going to do?" Pierce said.

"Throw it out. I've had it with Fort Lauderdale," I said. "At least I didn't have to lose my purity to finance your career. Let's get out of here."

We headed back to the hotel to pick up Trayf. "He was kind of cute, though, wasn't he?" I said.

"What?" Pierce said.

"Bill," I said. Pierce and Leopold laughed uproariously.

"You should get glasses, Maud," Leopold said.

"Whatever," I said.

"I thought you didn't like him," Pierce said.

"He bought me all these clothes," I said. "You guys didn't even notice. I suppose that's proof of your heterosexuality. And I took fifty dollars from his wallet. Maybe we should have hung around until he bleached my teeth?"

"Your teeth are very white, Maud," Leopold said.

"Oh well," I said. "It wasn't his fault that I was already in love with someone else."

"Who are you in love with?" Pierce said. "I forget."

28

Brian was standing in front of the Cross-Creek Hotel Inn with Trayf, looking very excited. "Can you believe it, the friggin' manager came by and fired me!" he said. "I can't believe it! This is dastardly, man!"

Trayf broke loose from Brian and came bounding over to the car. He put his paws up on my side of the Corvette and tried to lick my elbow, leaning in through the window. "How terrible! Poor Brian!" I said. "How come?"

"Because, like I said, I'm not supposed to keep a dog at the desk like that. Cool car. You guys hijack it, or what?" He came over to the window to look. "Phew!" he said. "Did one of you guys, like, make a doody in your pants or something?"

I opened the door to let in Trayf. "See you around, Brian!" I said.

"What about my underpants?" Leopold said. "They're up in the room. I washed them. And all those food snacks."

"You can wear mine," I said. "I got some new ones. Glow-in-the-dark. Let's get going."

"No, wait!" Brian said. "Can't I come with you guys? I never wanted to be assistant manager of a friggin' hotel. I wanted to be an astronaut. But they won't even let you into the program unless you're, like, some kind of nuclear physicist, man."

"What's with Trayf?" said Leopold from the back. I turned around. Leopold had his arm around the dog, who was staring at me. "Is he on drugs or something?"

I turned around. It was strange, but I realized the dog was looking at me with an almost swooning expression. He had fallen in love with me! This was very peculiar. Before, he was very loving toward me, but I was simply another member of the family. Now it was as if a frying pan had clobbered him. He gazed at me with such longing that a tear actually came into his eye and trickled down his muzzle. "Oh, no," I said. "Poor Trayf. Now it's happened to you, too." He wagged his tail and continued to give me that sappy look.

"What's wrong with him?" Pierce said, turning around.

"Nothing's wrong with him," I said. "He's just fallen in love, that's all."

"You're kidding," Pierce said. "With who?"

"With me, idiot!" I said. "Can't you tell? A dog has the exact same feelings as a person, that's the horrible thing. And just like with people, love can strike at any moment, unexpectedly."

"Yeah?" said Pierce. "I tell you one thing: it's not going to strike me."

"Yeah," said Leopold. "It's not going to strike me."

"Anyway," said Pierce. "I thought Trayf loved Lulu."

"He loved her," I said. "He was fond of her. He was fond of all of us, Mom especially. But not like this. This is that awful, gaga kind of love. Can't you see what's happened? It's that curse of Mother's. We've got to find her and get her to undo it."

"What curse?" said Pierce and Leopold simultaneously.

"Don't you remember, that day when Mom wished wishes for all of us, and said you would be a movie star, and you would open your own restaurant, and men would find me irresistible?"

"That's not a curse!" said Leopold. "I *want* my own restaurant!"

"Yeah," said Pierce. "Me, too. I mean, I want to be a movie star."

"If she undoes one part of the curse, she might have to undo the whole thing, Maud," Leopold said. "You better just get used to it. It's not so bad, is it?"

"And all this time, I thought it was just me," I said, opening the car door. "Well, as long as I know what's up, I might as well put it to use."

Brian was still standing next to the car, looking at me pleadingly. "So, que pasa, dudette?" he said. "Are we ready to hit the road? I've just got to stop by my place to pick up a couple of tapes and CDs."

"Brian, where's the manger who fired you?"

"He's inside. A real scumbag. Maud, please say you'll let me come with you. I have two thousand dollars saved up, that I was going to use to upgrade my scuba equipment. But you can have it, if I could come with you."

"Is there any way you could let us have the money without joining us?"

"Please don't say that. You won't be making a mistake. I'm reliable."

"You can't even hold down a job! You'd have to prove you're reliable and responsible."

"But if I can, like, prove that I'm responsible, you'd let me come and join you?"

"It will take a few years for me to believe that you're really a hard worker."

"I can dig it," Brian said. "I'll put in my time, if I have to. You're worth it. I could maybe come and meet you during my vacations though, huh? But I sincerely doubt he's going to give me my job back. He's really pizzed. He only planned to come in and see how I was getting along, but then he fired me and so he had to take over my shift. He stripped me of my name badge, too."

"No sugar!" Pierce said. "That really sucks, huh?"

"Could we maybe make a deal?" said Brian. "If he doesn't give me my job back, could I come with you guys?"

"That's cool," said Pierce.

"No, it's not cool," I said. "You'll get your job back. All of you, wait here."

I went into the lobby. The Senior Manger was in Brian's former position. He was a round fellow, soft, with a few pink tender pimples, who looked like he had been kept in a jar of mayonnaise. He looked at me suspiciously. "Can I help you?" he said.

"I think so," I said huskily. "It's all my fault."

"What is?"

"That you fired poor little Brian Trista!" I blurted, and leaned forward across the countertop.

"He knows the rules," the manger said, recoiling. "That dog wasn't even on a leash! It tried to bite a guest."

"Oh no," I said. "Trayf would never bite anyone."

"He did," the manger said.

I glanced down at his nameplate. "Oh, Mr. Coster!" I said, and started to cry. "Please don't penalize Brian. I had an emergency and didn't know what else to do! Brian was so kind, and I'm in so much trouble; I'm completely alone in the world, and it seems so wrong that a good deed should be repaid with punishment, though not unusual. Brian loves his job here, and I blame myself. You seem like a fair person—Brian has told me so much about you—he admires you so much—" Before he knew what was happening I had crossed the boundary of the counter and flung myself onto his lap.

There was nowhere to wipe my nose except the shoulder of his jacket, but I don't think he noticed, he was so nervous at having a person in a vinyl miniskirt and fishnet stockings sitting on top of him at his place of work.

Finally I got Brian's job back on a trial basis and a gift of fifty dollars from his own money; in addition, I explained that Brian had offered me two thousand dollars, but the banks were closed now, and in addition I did not want to take out Brian's entire savings account, so Mr. Coster took five hundred dollars from the safe, and said Brian could pay him back when the bank opened tomorrow.

"You are truly talented," I said. "I feel as if it's destiny that I met you. I know this sounds zany, but did you ever have the sensation that you were a termite, in a giant colony of termites, all doing their job, gnawing wood? And perhaps I was the Queen Termite, my pendulous sac extruding eggs by the millions."

He said he might be in Denver for some kind of massive confer-
ence of hotel managers, and wrote down the dates, and made me
agree to try and look him up. I also got his beeper number which he
normally never gave out, in case of emergency. He had been married three years and had possibly made a mistake, in that he had
known the girl since high school, and had never had any other girl-
friends, and he might have been wiser to spend some time being a
bit more free-spirited before settling down, although she was a very
sweet person and was studying to obtain a C.P.A. degree in addition
to working as a bookkeeper.

If I was planning to stay around the Fort Lauderdale area for a few
more days he would love to show me some of the sights, either at
lunch, or even in the early evening, for he knew of a beach that was
basically unknown to out-of-towners.

I went back into the parking lot, finally. It really was hard work
being a femme fatale, something men would never understand. Pierce
and Brian were leaning against the far side of the car, smoking a joint.
"Hey, where did you get that?" I said.

"The dentist gave me some last night," Pierce said.

A car stopped on the other side of the highway and began honking. "What's going on over there, Leopold?" I said.

Leopold peered out the back. "It looks like it might be Bethany,"
he said. "And Bill. I can't be certain, but they're pointing over this way."

"Quick," I said. "Let's get out of here. Brian, go back inside. You
have your old job back. Just don't screw up again." I tossed him a set
of keys. "A man will probably come inside looking for us," I said.
"Give him these keys to the Bronco. He's welcome to use it. He has
an assistant, Bethany. Here's a tip: she's a dental hygienist. They give
the best moofty-pooftys. Isn't that right, Pierce? It was lovely to
meet you, Brian. Oh, one last thing: I took you up on your kind offer
of money. I've borrowed five hundred."

"I think you should probably hurry, Pierce!" Leopold said.

We squealed out of the lot, nearly running over Brian. "What kind
of idiot would order a Corvette with automatic transmission," Pierce
muttered.

"I prefer it," I said.

"Can we go home now?" Leopold said.

Neither of us responded. "What's happening, Leopold?" I said. "Are we still being followed?"

"Yup."

"Gosh darn it!" I said. "I don't like being followed. We said our good-byes. Can't they leave us alone? We should call the police."

"How can you call the police?" said Leopold. "We'd have to stop."

"I don't know," I said. "Maybe this car has a car phone."

"It does!" said Leopold. "Right next to you!"

"Cool," I said. "I've never used a car phone before. Who could we call, beside the police?"

"They're waving at us to pull over," said Pierce. "What do you want me to do, Maud?"

"Step on it, Pierce! Lose them!" Pierce violently twisted the wheel to the right, a mistake because it turned out to be one way. Cars began to honk, gleeful and vicious. "All right, all right," I said as Pierce quickly exited onto another, two-way street. "So he made a little mistake. Big deal. Did we lose them?"

"Yup," said Leopold as the phone began to ring. "Telephone."

"I'm not going to get it," I said. "Pierce, you answer it."

"I can't answer it," said Pierce. "I'm driving, aren't I?"

"Leopold, you get it," I said.

"I'm not going to get it!" said Leopold. "I didn't get us into this mess!"

"Unfair," I said. "You're a part of the team. If you had any objections, you should have stated them earlier."

"Whatever," said Leopold.

I picked up the phone and jabbed some buttons. "Is that you, Maud?" said Bill Brinkman.

"Yes," I said. "What do you want?"

"I'm at a pay phone. Bethany's in her car. You've got my new Corvette. Bring it back and I won't press charges."

"Bill, you invited us to use your car. Now you're going to press charges?" I put my hand over the receiver. "Pierce, get onto the highway. This time, make sure you follow the directions west." I uncovered the phone. "Please, Bill, say you won't call the police." I was so terrified I started to cry. "I thought you said you loved me. Does this mean it's over? Love doesn't just go away like that."

"Where are you? Stay right there and I'll come and get the car."

"What?" I said. "I can't hear you, Bill. I'm losing you. I beg you not to harm me. My life will be ruined. My brothers' lives will be ruined. I'll call you very soon, Bill; and I'll never forget your kindness to me." I didn't know what else to say, and hung up. "Is there some way we can unplug it?" I said. "That way we don't have to hear the ringing."

"I don't get you," Pierce said at last, when we were back on the highway. "We had it made there. Brian and Bill were kind of cool, I thought. We were set up very well. I probably could have found that other guy, too, the one who gave me fifty bucks. He was nice! I could have got a job, like I said, working for that foreign car place, and you could have met plenty of other guys, if you didn't like the ones you already had."

"You probably miss Bethany," I said. "No doubt that was something very special."

"Who?" said Pierce. "Shut up! I don't know what we're driving around looking for, Maud, anyway."

"What are we looking for?" I said. "Fame! Glamour! Money! Admiration!"

"A home!" said Leopold.

"The nerve," said Pierce.

"That's right. Not some paved-over shopping mall that's supposed to be the United States of America!"

"It was only one state," Leopold said. "Florida. But it wasn't what I expected, though. They showed that movie, on TV, about a lady who went to Florida, and bought an orange grove. Everywhere there were woods, deer, oranges, canoes and people missing all their teeth. I didn't see anything like that."

"That's all gone now," I said. "Don't worry, this part of our lives is petty peas. There's bigger stuff in store for us, Leopold! Don't you know how rich people live in this country? After Pierce is a movie star, we can buy two hundred acres in some of the last wilderness in

America, and still have our home in Beverly Hills. It's only a question of time."

"I still thought it wasn't too bad," said Pierce. "I could have learned to play golf."

"Don't you miss our family?" Leopold said.

"Of course we do, Leopold," I said.

Trayf tried to worm his way over the back seat to get to me. He covered the side of my face with kisses. His breath was none too good. "He tried to bite some guest," I said. "I think he's gone crazy. This is awful."

"I think I see the police," said Leopold. "Yup. Actually, they're not too far behind us."

"Don't drive above the speed limit, Pierce," I said. "Maybe we won't be pulled over. I wish you had let me drive. Policemen like me."

"What do you want me to do?" said Pierce.

"Proceed like normal. Leopold, how far away are they now?"

"I don't know," said Leopold. "A mile? Half a mile?"

"Are the flashing lights on?"

"Yes, Maud."

"And are there any cars between us and them?"

"Lots."

"Then I'm afraid we're going to have to do something terrible. Using all of our mental strength, concentrate on a massive pileup occurring right behind us."

"Oh, gee," said Pierce. "It'll never work in time."

"Concentrate, now!"

"I wish we had Theodore to help," said Leopold.

"Don't speak!" I said. "Concentrate."

To my amazement, something did happen. Pierce passed a car just ahead. It was going fairly slowly; on the back were a number of bicycles, and on the roof something covered up with a huge black plastic tarpaulin. Maybe it was our concentration, or maybe the whoosh of air from our car, but in any event, as we passed it the black plastic came loose, and like a giant flapping bat, blew back and covered the front of the car behind it. The first driver stepped on the brakes.

The driver of the car that was covered by the tarp smashed into him. Bicycles went flying into the other lanes, along with the giant couch that had been on the roof. Beyond this I couldn't see too well; only heard screeching tires and smashing metal.

"I sincerely hope no one was killed or even injured," I said, worried. "Though I doubt we could be held accountable. But always remember, Leopold, whenever you kill something—be it your common housefly, mosquito or even a flea—that it may have a sex life richer and more passionate than you ever realized, let alone that you are crushing its dreams."

"I'm not a killer," Leopold said indignantly.

"Mmm," I said, not wanting to upset him, since once I had seen him frantically brush away a biting ant and step on it. "When you see a sign that says Georgia, Pierce, head in that direction. That's west. I'm not sure police from another state will know in a big hurry that we stole this car. After all, we do have the paper saying Bill lent it to us."

"What's happening behind us, Leopold?" said Pierce.

"It's a major pileup," said Leopold, reporting while he looked out the back. "All four lanes are closed; the cars are turned sideways. The police are far behind. Nothing is coming through."

"It might have been fun, to acquire some of those renegade bicycles," I said.

At least we were headed in the right direction. Leopold was in charge of map-reading, and selected destinations based on his own criteria, which I suspected were based on restaurants and eating places he had either read about or seen on TV.

In Atlanta, eating ribs in the parking lot of a barbecue shack, we saw a red-and-white 1965 Thunderbird convertible with a 4-Sale sign in the window, and Pierce suddenly announced the Corvette was having major transmission problems and would cost close to a thousand dollars to fix.

Before I knew what had happened he had traded our car for the T-bird. It was fun being in a convertible for a while; but there was no stereo, and the radio wasn't so good, and it kept overheating. "I don't get why you made the trade," I said. "This car has automatic transmission, too."

"Oh, shut up," said Pierce.

We drove for two days and nights, stopping to take naps on back roads, heading west—according to my directions—all the while.

In Mississippi we found a fried catfish restaurant and a thrift store where I bought each of us, including Trayf, sweatshirts printed with superheroes and comic-strip pictures. Trayf wore his backward, so that the fist smashing into the yellow star and the word KAPOW! was visible on his back. At least his pimples were covered. Leopold had Spiderman; Pierce, a picture of Roy Lichtenstein; and I had Richie Rich.

Unfortunately, the reason the sweatshirts were at a thrift store, selling for $1.98 apiece, was that they had been in a fire, and they smelled so much of smoke and gasoline, it was nearly impossible to breathe.

When we were eating at a diner, the waitress started sniffing all over the place, and dumped out the garbage, thinking maybe it had caught on fire, and ran into the kitchen yelling, "Is something burning back here?"

Finally she figured it out when six people sitting near us at the counter asked to be moved to tables. She looked at us suspiciously. "How ya doing?" Pierce said. She must have been too distracted to notice him before. Now her expression softened. Before we finished, she had given Pierce and Leopold each a free wedge of apple pie and half a T-bone steak for Trayf (who was waiting in the car) and slipped Pierce twenty dollars on the side, begging him to meet her that evening and she would give him all the additional leftovers she could save.

Her name was Polly and she was forty-seven years old. Pierce was all set to depart, and skip town with the twenty, but I insisted he spend the night with her (Leopold, Trayf and I stayed in a $19.95 Motel 86 on the highway nearby).

In the morning he turned up, white-faced and weary, but with two hundred dollars of her savings. "I had to promise to write to her with our address when we get to L.A.," he said. "She wants to come out and see me when we get settled. I hope you're grateful."

"Very," I said. "Though probably not as grateful as she. And just as soon as you get rich, you can mail her a check."

More days and nights passed. It was all becoming a blur. Outside Dallas I told Leopold we didn't have enough money (thirty dollars each) for admittance to The Great American Nightmare—a hundred-acre amusement park with roller coasters, carousels with vampire bats instead of horses, water-slides in dark caves, and high-speed interplanetary crack-the-whips.

"If we're careful, with the money we've got, we can get all the way to California," I said. "Don't you see? If we go in, we're down at least a hundred."

For an hour, though, Leopold cried and cried. "I'm sorry, sugar, I'm really sorry," I said. "I didn't even think you liked amusement parks. Maybe you're just crying for your lost youth."

"Maybe he's gone non-compost-heap-mentis," said Pierce.

"Clever, Pierce!" I said. "You made a clever joke!"

"I did?" Pierce said.

"Maybe I'm just suffering from too many hormones," said Leopold, when he was able to speak at last

The car broke down in Fort Worth and Pierce traded it for a 1971 Plymouth Valiant. "It's a semi-classic," Pierce explained. "Powder-blue inside and out; transmission is shot to hell in the T-bird, and we don't have time to fix it. We hang on to this one long enough, it'll be a real classic."

Most of the time Pierce drove while I slept, and vice versa. Outside Wichita Falls we were nearly swept away by a giant tornado. For three hours we crouched in the front seat, by the side of the road, while the sky turned mascara-black in midday.

Off the highway we found cheap motels for twenty or thirty dollars; one night we slept beside the car, parked behind some trees, on some blankets the car's previous owner had left in the trunk.

Just outside a campground where we parked overnight for fifteen dollars and used the public shower, there was a gas station where I met a man who agreed to fill up our car with gas if I would fondle his mashie niblick. "How do I know if you'll really do it?" I said.

"How do I know if *you'll* really do it?" he said.

"How do I know if *you* will."

We agreed at last he should fill up half the tank before, and half the tank afterward. I went with him around back, behind the men's room, and he unzipped his fly. It was a dark purple, very wobbly, and actually resembled some of the parts in the *Encyclopedia of Poultry*. "You poor thing," I murmured, and gave it a little rub. "Here's for good luck!" I added, and started to twist it between my palms. All of a sudden it got very hard and swollen and I let out a scream. "Ugh!" I said. "I'm getting out of here!"

The man grabbed my hands and held them in place, so I screamed again. Pierce was waiting around the corner and came running. He kicked the guy in the leg and the man let go of me. Also, the swelling went down right away. I took off running toward the car. "No, wait!" the man said. "I'm sorry! I made a mistake! I would never normally do anything like that."

"Shave your hideous beard, next time you try something like that!" I shouted. "Ya creep! Picking on the poor and disenfranchised!" I could tell he felt just terrible. I locked myself in the car with Leopold and the dog. At a distance I could see him chatting to Pierce, who looked threatening.

"He gave me fifty dollars," Pierce said, returning. "He says if you'll come out and let him apologize, he'll fill the rest of the car with gas, too."

"I don't care, Pierce," I said, wiping my hands on the seat. "Let's get out of here!"

Out the window of the car the landscape looked pretty much the same wherever we drove: strip malls and sparse patches of morose, desiccated trees, or oil rigs jerking off on what appeared to be fields of gravy. "From what I can tell, this whole country has been paved over," Leopold said.

"That's true in some spots," I said. "But this country is also full of spots of rare beauty. I've seen pictures on TV. The only problem is, the spots of rare beauty are for the rich people who can afford to buy them. That's why we're going to have to get rich."

"Rich, rich, rich," sang Leopold in his thin, high voice.

"Tell us, Maud, what it will be like to be rich," said Pierce.

"Yeah, tell us," said Leopold.

"Well," I began. "It's like this: you wear sweaters of the softest cashmere, in shades of golden brown, tan, lemon and other hues. Every morning you wake and find you've been sleeping on clean sheets. The bed is crisply made, but the sheets are soft. Portholes, I think they're called. Out the window in your bedroom, there's a beautiful view—trees, mountains, oceans, rivers, prairies, what have you. You get out of bed, ring a bell and drink cappuccino, caffé latte, espresso, or maybe herbal teas and fresh tropical fruit such as mango, papaya and pineapple. You never have to worry about losing weight, because you can always have a huge bowl of shrimps or lobster with cocktail sauce for lunch, which is low in calories! And everybody likes you; why? Because you're rich!"

There was a pause. "I don't know," Leopold and Pierce said simultaneously.

"Maybe I didn't explain it right," I said. "I'm sure there's a lot more to it than I can even imagine. You get to have a swimming pool, hi-tech exercise equipment, golf cart, padded hangers, English umbrellas with chestnut handles and lots of other things."

"The golf cart sounds kind of cool," said Pierce.

29

We drove through L.A. for hours and hours and there was nothing that looked familiar. It was getting late by the time we pulled into the lot outside the Fresh Juice Bar on Sunset Boulevard and went in. "Here we are!" said Leopold. "California, here we are! I'd like a large glass of the avocado, apple, strawberry, beet, lettuce and Green Magic algae juice."

"The combo?" I said.

"I'd like the carrot, apple, celery, ginger and banana frappé," said Pierce.

"Pierce," I hissed. "The combo drink Leopold ordered cost five ninety-five. That's all of our money. Let's not spoil this for him. Maybe he'll let you have a sip."

We sat at a table. The place was empty. Leopold looked out at Sunset Boulevard, slurping. Pretty soon a man came in. He couldn't stop staring at Pierce. He asked if he could join us. He said his name was Dennis. He told us—or, rather, Pierce—everything about himself. He was head of a record company, and his home, nearby, was originally a mansion built by some famous crooner back in the nineteen-twenties, whose name I didn't quite catch. He must have been rich; even though he was young, he had on a huge gold watch, and alligator shoes. "As soon as I get rich I plan to get alligator shoes—two pairs, or maybe three, like men's shoes in black, brown and orange," I pointed out.

Dennis ignored me. He asked Pierce a million questions. Since he seemed oblivious to me, I decided to let him struggle with Pierce on his own. Finally Dennis looked at me frantically. He looked like someone who claimed to know how to ride a horse, and who said he had a lot of horseback-riding experience, but when he actually got on the horse, he suddenly realized he didn't really know anything.

I got an extra straw for Leopold's drink. "You don't have a place to stay, you can stay with me," Dennis was telling Pierce when I got back.

"What's that sort of skunky flavor in your drink, Leopold?" I said, slurping.

"I think it might be the algae," said Leopold.

"I can stay with you?" Pierce said. "That'd be cool. I haven't had a shower in three days, man."

"Hey!" I said indignantly. "Just a second! What about us?"

"Oh yeah," said Pierce. "My little brother and sister."

"Relatives?" Dennis said reluctantly. "I have a guest house I suppose they could use until they find a place of their own."

He excused himself to use the men's room, and while he was gone Pierce changed his mind. "I don't want to stay with this guy," he said.

"If you don't like his place, we don't have to stay," I said. "But we can at least use his phone and see if Mother has contacted the police with her whereabouts. Maybe Dennis has a charming home. It certainly sounds like it. Besides, Dennis is in the music industry. It could prove to be useful for Theodore."

"I have a funny feeling," Pierce said.

"Come on, Pierce," I said. "I thought you agreed you didn't mind a little moofty-poofty, if you were the recipient."

"Huh?" Pierce said, looking baffled.

"That's where a man or a woman, but usually a man, sucks on a mashie niblick," Leopold said, laughing dementedly.

"Remember, Pierce?" I said. "You said it didn't sound too bad."

"Oh yeah," Pierce said. "I said that? Maybe you're right. It wouldn't be so bad, huh?"

"You just have to lie there. He probably has expensive, clean sheets, like I was telling you about, that have been ironed. You can pretend he's some girl."

"Why would I pretend he's a girl?"

"I don't know," I said. "Far be it for me to tell you what to pretend while Dennis gives you a moofty-poofty. Maybe Dennis doesn't even want to give you a moofty-poofty. How do I know what Dennis wants?" Snatching the jumbo cup from Leopold's hands, I drank the last few drops. "I guess you guys blame me, huh? That I said we would just get to L.A. and find Mother and the others. I didn't know it was such a big place. It didn't look so big on TV."

"Don't worry," said Pierce. "We're not mad at you."

"You're not?"

"We'll find them."

"Do you think?" I said, starting to cry. "I'm sorry. I didn't mean to start crying. Oh, I was probably awful to travel with. I'm sorry. And it's all my fault. And I'm hot, and grubby, and I don't feel so good, and I'm tired of strangers, and you guys are all I've got, and now you hate me."

"We don't hate you," Leopold said quietly. "We're used to you. We know you're crazy."

"Oh, Leopold, thank you," I said, giving him a hug.

Dennis came back from the toilet. He had tidied his hair and looked at Pierce hungrily. "So are you guys ready, or what?" he said. "Pierce, why don't you come with me in my car, and the others can follow."

"No," I said. "Pierce stays with us."

"Whatever," said Dennis with a shrug. "I hope you're not a murderer, but for whatever reason—I suppose with Pierce to protect me!—I'm not afraid."

"Stupid," I muttered.

"What?" said Dennis.

"I said, you have nothing to worry about. You have the sense to judge for yourself. My brother is going to be a movie star, and you'll be the first to have known him in California. He only has a minor criminal record."

"What?" said Dennis. "I still didn't hear you. I'm a little hard of hearing; probably due to my years of going to club concerts. You know what? I'm thinking, I'd love to have a little dinner party in your honor, Pierce."

"I don't want a dinner party in my honor," Pierce said.

"I heard that!" Dennis said. "I think you could be a little more agreeable. You don't know anyone here in L.A. and I'm trying to help you out. I have lots of connections. It's not such a bad idea. I don't know what you could be thinking!"

"He has a point, Pierce," I said.

"I don't think anything, Dennis!" Pierce said. "Now do you get it?"

Dennis sighed dreamily. "Oh, I can't tell you how I've longed to hear somebody say that," he said. "I'm sorry. You're right. I was out of line. Whatever you want."

"No dinner party."

"Fine. But please please, come with me. Don't ditch me, Pierce! You have no cash, no credit cards, you must let me help! I have a really terrific masseuse, Georgie. He's actually my Filipino houseboy. He can take care of you after your swim."

"That sounds nice," I said. Pierce looked like he was going to throw up. I glared at him. "Come on, Pierce, what's the problem?" I said.

"His jacket!" Pierce said. "Look at his jacket."

"What's wrong with my jacket?" Dennis said.

"The lapels," Pierce said.

"Oh, God, you don't like the lapels?" Dennis said. "This was an eight-hundred-dollar jacket. Oh, God, I feel like such an idiot. You're right. The lapels are awful."

"Dennis, do you have any drugs at your home?" I said.

"What sort of drugs?"

"Marijuana," I said. "My brother prefers marijuana, and good Scotch."

"I don't like Scotch," Pierce said. "Beer's okay."

"He loves excellent Scotch," I said. "Hopefully I've convinced him not to take heroin or cocaine, although who knows with him? You see, here's my theory: each human being is surrounded with an aura, which is sort of like an egg white. As the fetal chicken—the yolk—is to its white, so the human is to its aura. The egg white, you see, is food for the fetal chicken. The aura is spiritual assistance, or food, to the human. If you take heroin, you're devouring your own egg white—your own aura. It's very tasty to do this, but basically you've eaten yourself alive. When you're finished, you can never get it back, and it may be needed for something on the 'other side'—when you hatch, so to speak. Anyway, when your egg white is gone you have nothing left, and you can never get it back, and you're not so attractive anymore. Like a child who's eaten up next week's school lunches."

"I'm sure what you're saying makes sense to *you*," Dennis said.

"Bitch," I said.

"What's the matter, you don't agree with what my sister's saying?" Pierce said.

"Yeah," said Leopold, "you don't agree or something?"

"All I can say is, you two guys are the best!" I said, overcome.

"I'm sure *she* thinks what she's saying makes sense, but I certainly have plenty of marijuana at home, very nice stuff from Hawaii, all buds, and I just got some peyote buttons, which I haven't taken in years, but I thought might be fun, and I can easily arrange for some Scotch to be delivered, or stop on the way to pick some up, if you need it in a hurry," Dennis said.

"All buds, huh?" Pierce said. "Let's go. We'll follow."

"You see, if a child ate all next week's lunch, the other children wouldn't want to be friends with him or her: for one thing, he or she would be hungry and would try to beg lunch off the others. Of course some—the ones with low self-esteem—would be happy to hand over their lunch, just to have a friend. The same as some women with low self-esteem associate with a drug addict, and are happy to have their aura drained off, just because they feel worthless."

"Your sister—is she a little strange?" Dennis said to Pierce as we left.

"No," said Pierce. "*You* are."

"Yeah," said Leopold. "*You're* the strange one."

"I'll never forget the kindness you two have shown me," I said.

"Tell me," said Dennis, "do you really hate this jacket? It's almost brand new. I think I've worn it once. I'm just miserable."

I untied Trayf from the car-door handle and got in. Leopold squeezed over me, so all of us could be in the front seat. "He's driving a silver Mercedes," Pierce said. "He's got a forest-green Lotus at home, which isn't running at present. I said I'd take a look at it."

"He must be really rich," I said. "Oh, Pierce, if you'll just put out, we might have found our meal ticket."

"Whatever," Pierce said.

We followed the silver Mercedes for a few blocks. At a red light we were caught on the wrong side. Dennis's car disappeared out of sight. "Maybe he's pulled over," I said. I glanced at the car alongside us. "Leopold," I said. "I know I can't see very well. But look at that lady in the car next to us. Doesn't it look like Mom?"

Leopold peered across me. Then he stared straight ahead. Then he looked back. "It *is* Mom!" he said.

"You're kidding!" I said. "I thought I was hallucinating. What should we do?"

"Yell!" Leopold said. "Yell! Yell!"

"Mom!" I screamed. "Ma, look over here!"

She looked over in our direction. Then she unrolled the window.

"Where did she get a car with air-conditioning?" I said.

"Maybe it's that car Marietta had?" Pierce said.

"I don't think so," I said.

"A whole lifetime of fear, anxiety and worrying," my mother shouted out her opened window.

"Don't forget tidying!" Leopold screamed gleefully. He tried to scramble over me.

The light changed to green. "Where have you been?" my mother said. The cars behind her started to honk.

Trayf began to bark from the back seat. "Looking for you!" Pierce yelled. "Pull over, pull over up ahead."

We drove into the lot of a video department store. My mother got out and we all flung ourselves on top of her, including Trayf. "My darlings," she said. "Has it been so very awful?"

A woman I had never seen before got out of the car and stood alongside watching. She was Asian, around forty years old, with long black hair and approximately twenty necklaces around her chest and neck, made of huge amber, turquoise and silver beads. The necklaces looked very exotic, worn over a long, tight, black crepe dress. On her feet were silver leather platform boots. "This is Nancy," my mother said.

"Who's Nancy?" I said.

"She's my new friend," my mother said.

"In what sense?" I said.

"I'm a lesbian now!" my mother said. "I've had it up to here with men! Nancy and I are in love."

"Did something happen to put you off men?" I said.

"Edward escaped from the hospital."

"We know that," I said. "He kidnapped us, until we ditched him."

"My poor babies!" my mother said. "He's been on a rampage across the country. The papers said he was with a girl and a small boy, so I thought he must have murdered Pierce and gone off with you two."

"Oh no," I said. "They must have mistaken Pierce for him. We were fine."

"Thank God," my mother said. "The one who's really suffered is Edward's poor mother. She put up her house as collateral when bail was set. Now they're going to take it away. As soon as I can get the money for a ticket, I'm flying her out here to stay with us. But that's not the point. I've been sick with worry. You've taken ten years off my life. All this time I thought Edward was going to kill you any minute."

"I missed you, Mom," Leopold said. "I almost couldn't remember how dysfunctional you were. Now I'm happy you are."

"It was losing all my photographs in the trailer disaster that pushed me over the edge," she said. "There's no evidence of my entire existence. I was saving pictures of all you kids' fathers, to show you when you turned twenty-one."

"I turned twenty-one and you never showed me a picture," Pierce said.

"I couldn't find where I hid them," my mother said. "We were just racing to meet with a producer, about featuring you on one of those missing persons programs on TV. Theodore wrote a song about it. Do you want to come?"

"We don't need to go now," I said.

"Theodore will be disappointed," my mother said.

"Anyway," I said. "I sincerely doubt Edward would have murdered his own son, in the end."

"Oh, who even knows if Leopold was Edward's son," my mother said.

"You're kidding," said Leopold, looking pleased. "What are some of the other possibilities?"

"I'll have to think," my mother said. "I'll let you know."

"That's a beautiful necklace, Nancy," I said.

"Thanks," Nancy said. "I made it."

"You *made* it?" I said.

"Well, I collect old Tibetan and Russian necklaces and beads," she said. "Then I restring them."

"Ah," I said.

"Isn't she stunning?" my mother said. "She's been so good to me."

"Ma!" I said. "Since you became a lesbian . . . that means . . . you and Nancy have sex?"

"At first I thought: I can't have sex with a woman! Parts are missing! But after a while I realized: what the hell. Besides, we don't have sex all that often. Frankly, I don't have that strong a sex drive. And it's rather crowded, where we're living—we don't get that much privacy."

"Where are you living?"

"Nancy has a charming, somewhat run-down house in the Colony."

"The Colony!" I said with awe.

"I got it in the settlement," Nancy said. "And you? Where are you living?"

"What do you mean, where are we living? We just got here! We're living with you!"

"Of course my children live with me, Nancy," my mother said. "We discussed all that."

"But your children—they keep coming! And their friends, too!" Nancy said.

"We have a little one on the way," my mother confided.

"You're pregnant?" I said. "But . . ." I looked back and forth between Nancy and my mother. "How?"

"A little turkey-baster baby!" my mother said with glee.

"I always wanted a baby, but I've had a complete hysterectomy," Nancy said.

"Oh, how terrible," I said.

"I don't want your pity!" Nancy snarled.

"I've said the wrong thing," I murmured. "Forgive me."

"Oh, Maud!" my mother said. "You've grown up! How sophisticated you sound!" She kissed me on the cheek and turned to Nancy. "Don't be a bitch. Maud was only trying to sound sympathetic. How is she supposed to know what to say. If she didn't say 'How terrible,' you would have accused her of being cold and self-absorbed."

"I'm sorry," Nancy said. She took my hand. "I've only known your mother a week, and I've learned so much. We were together in another life, which explains everything."

"Apology accepted!" I said brightly. "But you must forgive me, if I say the wrong thing."

My mother looked at me admiringly. "She's really changed, Nancy. She sounds almost like a person."

I started to sniffle. "We're exhausted from our trip," I explained. "And in addition, you have to realize, it's a teeny bit of a shock to find my mother and now she's a lesbian. How did you two meet, anyway?"

"At our dojo," Nancy said.

"What's a dojo?" I said.

"It's a karate institute," Nancy said.

"I didn't know you studied karate, Ma," I said.

"There's a lot you don't know about me!" my mother said. "Do you think I have to stay exactly the same all the time?"

"I want to go to karate school, too!" Leopold said.

"Cool," said Pierce.

"This is going to be fun!" I said. "The Colony! I've seen reference to it, in literature."

"But Evangeline, where are they going to sleep?" Nancy said. "There's Marietta and Simon in the guest bedroom, Theodore, Fred and Shawn in the other bedroom, you and me in the master bedroom—there isn't any other space!"

"Who's in the guest bedroom?" I almost screamed in despair.

"Oh, don't worry," my mother said. "We'll work everything out." She averted her gaze and addressed the dog. "Trayf, Trayf, they haven't been feeding you, have they. You're so skinny!"

"He fell in love with me, thanks to your curse," I said. "He's lost weight because he's lovesick."

My mother looked blank. "A curse?" she said. "I doubt that. All right; kids, you follow us and we'll take you home."

Nancy got back into their car. "Come on, Evangeline, hurry up!" she said. "If we stay away too long, I'm afraid that friend of Theodore's will burn the house down."

My mother came closer and gave me a hug. "She's an interesting person, don't you think?" she said in a whisper. "On a scale of one to ten, I'd give her a three."

"I want to make a meal that symbolizes a real homelife," Leopold said. "Remember when Theodore found me that neat old cookbook at a flea market? It's gone now, but it was from nineteen seventeen. It was called *A Thousand-and-One Ways to Please Your Husband.* I wish I could remember more of it. There was one recipe, though, that I could try. Salmon croquettes. You take a can of salmon, mash it up, chop some onion, add an egg or two and form into patties. Fry these in a frying pan. On the side, mashed potatoes. Do you think the others will like that?"

"I'm sure they'll love it, Leopold," I said absently. We were driving up the Pacific Coast Highway. It wasn't as splendid as I had thought it would be, due to the fact that there wasn't a single part alongside that wasn't covered with houses. After a while there was a public beach, but a big sign stated PARKING LOT FULL.

"In nineteen seventeen, when *A Thousand-and-One Ways to Please Your Husband* was written, there was nothing in California except beautiful scenery," Leopold said. "They had all kinds of fruit, such as avocados, pomegranates and lots of other things. If only I could remember how, I could make avocado ice cream."

Ahead of us, Nancy's car turned into a little road going toward the ocean. A hundred yards down was a tollbooth. "You think they charge to get in?" I said. "Pierce, honk the horn and make them stop. We don't have a single dime left to our name."

Pierce honked the horn. At the tollbooth Nancy stopped. My mother hopped out of the car and came back to us. "Ma!" I said. "Do they charge admission to get into the Malibu Colony? We're broke."

"Oh no!" my mother said. "This is the security gate. Security is very tight. We don't want our privacy disturbed, here in the Colony. Nancy is speaking to Fred, right now, to make sure you guys get on the admittance list." She gestured to Trayf. He leapt into the back. Then she got in. I squeezed over, and Leopold clambered over me and climbed onto her lap.

"What's Fred doing here!" I said indignantly.

"He came out because of you," my mother said. "He's already been propositioned by three divorced ladies who have houses in the Colony, but he's saving himself for you. Luckily, thanks to Nancy, he got a job as a security guard. His starting salary is thirty-six thousand a year."

"Thirty-six thousand a year!" I said.

"That's only his *starting* salary, Maud," my mother said. "He's also writing a screenplay."

Nancy rolled past the gate and we followed. Pierce unrolled his window. "Hey, man, how ya doing!" he said. "Catch you later."

I shut my eyes. "I'm afraid I'm in love with him," I finally admitted.

"Oh, poor Fred!" My mother sighed. "Poor, poor Fred!"

"Enough already!" I said.

"Maybe you'll get over it? The poor man. Did you know, he put up signs, all over Los Angeles, looking for you? There was even an article about it in the L.A. *Times.* Everyone's rooting for him to find you. For his sake, I hope one or both of you loses interest."

"Nice," I snarled.

"Nancy was very taken with you, Leopold," my mother said blandly. "There's a chance she may want to adopt you. Then she'd leave you her house in her will."

"I might be a very lucky fellow!" said Leopold.

The Colony was a narrow road lined on both sides with houses that were not particularly large and were practically touching one another. "Is Nancy's house on the ocean side?" I said.

"Nope," my mother said. "Alas. There's a lot of things that need to be fixed, too, but we figured Pierce could do it."

"I thought you believed him dead," I said.

"In my heart, not really," my mother said. "I think I would have been more upset if something had happened to one of you children. I would have known it. Stop here."

"The piece of property even without the house must be worth quite a lot," Pierce said. "So, do you see a lot of movie stars out here?"

"Oh yes," said my mother. "Shawn's mother is one, although she hasn't been in a movie in years. She only starred in those Andy

Warhol underground-type films, anyway. But you'll find when you get to know some movie stars, they're just like ordinary people. Well, this is the place!"

"Who's Shawn?"

"Theodore's lead guitarist," my mother said. "He's living with us until the band gets on its feet."

"Where should I park?" said Pierce.

"Lord knows," my mother said. "I suppose you'll have to leave it out on the street, but I hope the neighbors don't complain. The people who live here like to think of themselves as free spirits, but the truth is, they all drive Range Rovers."

"This house actually looks quite nice," I said. Gray cedar shingles covered the facade; it looked a bit like a cuckoo clock. We followed my mother. A two-story living room was separated by sliding glass doors from a tennis court. "What's that terrible noise?" I shouted.

"Probably Theodore and Shawn practicing on the tennis court!" my mother said.

"Tennis?" I said.

"Not right now, sweetie," my mother said. "They're practicing their music."

"And where are Marietta and Simon?"

"I'm not sure. Upstairs, probably."

I ran up the stairs. One bedroom was empty. The door to the other was closed. I ran over and put my ear on it. "It's not going to hurt!" said a voice that sounded like Marietta's.

"Are you certain?" said a second voice, male, in an English accent.

"Just close your eyes and think of England!" Marietta said.

So it was true, then, about the two of them cohabiting. My heart, curiously, felt uplifted, maybe near my throat, though I couldn't figure out why—and certainly I would never let Marietta know.

I went back down. My mother was by the glass doors in back. "How could you let her, Mother?" I said. "Steal Simon. Now I'm going to have to kill her."

"You see," my mother said. "You haven't changed, after all. It's good to see that you're still in such a rage. I've always encouraged you not to squelch a single emotion. I think rage especially is very empowering. You can get a lot accomplished through rage. I've always wanted all my children to have a lot of negative emotions."

Theodore was standing with his back to me, plugged into a giant amplifier. I stood for a moment, listening. I couldn't say his music had improved, but he was playing it with a new authority and determination. Probably it was something other people would get used to and even learn to love.

I tapped him on the back and he turned around. He looked older, wiser, toughened-up, beefier, more mature, the boyishness nearly gone. His face, at first tense and worried, filled with relief and he broke into a grin. We hugged and he shouted in my ear. "Maud, do you know what living hell I've been through, trapped in the car with her all the way across the United States of America? Do you have any idea of what I've been through, the men I've had to drag her away from in bars, her new acquaintances made at bus stops and public toilets? Thank God you're back."

Pierce and Leopold crowded around. "How're you doing, man," Pierce said, embarrassed to be caught in an emotion-charged situation. "How's your, uh, arm?"

"I can't believe you remembered!" Theodore said. "It's fine—just a little bent."

"Who's your friend, the handsome ukulele player?" I said.

"Hi," said the youth, coming over. "I'm Shawn. Spelled X-e-a-b-h-o-i-g-h-a-n. Spelled Xeabhoighan, pronounced Shawn."

"Oh, who cares about that?" I said.

"It's important," Xeabhoighan said. "It's a Swahili/Gaelic spelling. See, I'm half black and half Irish. My father was a Black Panther, and my mom an underground-movie star."

"Yeah?" I said. "And my father was the keeper of the Eddystone Light."

"Cool," said Xeabhoighan.

" '*My father was the keeper of the Eddystone Light,*' " Theodore sang. " '*And he slept with a mermaid one fine night. / Out of this union there came three. / A porpoise and a porgy and the other was me.*' "

" '*Yo ho ho, the wind blows free.*' " Pierce sang the chorus. " '*Oh for the life of the open sea.*' "

"Can your brother play an instrument?" Xeabhoighan asked Theodore. "Would he maybe want to join the band?"

"No!" I said. "He's got other plans."

"Why don't you let him decide?" Xeabhoighan said. He wasn't tall, and I could have punched him, if I had still been that sort of person. He had the delicate good looks and long golden dreadlocks of a boy who had always been pampered; still, that was hardly his fault, was it? I figured I would take care of him later. He looked like he had grown up being served bowls of raspberries by a Mexican maid, in a house with central air-conditioning. Even though his hair was tangled, it was accustomed to expensive emollients, and I could see that whoever snipped the ends probably charged a hundred and fifty dollars. "Theodore's told me so much about you guys," he said, peering at all of us closely. "I feel like I know you all, already. You want to clear the equipment away so we can play some tennis?"

"We don't play tennis," I said. Xeabhoighan looked shocked.

"I always wanted to play tennis, though," Pierce said. "Maybe you could teach me."

"You always wanted to play tennis, Pierce?" I said. "I didn't know that. I never saw you as the tennis-playing type."

"Things are going to be different now," Pierce said.

"Oh, gosh," I said. "Then what's going to become of me? Maybe I could have a trained dog act. It doesn't look like there's going to be enough room here for me to start raising emus or ostrich. Where's Lulu, anyway? Where are the puppies?"

"I have to lock them in the cabana while we practice," said Theodore. "Otherwise the puppies piss on our equipment."

"Is that the cabana?" I said, pointing to the little pink-and-blue–striped shed at the back of the tennis court. "I've never seen a cabana before. Isn't it cute? Come with me, Trayf. You can have a reunion with your bride."

I went across the court and opened the cottage door. Seven dogs poured out. The five puppies were bigger; I almost wouldn't have recognized them. One had grown a black crest of hair on his head, but otherwise was a stark-naked slate-gray. He spun around and around in a circle before crashing into the wall.

"Two are Fred's, two belong to Simon," Theodore said. "Unfortunately that puppy—we call him Peeve—is autistic."

"Oh?" I said. "I might be interested in keeping him—as a pet project. What did they end up naming the others?"

"Romeo, Pansy, Beep-beep and Alphonse Daudet."

One, a girl, was pink with brown spots. One was dark black, with a strange tuft of hair on one side. One was what I would have termed a lavender hue, and the last was palomino. There was also a tiny black Chihuahua. The pups were friendly enough, but obviously didn't remember me; only Lulu let out a yelp and toppled over on her back, swooning at the sight of Trayf. Absence had made her fonder of him, at least temporarily. "Aren't they sweet?" I said. "Whose Chihuahua?"

"Marietta's," Theodore said.

The Chihuahua leapt into my arms and began plastering me with kisses. "Oh, you poor neglected darling," I said. "Don't you have anybody to love you?"

"Handsome!" a voice shrieked behind me. "Handsome, come here at once! That's my Handsome, Maud! He's never been neglected for one single second his whole life!" I turned around, scanning the ground for a useful weapon.

31

"You sea slug," I said as Handsome leapt from my arms. "Invertebrate!" Marietta was even thinner than before, wearing some kind of drab linen or flax skirt in a mud color with a black turtleneck and a wide black alligator belt with a silver buckle. Boring, yet tasteful and rich in appearance. "Is that real alligator?" I said.

"You don't think I'd wear fake alligator, do you?" she said.

"Reptile!" I said. "You haven't changed a bit, have you? You stole my boyfriend from me! How could you?" I stepped forward and started to throttle her. She shouldn't have lost so much weight if she wanted to be able to defend herself. "How could you! You deliberately sent me off in the car with Pierce so you could keep Simon for yourself! G. Dash D. knows what lies you told him!"

"Stop, fiend!" Marietta said. "You're hurting me!" She let out a squeal like a rabbit being decimated by a fox. Even while she was yowling she reached under my shirt and gave me a vicious pinch, so that it looked like she was passive and defenseless, only she wasn't. I screamed and pulled her hair. Just then I noticed Simon had arrived and was standing helplessly in the doorway.

"Oh, Simon!" I said, letting go of Marietta and running over to him. "How could you do this?" Marietta came up behind me and put her arm around me so that it seemed she was being affectionate, only what she was doing was digging her sharp fingernails into my neck. "Ow!" I said, and turned around to punch her.

"I was only trying to make up!" Marietta said. "Look at her, Simon, she's crazy! She attacked me for no reason."

"No reason!" I said. "She stole you from me! The mendacious bitch!"

Marietta began to sob. She ran over to Simon and wrapped herself around him. "Don't fight over me, girls," Simon said weakly.

" *'I will slay this Pau-Puk-Keewis,'* " said Marietta, " *'Slay this mischief-maker!'* "

Simon patted Marietta absently. "Why don't you recite some of your original material now, beloved?" he said.

That's when I burst into tears. "You said you loved me!" I said. "You wanted to take me home to meet your parents."

"Oh, Maud, that's just an English expression," Simon said. "Marietta said you and Freddy de Gaillefontaine were an item, and when he came all this way out here to look for you, I didn't think you were serious about me."

"Bitch!" I flung myself on Marietta again. "You know Fred is inappropriate for me. It's not my fault that he, like so many others, found me irresistible."

"Oh?" said Marietta. "Why don't we have a little honesty around here? Why don't you admit, once and for all, how you really feel?"

"Maybe," I said reluctantly.

"And poor Simon was all alone, and lonely, and so kind to come all this way out here to share the driving with my demented family," Marietta said. "Knowing full well you never really cared for him as he should be cared for."

"As if you're not just out to snare yourself a title!" I said, starting to dance and feint in a circle around her.

"Keep your guard up, Marietta!" Simon suggested. "Tuck your chin down low!"

"Girls!" My mother came out onto the tennis court. "Are you fighting already? I can't stand it! I just hope this new baby turns out to be a decent human being. I keep trying and trying but I can never seem to get it right. All I ask for is some mature, interesting conversation. Is that too much to request?" Pierce, Theodore, Leopold and Xeabhoighan stood cackling merrily. Only Simon looked distressed and frightened. "Hold Maud's arms together, Pierce, until she calms down," my mother said. Marietta glared at me triumphantly.

"Should I pour some water on her?" said Leopold.

"I remember in the old days," my mother said. "My grandmother used to talk to me about the art of conversation. It consisted of a back-and-forth speech pattern, in which the various parties would exchange ideas on literature, the arts, newsworthy events and so forth. Sometimes one party would ask a concerned question regarding the other's health or activities; the respondent would answer and then, shortly thereafter, pose a similar question to the first party."

"Poor little Leopold," Simon said. "All this arguing can't be good for the chap. Why don't you come with me into the kitchen? I can show you where all the cooking things are, and there's a TV set."

"Oh, goody," said Leopold. "I can begin making dinner."

"Is it going to be oily?" my mother said. "I don't like oily food."

"Where's the beach?" I said. "I wouldn't mind going to the beach."

"Yeah," said Pierce. "I'd like to see the Atlantic Ocean at last."

For a few seconds none of us spoke, but grinned admiringly at Pierce. "I'll take you guys," said Theodore. "Though I dread to think what's in that water. Did you know the Mississippi River was recently discovered to contain .04 percent caffeine? No sewage treatment can remove it. Someday we'll be swimming in a sea of secondhand coffee."

"Is the Mississippi nearby?" said Pierce. "I didn't know that."

"Maud, I think I'll make up the couch in the den for you to sleep on," my mother said. "Pierce, if you help me carry the futons down from the attic we can move them into the cabana and you and Leopold can sleep out there, if you don't mind using the bathroom off the kitchen. Isn't it wonderful, that we're all together again? Please don't fight. Without each other we have nothing."

"Yeah?" I said, still angry. "If not for my family, I could have stayed in Florida with a dentist."

"Oh, how bourgeois," Marietta said with a tinkling laugh. "Wait until Simon hears that. A dentist? In Florida?"

"Children, children," my mother said. "I beg you, keep your voices down. Nancy is trying to have a nap. You know she's used to a calmer existence."

"This Nancy—is she so very difficult to get along with?" I said.

"She didn't used to be," Xeabhoighan said thoughtfully. "I've known her for ages, well before you all came along."

"It's just that she's overdosing on estrogen," my mother said. "The doctor started her on these arm patches, and she's all hepped up."

Theodore showed us where to squeeze between two houses across the street to get to the ocean. The sand was gray and covered with old plastic milk bottles and rings that held beer cans together. From the shore, the facades of the ten-million-dollar properties, with their wooden decks and sliding glass doors, were not all that imposing. We walked down the strip of sand. At the end was a giant fence, either to keep the tourists out, or to keep the residents in. "More like a leper colony," I said. We turned back.

"Wonder how the water feels," said Pierce, taking off his work boots and dipping his toes. "Geeze, it's freezing. Will I get into trouble if I go swimming in my underpants?"

"Don't you have a swimsuit?" Theodore said disapprovingly. "We'll have to take you shopping. I think Versace is having a sale."

Pierce stripped down to his jockey shorts and strode across the beach and through the little waves. "But remember when the trailer collapsed and Pierce said he couldn't swim?" I said. It was true that now Pierce did not cut all that graceful a figure. He went in up to his chin, dog-paddled a few strokes and floundered around.

"Maybe he's committing suicide," Theodore said.

"Theodore, don't say that!" I said. "Do you think? Why would he commit suicide now, when he's close to the verge of making it?"

"If he has low self-esteem, even the thought of success and accolades could make him very self-destructive," Theodore explained. "He would feel he doesn't deserve it. Look at James Dean, for example."

In unison we began to bellow: "Pierce! Pierce! Come back!"

Pierce trudged back to shore. "What's the matter?" he said.

"You can't swim!" I said.

"Oh," he said. "I kind of forgot. I remembered I had been in some water, but I forgot it was by accident when the trailer collapsed." He guffawed. It was good to hear him guffawing again. It seemed like the whole time during our trip, he had hardly guffawed at all. Maybe he had been under more pressure than I had given him credit for. "Hey, what's going on up there?"

Theodore and I turned around. A crowd had collected on the deck of the house just behind. There were at least eight people. A man dressed in white was beckoning us. "Uh-oh," I said. Two of them were looking at us through binoculars.

"Oops," said Pierce. "You think they're mad because I'm just wearing my BVD's?" He glanced down. "What, am I exposing myself or something? There's nobody else on the beach, what do they care. Bunch of perverts."

"Oh, that's just Barry," Theodore said.

"Who's Barry?" I said.

"He's a multimillionaire producer," Theodore said.

"What kind of producer?" I said. "Movies? Magazines? Music?"

Theodore shrugged. "I guess."

"What do you mean, you guess? Which?"

"Everything, Maud," Theodore said. "He's not even a millionaire. He's a billionaire. He owns everything."

"Nobody can own everything," I said.

"He does," said Theodore. "There are people here who own everything. Everything that's important, that is. You'll find out. He's ready to listen to my demo tape, anytime."

"So why don't you give it to him?" I said.

"I'm not ready yet!" Theodore said.

"Of course you're ready!" I said. "Don't tell me you're not! Oh, God, I don't believe it. Theodore, you're really sick."

"Hey, don't call me sick!" Theodore said. "Stupid slut."

"Yeah, you can be kind of vicious, Maud," Pierce said. "Theodore knows what he's doing. I don't see the sense in calling him sick."

I was ready to cry with frustration. It was exasperating, not to have everyone obey my every command. Theodore put his arm around my shoulder. "Come on, Maud," he said. "He wants us to come visit."

"Hold on," Pierce said, grabbing his clothes from the sand and starting to get dressed. The crowd on the deck began to wave. It looked like they were signaling No.

"I don't think they want you to put your clothes on, Pierce," I said.

"Aw, the heck with that," Pierce said, getting back into his jeans. We walked up the wooden steps. "Hi, Barry!" Theodore said. "This is my brother, Pierce, and my sister, Maud."

"Where have *you* been?" Barry said, looking at Pierce.

Pierce got out his cigarettes. "We just arrived," I said. "We were driving cross-country."

"I'd really rather you didn't smoke," said Barry.

"What are you talking about?" I said. "We're outdoors! On a windy beach! He's downwind from you! Cigarettes are legal!"

There was a woman wearing a purple and orange caftan. "Your brother and sister are *g-o-r-g-e-o-u-s!*" she told Theodore. "Anyway, your brother is; your sister is just another pretty face and figure, of which we already have a million." She turned to Pierce. "I want to know everything about you. I take it you're an actor?"

Pierce didn't respond. For some reason he felt obliged to offer a public demonstration of snorting and rubbing his nose with thumb and forefinger. Then he lit his cigarette. I could see he was beginning to go off a little bit, which he tended to do in moments of stress.

"Of course he's an actor!" I said. "Everyone who sees him is hypnotized!"

"Has anybody seen you yet?" said Barry.

"No, no one's seen him yet," I said. "We just got here."

"And your brother—he doesn't speak?"

"Rarely," I said.

"Don't talk about me like I'm not here!" Pierce said in a surly voice.

Everyone looked uncomfortable yet secretly pleased, as if this was how they had hoped he would sound. "I'd be interested in representing you," said the woman in the caftan.

"Aren't you lucky!" said Barry. "Merry's the best in the business. I've never known Merry to represent anyone before who was just a beginner. You don't have any credentials to your name, do you?"

Pierce scratched his crotch. "No, he hasn't done anything yet," I said. "But I know he'll be good. I'm wondering . . . Merry, while you represent Pierce, can I watch how you work?"

"Hhhmmmph," Merry snorted. "We'll see about that."

"He hasn't done any . . . dinner theater?" Barry said. "High school plays? Things that may come back to haunt us? Summer stock? Mention it now, please."

"He hasn't done anything like that!" I said. "Are you using those things as a euphemism for pornography?"

"Pornography's not a problem!" said Barry, contemptuously. "I'm talking about a television commercial for, say, hemorrhoids. *That* could conflict with the image we have in mind. He'd be perfect for that . . . what's-it-called, Merry, that movie we were thinking of doing?"

"He'd be divine," said Merry. "Of course, we don't know if he can act."

Barry laughed. "Merry, you're a riot," he said dryly.

"What difference would that make?" I said.

Barry looked at me appreciatively for the first time. "Exactly," he said.

"Oh, God," Merry said, peering up the beach through her binoculars. "Here comes that redheaded security guard. I had a good part for him on a TV detective show. But no, he wants to *write*. I can't imagine what's wrong with him."

"That must be Fred," I said. "Oh, Pierce, it's so sad and pathetic—he's probably come to look for me."

"Is he related to you?" Barry said.

"No!" I said.

"A friend of yours?"

"Oh, no."

"But, Theodore," Barry said. "Didn't you say the security guard was living with you?"

I felt a compulsion I couldn't control, to go to Fred at the far end of the beach. "I better go get him," I said. "He looks kind of lost. Come on, you guys—let's go."

"Wait!" said Merry. "How can we reach you? How can I get hold of you?" Pierce didn't answer.

"We're staying across the way," I said. "At Nancy's."

"Where I live," said Theodore.

Merry took a few steps toward Pierce. She looked aggressive, yet loving, like the female scorpion who is tender with her mate until mating is complete. Then she eats him, slowly, thoughtfully, part by part. Scientists know this; they just haven't been able to figure out what it is she is thinking while she eats. "Are you sure you're interested in being a movie star?" she said. "You're not just wasting my time?"

"I don't know," Pierce said with a sigh. He glanced at Merry and Barry and averted his eyes. "I might rather be a car mechanic. I like cars. I like foreign sports cars. I've seen a lot of foreign cars around here."

I groaned. "Of course he wants to be a movie star," I said. "He's just playing it cool." Then I noticed Barry and Merry weren't even paying attention. They were staring at Pierce, even more impressed.

"I've found, in the movie industry, the people that do best are the psychopaths. Are you a psychopath, Pierce?" Barry said. Pierce didn't answer.

"Of course he is, Barry!" Merry said. "Just look at him."

"It's really a job for people who need to be the center of attention all the time," Barry said. "Under other circumstances, movie stars might have been serial killers, or other kinds of criminals."

"That's definitely like Pierce," I said.

Fred arrived at the bottom of the steps and Pierce went down to greet him. "How ya doing?" he said, sticking out his hand. "Long time, no see, man."

"He's too divine," Merry said wistfully. "Your brother—is he straight, or gay?"

"Don't worry, Merry," I said. "He's very easygoing."

"How perfect," said Merry. "Tell him I'll pick up the two of you at seven tomorrow morning. I'll have him meet with the director."

"Seven in the morning!" I said. "Are you kidding?" She glared at me. "I'll do my best. Tell me. I can't see so good: do you really think Fred is good-looking?"

"The security guard?" said Merry. "He's a man, isn't he? Isn't that enough? *And* tall, with a flat stomach. However, I will add that you rarely see a redheaded man so attractive—if you like redheaded men. There's plenty of work out there for him, if he'll only come around to my way of thinking. He promised he'll let me try him out, soon."

"What's he waiting for?" I said.

"He wants to finish his screenplay."

"Oh, he'll be finished quickly!" I said. I went down the stairs. Before I knew what I was doing, I had tripped and flung myself into Fred's arms. "Excuse me," I said. "I really must get glasses. I didn't notice you were here."

I didn't get a chance to finish the sentence, because our coral seas were glued together. Finally I pulled myself away. "Did you know there's a type of leech that uses his mashie niblick—well, it's not a mashie niblick, exactly, but a tube-shaped organ—to penetrate his girlfriend's skin anywhere he likes?" I said. "He sticks his semen into her any old place. The little sperm then have to find their own way to the eggs. Leeches may even have their own individual personalities, for all I know."

"I wasn't aware of the sex life of the leech," Fred said. "But I do know that when a squid is placed all by itself in an aquarium, it gets so depressed that it goes crazy and kills itself by eating its own arms."

"If a squid can get so depressed it grows suicidal, then it must also be capable of great happiness," I said. "You know how the female spider usually eats the male after mating? There's a type of male spider that has figured out how to avoid this problem. The male ties up the female, temporarily, in a silk cocoon. That way he can take the time to find her Edith Sitwell at his leisure. I can get used to anything for love, I guess." I sighed and accidentally poked my finger in Fred's ear, trying to stroke his hair. "Even though I don't really believe in it."

Involuntarily, Fred winced. "You don't sound exactly like your old self," he said. "Maybe you've changed, a little bit?"

"Maybe," I said. "I can't help it if I have no morals. It could be my genetic makeup, or environment. In any event, believe me, it's not easy. But I'm trying to grow—as a human being, or whatever—all the time. Hey, did you know that the dog, the ferret, the bear, the walrus and the whale all have bones in their mashie niblicks?"

"Mmmmmm," Fred said. "But the sex organs of the snail are in their heads."

When he kill the Mudjekeewis
Of the skin he made him mittens,
Made them with the fur side inside,
Made them with the skin side outside.